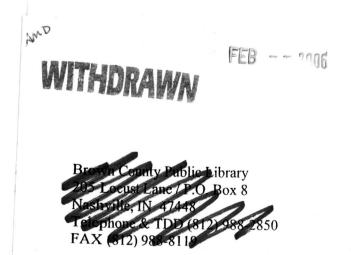

ESCAPE CLAUSE

ALSO BY JAMES O. BORN

WALKING MONEY

SHOCK WAVE

ESCAPE CLAUSE

JAMES O. BORN

G. P. PUTNAM'S SONS　　　NEW YORK

G. P. PUTNAM'S SONS
Publishers Since 1838
Published by the Penguin Group
Penguin Group (USA) Inc., 375 Hudson Street, New York, New York 10014,
USA • Penguin Group (Canada), 90 Eglinton Avenue East, Suite 700, Toronto,
Ontario M4P 2Y3, Canada (a division of Pearson Penguin Canada Inc.) •
Penguin Books Ltd, 80 Strand, London WC2R 0RL, England • Penguin
Ireland, 25 St Stephen's Green, Dublin 2, Ireland (a division of Penguin
Books Ltd) • Penguin Group (Australia), 250 Camberwell Road, Camberwell,
Victoria 3124, Australia (a division of Pearson Australia Group Pty Ltd) •
Penguin Books India Pvt Ltd, 11 Community Centre, Panchsheel Park, New
Delhi–110 017, India • Penguin Group (NZ), Cnr Airborne and Rosedale
Roads, Albany, Auckland 1310, New Zealand (a division of Pearson New
Zealand Ltd) • Penguin Books (South Africa) (Pty) Ltd, 24 Sturdee Avenue,
Rosebank, Johannesburg 2196, South Africa

Penguin Books Ltd, Registered Offices:
80 Strand, London WC2R 0RL, England

Library of Congress Cataloging-in-Publication Data

Born, James O.
    Escape clause / James O. Born.
        p.   cm.
    ISBN 0-399-15334-9
    1. Police—Florida—Fiction.   2. Florida—Fiction.   I. Title.
    PS3602.O76E83   2006   2005048722
    813'.6—dc22

Printed in the United States of America
10   9   8   7   6   5   4   3   2   1

BOOK DESIGN BY MEIGHAN CAVANAUGH

This is a work of fiction. Names, characters, places, and incidents either are the
product of the author's imagination or are used fictitiously, and any resemblance
to actual persons, living or dead, businesses, companies, events, or locales is entirely coincidental.

While the author has made every effort to provide accurate telephone numbers and Internet addresses at the time of publication, neither the publisher nor
the author assumes any responsibility for errors, or for changes that occur after
publication. Further, the publisher does not have any control over and does not
assume any responsibility for author or third-party websites or their content.

THIS ONE IS FOR NEIL NYREN.

FOR OBVIOUS REASONS.

ACKNOWLEDGMENTS

Many thanks to my fine agent, Peter Rubie.

To Tony Mead, the operations officer for the Palm Beach County Medical Examiner, for his guidance about medical matters.

To Steve Barborini, Special Agent with the Federal Bureau of Alcohol, Tobacco, Firearms and Explosives. One of the best agents in the most effective Federal agency in the country. For help with several books and years of keeping me in line.

And to all the cops who have supported my efforts in my new career. These books are for every cop who ever wanted to say or do something just to annoy the criminals.

ESCAPE CLAUSE

 **BILL TASKER TOOK HIS DAUGHTER'S HAND AS** they crossed the parking lot heading into the Bank of Florida branch in Kendall, just south of the city of Miami. The blond eight-year-old saw a license tag from Quebec on a rust-riddled Nissan pickup truck and turned to her father and asked, "What's that mean?"

"Je me souviens?"

"Yeah, what is it?" Her blue eyes wide.

"French."

"But, what's it mean?"

"Not sure, sweetheart, but I think it means, 'I brake for no apparent reason.'"

She gave him one of her looks.

"Or it means, 'I drive slow in the left lane.'"

She kept her look until he laughed and then asked him again, "What's it really mean?"

"I think it means, 'I remember.'"

"Remember what?"

Tasker shrugged. "I dunno, baby. Maybe they should remember not to start a war with the English."

She gave him another look, but seemed satisfied with the answer as they pushed open the tall, glass front door and walked inside.

The smell of banks bugged him—that fake, clean, antiseptic odor. Just like the fake nice furniture—the expensive-looking veneer pasted over cheap pressboard designed to be replaced every few years when the constant swarm of people turned it black with dirt. After a couple of minutes, his biggest concern was that Emily would damage some of it. When they were fifteen people back in line, she had dropped to the floor to do a full split. Now that they were ten people back, she was leaning on a stool with one hand and lifting her whole body off the ground in short bursts.

"Look, Daddy," she said, as her entire body floated off the ground, muscles straining, balancing on her left hand.

Bill Tasker smiled and said, "That gymnastics class is paying off."

An older Latin man next to Tasker said, "That is a real talent." He was sincere and Tasker had to admit he was proud of the athletic ability of his youngest daughter.

She lowered herself with control and stepped back to her father in line. "What are all those stars for?" she said, pointing at a large poster.

Tasker said, "Those are asterisks. They mean free checking costs six bucks a month, and four percent interest on a CD is really two and a half."

She looked at him in confusion.

He smiled and said, "It just means that when the big letters say something, you have to read what's at the bottom of the page, too."

She shrugged, just happy to have a few minutes with her dad. He felt the same way. He saw her and her sister, Kelly, at least once a week even though they lived with their mother seventy miles north in West Palm Beach. They stayed with him in his town house every other weekend, and then he visited one or two nights a week for dinner. Their mother seemed to appreciate the visits as much as the girls.

Today was an extra weekday—a teacher's planning day in Palm Beach County. Tasker had taken a rare day off from work just to spend with them, directly addressing his ex-wife's contention that he focused more on work as an agent with the Florida Department of Law Enforcement than on the girls and her. A belief that was, unfortunately, built entirely on fact. Police work, especially investigations, required an alarming amount of time. FDLE tended to get involved in the biggest of cases and there often wasn't time to just take off and see your family. As he and the girls grew older, he realized what a mistake that was.

He could watch either of his girls all day long. Granted, Kelly, the oldest, had a much more refined streak and mature attitude, but he thought of her as perfect. Emily was almost like the son he never had. He took in a deep breath of recycled air, appreciating the fact that he had a day with them he had not expected.

Emily playfully started to pull on his arm and climb off the ground, but he stopped her. He hated to admit it but the toll of the last six months had caught up to him. Among his other injuries during a hunt for a fugitive, he had torn the ligaments in his left shoulder. The fugitive, Daniel Wells, had been wanted for the bombing of a cruise ship. Tasker had allowed him to slip through his fingers once and, determined to catch him, had made an ill-advised leap into the back of Wells' speeding pickup truck. He felt the result of his exit from the moving truck every day. The new scar on his forehead didn't bother him, but chronic pain was starting to mount up. He still hadn't started back to practice with the Special Operations Team.

Tasker and his daughter exchanged small talk and played games until they were near the front of the line. He had allowed the day off and the attention of his daughter to relax him more than he'd been in months.

Out of nowhere, Emily said, "That lady is pretty. Would she be fun to go out with?"

Tasker's eyes followed her finger to a petite Latina with layers of lustrous light brown hair and dark, intelligent eyes. She was cheerfully directing the tellers as she calmed the impatient crowd. Tasker noted that she had a touch too much makeup, then caught himself. That picky attitude might explain why he'd been celibate for almost six months. He had to admit he'd been lonely, due to this shit-heel, critical attitude and the fact that he was still hung up on his ex-wife.

"Why would you ask that, beautiful?"

She shrugged her tiny shoulders. "Mom goes out with Nicky sometimes. Kelly and me want you to be happy, too."

He ruffled her hair and smiled. "I am happy. You guys make me happy."

"But she'd make you happy, too, wouldn't she?"

Tasker looked back at the vivacious, radiant bank manager with the extra eyeliner. "I'm sure she's a nice person."

"Will you ask her out?"

"Let's see when we get up there."

"So you might?"

He smiled and let out a little laugh. Before he could answer, though, a blast of warm, humid South Florida air hit him as the front door swung open. He looked up and . . . couldn't pinpoint the feeling exactly, but his hand almost instinctively came to rest on the small, green belly bag that concealed his off-duty Sig P-230 automatic. Two men in their early twenties stood next to the door, talking. Tasker scanned them from their ratty Keds to the grubby University of Miami ball caps on their heads.

They looked up at the security cameras and then up and down the row of tellers. They never even looked at the customers. Tasker knew what they were up to. The only question was whether they had the balls to go through with it right now.

Every instinct told him to draw now and preempt what was coming, but Emily's presence at his side slowed him, as did the other innocent bystanders. Unless there was an immediate threat to someone's life he shouldn't worry about a bank losing money. Besides, maybe these guys were just workmen assessing a painting job. Oh please, he was thinking like an attorney now.

His heart rate picked up as he watched the two men, dressed in jeans with unbuttoned shirts over T-shirts, separate, one staying near the front door, the other heading toward the counter. He noticed the tattoos on the neck of the guy walking toward the counter. The other had both ears and an eyebrow pierced. He wanted to give a good description when the Metro-Dade detectives asked him what he had seen.

He turned to Emily. "Hey, let's play a little game."

She immediately lit up.

"You try and hide where I can't see you, under that table with the marble-looking top." He pointed to a table in the small loan area twenty feet from the line. "You stay there, out of sight, until I come over and get you."

Without hesitation, she scurried over to the empty loan area and disappeared under the table.

Tasker took a step to the side, moving out of the line, then started to step forward past the few remaining customers toward the counter and the would-be robber. As he took a step, he felt a hand on his shoulder.

"Where do ya think you're goin'?"

He turned quickly, and at first thought no one was there, then looked down and found that an elderly lady, not much taller than Emily, had reached up and grabbed him.

"No cutting in line. We've all been here awhile." She had a sharp New York accent.

"Yes, ma'am, I know. I wasn't cutting in line." As he was about to turn back, he heard a loud voice.

"Nobody move."

It was one of the men he'd been watching. He stood next to the counter and held a large-framed revolver. The other man blocked the front door, with a much smaller revolver in his hand. It looked like a Smith five-shot .38.

Tasker's stomach flipped as he glanced back to the table Emily was under. He didn't see her. Good. He stood still, letting this thing unfold. It was the smart move, keeping everyone out of the line of fire, but it went against his nature.

The robber at the counter turned to the tellers and started barking commands as he pulled out an empty pillowcase from somewhere under his open shirt. "Fill this quick. When it's heavy enough, I'll leave and you can go back to business. You fuck with me and I'm gonna pop a cap in somebody's ass." He tossed the pillowcase to the closest teller, who immediately started shoveling cash from her drawer into it. She passed it to the next teller, who did the same.

Tasker zeroed in on the redneck accent and figured him for a Homestead thug who'd watched too much TV where people were always popping caps and holding their guns sideways. That shit annoyed Tasker as much as robberies.

He stole another glance toward Emily's table and still saw nothing. Poor, tiny Emily was probably squished in the corner, terrified.

The man at the counter banged the grip of the revolver on the counter saying, "C'mon, c'mon," as his eyes darted around the bank's lobby and the pillowcase made its rounds. His partner appeared much calmer, watching the people in line and occasionally glancing out the door. His head bobbed to some private beat in his brain.

Then things changed. The small, pretty manager Emily had fancied as a stepmother took the case from the last teller and approached the robber. The pillowcase was stuffed with cash now. She struggled with the heavy bag as she handed it to him, then took a short step backward. She stood silently, her brown eyes taking in every detail. Tasker wasn't the only one gathering a description.

The robber set the bag on the counter and dug through it with his free hand. After a few seconds of searching, he froze, then yanked something from the bag. Tasker could see it was silver-colored, probably a dye pack. The man heaved it across the tellers' space, causing one of the younger female tellers to let out a yelp. The robber stared at the manager silently and raised the gun to the young woman's head.

"Think we're stupid?" he shouted, sticking the gun barrel in the middle of her delicate forehead.

She remained placid and said, "I'm sorry, it—"

Then he pulled the trigger, the sound of the gun echoing hard on the tiled floor of the bank. The bank manager's legs went limp and she dropped straight to the ground, her long brown hair floating over her face as she fell. Everyone gasped, and for an instant the bank was as quiet as a library. Then came the screaming. The noise seemed disconnected from the people making it.

Tasker took the moment to grab a look at the punk with the piercings at the front door, who appeared startled by the violence, then to each side. These people were in danger if he took action, but by the look of the guy at the counter, they were in danger if he didn't. He took one last peek at Emily's hiding place and didn't see her.

The shooter stood over the manager, staring at her body. He still had the gun up pointing at the tellers. His gaze came up as he looked for a new person to order around.

That was it. Tasker decided to take advantage of the confusion by reaching for his pistol.

He stepped away from the crowd and yanked a string that opened the front of his bag, revealing the pistol in a holster and a yellow badge patch with the word POLICE under it. He drew the flat gray Sig smoothly, bringing it directly on target without a sound, then fired at the gunman. He was worried that the small caliber might not have enough stopping power, so he reverted to his years of SWAT training and automatically fired three times, twice in the body and once in the head. He caught the robber before he could aim his revolver. The round in the head stopped every brain function the man had and the gun slipped to the floor a second before his dead body.

Tasker didn't pause. Blocking out the screams and movement of the customers, he pivoted and dropped to one knee, his pistol sight coming onto the chest of the man at the door, his eyes wide, his Adam's apple bobbing up and down like it was broadcasting a redneck Morse code.

Tasker assessed his target and saw the young man hadn't raised his gun; he just stood there in horror.

Tasker raised his voice above the chaos and, once again following his training, said, "Police, don't move," in a clear, direct tone.

The man froze. Tasker stole a look past him toward the front door. No one else was coming in. The bank seemed to quiet down as if on cue.

"Drop the gun, now." Clear, not panicked. That took effort.

The small revolver clanked on the tile floor.

"Step toward me, now."

The man stepped toward Tasker, and more important, away from the gun.

Tasker stood, keeping his pistol on the man's body, and said, "On the ground and spread your hands."

The man complied and then everything rushed into Tasker's head at once as he came out of his tunnel vision.

He stepped to the man and searched him roughly with one hand as he held the gun to his head. He leaned in close and asked, "How many more?"

The young man shook his head violently and said, "Just Vinnie the driver, but he ain't got a gun."

Tasker touched the barrel of his gun to the man's head. "If you move when I stand up, you're dead meat. Got it?"

The man nodded his head vigorously.

Tasker backed away until he was next to the robber he'd just shot. There wasn't much blood because of the head shot. His heart had stopped getting the signal to pump before he'd hit the ground, but Tasker reached down to check his pulse anyway. Nothing. He picked up the two dropped revolvers and held them with one hand. He hopped onto the counter, still watching the prone man, and then turned to see the young manager sprawled at an odd angle on the carpeted floor. One neat, nearly bloodless hole in her forehead. He didn't risk losing his line of sight to the remaining robber to check her. She was dead.

Then he sprang down and darted past the line and looked into the loan area.

Emily's face was white as she crouched on the far side of the table.

In the distance he could hear the sirens.

**2** CAPTAIN SAM NORTON OF THE FLORIDA DE-
partment of Corrections stood outside the fence with his
best friend, Sergeant Henry Janzig. They were at the edge
of the housing units provided to the staff of the correctional facility.
Most people called it Manatee Correctional, but he referred to it as "the
Rock," because the goddamn State of Florida hadn't named it properly.
Manatee! What kind of a name was that? The outer fence of the close-
custody facility was right behind them and the start of the trailers and
prefab houses used by the staff were in front of them.

Norton squeezed a little packet of sunscreen into his hand and
smeared it over his pale nose and cheeks.

Janzig grunted. "Thought only women used that shit away from the
beach."

"Skin cancer, you old coot. We all got to worry."

"You read too damn many magazines."

Norton smiled. Sometimes he looked at his older friend Janzig with
his weathered face, gimpy hips and little gut that hung out over his thick
leather belt and hoped he didn't end up the same way. Janzig didn't much
care about exercise, and his years of standing on hard prison floors had
ruined his hips and made his knees as supple as a two-by-four. He got his
aerobics by riding roughshod over new correctional officers and occasionally beating the living shit out of an inmate. Norton tried to take

better care of himself. It was tough, against the examples of the older Department of Corrections officers, including his own father.

Janzig pulled out a pack of Winstons.

Norton stepped away and said, "C'mon, Henry, don't ruin the fine fresh air God has provided for us out here."

The older man looked at the corrections captain and said with this old Florida twang, "Don't ruin a good smoke for me. You fuckers done got smoking outlawed in every fuckin' building in the state. This is what I'm down to."

Norton smiled. Both men kept their eyes on a trustee wearing an orange shirt over his normal-issue gray facility shirt. By definition a trustee was not an escape risk but any time one worked outside the fence he had to wear the orange shirt. Every inmate aspired to being a trustee because of the better privileges and the freedom to be outside once in a while. Both Norton and Janzig had their suspicions about this trustee, though. His name was Mike Matulis and he was serving an eight-year sentence for stealing air conditioners from the back of appliance repair trucks. Norton knew you didn't get eight years for theft, so he had looked at the man's record and seen a string of burglaries over the years. Matulis had claimed his wife's spending on their four boys had driven him to crime. Norton knew how a wife's spending habits could affect you.

It had taken Matulis three years to work his way up to a trustee. That was about average. Some made it quick, if they did the right people favors, but most inmates never got to trustee status. And few who made it risked doing something to lose trustee status. Matulis appeared to be the exception.

Now the two men stood silently with Norton's personal pet German shepherd, Hannibal. The beefy captain tossed a rawhide bone for the big, hairy dog every afternoon at right about this spot so no one noticed anything unusual. Janzig usually joined him. It was the one place they weren't afraid of people overhearing their private discussions.

Norton thought that Janzig looked like a World War II veteran, even though he was only fifty-seven. He wobbled on his slightly bowed legs and was missing the end of his left ring finger. The old sergeant always claimed an inmate had bitten it off in a fight at Union Correctional. Norton knew the truth: He had tried to adjust the wheel of a running lawn mower and gotten too close to the blade.

Now Janzig ran his right hand through his thinning hair coated with oily gel. "What d'ya think, let 'im go now?"

Norton kept watching the trustee as he went about his assigned job of picking up trash around the middle row of trailers. "Not yet. He's gotta go inside to confirm he's the thief."

"Who else is it gonna be? I mean it makes sense. Tall som-bitch can reach up and try any door without goin' up the stairs."

"Might be one of the other trustees that works out here."

"One of them niggers that comes out here to clean up the dog shit?"

Norton gave him a severe look. He didn't have to say anything. Everyone who knew him knew how he felt about that word.

Janzig shrunk slightly. "Sorry, old habit. Didn't mean nothin.'"

Norton nodded, but said, "Just want to make sure Matulis is our thief."

"It's him, all right. I garun-damn-tee-it."

"Don't worry, Henry, if it's him, we'll deal with it. Terry's wife is pissed she's missing that watch and ring. I wanna know where he's stashing this shit, too."

Janzig grunted and tossed the bone for Hannibal to chase so they looked natural.

Norton said, "What about our other problem?"

"Which one? Since you got us involved in all the shit, we seem to have more problems than ever."

"I mean Luther Williams."

"Why's he a problem?"

"He could talk."

"Not while we got him here. Shit, you made him a damn trustee. He'll keep his yap shut. Besides it's too soon to have anything happen after Dewalt's body bein' found."

Norton nodded. "But we didn't have nothin' to do with that. You told me you didn't even ask anyone to kill him."

"I didn't, I swear. It was just good luck."

"Not if his parents don't shut the fuck up. They might send someone to look into his death. That wouldn't be good for anyone. We don't need no strangers around right now."

Janzig nodded his head now. "You tellin' me we couldn't scare off anyone who looked to cause us trouble?"

Norton's creased face eased and he said, "Guess you're right."

From the direction of the administration buildings, Norton noticed the tall, gawky form of one of the younger correctional officers, Lester Lynn. He didn't like his quiet time with Hannibal and Janzig interrupted and wished people would figure that out.

"Excuse me, Captain," said the thin man in the standard brown-and-white uniform.

"What is it, Lester?"

"I was just leaving from my shift in the hatch."

"Uh-huh." He knew where this was going.

Janzig cut in. "Want a medal? You made it through the seven-to-three shift without lettin' one of the nuts escape."

"Yes, sir. But I wanted . . ."

Norton gave a hard look to Janzig. Sometimes the old sergeant could be a little rough on officers as well as on inmates. In an easier tone, he said to Lester, "I know what you want, son."

"You do?"

"Want another shot at the control room."

"Yes, sir."

"No spots open right now."

Lester's Adam's apple bobbed. He looked down at his long feet.

"I know I said that if you done a good job in the psych ward you could move to the control room after a year."

"And I done a good job, sir. No problems when I was in there."

Janzig said, "Linus Hardaway didn't try to get friendly with you?" He cackled through his ill-fitting upper bridge.

"No, sir, Sergeant Janzig. He's in his room all quiet."

"All quiet?" asked the sergeant.

Lester's face turned red. "Except for the thumping noise."

"You mean humpin' noise." Janzig wailed at his own joke. Even Norton had to smile, seeing the old man's glee at his cleverness.

Norton said, "Okay, Lester, you can have an overtime shift on Sunday afternoon. We'll see how you do."

The young man brightened. "Yes, sir. Thank you, sir," he said as he backed away, like he didn't want to give the captain a chance to change his mind.

After Lester was out of earshot, Janzig said, "You think that boy is ready?"

"We're gonna give him a test right there on Sunday and find out. You set something up."

The old man just nodded, then turned back to see if he could spot the trustee.

Norton said, "Look there. See, we got 'im now." He watched as the tall trustee casually walked up the three steps to a trailer occupied by one of the officers who worked lockdown. In less than a minute, he was back outside and picking up trash like nothing had happened. Norton didn't like it when people thought he was an idiot. Especially inmates.

Norton knelt down to his furry shepherd and attached the leather leash to the dog's collar. The two men walked the dog toward the trustee, who held a black plastic garbage bag.

"Hey, Matulis. What're you doin'?" asked Janzig.

"Picking up trash, sir." The forty-five-year-old man was tall and fit, with close-cropped black hair and a thin Fu Manchu mustache. He'd be a handful if he wanted to.

Norton didn't reach for his ancient hard plastic nightstick. Janzig hadn't even bothered to bring his along. They both knew what was going to happen.

Janzig said, "Lot of trash inside the trailer?"

The inmate froze. His eyes shifted from one side to the other. "What do you mean, sir?"

Janzig wasn't imposing physically, but his voice could convey threat. "I mean I just saw you go inside that fucking trailer. Why?"

The inmate shook his head. "No, sir, Sergeant Janzig. I just grabbed an empty plastic bag off the steps."

Norton kept quiet and used his best poker face. That unnerved people more than anything.

Janzig said, "Look, asshole. We ain't got time for this. You went inside and stole something. You did it last week when you was out here. We want the ring and watch from last week and whatever you took now."

"But . . ."

"No buts, asshole. We want them now."

The inmate started to shake.

Hannibal let a low growl come from the back of his throat.

The front of the inmate's pants stained slightly as he pissed himself.

Norton said, "Calm down, boy. We'll work this out."

The inmate swallowed hard and let out a deep breath. "We will?"

Norton nodded. "Yeah, but not here. You trot back to the admin building and wait for us."

The inmate straightened. "Yes, sir. At admin." He turned and started off in a jog.

Norton called after him. "And, Matulis."

The inmate turned slightly.

Norton released Hannibal, who started after the trotting inmate, then said, "You better run hard."

The man took off in a full-out sprint as the big shepherd closed the distance quickly.

Janzig said, "I say one."

Norton smiled. "No way. Hannibal is up for this. I'll lay ten on both of them bleeding."

Janzig stuck out his hand. "You're on."

They started to walk calmly toward the fleeing inmate with the dog on his heels. Norton appreciated the inmate's speed, but it wouldn't matter soon.

At a full gallop, Hannibal poked his massive head between the inmate's legs, and with one snap of his jaws on the man's groin brought him to an abrupt stop. Matulis pivoted in midair as his face slammed down into the hard ground.

Matulis' scream seemed to penetrate the buildings. Norton looked up at the nearest tower and waved off the officer who had already raised his rifle at the sound outside the fence. The officer turned his attention back to the yard without hesitation.

Hannibal now had the man cleanly by his testicles, shaking him like a stuffed toy. Then, after tossing the screaming man a few feet away, he used his teeth to shred the gray prison pants. The dog raced back toward Norton, then, when he had his master's attention, ran back to the prone inmate and quietly sat next to him, panting lightly.

Norton and Janzig didn't rush to get to the injured man. Norton stopped to rub his dog's neck. The only issues left were where he had hidden his loot and who would win the bet.

Janzig kicked the inmate's hands and said, "Move those hands, Matulis."

Hesitantly, the man complied, revealing a shredded pair of pants with blood flowing down his exposed legs.

Norton leaned over and inspected the man's genitals, which were covered in blood. "I don't know, Henry, but it looks like both his balls are bleeding to me."

Janzig took a closer look, too, and said, "Damn," as he pulled out his wallet and handed his friend ten dollars.

"You gonna tell us where the shit is now?" Norton asked the writhing inmate.

The man just nodded his head and kept saying, "Yes, sir, yes, sir. Yes, sir."

Bill Tasker sat in a deep, comfortable chair, trying to figure out who the guy in the suit was and why he was at the Miami FDLE office. The director of the Florida Department of Law Enforcement's Miami Regional Operations Center was clearly annoyed to have the visitor and this caused Tasker some apprehension. As one of the chief law enforcement officers in the whole state, the director didn't waste time playing politics or gaining favor with others. Tasker liked his direct approach on most subjects, but today he seemed a little subdued.

The director said, "Billy, you doing okay?"

He shrugged. "Sure, boss."

"Billy, this is Ardan Gann from the governor's office."

Tasker stood and shook the bald, older man's hand. His face was smooth and tight like someone had yanked on the back of his neck. He had on a dark Brooks Brothers suit with a red power tie. He wasn't a flunky for the governor, that much was clear.

Gann nodded without saying a word.

The director said, "You did a great job in the bank. Lot of guys would've panicked. You kept cool and we're proud of you."

Tasker felt a chill rocket down his back. He'd been a cop long enough to know that statements like this were always followed by a "but." He blurted out, "Oh my God, what's wrong?"

Gann, the governor's man, spoke, cutting off the director. "Agent Tasker, we find ourselves in an unusual position."

Tasker held his mouth and let his eyes bore into the man.

"You see, the state attorney's office is at something of an impasse. Metro cleared you in the shooting, but the civilian review board has some questions. They would prefer to let the whole thing drop, but it's an election year and the state attorney herself is facing stiff opposition. She needs to be seen as doing something. At least bringing the matter before a grand jury. It all goes back to the review board's questions."

The director said, "They always have questions."

Gann nodded but didn't seem to want comments at this point. "That's true. Their first priority usually is not the public but rather to make it look like they're doing something. Do you follow me?"

Tasker nodded and allowed him to continue.

Gann was cool and he had a voice and delivery like a funeral home director. "The questions revolve around the idea that you could've not gotten involved. The reasoning was expressed that after the robber killed the manager, he would've fled without further bloodshed."

Tasker shook his head. "That's stupid."

The director held up his hand from behind his desk. "Now, Billy, let's keep this professional." He looked at Gann and said, "That's bullshit."

Gann shrugged. "No one is saying they're right. It's just a civilian review board. They don't have to follow facts."

Tasker said, "What did they want me to do? Let this guy flee?"

"They said that if you had allowed the robber to exit the bank, then a subsequent investigation would have identified him and he would not have been gunned down. Or as one review board member said, 'executed.'" He paused. "They sounded more concerned with the young robber's life than anyone else's."

Tasker was about to answer when his director spoke up. "If a member of the review board used the word 'executed,' the governor should remove someone so inflammatory and uninformed." His dark complexion flushed red.

Tasker was impressed with the support and with the professional comments coming from a guy who had been on the Special Operations Team with him years before.

Then the director added, "Assholes like that make our job fucking unbearable."

That sounded more like the director that Tasker knew. Now he spoke for himself. "Mr. Gann." He paused and gathered his thoughts. "Having been in a position where I was in legal limbo for an extended period, I would say to you, if the state attorney is going to charge me, she should do it now. If not, allow the grand jury to issue a no true bill and let me get on with my life."

Gann said, "I was going to tell you we have an alternative."

"To what?"

"To the entire grand jury. Clear you right now, no questions asked."

"How?" asked Tasker, looking for the trap.

"We need help and FDLE is in a position to provide it." He looked at the director, then back to Tasker and said, "The Dade state attorney needs some money and we have a grant being held for them. FDLE helps us, we help the state attorney and they help FDLE. Everyone wins."

Tasker added, "Except me."

The director looked at Tasker. "Billy, that's not fair. Hear Mr. Gann out."

Tasker stood, and felt his blood race through his head. It was starting to feel like he was being singled out. The word "persecuted" came into his mind. "It was a good shoot. I had no choice and I did it in defense of life. That's what the statute says, isn't it?" His voice was louder than he had intended.

"In the era of kinder, gentler police work, review boards don't want to hear shit like that." The director stood up and walked from behind his giant desk. "C'mon, Billy, it's not what it looks like. Of course it was a good shooting. I just felt you needed a break and this way you can help yourself, help FDLE and not have to hassle with a civilian inquiry. Listen to the assignment. It's voluntary. You think someone is trying to hurt you, turn it down. But this was my idea, too. I'm worried about you. This could work out."

Tasker took a deep breath. "How?"

Gann said, "Are you familiar with Manatee Correctional in Gladesville?"

"I've heard of it. Never been out there. It's only been open a few years, right?"

"Four years, to be exact."

"What has a state prison got to do with me?"

"An inmate was killed there about five weeks ago. The county looked into it briefly and the Department of Corrections is continuing the investigation, but so far no one has determined the identity of the killer."

"Why's the governor interested in a single homicide in a prison? They happen all the time."

"In this case, it's the victim. A young man named Rick Dewalt."

"And?"

"His family has ties to the governor, and they don't believe it should be that hard to find a killer in a confined space like a prison."

"Except that there are a thousand potential suspects and no one will help with the investigation."

"See, you've already caught on to our problem."

"What's the story on Dewalt?"

"His father is a big contributor to the governor's campaign and a local builder in Palm Beach County. The son went to Central Florida for a few years to major in mathematics, even did a semester at Oxford, but too much partying and a wild girlfriend led him down another path. After a few years as a land surveyor, he got involved in marking landing strips for planes loaded with cocaine. Got off the hook once with three years' probation, but got caught again and the judge sent him to Manatee for ten years. He had only been there a year when they found him outside the lockdown facility, choked to death."

Tasker looked at him, not sure he knew how to speak to the buttoned-down governor's aide. "What do you think I'll turn up that others have missed?"

"Doesn't really matter."

"Pardon me?"

"Just have to convince the family we're doing all we can."

Tasker had seen these types of investigations before. They were usually pawned off on an agent who didn't have anything big going on. It was an incentive to hardworking agents to be involved in major cases all the time.

The director stood up behind his desk. "Billy, I'm the one who floated your name. You need this. Not just because it shuts up the stupid review board, but because it gets you away from Miami for a while. You've had a lot of shit happen the last few months."

Tasker looked from his boss to Gann. "I'll have to commute out there?"

The director said, "No. No commute. Temporary duty. We have some state employee housing out there." He walked around the desk and put his arm around Tasker. "Look, Billy, like I said, you been through a lot. The FBI shit, the Daniel Wells case and now this shooting. Jesus, there hasn't been a month in the last six you weren't either under investigation or recovering from on-the-job injuries. You need a break. Find out what's important. I'm personally worried about you, Billy. I could get anyone to look into this thing. It just happened to come up and you need this now." He slapped Tasker on the shoulder. "A few months in the country will be just what the doctor ordered."

Tasker just looked at him.

The director said, "I'm serious. The psychologist we hired agrees. You're on the edge. He's afraid you're starting to see everything as your duty. He's opposed to you coming back to full duty right now."

Tasker nodded as he accepted his fate.

The director added, "It's even in the same county as your kids."

Tasker realized that even with all the reasoning, it still wasn't a request. He immediately started thinking of what he should pack.

3 TASKER LET HIS FULL ONE HUNDRED AND eighty pounds bounce onto the trampoline and watched Emily fly ten feet into the air. He hit the next one and she landed on her butt and laughed for a full twenty seconds. He was taking extra time with her since the shooting. Her mother had sent her to a counselor and Tasker worried every night how the incident might have affected her. Right now it didn't appear to be much of an issue. He flopped next to her, making her pop up again, only this time not as high.

Kelly, his ten-year-old, climbed onto the trampoline and started to bounce her sister, too, causing them both to giggle wildly. Tasker could see that Kelly was concerned about her younger sister, too. There had been none of the usual petty rivalry or bickering since the morning Emily had seen her dad shoot a man three times.

Sometimes, when he least expected to be thinking about the shooting, he found himself staring at the lifeless young man's face or thinking about how his mother must be feeling. Late at night he'd feel anger at the robber for killing the pretty bank manager. Lately he'd focused his anger on the inept and useless civilian review board. They were just making noise more than anything else. But the noise hurt. After doing what he thought was right, he was being second-guessed by a bunch of people who had never even heard a gunshot. He worked hard to bring his consciousness back to the present and play with his girls again.

He scooted to the edge of the trampoline.

"Please, Daddy, a few more minutes," they both pleaded.

"Give me five minutes to talk with your mom and I'll be back." He leaned over and playfully bit Kelly on the big toe, then walked to the covered patio behind the house.

Donna, his ex-wife, handed him a glass of punch. He took a sip, then looked at her. "What's this?"

She smiled that brilliant smile and said, "Rumrunner."

"I shouldn't."

"It's Saturday, you've earned it."

"But I'm in the state car. I got that drive out to Gladesville." He shrugged and took another sip.

"Why are you going out there on a Saturday, anyway?"

"Why, want me to stay?" He smiled and wiggled his eyebrows. In case she said "no," he could claim he was joking.

She cocked her head like a puppy, but didn't answer.

He took the hint and answered the question. "Want to settle in and look around. Monday I hope to hit the ground running."

"You never change. Whatever the assignment, you go a hundred per-cent." She didn't smile now. They had already had a "discussion" about the bank shooting. As upset as Donna had been that Tasker would do something that dangerous with Emily present, she'd realized he was even more upset. He had always been hard on himself, and in most cases he deserved it, but in this case he'd weighed the options and done what he felt he had to do. His ex-wife saw that and had told him she knew the anguish he felt over it. He was just happy that this was an easier "discussion."

He sat in a lounger and took another sip of his rumrunner, letting Donna's mind wander to a more pleasant subject than his focus on his work. Finally he said, "At least Gladesville is closer when the kids visit."

"You want them to come out to the Glades?"

"Yeah, I'll be out there awhile. I didn't expect not to see them."

She brushed back some strands of her naturally blond hair. "It just seems so isolated." She shrugged her bare shoulders and gave a slight shudder, as if the thought of being an hour away from a mall might cause permanent internal damage.

"Where was the murder? Which prison?" she asked.

"Manatee Correctional."

"The one just past South Bay?"

He nodded. "Yeah, in Gladesville."

"How tough can a prison named 'Manatee' be?"

"We laughed about that at the office a little."

"It's just so far away."

Tasker offered, "It's still Palm Beach County."

"No one thinks of it like that. But I suppose it won't hurt the girls to see someplace new. And this homicide investigation won't put you in any danger. The crime already took place. That'll be a nice change, not worrying about you."

"I haven't done too many homicide investigations, but this is a little different. It's more of a historical investigation. The crime scene is gone, all that's left is photos and reports."

"No one shoots at you or tries to blow you up when you're doing a historical investigation."

He nodded, absently reaching up to massage his sore shoulder then finger the scar on his forehead.

"That's at least a step in the right direction."

Tasker smiled, looking at her clear, blue eyes. He wanted her to ask him to stay the night. He said, "What about you? Will you come out?"

She smiled at the invitation. "We'll see. I don't want to give you the wrong idea if I do."

"What's the wrong idea?"

"That we're back together. I'm not ready."

"I know, I know. Until you're sure Nicky Goldman isn't going to land the biggest class-action lawsuit of all time, you want to keep your options open."

She punched him hard in the arm. "You know that's not true. Nicky and I have something small and sweet."

"Not unlike Nicky himself."

She punched him again.

uther Williams looked in the mirror as he spoke to the younger inmate. Luther liked to make sure he was as sharply dressed as could be
managed in the standard gray correctional tunic. He also had his favorite
weapon, a thin strip of metal with an extremely pointed edge that used
to be some form of oil dipstick for a vehicle. He had given two packs
of Camels, eight dollars and a month's worth of protection for the
fine weapon. On the street it would be effective, but in here it was the
equivalent of a nuclear weapon. It slipped into his waistband whenever
needed and unless he was going out the gate as part of his trustee duties
and passed through a magnetometer, no one suspected him of being
armed.

He kept his gaze in the rough, round mirror mounted on the wall
next to his bunk as he spoke to the thirty-three-year-old black man
standing next to him in his dorm.

Leroy asked, "What d'you need that long ass shiv for?"

"Purely for protection, my boy."

"Protection from what?"

"Not what, who. You never know who is going to try and get over
on you in here."

Leroy shifted in his heavy work boots. "Anyway, you said you knew a
way out of here if someone was willing to risk it."

"Yes, Leroy," started Luther, "I know of a fault in the system. You
could get out." He always worked to keep his voice calm and soothing.
It never hurt to lull people with whom you were dealing.

"What'll it cost me?"

"Why do you assume that this consultation will cost you?" Luther reverted to his lawyer's persona during any formal business negotiation.

"Because you ain't known as a charity."

Luther smiled as he considered the younger man's comment. "I suppose not. But let's say this is my way of helping out another brother."

"Like you helped out Tannis Brown."

"Mr. Brown tried to steal from me. He was warned about that and chose to ignore the warning." Luther looked at the other man for emphasis. "I'm sure when Mr. Brown gets out of the infirmary, he will understand the rules better."

Leroy Baxter nodded his head. "Then what zactly is this fault in the system?"

"I'll tell you when you're ready to go. It'll be easy if we do it near the six o'clock shift change."

"What day?"

"Thursday or Friday."

"And you'll just help me—you don't want to come?"

"I have an appeal that may release me. I can't risk it now. But you, facing what?"

"Twenty-five years."

"As a young man you need to be outside. Sow your oats."

"Never worked no farm."

"Then perhaps an education. Look what a good education has done for me." He spread his arms and looked around at the large, smelly dorm. Then he realized Leroy Baxter didn't really appreciate sarcasm.

Tasker drove through the south end of West Palm Beach, cutting down some streets between Olive Avenue and Flagler Drive on the intracoastal waterway. He liked seeing the houses he had known as a kid. He'd been inside dozens of them, from the old Moore house on Palmetto to the Hutcheon house on Ellamar. He thought about the loud Hutcheon kids and smiled. One of them even worked for FDLE now.

He turned west on Southern Boulevard, in front of the ornate Greek Orthodox church, knowing he had a long ride out to Gladesville about seven miles past Belle Glade. From the intersection of Flagler and Southern, he could see the old Post mansion, which had been turned into a club by Donald Trump. Trump called the club Mara Lago, which had been the mansion's name when Tasker was growing up. He'd never been past the entrance, which used to have thorny plants and glass glued on the top of the walls, but he didn't like Trump coming in and turning it into a club. Maybe it was his general distrust and dislike of developers. He had a hard time accepting change in the town where he grew up.

After fifteen minutes on Southern Boulevard, he passed Lion Country Safari, then he hit the rural farming area west of Loxahatchee and the start of the massive sugarcane fields. There was no way to get lost even though he wouldn't have minded delaying his arrival. It was one road with few turnoffs and miles and miles of cane fields on either side of what had become State Road 80.

The open road, void of vehicles, encouraged him to ease his state-issued Monte Carlo up over eighty, then a little bit faster. The well-sealed, newer car was one of the nicest vehicles he had been assigned over the years. Due to the amount of surveillance they were asked to do, most FDLE agents had cars that blended in with traffic. Fords and mid-level GMs like the Monte Carlo were the most common FDLE cars, with a new group of pickup trucks being moved into the fleet. Most of the supervisors had Ford Crown Victorias, which were often used when agents were assigned to protect the governor or some other dignitary.

The car hummed along as Tasker let his mind wander. He wasn't in a particular hurry, but he had already seen enough cane fields and straight roads to last awhile. He cranked up the Rolling Stones' "Start Me Up," then fell into a comfortable zone where the occasional images of dead bank managers and robbers from Homestead didn't seem likely to pop into his head. He was so comfortable he didn't notice the Florida Highway Patrol trooper racing up behind him until the blue lights filled his rearview mirror.

"Oh shit," Tasker muttered, shocked he could have been so unobservant. He pulled the car onto the rough shoulder of State Road 80 with a field of swaying sugarcane starting twenty feet away. He sat motionless with his hands on the wheel and watched the tall trooper with a wash-and-wear haircut slowly ease out of his brown-and-tan Crown Vic. The guy already had his metal ticket book in his hand and he didn't look like a friendly public servant.

Tasker hit the power window and looked over his shoulder, smiling up at the trooper, who looked like an older Boy Scout or a Wendy's manager.

The trooper just stared down at him for a moment, then said, "Do you have any idea how fast you were going?"

Tasker realized the trooper had no clue he was a cop. He figured once the guy found out it would be old home week and he'd be on his way. Possibly with a marked, trooper escort.

"No, sir. I know I was speeding, though."

"How do you know that?"

"Because I was surprised anyone could catch up to me." He looked up and smiled, thinking the trooper would appreciate his sharp sense of humor.

"License and registration."

Guess not. "Look, Trooper"—Tasker looked up at his name tag—"Miko. I was just joking."

The trooper cut him off. "Is safety a joke, sir? I own this highway and it's my job to keep people safe who aren't traveling at ninety-three miles an hour."

Tasker flinched. "Ninety-three. Okay, that is a little quick."

"License and registration."

Tasker hated flashing his badge. He had, however, learned more subtle ways of getting across that he was a cop. "No problem." He placed both hands on the wheel again so the trooper could see them, and added, "I do have a loaded gun in the car, sir."

The trooper had some years on him and knew not to overreact. An armed criminal rarely tips off a cop that he has a gun. The trooper leaned down to see the entire interior of Tasker's car.

The trooper's eyes scanned the front and back seat, then he said, "Why do you have a loaded gun?"

"I'm a cop."

"Do you have any ID?"

"Yes, sir."

"Slowly reach for it and show me."

Tasker knew he had seen the 800-megahertz radio controller under the dash and the small control box for the siren and PA secured under the hood. He reached into his rear pocket and pulled out his credential case and flipped it open so the trooper could inspect it.

"I thought you said you were a cop?"

"I am. Look, with FDLE."

"The state considers you cops?"

Tasker realized he had walked into one of the oldest and oddest rivalries in police work and had set up his opponent with a soft pitch that he hit out of the park.

Tasker allowed a slight smile at the dig and said, "Last I checked, I was certified."

"You guys have uniforms?"

"Nope."

"Work shifts?"

"Nope."

"Drive marked cars?"

"Obviously not."

"Then how can you call yourselves cops?"

The tall trooper clomped away without issuing the ticket. But Tasker still felt the jab.

After slowing down for the next twenty miles of fields, Tasker could see buildings sprouting on the south side of State Road 80. Finally he came to a crossroad that forced him to turn right or left. He took the left toward downtown Belle Glade.

To his right was the warden's residence for Glades Correctional, the first state prison built in the area, which sprawled out behind the two-story house. Tasker knew the prison from occasionally interviewing prisoners or helping the Department of Corrections with an investigation of corruption at the large, medium-security prison. Elmore Leonard's book *Out of Sight* was partially set there, based on a true incident. Six men had tunneled out from the chapel and made their escape. It had happened before Tasker was hired by FDLE, but the stories were standard FDLE lore.

After another curve of the road, he passed the sugar companies' administrative buildings, saw the water tower for the nice little town of South Bay, then, cutting through the town of Gladesville, Tasker saw the larger, more imposing structures of Manatee Correctional state prison. This was the close-custody prison where a twenty-eight-year-old land surveyor named Rick Dewalt had been killed. Tasker would do all he could to find out who had killed him.

Luther Williams stopped as he entered the dorm. A few inmates were sitting around the last bunk on the left. They were probably playing dice, but he couldn't tell from where he stood. That was intentional, to keep the correctional officers from hassling them. The reason he was waiting was that the only other inmate present was Vic Vollentius, a nominal member of the prison's best-known white gang, the Aryan Knights. A bald, fit man near forty, Vollentius was the only Knight housed in this dorm.

Lately, Luther had noticed some added scrutiny from the Aryan Knights, but he didn't know why. Having this dumb-ass in front of him made him wonder if he was paranoid or observant. His right hand rested on the tip of the handle to his shiv.

Luther kept his eyes on the man, noticing the tattoo that sprawled off his neck to some place under his white, plain T-shirt. Vollentius kept his blue eyes on Luther, too.

"You need something?" asked Luther.

"What would I need from a . . . a . . ." He paused as he saw Luther's expression.

For his part, Luther realized this idiot was just trying to see how far he could push things.

Luther said, "You and your pals seem interested in my activities lately."

"You might think you're more important than you really are."

"That may be, but I hope none of you would be stupid enough to cut in on any of my action."

Vollentius feigned being hurt. "You got me all wrong, Williams. I don't cut in on anyone's action. Too much work." He stepped closer. "But you better keep your shit straight, because if I get the chance, I'll sell you out. Maybe to Big Tony in Dorm G or maybe to Sergeant Janzig for a little extra visiting time."

"You would learn, Mr. Vollentius, that I don't appreciate such activity and that you would be well advised to mind your own business."

"What if I tried to sell *you* something?"

Luther looked at him. "Like what?"

"Like why you're getting special attention lately."

"How much?"

"An ounce of your coke."

"An ounce?" Luther was stunned.

"And not a gram less."

Luther smiled and said, "I'll take my chances."

**4** TWO MILES WEST OF THE PRISON, BILL TASKER
found the small gravel road marked Dead Cow Lane and
turned left. He knew someone with a sense of humor must
have named the road, but he was surprised the state had made an official
sign for it. This was going to be home for the next few weeks.

The road cut through another cane field, then opened into a complex
of nine small apartments in a U shape with three on each side and three
in the rear. The white clapboard building had two parking spots in front
of each unit on a coarse lime-and-gravel parking lot. He knew the state
owned it but had no idea who lived there.

Pulling into the spot in front of number 3, the rear corner unit, he
stepped out of his Monte Carlo and stretched, taking in a deep breath.
He tried the door, as he had been instructed to do, and stepped inside.
An envelope with the keys and some information were on the small
table next to the front door. So far, so good.

A quick inventory of the one-bedroom apartment showed it to be
furnished as promised, and free as advertised. Other than that, he wasn't
too thrilled. The bedroom had a double bed, dresser and straight
wooden chair. The living room featured an old couch with a block of
wood holding up one corner, a coffee table and a small hutch with a
large, portable TV sitting on top. The kitchen had a new refrigerator, at
least, a standard 1965 plastic-covered table and four mismatched chairs.

On his way back to the car, a young dark-skinned woman, who obviously knew she was good-looking, took her time strolling toward the door of the apartment next to his and nodded a greeting. Tasker smiled and nodded back as the young woman in the damp T-shirt pulled a wide box from the passenger seat of an old Ford pickup truck. She was petite, but no one would mistake her for a child. Her dark eyes cut to the side to get another look at her new neighbor.

She stopped and said, "Hi."

He smiled. "Hi."

The woman said, "I'm Billie."

He hesitated and said, "So am I." When she just stared at him, he stuck out his hand and said, "Billy Tasker."

She set down the box, which didn't look too heavy, and placed her tiny hand in his. "I'm Billie Towers."

"You live right there?" He tried to keep the hope out of his voice.

"No, my boss does." She eyed him and said, "But I wish I did." She picked up the box and started to walk, saying over her shoulder, "See you around, Billy Tasker."

He stood there grinning and then wondered what a Saturday night in Gladesville was like.

Tasker ate half a slab of pork ribs at a simple barbecue joint that looked like it used to be Sonny's, but now was called Sonny Boy's. They hadn't even taken down the original sign, just tacked up a "Boy's" next to it. He decided to wait for recommendations before trying the out-of-the-way places. About nine, he cruised the small, quiet streets of Gladesville until he found a building that looked like some kind of sports bar, named the Green Mile. He smiled at the local community's support of the prisons.

He parked his state-issued Monte Carlo in the dirt-and-gravel lot, then walked past about thirty cars to the front door, noticing a large number of pickup trucks and older Fords.

The wooden steps leading up to the front door rattled as he hesitated on entering the busy establishment, but then a heavy woman in a huge T-shirt opened the door to come outside and the blast of music surprised him. He'd expected country-western but heard some funky Donna Summer disco rip-off. He shrugged and stepped inside. The large single room had a bar in the center and two dance floors with a dozen couples dancing. The wood floors and high rafters gave the place a barn-like feel, but Tasker realized the same building in Delray Beach would have a retro, classic feel. It wasn't what he'd expected, but after thinking about his run-down apartment on Dead Cow Lane, he decided he'd stay for a beer.

As he approached the bar, it felt like people were staring at him. He looked around and was surprised to see a good mix of people: black people eating at the tables along the edge of the dance floors, white couples dancing. The bar had a good crowd. Somehow, without ever spending a lot of time in the western county, Tasker had come to the conclusion that it was a backward, racist, segregated area, but he was happy to have his prejudice proved incorrect. He realized it must be the same for those New Yorkers who felt that way about Florida as a whole without really knowing the state. It made him mad when they did it, so he resolved to give places and people a fair shake before labeling them redneck, backwoods shitholes. Like some of the towns farther out US 27.

A thin, rough-looking bartender with a mustache like an old-time Mexican bandit looked at him without saying a word.

Tasker said, "What do you have on draft?"

The man had a good Florida cracker accent and said, "We got both kinds on draft. Bud and Bud Light."

"What about in a bottle?"

"We got everything in a bottle."

"What's everything?"

"Bud, Bud Light, Mich and Icehouse."

Tasker ordered his Icehouse and found a stool. He still caught people staring at him, but realized that new people didn't pop in every day out here.

After about ten minutes, a stunning black woman, almost as tall as he was, took the stool next to him. She had a light complexion and the most perfect almond-shaped brown eyes he had ever seen. She looked at him and smiled, but then immediately faced the bar. Her girlfriend slid onto the stool on the other side of her. Her friend was very dark, with unnaturally straight hair that reflected the lights off the high ceiling. They spun around on their stools to face out onto the open floor like they were checking out the crowd.

Tasker had never been the kind of guy to talk to a woman he didn't know at a bar and hadn't really dated since his marriage to Donna. His last attempt at dating had been a girl from work named Tina Wiggins, and it hadn't worked out at all. He took the occasional glance at the two women to his right. Each was attractive in her own way. They started to talk about the men in the room, making slightly snide comments about height and weight.

The woman farthest from him spoke like she had been raised in a rap video. She said loud enough so everyone at the bar could hear, "I'm tired of short men. I need me a tall man for a change."

The woman next to Tasker slapped her friend playfully, then glanced back at Tasker, who smiled.

Her friend caught the smile and turned to him, "Who're you smiling at? I *know* you don't think we'll talk to you."

Tasker smiled at the comment. He was old enough to know better than to argue with someone as loud and obnoxious as this woman. He turned back to the bar and picked up his beer.

Then the incredible happened.

The young woman next to him—he thought she might be twenty-eight—turned to him with her hand extended and said, "I'm sorry, she doesn't mean anything. She just likes to show off."

Tasker set down his beer, shook her hand and said, "I hadn't noticed."

The woman laughed as her friend sprang up to confront a man who was staring at her across the dance floor.

The woman next to him said, "Hi, my name is Renee."

"I'm Bill." He held her gaze.

"I've never seen you around here before."

"My first day in town."

"Just passing through?"

"No, I'm here for a while."

"What on earth for?"

Just as he started to answer, he felt a hand on his shoulder. He turned to find a squat but muscular black man, with two friends who were taller and less threatening-looking, behind him. The leader had an array of freckles on his cheeks that captured Tasker's attention. His lighter skin had no continuity to it. His neck was darker than his face, and his forehead blended into his reddish-tinged hair.

Renee spoke across Tasker as they both stood. "Rufus, you had your chance. I can talk to whoever I want."

The man glared at her. "This don't concern you." He looked at Tasker and said, "Who're you?" in a surprising Bronx cadence.

Tasker assessed the three men and decided he wouldn't stand much of a chance if things went bad. The most he could do was get in a few shots and then take his licks. Since it sounded like a domestic, he couldn't be sure his new friend Renee wouldn't jump in if he started swinging at her boyfriend or whatever he was. He was still weighing his options . . . when a fist whipped past his face and smashed into the man's nose. Tasker turned his head to see the pleasant girl he'd just been talking to, Renee, swing with her other fist and knock the man off his feet.

She looked at the other two. "Take Rufus outta here."

They hesitated.

"You want some, too?"

With that, they reached down at once and helped their bloodied comrade to his feet, then shuffled toward the door.

She looked at Tasker, his mind mentally agape, and said calmly, "I'm sorry, I better leave before someone calls the cops."

Tasker stared at the lovely, athletic girl as she gathered up her purse and a friend came to hurry her along.

Tasker stammered, "But wait, when . . ."

She smiled and answered his half-asked question. "Don't worry, it's Gladesville. We'll see each other soon."

She was out the door before the bartender could investigate the incident.

5 IT WAS MIDDAY ON SUNDAY IN GLADESVILLE.
Even though he'd just read the *Palm Beach Post* as he had
most of his adult life, it didn't feel like Palm Beach County.
He had the small window-mounted air conditioner off and all the windows open. In front of him on the floor were photographs of Rick Dewalt's body next to a squat cement landing inside the walls of Manatee Correctional, the angle of his head and legs reminding Tasker of a discarded doll, the corpse's arms secured behind his back with a length of rough tan rope. In addition to the crime scene photos, Tasker had the autopsy photos and the investigative reports written by one R. A. Chin, inspector. The reports were well written and concise, but the investigation had failed to turn up much.

He looked over the scattered paper and then froze as he saw a small gray creature with a funny yellow streak on its hindquarters, as if it had bumped into paint, slowly creep across the floor on the far side of the room. The mouse didn't look threatening but he didn't like the idea of another mammal in the house, and he looked around for something in arm's reach with some heft. The only thing was his paperback Florida State Statutes book. He kept his eyes on the mouse and slowly brought it up, but then just as he winged it, someone banged on his front door. The book hit wide right and the mouse took off like a tiny missile out of sight into the lone bedroom.

Tasker turned to the door to find a short man in his mid-fifties standing outside the screen.

Tasker stood, hoping the man didn't realize what he had been trying to do.

The man said, "You chase him out of here and I'll end up with him in my apartment." He smiled. "I designed a humane trap for the little critters. Nothing fancy. Just a hamster cage that will shut when he comes in for the food. More work than throwing a book at them, but not as messy."

Tasker opened the door and offered his hand. "Bill Tasker."

The man said, "Warren Kling. I live next door. What god-awful state agency do you work for and what did you do to get sent here?"

"FDLE, and I did what anyone would do. I said, 'Sure, I'll go out to Gladesville.'"

"But what for?"

Tasker shrugged. "Looking into a death at the prison."

"A murder?"

"Looks like."

"Now that's interesting."

Tasker shrugged again. "What about you?"

"Archaeology led me here. Seminole camps. I'm a professor of Native American studies—lot of interesting sites out here."

"I think I met one of your assistants."

"Only have one. Not many men miss her."

"You can send her by to drop off stuff anytime you like."

"Actually, I try not to. Every time she leaves the site I don't see her again for hours. You know young people."

"Where do you teach?"

"University of Florida."

Tasker frowned.

"Don't tell me," the professor said.

"'Fraid so, Doc. Florida State, class of 'ninety-three."

"Hell. Just when I thought this place couldn't get any worse."

"I agree." They both laughed and immediately Tasker felt better about his stay. Their schools might be fierce rivals, but at least he had a neighbor worth talking to.

Billie Towers peered over the steering wheel of the noisy Ford pickup that the University of Florida had provided Professor Kling for his crazy dig. Who really cared if her ancestors settled here near Gladesville or out west in Big Cypress? She'd been raised on the Hollywood reservation and she didn't give a shit. All she really cared about was a reason not to live on the reservation again, even if it did mean a fat stipend from the Seminole tribe of Florida. When she did think of the reservation outside the beach town of Hollywood, all she could remember was her father bringing home a different tourist lady every night and his friends' eyes following her as she raced through the house to find refuge at the local arcade or school event. She'd learned early that men appreciated her for things other than her intelligence.

Now she felt the truck's engine stutter as she drove past one of the many abandoned sugar company offices.

"Shit," she said as she pounded on the cracked blue steering wheel. The pickup reacted by cutting out altogether. Billie assessed the situation. She could turn and coast into the empty parking lot of the office building, where she would be safe, or just pull to the side of the road. Although she'd be near traffic, she figured someone would see her, and if that someone was male she was confident she'd be rescued.

She bumped onto the shoulder of the four-lane highway and didn't waste any time scooting out of the truck. She checked her hair in the side mirror, tied off her T-shirt to show her defined abs, and, satisfied she was ready, turned and faced the highway. Before she could walk to the rear of the truck, two vehicles nearly collided trying to turn off the road.

A new Dodge pickup truck with a tall, cute guy about twenty-five stopped just past her. His smile reflected the bright sun and a confident strut as he came toward her, and his brown hair, stylish and a little showy, must have been cut by someone in the city. Behind her, a heavy man around fifty-five slowly plopped out of a four-wheel-drive Chevy truck. The two opposite specimens of men met Billie at about the same time.

"What's the prob?" asked the younger man.

Billie held up her hands and shrugged.

He smiled and said, "I'm Chuck."

Billie was about to answer when the other man said, "What year is the truck?"

"'Ninety-five, I think."

He didn't reply, just walked right past them to the front of the truck and popped the hood. He grumbled as he poked around, then stopped to scratch the gray stubble on his chin and tilt up his black number three memorial hat.

Billie and Chuck waited for a passing semi, then joined the other man. Billie liked watching Chuck's walk and the sway of his hips.

When he looked in the engine compartment, Chuck said, "Man, look at that antique. We should just leave it here."

The older man said, "Crank it for me."

Billie crawled in the cab and tried it a few times without success. She rejoined her new friends.

The older man said, "It's the alternator. Happens all the time with these Fords."

Billie looked at Chuck, hoping he'd know what to do. He still looked good, just not as smart.

Billie said to the older man, "What should I do?"

"Don't know. Auto parts store is a few miles back." He looked at his battered Timex. "Could take a while."

Chuck said something, but Billie knew who could rescue her now and didn't listen to the young man's comments. She said to the older man, "Is there any way you could help me?" She smiled and looked up at him.

"I guess I could do it, but it'll cost sixty bucks for a rebuilt alternator."

Billie checked her front pocket. She had a twenty the professor had given her, but that was it. Suddenly she remembered Chuck and turned. "I only have twenty. Shoot, I don't know what to do." This time she let her head rest against the tall man's chest.

Chuck immediately dug in his rear pocket and yanked out a nice leather wallet. "I only have thirty."

Her face sank.

"But I have an American Express." He pulled out a Gold card. "See, I can cover it."

"Thank you so much." She hugged him, then hugged the older man, too.

The older man said, "I'll start to pull this one off, you go to the store."

As Chuck turned to head to his own truck, Billie added, "Could you pick me up a Big Mac on the way back?"

As Chuck cheerfully trotted away, Billie smiled. She knew her strengths. Now all she needed was some cash so she didn't have to rely on them all the time.

Captain Sam Norton liked to imagine he was a lord looking over his castle when he stood high in the control room of the Rock. The facility didn't have an electric chair, but they still killed inmates on a fairly regular basis. Two this year when they tried to escape through a hole in the west fence. With a damn name like Manatee, you had to throw a scare into the residents once in a while. Norton had been at Glades when the six had tunneled out. The experience had been embarrassing to the department, but he had found it to be the most interesting month of his whole career.

Now Captain Norton looked out over the empty yard. He was pleased to see no movement. As the senior man on duty, he had just ordered a full lockdown, which meant most of the inmates of the Rock were shut in their cells and no trustee was allowed to wander from a workstation. Captain Norton held his beefy five-foot-eight frame still as he looked out from the control room. He smiled because he hadn't ordered the lockdown for safety reasons or to fix some fault in the fence.

He'd done it because he was sick of looking at the miscreants that the good state of Florida had sent to him, here at the toughest facility south of the Florida State Prison in Starke. Even if it was named after a damn waterborne cow.

Norton had a lot on his mind. The damn FDLE agent was coming to look into Dewalt's death. His business plan could go out the window if he didn't take action, and, like most men, Norton was finding that relationships, no matter how quiet you tried to keep them, were a pain in the ass. He was tired and it was time to test the kid, Lester Lynn, in the control room. The boy had pestered him for months about getting out of the psych ward and into the control room. Some officers liked the tech-heavy room where you could look into almost any corner of the facility. Due to limited manpower, Norton had assigned only one officer per shift to the room, so it was not as all-seeing as it should have been. Norton also had his doubts about this boy Lynn. He needed the right officer in the control room, not just any officer. Some of the other, more experienced officers said he was okay, but there was only one way to find out.

"How long we locked down for, Cap?" asked the young correctional officer. At twenty-four, he was still eager and in pretty good shape. That might last two more years, tops.

"Why do you care? They're down for a while, Lester. You just keep an eye on that board and shut your yap." The captain stood back and watched the young man carefully.

Norton checked his watch and knew the test would start in less than a minute. He walked out of the control room without comment. He pulled out his personal cell phone and called Janzig. "I'm out, Henry. Put on your show." Norton couldn't resist walking down the hallway to peek out the window. He knew young Lester would see the same thing over a monitor. The question was, would he report it?

Norton watched Henry Janzig walk into one of the outdoor walkways with an inmate. It looked like the old pot smuggler from Dorm D. The thin, white boat captain had gone along with the shows before. The fifty-seven-year-old short, puffy Janzig wobbled like a kid's toy as he followed the inmate, then stopped, pulled out a solid nightstick from his belt and whacked the inmate across the back, dropping him to his knees. Then, when he was down, Janzig clubbed him three times over the shoulder and head. Janzig looked up at the monitor and shook his head as a warning to Officer Lynn.

Norton had seen Henry Janzig scare many a new correctional officer with that look. He thought the inmate overacted a little, but seeing it on a monitor without sound, it had to look real. Norton smiled as the inmate pretended to stagger to his feet and walk toward his dorm.

After ten minutes or so, Norton had not been raised on the radio or called on the phone. He walked back into the control room.

"Any problems, Lester?"

The young man remained cool and looked straight ahead. "No, sir. Everything is quiet."

Norton smiled. This boy might be able to join the club, he thought.

He walked down into the yard, nodding to the officers on the towers, standing with their scoped, high-powered 30-06 rifles leaning on their hips, ready for action. He was the boss here and wanted things to run smoothly. He took his job seriously and expected the same from the men and women who worked under his command.

He stopped in front of Dorm A near a female officer writing a report on a picnic table just outside the door. Her body looked square in the bland tan-and-brown uniform issued by the state. Her straight brown hair hung down around her face as she leaned into the paperwork.

"Anything new, Rosalind?"

She looked up. "No, sir, Captain. Just writing up a work order for the air-conditioning in the dorm. It's not working right."

"Don't worry about it now, Rose. They're down for the afternoon. They won't complain."

Norton was tired of this new breed of correctional officer, all concerned with inmates' feelings and well-being. He had started when he was nineteen and spent a total of twenty-two years among the most hardened criminals. He couldn't care less what they thought of being locked down on a pretty Sunday afternoon.

Rosalind said, "Won't be like this if they put in a private prison."

"Don't you worry about that. They won't take these kind anyway. We'll always have us jobs."

"But what about the money goin' to private prisons? What'll we do if they can run 'em cheaper?"

"One thing at a time, Rose. They're just looking for a site for the prison. Whatever happens, it's a long way off." Norton turned and headed toward the main gate so he wouldn't have to listen to the girl yak. He walked through the administration building and then out the side exit to the housing. He had four hours left on shift and needed a break, so he headed to his private quarters. The two sergeants on duty knew to call him if there was trouble. Janzig was the most dependable son of a bitch he'd ever met. If he had to, he could jog the four hundred yards from his little state-provided house back to the prison. As he came to the rear of the house, he heard the big air conditioner on the roof cranking full blast and knew he still had a guest. A smile crossed his lips as he thought about what he might do on his break.

6 TASKER PARKED HIS STATE-ISSUED GOLD MONTE Carlo in the visitors' lot of Manatee Correctional and walked the quarter mile on hard-packed limestone to the administration building. The distance was an intentional design so that cars couldn't be brought close to the outside perimeter fence. At the front office, he pulled out his FDLE badge and credentials and waited for an escort, while straightening his tie in the reflection of a glass picture frame that held an aerial photo of the prison. He'd purposely left his Sig in his car so there wouldn't be an issue and worn his light, comfortable, blue blazer. Even winters could be warm in the Glades. He'd left his state-issued ASP, too. The collapsible metal nightstick usually sat in his right rear pocket when he had on a coat, so it was hidden. The stick had helped him out of more than a few jams. He'd figured he was safe in the administration building of a prison, though, and locked it up.

After less than a minute, a young correctional officer with a crew cut and thick-rimmed glasses opened the door and said, "This way, sir."

Tasker followed him through a maze of clean hallways with thin, industrial carpet, where several trustees in orange vests ran vacuum cleaners and wiped windows. At the end of the longest hallway, an open door showed a large office with dark oak furniture. The sign above the door said WARDEN in large gold letters. The young correctional officer stuck his head in the open door and nodded to a tall, well-dressed black man behind the gigantic oak desk.

"Agent, Tasker. I'm Robert Stubbs, warden of Manatee." He extended his large hand, then guided Tasker to a chair at a conference table.

The warden said, "This is Captain Sam Norton."

Tasker shook the hand of the shorter, sturdy-looking, uniformed captain. His brown eyes briefly appraised Tasker, then showed his lack of interest.

"And this is Inspector R. A. Chin."

Tasker turned his attention to the figure at the far end of the table, and then froze. The inspector had been facing the wall, talking on the phone, but then turned, and Tasker saw that Inspector R. A. Chin was a female. A tall, beautiful female. Whom he had already met.

"We're old friends," she said. Then Renee leaned across the table, took Tasker's hand and grinned at his shocked expression.

The warden said, "We're happy to have you here, Agent. Inspector Chin will be assigned to work with you on the case."

Norton mumbled, "What I want to know is, why're you here for this murder and not one of the other six unsolved ones we've had in the last four years?"

Tasker shrugged. "I was assigned, that's all I know."

Norton said, "Oh, F.I.G.M.O."

Renee cocked her heard, "Figmo?"

Tasker smiled because he was very familiar with the phrase.

Norton answered her. "Fuck it, I've got my orders."

Renee smiled.

Norton turned toward the door. "This don't really involve me, so I'll leave you two to handle it." He looked at Tasker. "Please don't get in the way of daily operations. That *is* my business."

It took great self-control for Tasker to wait the five minutes until after they'd left the warden's office before he started questioning the lovely and mysterious R. A. Chin, also known as Renee. The narrow hallway crowded with staff and trustees wasn't the right setting, either. Finally they came to a set of offices and, inside one of them, Renee turned to face him.

"I know, I shouldn't have sprung it on you, but when you walked in and I recognized you, I turned on purpose. I still like the look on your face." She smiled, revealing perfectly straight white teeth with only one flaw: her second tooth in the front had a chip that cut it at an angle. It was dazzling regardless.

"You did surprise me. And I know you enjoyed taking me the long way so I couldn't speak until now."

"You're very observant. You're right, we could've turned right and come in over there, but where's the fun in that?" She leaned back on a solid oak table and casually crossed her long legs. She wore Dockers pants and a polo shirt with the Department of Corrections DOC logo across the pocket over a T-shirt with sleeves that came to her elbows.

"I'm afraid of what other surprises you have in store for me."

"None, here. I was told to be your tour guide, liaison and interpreter."

"For what language?"

"Prison-speak. Our correctional officers and inmates have their own language of acronyms and shortcuts."

"And this way the warden knows everything I hear."

"You are smart."

"You treat all your visitors like this?"

"If they're under orders from the governor." She smiled and winked. "Anytime someone is in a position to say something positive to our administration, we try to take care of them."

"And I'm sure the fact that you're a knockout has nothing to do with you helping me with my investigation. What was the plan if I was gay, Captain Norton would be my liaison?"

She laughed at that, then said, "If you were gay, I'm quite certain the good captain would have you beaten. He's five feet eight of sour mood and limited patience. I was the only choice. First of all, that's what inspectors do, and second of all, Sam Norton has no use for anyone but his cronies."

"I'll keep that in mind."

Renee kept her perfect brown eyes on him and asked, "Any questions so far?"

"Actually, a few."

"Ask away."

"Okay. I thought the head of a correctional facility was called the 'superintendent.'"

"That was the title until a few years ago. Then a new Secretary of Corrections wanted to go old-school and make the titles sound tough, so he changed it back to warden."

"I'm guessing this prison was named under a different secretary."

She smiled. "You don't think Manatee sounds tough?"

"As tough as Snapper or Key Deer prison, not as ominous as Union or Starke."

"Starke isn't a prison, it's a town, and I wouldn't express your views on the prison name in front of Captain Norton or some of the other veterans, who wanted this place called Hell or Bleak prison. They never use the name 'Manatee,' just 'the facility' or sometimes 'the Rock,' because they liked the movie."

Tasker snickered at the thought of grown men ashamed of the prison's name. "How do you like working for the DOC?"

"Good outfit. Tough job. Think I'll stay, though."

"I expect you'll move up the ladder."

Renee Chin flashed that pretty smile and said, "Maybe. One day." She paused and said, "We're all waiting to see what effect the private prison has when it goes into operation. We may lose people to the corporation running it."

"But that won't be a maximum security facility."

"No, but plenty of people are worried around here."

Tasker inspected the long room. Four tables were spaced before a permanent walkway into the next room, which lined with books. "What's this room for?"

"Study room for the law library."

"For the prisoners?"

"No. The trustees can look things up and then deliver the books to each cell. If we had this inside the walls, the prisoners would be hiding things in the books and using them for exchanges all the time."

A trustee came out of the main library room with an armful of books. The older black man looked like he was in good shape and had been around the block. There was something familiar about him, though, as he waited for Tasker and Renee to move so he could get by. Unlike the other trustees, this man made no effort to be friendly or deferential.

Renee turned to the solid man. "Who're all those for, Luther?"

"Sergeant Janzig said that Dorm C could have a garden. These are texts on such activities as relate to the endeavor."

Tasker heard the voice and use of language and snapped to attention. "Cole Hodges?"

The man slowly looked at Tasker. "In here, they call me Luther Williams, Mr. Tasker." He paused to look at Inspector R. A. Chin and said, "Special Agent Tasker and I are acquainted."

Renee kept her eyes on him. "I see." She looked at Tasker and said, "You just know everyone, don't you?"

Luther Williams took his time walking to Dorm C. It was quite a shock to see the cop who'd figured out who he really was and then, indirectly, had him sent to this hellhole. He had had a fine life as "lawyer" Cole Hodges after he escaped from the Missouri State Penitentiary over twenty years before. When things had gone bad with his community action group, the Committee for Community Relief, he tried to flee with the million five he had skimmed, but other people had wanted the money, too. When it was all said and done, this state cop had been the only one smart enough to realize he wasn't the prominent attorney he'd pretended to be. A quick plea on his part had gotten him ten years Florida time, to be followed by twenty more in Missouri. He'd taken it because he'd figured on a shorter sentence, much shorter, and knew he could hide a hell of a lot better in Florida, with the contacts he had and the other money he had stashed, than in Missouri. This smart cop might prove valuable.

Coming toward him on the walkway was the largest of the Aryan Knights. Luther stayed clear of them mainly because he didn't need the aggravation. He thought about Vic Vollentius' message. It was vague, but enough to put him on edge. He still wasn't afraid of any man, no matter how many weights the guy lifted or how often he shadowboxed in the yard. This one was tall, maybe six-foot-three, and had a lot of meat on him, not much of it fat. He gave Luther a hard stare from more than thirty feet away. Luther couldn't figure out what had turned these morons so nasty the last few weeks, but he was getting tired of it. In the cafeteria he had been jostled by two of the Knights, and now Vic Vollentius seemed to be keeping a close eye on Luther's activities.

As the younger man came closer, he shifted more toward Luther, who refused to give up ground to this monster. Then, when they were next to each other, the Aryan Knight leaned into him and bumped Luther hard, almost off his feet.

Luther wasn't the chatty type. He knew this was an assault on his stature. The big Aryan Knight stopped and stared, like he was daring Luther to take action.

Luther kept calm, and placed his hands on his waistline, where his belt should be and the long, thin metal strip he used like a fencing foil was hidden. Luther looked past the Knight's shoulder and nodded to the empty space. When the Knight turned to see who was coming up on them, Luther jerked the end of the foil and, by the time the Aryan Knight had turned back around, shoved the metal strip deep into the man's right bicep.

He withdrew it instantly and quickly pulled it between his two fingers to remove the thin sheen of blood.

The wounded man grasped his upper arm. "Motherfucker. You're gonna pay for that."

"Now?" Luther could not help but smile. He knew the wound wasn't lethal but it affected this man's head. He obviously loved his big, defined biceps and didn't know what having a metal strip run through them would do.

The big man said, "Soon. Your time is coming soon, jungle bunny."

Luther chuckled. "Jungle bunny. That's the best you can do? C'mon, son, I grew up in the sixties in East St. Louis. I've heard nuns call me worse names."

The man backed away, still clutching his injured arm.

Luther secured his weapon and continued on his way like he had just stopped to chat with a friend. He was at Dorm C a few minutes later.

As he entered the forty-bed dorm with the observation cage in the middle, which was now, due to budget cuts, unoccupied, he announced to the lounging inmates, "I have reading material to enrich your minds." He smiled as their heads turned. He opened one book and took out a bag, which had been flattened inside. He held it up and shook it as the white powder fell to one corner of the clear plastic. "And something to expand your consciousness."

He smiled as they lined up, some stopping to dig in their stash holes for money.

He knew he'd make a living wherever he landed.

7 TASKER LOOKED OUT OVER THE YARD FROM Renee's second-story office just outside the perimeter fence of Manatee state prison. The eight main dorms, eight secure dorms and the lockdown building were all in view. About thirty inmates were in the exercise yard, the most ever allowed at one time. It kept down the trouble and the chance to plan escapes. Since the famous Glades prison escape of 1993, rules for pleasant treatment and inmate exercise needs had been scrapped.

Renee, sitting behind her neat and orderly desk, said, "So where do you want to start? The crime scene? Interviews?"

He turned from the window and said, "First, I'd like to know how a black woman in Gladesville ended up with a name like Chin, then I'd be interested in how you learned to punch like you did the other night in the bar."

She smiled. "First, I was born in Jamaica, where twenty percent of the population has some Chinese DNA and odd middle or last names. And, second, I have two brothers and six years as a correctional officer and inspector." She kept her smile. "Now you can tell me about Luther Williams."

"Nothing to tell. He was an active crook in Miami and an escaped convict and we arrested him."

"I heard he was known as Cole Hodges, had assumed someone else's identity, but that was it. He behaves, you know. He's one of the few really bright guys out here."

"Yeah, he's smart. He copped a plea that included no one looking into what happened to the real Cole Hodges. I guess the state attorney figured he'd be behind bars until he died."

Renee said, "Out here, almost everyone is behind bars until they die."

Luther Williams was still a little annoyed and concerned that the Aryan Knights had suddenly seemed to realize he was black. They hadn't bothered him until the last few weeks. Why now? He carried those thoughts with him as he entered the visitors' center. He was now annoyed at his visitor. He had told her not to come early. He wanted the guards to get used to her coming late on visiting days. He was angry but couldn't show it as he entered the room where certain prisoners received non-relative visitors through a thick sheet of glass and a telephone. Not even these Neanderthal guards would believe this woman was related to him. She wanted to be and he'd marry her if it would help his plans, but right now this tall, hundred-and-sixty-pound lump of white flesh obviously showed no signs of shared DNA with Luther. The best he'd be able to do is a relation by marriage, which didn't really thrill him.

He sat at the small counter in the hard wooden chair and picked up the handset for the intercom as she did the same. He feigned a smile, showing off the store-bought teeth he had been able to afford a few years ago. "Hi," was all he started with.

A broad smile sparked across her pretty face. "It kills me not to see you for a whole week."

"Rules of the institution, my dear."

"Rules that break my heart." She gazed at him with her green eyes.

He thought, Rules that keep me from having to look at you more than once a week. But instead he smiled again. "There is an opportunity on Sundays as well. You could come at the same time."

"Really? I could come earlier in the day so we could have more time together."

"Believe me, four-thirty is the best possible time."

"I'll be here."

He forced a smile and said, "What news of the world do you have for me?"

"You probably heard about the amendment to reduce class size coming under fire."

He frowned. "No, my dear, I didn't mean that. I get to read the newspapers. I meant about my remaining business interests." This woman had fallen for him based on news stories she had seen about his past. She felt he had changed and bettered himself and was not being given a proper chance to get ahead in life. In turn, he had made her the manager of his few remaining business interests and pretended to love her as much as she loved him.

She looked at him and put her masculine hand to the glass. "Everything is fine. All the rent on the apartments is up to date and the gas stations are all doing well. Herbert says he wishes you were able to talk to the wholesalers because they don't show him the respect you got."

"You tell Herbert to start paying one of the gangs, maybe the Eighth Street Boyz, a few hundred bucks to show their faces to the wholesaler once in a while. Maybe have them stop his truck and explain it. Tell him to do that, then for him to come see me in two weeks."

"But then I won't be able to visit that week."

"A tragedy, my dear, to be sure, but necessary."

She accepted the news, then said, "I had a check sent to Florida A and M for Teresa. It'll look like it's part of the scholarship."

"Excellent."

"Why don't you tell her who's been providing for her for so long?"

Luther stared at her. "I'm not particularly proud of my situation at the moment. Perhaps if things change."

"The girl has a right to know who you are."

"I have a right to handle it as I see fit."

She cast her head down and nodded, then returned her hand to the window.

He placed his hand opposite hers. "One more thing. You need to time it to come right at four-thirty from now on, no excuses."

"Why?"

He twitched slightly and let his nostrils flair. "Because I just told you to."

Tasker used his afternoon to visit his odd but pleasant neighbor, Warren Kling, at his archaeological dig. They stood in an open field ringed with sugarcane big enough to hold a football stadium with a full parking lot. Tasker waited while the portly figure finished a call on his tiny cell phone.

Kling nodded as if the person on the other end could see him. "I know, I know, Rick." He listened to his caller. "No problem the dig will go that far. I promise." He listened to his caller and said, "No, Rick, it doesn't. Seminoles are not Florida's original people. They came from other territory, so they aren't considered OPs." Then after only a few seconds, "I have company. I'll call you later."

The pudgy man shrugged at Tasker, saying, "Sorry, business."

Tasker waved him off and said, "You got plenty of room out here." He snapped a couple of photos with his digital camera.

"My site is right here and probably drifts a few hundred feet that way." He pointed into the open field. "That's one of the sites they're considering for the private prison you hear everyone talk about."

Tasker looked over at a crude, hand-painted sign with the numbers 19650 scrawled on a flat piece of wood. "Is that to identify the site?"

"Yeah, I guess it's the address on US 27."

"Where's the other site?"

"Three miles down the road."

"What's the difference?"

"The difference is if one owner can sell to the state rather than the other. Lots of money involved."

Tasker looked out at the rabbits, which appeared to be swarming to something now, if rabbits actually swarmed. "They displace a lot of rabbits when they cut the fields."

"You have no idea. If the PETA people saw what happens, they'd invade and kill all the migrants out here."

"What happens?"

"They burn the fields to make the soil last longer. When they start the fire, the bunnies all run to the edge of the field in a tiny herd. The local kids get a dollar apiece for the rabbits, for their pelt, feet and, in some cases, meat. The kids take a four-foot stalk of cane and smash them as they run from the fire. See." He pointed to dark spots on the ground. Hundreds of dark spots.

"What are those?"

"Rabbit remains. The spots can stay for a year or more. The ones by our apartments are from last season."

Tasker looked out over the field at all the bunnies. "How are there still so many?"

"They screw like rabbits."

Tasker nodded at the obvious response.

Later, Tasker sat in a folding canvas chair under a wide plastic cover, surveying the series of shallow trenches, digging tools strewn on the edges. He took a photo of the site and one of the professor climbing out of a trench. Then he took one of the professor with the wide-open field behind him.

"What're you, a professional?"

Tasker smiled. "It's digital. My kids gave it to me, so when I remember it I snap a lot of photos. The storage card is filling up."

"I'd never figure something like that out."

Tasker smiled, then looked around the dig. "Okay, Doc, what have you turned up? Incas? Leif Eriksson's first expedition?"

The professor smiled. "You're pretty smart considering where you went to school." He flopped into the chair next to Tasker. "No, what Billie and I have uncovered here are the remnants of the Seminoles who fled the third Seminole war. I always thought they had an interim home before settling in the Big Cypress farther south and west, but never had any proof. Every day we find more to support my hypothesis."

Tasker heard a vehicle approaching.

"Here comes Billie. What do you think of her?"

"Very pretty."

"Wish she was a little less pretty and a little more motivated."

Tasker stood out of habit as the small pickup truck came to a stop next to the tent. Strands of hair fell over her small, delicate features. She looked like a gymnast, her muscular body moving under jeans and a tank top. Her jet-black hair shone in the sunlight as she smiled at the professor.

"Billie, you remember Bill Tasker."

She smiled and nodded.

Tasker said, "You surprised me the other night. I didn't expect a 'Billie' to look like you."

She bowed her head slightly and said, "I didn't expect a cop to look like you."

8 BILL TASKER STROLLED ACROSS THE OPEN YARD of Manatee Correctional. He never strolled. He walked fast, trotted and ran. This was a new feeling. Although the sun was shining and the temperature a perfect seventy, the only reason he wasn't racing to his destination was that Department of Corrections Inspector Renee Allison Chin was walking alongside him. He was on official business, but times like this reminded him why he liked his job so much.

In his right hand he held a folder with thirty-two crime scene photos of the body of Rick Dewalt. The young man's body lay next to a cement landing with three steps that led to the common door to lockdown and the psychiatric ward. The photos gave him a good sense of the position of the body and the marks around his neck, but not the feeling for the location. He wanted to see if, by looking around the compound from the site where Dewalt had been found, it might give him an idea why his body had been left there. Was he killed there? Was the location hidden from normal view? That was why he was physically in the prison, to get a firsthand look at the circumstances of the death.

As they came to the long, blank wall with its one door, Renee said, "One of the officers found him here about ten in the morning. I responded almost immediately."

Tasker nodded. "Your reports cover all that pretty well. Did you ask any of your sources?"

"Sources?"

"Um, snitches, I mean, informants. Everyone calls them something different."

She smiled. "And you're sure I have informants in the general population."

"You're too competent not to."

She kept smiling. "Yes, I have talked both formally and informally to my regular sources of information." She looked at Tasker. "Does that sound more like a cop? Sources of information?"

"That's our politically correct term."

"In here people are always looking for an angle, so they share the one commodity they all have: information."

Tasker nodded and then stood on the cement landing looking down on the ground where the body had been found and then up and around the yard. "This is a little isolated, but I'd be worried about someone seeing me if I was choking someone here. That usually takes a few minutes."

"So you think someone dumped the body here?"

"Too early to tell. I'll talk to the ME and try to keep an open mind. What's your take on it?"

"I always thought Dewalt was killed somewhere else, but we have no clue where."

"He worked as a trustee inside here, right?"

"Yeah, he switched between psych and lockdown, cleaning up and keeping sodas in the coolers for the officers. That sort of thing."

"No time log when he came and went."

She shook her head. "The trustees have to be available, but the officers send them all over on errands."

"He didn't owe anyone money or have bad blood with anyone?"

"Not that I could find out. He was real low-key. As you probably know, his dad is a rich land developer. I don't think Rick Junior was ready for life on the inside. He tried to fly below the radar whenever possible."

"I know most of that from reading your reports." He looked at her and grinned. "R. A. Chin."

She laughed. "I just always sign things that way. Sorry if your mind wasn't open enough to think I might be a female."

Tasker smiled and went back to his review of the photos as he thought, And some kind of female, at that.

Two hours later, Bill Tasker pulled into a spot right in front of the small structure in the parking lot of the Palm Beach County Sheriff's Office, which housed the medical examiner's office. The two-building facility was known by most detectives and agents in the county, and so was the building's most interesting occupant, Assistant Medical Examiner Dominick Freund. Tasker waited at the front until the operations officer, Tony, escorted him in.

"The doc is in the procedure room," said Tony. Each of his strides made up two of Tasker's. He had that perpetual stoop really tall guys develop as a defense against low ceiling fans and other obstructions hung by short people. He turned his usual smiling face to Tasker and said, "Haven't seen you around for a while."

"I was transferred to Miami four years ago."

Tony grinned and said, "I guess I did see something about it on the news." He led Tasker through a small outdoor walkway from the administration building to the rooms used for evidence storage and procedures.

Tony said, "He's just finishing up."

"That's good."

Tony smiled and said, "Everyone says that."

Tasker followed him into the large room with four separate stations. He'd hate to see a time when all four were being used. At the far station, his friend Dom Freund was lifting a bucket and preparing to dispose of the contents.

"Still have the problem, huh, Doc?"

Freund turned. "Billy Tasker. You back up here now?"

"Nope. Believe it or not, I'm out in the Glades for a while."

"You find airstrips again?"

"Looking at the death at Manatee about six weeks ago."

"I remember it a little. Let me clean up and I'll get my notes in the office."

Ten minutes later, after catching up on family matters and Freund's need for buckets during autopsies, Tasker settled into a comfortable high-backed leather chair in the assistant ME's cluttered office.

Freund read over his notes and reviewed a few photos and said, "Yeah, I remember it now."

"What can you tell me?"

"He died of asphyxiation due to ligature strangulation." The ME looked up at Tasker and added, "That is, a weapon was used to choke him, not someone's hands."

Tasker said, "Thanks, Doc. Went to the police academy, remember?"

"Most of you FDLE guys are a little slow on the uptake. Just making sure." He smiled and continued with his analysis. "Based on the marks on his neck, probably by a belt or thick cord."

"How do you know that?"

"Wide mark and the object didn't dig into the sides of his neck deeply like a rope might have. Plus there are no strand marks like a rope might leave. His hands were very loosely tied. Didn't show marks of a struggle."

"Wouldn't he have struggled if someone was choking him? I mean, that takes a minute or more."

"If the initial pressure was strong, he could have lost consciousness almost immediately. I have to look at the totality of the circumstances. He was outside, there was no lividity in his extremities. If he had been hanging like a suicide, the blood would have pooled in his hands and feet. Blood will go to the lowest point without the heart pumping."

"Okay, then what's your theory?"

"I'd say someone looped the murder weapon around his neck and pulled. He might have been choked right from the stairs where he was found."

"Almost sounds like someone was trying to make it look like a suicide, but something went wrong."

"Like what?"

"Maybe someone saw them and they had to abandon the body right where it lay."

"You cops have to have a theory for everything."

"He's dead. My theory right now is that something killed him. Can you help me with anything past that?"

"Nothing except you have your work cut out for you out in that snake pit."

9 BILL TASKER PARKED AT THE END OF THE wide circular driveway, saw a Corvette and a four-wheel-drive Toyota truck parked in close to the garage and a big four-door Cadillac in front of the entranceway. Tasker took in the massive two-story structure with the glass inlaid walkway as he fumbled with his steno pad to make sure he had the right house. He was pretty sure a successful land developer would live in a place like this. It wasn't a Palm Beach mansion, but out here in Wellington, an upscale community with its own polo grounds, this place looked nice.

A small woman about fifty answered the door with a smile.

"Mrs. Dewalt? I'm Bill Tasker, we spoke on the phone."

She nodded and motioned him in all the way.

As he entered the silent house, he could tell that this woman had taken her son's death hard. She still hadn't said a word as he followed her through two giant rooms toward a series of open sliding glass doors and a patio surrounding a pool with two separate water fountains.

"Rick, the state policeman is here."

Tasker saw the wide man with round wire-rimmed glasses stand and turn to greet him. He had a bottle of bourbon and a half-filled glass by a stack of contracts. Tasker would've bet he never drank during the day a few months before.

After settling in, Tasker started with simple questions about their son's background and how he ended up in a state prison. He had already looked at the few belongings Rick Dewalt, Jr., had left behind at Manatee. A few pieces of jewelry, a cheap watch, things like that. Nothing that gave any indication about the young man's history or family.

Big Rick Dewalt, as he was sometimes called, said, "You cannot tell me pot is not a dangerous drug. If it weren't for marijuana, little Rick would've graduated from UCF and gone on to teach. The boy had a gift for mathematics."

Mrs. Dewalt just nodded and stifled a sob.

"Did your son talk about any problems he was having out at the prison?"

"All he had was problems. You saw the scum out there. No place for a decent white man to get sent. As much as I paid the fucking cutthroat lawyers, you'd think they coulda done better for him. But no, the Department of Corrections acts on its own. Judges don't influence them."

"Was your son bitter about jail?"

"He knew he brought it on himself, if that's what you mean. No one else to blame."

Mrs. Dewalt said, "No one but the people that kept getting him hooked on drugs. He was in rehab four times. Finished it, too, then someone would always get him using drugs again."

Big Rick Dewalt nodded. "Almost as expensive as the goddamn lawyers, that rehab shit. Every place more expensive than the last. It was just another scam. Everyone is out to make a buck."

Tasker made a few notes. Nothing useful. He worked hard not to ask if developing Florida land was a scam, too. As far as he knew, that's all it was. Part of the scam included buying off county commissioners or whoever else could approve the use of what had been wetlands or preserves. Tasker stuck to the point.

"When was your last contact with your son?"

Mrs. Dewalt said, "I visited him the day before they found . . ." She finished with a sob.

Big Rick Dewalt said, "I saw him when he was sentenced."

"You never visited Manatee?"

"No." He glared at Tasker, almost daring him to inquire further. Then he added, "I spoke to him on the phone from time to time."

"What sort of things would you talk about?"

"Just catching up. He was a land surveyor, so they used him to mark out new construction projects now and then. We'd talk about that sort of thing."

Tasker stared at his pad, trying to decide where he was going with the next question. Then the half-in-the-bag businessman said, "Don't get me wrong, Tasker. He was my son. But I have two other kids to worry about. A nineteen-year-old at Florida Atlantic and a twenty-four-year-old at Stetson. Little Rick chose to throw away his life. I don't have enough time to waste on someone like that."

Tasker nodded, still silent. There was something up with this guy, but Tasker had no clue what. He turned to Mrs. Dewalt. "Did he seem all right to you? Was he particularly despondent?"

Her hair had a slight gray tinge to it and her eyes had gentle wrinkles around the corners. She looked like she had laughed a lot at one time. Now she asked, "How do you mean? He was always down when I visited him."

"Anything. Anything worse than usual?"

"Well, he said he'd like to end it all. But he said that all the time."

Tasker thought about it and was about to ask if she thought he'd committed suicide when Big Rick said, "Guess someone ended it for him." The big man stood and said, "That's all we care to say about our son right now, Mr. Tasker. Just find out who killed him, so we can lay the whole thing to rest."

Tasker knew the end of an interview when he heard it.

That evening, Tasker scurried around his little apartment picking up clothes and generally trying to make it presentable for Donna and the girls. He had spent the afternoon considering his encounter with Big Rick Dewalt and his quiet, ghostlike wife. He had the idea that the senior Dewalt was more embarrassed by his son than saddened by his death. Tasker figured the wife was the one pushing for answers to her son's death. Big Rick looked like he would rather be filling in part of the Everglades for more condos.

Donna had reluctantly agreed to drop the girls off for the weekend if he could drive them back Sunday afternoon. With his visits to the medical examiner, the sheriff's office and the Dewalts, the week had flown by. His only regret was that he hadn't seen much of Renee Chin. Not officially and not socially. But he hoped both situations might change soon.

He glanced at the hamster cage that Professor Kling had made into a trap as he hustled some newspapers to the garbage. He had looked in the cage every day since Kling had given it to him. Tasker had begun to doubt its effectiveness, but now he stopped to stare in amazement. The little mouse with the yellow stain was now calmly munching on some peanut butter the professor had used as bait. The trap had shut and the vermin was secure. Tasker smiled as he heard a car pull up.

He met his ex-wife as she came up the three steps onto the old wooden porch he shared with Professor Kling. His girls both darted from the car up the steps in front of the professor's apartment and into his arms. He crouched and kissed them both on the heads, then the cheeks. As he stood, Donna leaned in for a kiss and turned her head to the side. He delivered a platonic peck on the cheek and knew what she had planned this weekend.

"Have time to come in?" he asked.

"Sure." She stepped through the door before him. Following her was never a problem. As pretty as her face was, her rear view was just as spectacular. She stopped in front of him midway through the door.

"Billy, what did you do?"

He hesitated, then peeked in at the girls, both of whom were kneeling by the cage and cooing at the trapped mouse.

"I, ah . . ." He didn't want to tell her the truth because he was afraid she might not let the girls stay in an apartment with rodents on the loose. "I needed company and knew the girls would get a kick out of it."

"What's his name?" asked Kelly.

"Ah, well, I call him Mousy," he finally stammered out.

"Can we rename him?" asked Kelly.

"You bet."

Donna turned to him. "Billy, that thing isn't coming to my house when you move back to Kendall."

"That a question?"

"No."

"Then I guess it's coming to Kendall with me."

"Can we hold him?" pleaded Kelly with a quick second from Emily.

He was caught short. "Ah, not right now. He was a little sick when I first, ah, picked him up, and a vet should take a look at him."

"Can we take him to the vet in the morning?"

"Ah . . ." He looked at Donna and then the girls and just nodded his head. "Sure."

He heard another car and turned his head to see Professor Kling and Billie heading to his apartment. The older man looked up and smiled.

"Hello, my FSU friend. Finally have some visitors?"

Tasker motioned him up, then inside, and made introductions. Billie scurried on to the professor's apartment with something in her arms. When the professor stepped toward the girls to see the cage, Tasker realized his danger.

"Ah, Professor, tell Donna about your dig. It's really fascinating."

The professor ignored Tasker, leaned over and lowered his glasses. "I say, my boy, it worked."

"What worked?" asked Donna, now suspicious.

Tasker immediately said, "He fixed this cage so I could use it for the hamster I bought the girls."

The professor turned to him. "The hamster?"

Tasker blinked his eyes hard and said firmly, "Yes, that hamster."

"But—" was all the professor got out when they all heard a deep howl like an air raid siren.

"What's that?" asked Donna.

Tasker knew the sound and what it meant. "Escape at Manatee."

Luther Williams' heart raced as he watched correctional officers swarm to the front gate and a man with three hound dogs on leashes hustle to the partially open gate access. It had taken them a lot less time than he had calculated to discover the breach and react. And their reaction was much more specific and effective than he'd ever thought possible. He watched the men rush through the gate, and two officers, armed with big, black Remington 870 pump shotguns with extended magazines, stood by the open door so only authorized personnel left that way.

"Damn," Luther muttered to himself as he clicked the stopwatch he was holding and sat back on his stool next to Dorm A. He had spent a month convincing that moron Leroy Baxter from Daytona to attempt an escape. When the young man had come to him that afternoon, Luther explained that a wedge on the correctional officer's single door at the right time would lock it open enough for someone to slip through. He had done it solely to see how the guards handled an escape. Now he had his answer: They handled it well. Two minutes from the moment the armed robber had casually made his way out the jammed door that no one noticed until the alarm sounded. Four minutes and fifteen seconds later, the guards, with dogs, were hot on his trail. The boy didn't stand a chance. They'd run him to ground inside an hour. That made Luther's chances even harder.

He immediately set to work on his own plan.

Captain Sam Norton, a twenty-two-year veteran of the Florida Department of Corrections, stood next to the dog handler and felt the weight of his shotgun in his hand. He loved this. He'd allow escapes every week if it wouldn't cost him his job. He'd been at Glades when the six had dug out and it had been the best time of his whole career. This was the third attempt in the past year and only the second to get off the facility. He'd be there when they ran this convict down. He had to be, he was the boss.

"Okay, Lester, you and your boys cover the field behind the prison. Take the sheriff's dogs out there. Tommy, you start checking all the outbuildings on the grounds." He knew this sucker wasn't in any outbuildings. He knew that ice-cold robber had shaken his black ass right toward Gladesville hoping to get a ride or jump on a semi-tractor-trailer. "Cletus, set your dogs toward the town and I'll go with you." He looked around at the men. *"Now,"* he barked, and, as expected, everyone kicked into high gear.

Just as he started to trot with Cletus and the dogs, he saw Renee Chin coming out of the admin building with a service revolver in a holster on her hip. It burned his ass that inspectors were issued handguns and could carry them off the prison grounds. He let his frustration slide with Renee Chin. He liked her being close when things went bad. Not only to impress her, but to protect her, too. This time he thought it'd be better if she was well away from the action.

He stopped to face her and pointed toward the rear fields. "Help Lester in the back field. He's got a deputy with a sheriff's dog. The tower guards at the Rock will cover you."

She nodded and started to move in an easy lope with those wonderful long legs toward the uncut cane field. Norton caught up with the hounds heading toward Gladesville and apparently already on the fleeing man's scent.

'll be right here with them," he said as Donna shook her head again.

"No way," she said from the driver's seat, the girls crying in the back of the van. "It's too dangerous until they catch that guy. Besides, you want to get out there and help. I know you."

"Traditionally, prisons catch escapees in the first ten hours."

"Maybe we'll be back tomorrow then," she said, putting her van in gear and starting to back out.

He stood and watched, almost saying, At least let them take their hamster.

She waved and made an apologetic shrug as they turned for the long road headed to US 27.

He stood watching them when he felt a hand on his shoulder. He turned to see Billie Towers standing next to him, her full lips in a slight pout. "Sorry they had to go. Is there anything I can do to help?"

Tasker couldn't keep the smile from spreading across his face. Despite what he wanted to say, he shook his head. "No, thanks, Billie. I gotta get over to the prison and see if they need a hand." She had a worried look, but Tasker got the feeling he wasn't the one she was concerned about.

10 ON THE SHORT DRIVE FROM HIS APARTMENT to the facility, Tasker called the prison admin office but the phone just rang. Then he scrolled down his phone list to the newest entry: R. A. Chin. She answered her cell phone on the first ring.

"Go ahead." She was all business now.

"Renee, it's Bill Tasker. I heard the siren. What can I do to help?"

She sounded distracted. "Bill, I'm in a sugarcane field on a wild-goose chase now. Sam Norton was headed toward town with some dogs. See if you can find him."

"How many are out?"

"Just one. Leroy Baxter. He's got a violent history, but hasn't been a problem for us. Looks like he slid a wedge into a side gate and slipped out."

"I'll call you after I find Norton."

"Bill!" She shouted it to keep him from hanging up.

"Yeah?"

"Be careful."

He appreciated someone being concerned for him. Billie Towers had said the same thing as he bolted from the apartment complex a few minutes before. She had slipped him her phone number and told him to call when he was done for the night, if for no other reason than to let her know he was okay. He'd smiled and told her he'd probably be right back anyway, that's how escapes worked. Searching for an escaped convict is the kind of job he was made for. Simple, direct and with an obvious gauge of success. If the convict ends up in custody, the mission is accomplished.

He slowed near Gladesville as he headed east on US 27. Near the prison he turned toward town and immediately saw a DOC pickup truck, one of the trucks usually circling the compound, slowly cruising up one side of the road. Tasker pulled alongside and lowered his window.

He held up his open badge and said, "Bill Tasker, FDLE."

The middle-aged man just looked at him.

Tasker paused and said, "I'm looking for Captain Norton."

The man pointed up ahead and toward a line of industrial-type shops with a warehouse complex behind them.

Tasker punched the gas and darted into a parking spot in front of a cabinetmaker's shop, which had closed for the day. As he stepped out of the Monte Carlo, he could hear the dogs barking behind the building. He went to his trunk and pulled out a FDLE raid jacket so he could be clearly identified. He also took off his belly bag with his small Sig Sauer .380 inside and used his tactical belt with his issued Beretta .40 caliber in a holster on his hip. He checked the automatic and saw there was a round in the chamber. Finally he stuck his ASP in his rear pocket. Not only could it be used as a nightstick, it was handy for searching through piles of debris or other things he didn't want to stick his hands into. Finally, with all his gear in order, he headed around the line of four shops.

He spotted two men with shotguns as he rounded the building. One man turned quickly and Tasker froze so he could see he was a cop.

The other man, Captain Norton, waved him over. "What're you doin' here?"

"Just here to help."

"I think we can handle this."

"I'm out, an extra man never hurts."

Norton shrugged, apparently not awed by FDLE's reputation or position in law enforcement. Tasker stood next to the DOC officers and watched the dog handler work a section of the warehouse.

Norton turned to Tasker. "Okay, Mr. Special Agent, why don't you stay with Cletus and the dogs and we'll run 'round back. We think he's in them warehouses and if you guys go in you'll likely flush him out to us."

Tasker nodded and walked toward the man holding the leashes of the three dogs. He was heavy, with all of his extra weight in his belly. His red T-shirt didn't cover the mound of flesh above his belt line.

"Cletus, I'm Bill. Captain Norton told me to go with you and try to flush the guy toward him in the back."

Cletus turned his head to one side and spit out a giant dark chunk of chewing tobacco. The brown juice dribbled down his chin. He looked at Tasker and nodded, turning toward the opening to the rear warehouses. The dogs continued to bark and strain at their leashes.

Tasker drew his pistol and started scanning each area carefully. The dogs seemed intent on the warehouse farther back, and Cletus let them pull him that way at a pretty good pace. They cleared two rows of warehouse units in less than a minute and could see the rear exit. Then they heard a quick shout and a shotgun blast. Tasker recognized the hollow sound of a double-ought buckshot round.

Leroy Baxter had been inside Manatee for two years and knew he wouldn't see freedom for at least eighteen more. He'd pleaded guilty to a series of armed robberies in Daytona, where he would rob check-cashing stores and biker bars on a rotating basis. He always wore a blue mask at the check-cashing stores and a bright red mask at the biker bars, thinking everyone would figure there were two separate robbers. His plan might have succeeded if the police hadn't found both masks when he was arrested after a short car chase from a biker bar.

Leroy was actually relieved when he was only charged with the robberies because he had also killed two separate couples in the same month he had been robbing the stores. One couple was a Canadian husband and wife on their honeymoon. The man had been a smart-ass and the woman a piece of ass and when he'd tried to show the woman the benefits of some Florida lovin', the man had gotten froggy and Leroy had had to shoot him in the face. He hadn't meant to shoot him in the face, but he'd moved so fast it just happened. The woman started screaming and wouldn't stop, so Leroy had shot her in the face, too. Then he'd put them in the trunk of their rented Ford Taurus and dropped them in one of the deep lakes out near Apopka. A few days later, he started seeing reports on the TV about how the couple was missing from Orlando. The Daytona trip was just a day trip and no one even knew they had come to the coast. What luck.

The second couple Leroy killed was on purpose. He had walked into a check-cashing store and seen this old dude and a young woman cash a couple of checks and walk out with a load of cash. Leroy just followed them back to one of the cheesy motels on the north end of the beach and watched their room. After an hour, he slipped up to the second-story outside room and knocked on the door. The man had called out without opening the door. "Who is it?" Kinda pissed off.

Leroy said, "Your bathroom is leaking into the first-floor room. I need to check it real quick."

When the man opened the door a crack, Leroy had the pistol waiting at face level. The man didn't hesitate to raise his arms and step away from the door. Leroy stepped inside and closed the door. The old, fat man stood with his hands up and a small towel wrapped around his waist. The woman was frozen in the bed with the covers up to her neck. As Leroy stared at them, the man's towel dropped to the floor.

Leroy motioned toward the bed with his .38 revolver. "Get in the bed with her."

"Just don't shoot," the man said, his eyes focused only on the gun barrel.

"Do what I say and no one'll get hurt." He watched the man lie down, then said to him, "Take the covers off her."

The man complied without any hesitation, exposing the much younger woman, who was naked under the covers. She had a tight body with big, fake tits that stuck straight up even though she was on her back. Leroy immediately felt his interest in her.

"Where's the cash?"

The man just stared at the gun.

Leroy repeated, "Where is the cash?" This time he spoke slower.

The man knew there was no use. He nodded at his pants hanging on a chair by a small old desk.

Leroy backed up to it with his gun still pointed at the naked couple and felt the pockets with his free hand. He found the wad of hundred-dollar bills and stuck the three-inch stack in his pocket. Now that business was over, he thought he might have a little fun. He stepped to the woman's side of the bed and looked down at her. She didn't look nearly as scared as the man. He smiled and used his free hand to unzip his loose pants.

Then the woman spoke. She had a thick New York accent and he wasn't sure if she was talking to him or to the naked white man next to her.

She said, "I ain't gonna fuck no nigger."

Leroy didn't need that kind of shit. At the time, it was the start of a new century and he thought that kind of attitude had been left in the old century. Besides, he had a gun. He didn't hesitate. He just pointed the barrel to within three inches of the woman's good-looking nose and pulled the trigger. The pop drowned out the man's yelp. Then Leroy just pointed the gun at the man's temple and jerked the trigger again. Now he had the cash and no witnesses. He had also showed this fine-looking bitch how certain words could hurt. He had stepped outside and casually walked to his car and no one had ever asked him a single question about the double murder.

The news had said it was a drug deal gone bad and covered it for three or four days, but that was all. So Leroy always thought he'd gotten off pretty easy for four murders and six robberies all in one month. Too bad his little vacation from prison hadn't lasted any longer.

He had heard the dogs and scampered out the rear when he saw Captain Norton and Sergeant Janzig standing there with shotguns like they were waiting for him.

Leroy raised his hands slowly and froze. Neither man pointed a gun at him. Captain Norton just raised his hand and motioned him to come to him like they were in the cafeteria and the captain needed to talk to him.

Leroy relaxed and started to stroll over to the notoriously surly man. He saw the captain say something to the sergeant and then smile slightly.

Leroy smiled as he came closer, relieved neither man looked nervous and hadn't even bothered to threaten him with their black shotguns. He put his hands on his head because his arms were a little tired and said, "I guess you got me," as he stopped a few feet away from the armed DOC officers.

The captain said, "Leroy, I thought you were tougher," and then tossed something on the ground at his feet.

Leroy looked down at a crude shiv made from a straight piece of metal about ten inches long with a swath of cloth wrapped around it.

Captain Sam Norton looked at Sergeant Henry Janzig. Norton remembered when his friend had passed his test to enter the little club of trusted officers by keeping his mouth shut about a fucked-up inspection for which Norton had changed some crucial findings before the report had gone to Tallahassee. Now his friend saw the inmate. He shook his knotty head and looked at the captain with that constant scowl. Janzig actually had a good disposition if you were one of the three percent of the population that didn't annoy him.

Norton said, "Told you so."

The sergeant nodded and pulled out a five-dollar bill from his front pocket. "Shit, that's fifteen bucks I lost the last two weeks."

"You'll make it back up."

"I thought he'd go out the front."

"Henry, you spend too much time with them white power shitheads. Other people do other things."

"You sayin' a white man woulda gone out the front?"

"I'm sayin' you got to get inside people's minds. Think how they think, not think how they look."

"You been readin' one of your crazy textbooks again?"

"Reading ain't a sin, Henry."

The tubby man shrugged his rounded shoulders.

Now Norton changed his tone. "You know, Henry, we could kill two birds with one stone."

"How's that?"

"What if this boy here killed Rick Dewalt?"

Janzig gave a little smile. "Get that FDLE agent outta here faster."

"No shit. The longer he's around, the more chance he has to screw things up."

"We're gonna need to know what he thinks about the Dewalt thing and when he's leaving."

Janzig turned to Norton and said, "How we going to find that out?"

Norton smiled. "I got an idea."

They turned their full attention back to the inmate.

Norton said, "What d'you think, pipe or shiv?"

The sergeant looked at the surprised prisoner in the gray uniform, who was now stopped and raising his hands. "I'd say shiv. Looks more threatening."

Norton nodded and signaled the escapee to come toward them. The man complied easily and casually walked right to them.

Norton was disappointed the second he saw that Leroy Baxter wasn't even going to run. At least he'd won the bet that he'd come out this way.

As Leroy stopped in front of them, Captain Norton said, "Leroy, I thought you were tougher." Then he tossed a shiv he'd taken from some inmate over the years onto the ground next to Leroy. Calmly he watched the black man look at the discarded weapon, and with one hand he leaned the shotgun down at an angle and discharged a round into Leroy's face from less than a foot away.

Tasker ran from the front when he heard the shotgun. He raced through the last exit to see Norton and a short, tubby sergeant standing over the prone body of the escapee. Tasker slowed to a walk as he saw the two DOC men were unharmed.

"What happened?" asked Tasker.

"That official?" asked Norton.

"What?"

"That question."

Tasker was confused. "Why?"

"'Cause if FDLE is investigating this shooting, I need my PBA attorney."

"Why?"

"Just the way it is."

Tasker stared, wondering what had happened. He had a pretty good idea—that is, if he didn't jump to any conclusions. There was a dead guy on the ground with his face now just a mass of blood and flesh. Tasker could see several of his teeth still intact in a mouth rimmed with torn and bleeding lips. There was a homemade knife to the side. Norton and the sergeant stood calmly a few feet away with shotguns. Tasker didn't have to be Stephen Hawking to add up the pieces.

Tasker said, "Guess he really didn't want to go back."

Norton nodded. "Or he really wanted to see me stuck like a pig."

"He charged you with a knife?"

"We was looking over that way and he surprised us." Norton looked out over the complex of storage units and said, "That's all I'll answer right now."

**11** IT WAS NEARLY MIDNIGHT, ABOUT SIX HOURS since Tasker had stood over the dead body of the escaped inmate, and Captain Sam Norton had essentially said, "I don't feel like talking about it."

On the bright side, he was now sitting in a booth in Gladesville's only all-night diner, with Renee Chin sitting across from him eating a fruit plate. He couldn't hide his fascination as she finished the last scraps of a peach.

She looked up and giggled as juice ran down the corner of her mouth. "What're you staring at?"

"Nothing. Just happy you could meet me. Sometimes shooting scenes take a long time to clear."

"Things are simpler out here. One corpse. One city detective. One hour to wrap up. It took me twice that long to forward a report to our headquarters in Tallahassee."

"Norton seemed pretty calm."

"Been here before. He shot an escapee at Glades and shot two inmates in a fight at Union Correctional." She looked at him with those clear dark eyes. "Why weren't you involved in the investigation? I thought FDLE could look into anything?"

"Not me. I called Miami and they said for me to focus on the death investigation of Dewalt. Nothing else. They said someone would catch up with the Gladesville detective to review everything."

She nodded.

Tasker asked, "You know the homicide guy for Gladesville?"

"Homicide guy, burglary guy, fraud guy. I know 'em all."

"Good guys?"

"Same guy. This isn't Miami. Gladesville only has twenty-two cops. One of them is the detective."

"Okay, is that guy any good?"

"Yeah. Tough, too."

"Really, what's tough mean to you?"

"He gave me this." She smiled and pointed to the chipped tooth he had noticed earlier.

His head popped back in surprise. "You were arrested?"

"In love."

"It was a domestic? He hit you and he's still a cop?"

"Actually, it was more like I hit him. Several times."

He stared at her.

"With a shovel."

Tasker remained silent.

"And then a rake handle."

He kept his gaze, sensing something else coming.

"The handle broke in half on his head, flew up and hit me in the mouth." She smiled again, feeling the broken tooth with her tongue. "Then the bastard even drove me to the dentist."

"Hate to ask what he did."

"Fooled around on me."

"On you? He must've been deranged."

She gave him a sly smile. "It's hard to tell when you're being sarcastic."

"Because I'm not. He'd be a fool to cheat on you."

She shrugged. "All ancient history now. I avoid the woman. In fact, I never even met her. Just saw her in his apartment. And now I slug him every chance I get."

"At least he knows you still care."

"Only happened last Thursday."

Tasker nodded, somehow sensing that laughing might be inappropriate.

Just then, the man who had accosted Tasker in the sports bar his first night walked in the front door and immediately saw them together. He turned and marched in their direction. Even from across the room, Tasker could see the bruise around his eye from where Renee had clocked him Saturday night.

Tasker tensed and put his hand on the belly bag containing his Sig Sauer.

The man said, "Wondered where you'd gotten to, girl." Even using local phrases, he sounded like he had just left Yankee Stadium.

Without a word, Renee flicked a back fist at the man's nose and caused him to take a step back, then bump a chair and lose his balance. Renee looked at Tasker and said, "Sometimes instead of a simple slug, I use a back fist." She looked down at the man. "And that's Gladesville's ace detective."

L uther Williams lay in his bunk silently looking up into the dark shadows on the tin roof above him and listening to the sounds outside as men returned to their posts from the search for the escaped Leroy Baxter.

Luther wasn't sorry the armed robber had been killed in the escape. The man needed to be. More important, the guards would think that killing the escapee would be a good enough message to others and wouldn't worry about increasing the security. He was still upset that they had reacted so quickly. He had already heard the rumors that Nasty Norton had killed the man. Word was that Leroy had fallen on him with a foot-long shiv and tried to carve out his eye, when the captain had blown his face off with one of their new Remingtons.

This was still not an issue. He had had his questions answered and decided that they might not expect another escape attempt immediately. He'd prove them wrong. He still wasn't sure if he was better off using his trustee status and leaving from the admin building, or using some other mode. As he lay there in the dark, he considered his many options.

T asker felt crammed against the wall as Rufus Goodwin filled them in on what he thought about the death of the escapee early that evening. The short, wide man hadn't hesitated to join them despite Renee's repeated physical assaults. His light, splotchy complexion and oddly arranged freckles made it difficult to guess his age. His hair had almost a red tint to it.

Rufus, in his gravelly voice and sounding like a local color announcer for the Jets, said, "Clearly a good shoot. The homemade knife, the shiv, was next to the dead man's body. Old Norton put all nine pellets from the buckshot round right in his face. He wasn't fuckin' stabbin' nobody."

Tasker nodded and said, "You sound like you had some experience up north, maybe NYPD?"

"Me, nah."

Renee chimed in, "New Yorkers. You can't even get away from them out here."

Rufus said, "And still I become the town's first detective."

"By outshouting everybody else."

"By puttin' perps in jail."

Tasker listened but was more interested in how this average looking small-time cop had landed a girl like Renee and then made her mad enough to keep smacking him.

Rufus slid out, making no effort to pay for his coffee, and turned back to Tasker.

"Sorry for the misunderstandin' the other night."

Renee cut in, "Sorry 'cause your eye is sore?"

"No, just sorry." He looked at Renee like he knew he'd screwed up a good thing. She returned a look that meant *Don't come too close.*

Renee couldn't resist and said, "How's the new girlfriend workin' out?"

Rufus dropped his head and said, "Told you it was a mistake. Not a girlfriend and never will be."

"A little young for you anyway."

He looked at her and said, "So were you."

Tasker rolled up to his apartment about two in the morning. He planned to race into West Palm tomorrow and pick up the girls. Donna had agreed pretty easily. He figured she had a hot date and didn't mind him taking them for one night. First thing in the morning he'd drop off the mouse, which from now on would be called a hamster, at the vet's to make sure it had no diseases.

He took the rickety steps slowly, his tactical belt with his service Beretta in the holster, slung over one shoulder. Sensing something out of order as he stepped onto the porch, though, he froze. He had that funny feeling he got when there could be trouble nearby. Like at the bank. He paused, reaching for the pistol hanging from the belt. He tried the door and it was unlocked. Was he being paranoid? He looked at the gun in his right hand and pointed the Beretta model 92F, .40 caliber, in front of him.

He shoved the wooden door and let it open on its own, creaking along the way. He stood silently to one side of the open door, letting his eyes adjust to the darkness. Quickly, without a word, he slipped through the doorway and to one side to stay out of what cops called the "fatal funnel," the area in front of an open door. Especially a doorway that could cause a silhouette.

Inside, he edged toward the table when suddenly he saw a figure move on his couch.

"Police," he barked, bringing the pistol on target and dropping to one knee.

"Bill, it's me."

He stood slowly and backed up to the wall near the light switch and flicked it on. He exhaled audibly and lowered his pistol as he said, "What're you doing here?"

Captain Sam Norton sat on the porch of the small house he rented from the state on the prison grounds for $36 a month. As a captain with no dependents, he was entitled to certain housing. It wasn't fancy, but it was clean, dry and had good plumbing and air-conditioning—two things vital in the Glades. When his wife and kids had stayed with him, he usually got another bedroom, but when she'd gotten tired of living in towns like Starke, Belle Glade and Gladesville, she'd decided to take the two girls and live in Fort Lauderdale with some tall, bald, *Sun Sentinel* reporter she had met. Now, when the girls came to visit, they had to share a room. It killed him when they'd tell him how the house in Fort Lauderdale had a nice yard and they each had a room. One day he'd be able to afford something nice for them. Maybe even something nice enough for his wife to want to come back.

He popped the top of a can of Budweiser. This was unusual because as a rule Norton didn't drink. He'd seen what alcohol had done to his father. The man could've been a prison administrator in Tallahassee instead of a no-account sergeant at Hendry Correctional until cirrhosis killed him at fifty. Norton's mom had had to live with his sister in Deland because his father had not provided like he should have. Norton didn't intend to make the same mistake. His girls were going to have a decent life no matter what it took.

He'd had some fun tonight. That boy had caused a lot of trouble on the outside and hadn't been punished nearly enough. He had heard what the snitches at Manatee had said. Leroy Baxter had shot a woman for calling him a nigger. He was proud of it. Norton didn't really care because he never really cared for that word. If you had a problem with someone, white or black, you dealt with that problem. You didn't have to use some cheap trick like a word to knock someone down. He had done that with his fists. Tonight he had done it with a shotgun. Maybe it was because his two daughters were half-black, but he had no use for racists. Maybe it was because of who he was dating now. Good looks and a personality had nothing to do with color. He was always insulted when people assumed a white correctional captain living in the Glades was a racist. It just wasn't true.

If Henry Janzig worked it right, and Henry usually did, that hotshot FDLE man would be convinced that poor old dead Leroy Baxter killed Rick Dewalt. Then they'd be left in peace to do their own business.

The shooting was already investigated and cleared. Maybe not officially, but he knew he could count on old Rufus Goodwin to do the right thing. He knew he'd get the standard, minimum three days off on administrative leave. It was supposed to be for mental health, but Norton didn't care. He had business to take care of in the next three days. If he didn't get a handle on some of the things he had planned, it could get out of hand. If he didn't get on top of this thing, the whole affair could cause him to develop an ulcer.

Tasker sat on the couch staring at his surprise visitor. He was a little shaky mainly because of what he could've done.

Tasker said, "You scared the shit out of me."

Billie Towers brushed her shiny black hair from her small face and said, "Believe me, you surprised me, too."

"How'd you get in?"

"I hope you don't mind. The key to the professor's apartment fits yours, too. In fact, before you moved in, when we worked late, I'd stay here some nights. After you left this evening, I was worried, so I asked him if he thought you'd mind if I waited inside for you a little while. I guess I fell asleep. I'm sorry."

"Nothing to be sorry about, you just startled me, that's all."

"I have a friend at the prison who said they shot the escapee. I thought you'd be back right after that."

"I went out to eat and talk with some people."

She placed her delicate hand on his leg and leaned into him. "I guess you're too tired for any more guests."

Suddenly he didn't feel tired at all. In fact, he felt invigorated.

He also realized he still held his big Beretta in his right hand. "Let me put this up." As he stood up, she followed him into his bedroom.

She stopped at the doorway and said, "Must've been scary out there."

"A little," said Tasker as he opened the drawer to his nightstand and pulled out the thick novel he'd been reading. He slid the gun behind the book and closed the drawer.

Billie said, "You always keep that there?"

"Just in case. I pull it out for enforcement duty, but most of the time just carry a little .380."

"Good thing you didn't have to use it tonight."

"The captain at Manatee seemed to handle things fine."

"I heard. At least he's okay."

"Norton? Yeah, he seemed fine."

"And you're okay."

He nodded. "Yep, no problem, I didn't pull the trigger."

"Have you ever shot anyone?"

"That's one of the reasons I'm out here."

"Did you . . ."

"Yeah. He died at the scene of a bank robbery."

She looked sick to her stomach. "Does it ever bother you?"

He shrugged. It did, but he didn't think it was anyone else's business, really. And he didn't want to sound like a whiner. "Sometimes, I guess." He led her back out to the couch and they got comfortable. "It was nice of you to check on me."

"Sure." Then she said, "Tell me about your assignment out here. The professor says you're investigating a murder."

Tasker shrugged and started talking business without even knowing it.

Sergeant Henry Janzig waited until things had quieted down around the Rock before he ventured up into the administration building, which was now dark and silent. He knew exactly where he was headed and exactly what he would do. The question was what would he use to accomplish his task.

He would have preferred to do this Saturday or Sunday morning, but knowing how thorough Renee Chin could be, he'd decided he better not wait. He slipped into her office and prayed she didn't lock the little storage room she used for evidence. He relaxed when he saw the door to the room wide open. He sat at her desk for a moment, dreaming about what an easy job this would be. Off your feet, solving crimes that no one cared about. No one outside the prison walls cared if one inmate stole from another or even if one killed another. Shit, Janzig spent most of his life working within the walls and he didn't even care.

He looked at a photograph of a black couple in their mid-fifties. Must be her parents, he thought. He could see where she got her looks. The

woman in the photo had fine bone structure and a pretty smile. He just
didn't go for the coloreds like his friend Norton.

He stood up, stretching his aching back and massaging his throbbing
hip. He limped into the storage area and flicked on the overhead light.
Lined up on the shelves on one wall were dozens of plastic bags. Most
were open. One or two were sealed with a heat sealer. He didn't know
why. He knew they were filed by date and went to the last row, three
bags from the end. He found the bag marked DEWALT, R. Inside were a
dozen or so personal items the goofy kid had had by his bunk at the time
of his death.

Janzig shook the bag, then poured out the contents onto an empty
shelf. He rooted through the small stack of items, looking at a Casio
watch, a ring and a small bracelet with no markings. Then he stopped
and picked up a pendant about the size of a Kennedy half-dollar. He
wondered if they were still in circulation. The front of the pendant had
a profile of a face on it. The back of the silver base had an inscription:
Ricky Dewalt, Third Grade.

Out loud, Janzig said, "Perfecto." He snatched up the pendant,
scooped the other stuff into the bag and tossed it back on the shelf.

"Case closed," he said, as he shut off the light and headed toward the
entrance to the prison. He was almost done for the night.

 **12** IT WAS A PERFECT AFTERNOON. NO CLOUDS IN the sky. The temperature about seventy. Tasker had risked the wrath of Florida State Trooper Tom Miko patrolling somewhere on State Road 80 by pushing his Monte Carlo past the specs laid out in Detroit. He raced into West Palm Beach and picked up the girls after just a few hours' sleep. Now, in the backyard of his temporary residence, he felt like a real father and had no problems on his radar. He stepped back and let the Frisbee sail high and slow over the girls' heads all the way to the edge of the cane field behind the apartment complex. The backside of the apartments had another covered porch that looked out over a half acre of trimmed grass. It was perfect for the girls to run and play. On the porch that led to his kitchen, Hamlet the fake hamster, newly named by Emily, had been cleared by a vet and now sat in his cage under the low roof. Kelly had wanted the mouse to feel included in the family activities. Next to the mouse, Professor Kling sat in a reclining Adirondack chair going over some paperwork and occasionally shouting encouragement to the girls.

The professor's assistant, Billie Towers, seemed to appear and disappear in an instant. Tasker had hoped she might be around today. After talking half the night with her, he thought they had some connection. With age and experience, he had realized something most men never do: He had no clue what women were thinking or what they wanted.

The best he could do was appreciate the fact that pretty ones even spoke to him, if only occasionally.

Tasker even felt good to be a little tired. He had not gotten much sleep, but didn't mind. Billie had seemed genuinely interested in his work and he liked her rosy, mid-twenties attitude. He had even talked about his feelings for his ex-wife. Billie said she had seen her, but had avoided meeting her. She didn't like the way some women reacted when she was around their men. Tasker could see why some women would feel threatened by the Seminole coed. Her thin body was certainly not shapeless and she had a grace to her movements that almost seemed like a dancer's. After some of his recent experiences with graceful women, he had even asked her if she ever danced, not insinuating that he meant a stripper but letting her answer the question that way. She had been at the University of Florida five years—since she was nineteen. Just naturally graceful.

She had left sometime after four, even though he had offered to sleep on the couch if she wanted to rest before driving. She'd declined the offer and seemed none the worse today.

Tasker took a break and walked back to the porch.

"What're you working on, Professor?"

The older man smiled. "Just surveys and sketches of my dig. My benefactor wants an idea of how far the artifacts might extend from my current spot."

"Does it look big?"

"If I can keep digging, I'm sure I can show that a whole village existed here, far east of where everyone says were the original settlements of the Seminoles who fled the war."

"What could stop you from digging?"

"You name it. Time. Money. The university's priorities."

Tasker smiled and said, "I'm just glad you're here for now. I'd hate to think about the possible neighbors I could have." He meant it about the nice college instructor, but when he heard a car door and a moment later saw Billie Tower's smiling face, he knew there were other reasons, too.

Renee Chin kissed her grandmother on the cheek and headed into the living room crowded with her family. They all shared a common name, the light skin and oval eyes from a paternal great-grandfather no one had ever met in person. She plopped down on the long couch in the fashionable house located an hour south of Manatee prison near US 27 in the town of Weston. It was about ten miles from the house in Miramar where Renee had grown up. After her four years in Tampa on a scholarship at the University of South Florida, Renee's parents had used the money they'd accumulated from their small but swanky restaurant, Black China, to buy the expansive house here in the upper-class neighborhood in western Broward County. Although the menu and brochures for the restaurant had said it was owned by Albert Chin, no one had ever suspected that the elderly black man who did the books was actually the owner. He had been careful twenty years ago to hire a head chef named Chin. He had found that unlike in the old joke, a Chinese phone book didn't have that many Chins, and so when he found one who could cook, he held on to him.

Renee leaned against her mother, who patted her head.

"Child, you didn't have anything to do with the escape from Manatee Friday night, did you?"

"No, ma'am, not really. I was out in a field looking for him when they shot him."

"How a girl as smart and beautiful as you expects to find a man out in that hole, I'll never know. I mean, no decent men ever come through town out there, do they?"

Renee smiled slyly. "You'd be surprised, Mama."

Her mother sighed. "Not a prison guard."

"No, ma'am, a FDLE agent."

Tasker rolled up on his old house off Forest Hill Boulevard at about six o'clock Sunday evening. Both the girls had dozed off in the car. Part of it was all the running around they had done and part was that he had blown off their bedtime, allowing them to watch all of *Saturday Night Live* before falling asleep in his bed. He had even felt confident enough to consider asking Billie Towers to have dinner with them Saturday night, but then decided it probably wasn't a good idea to have a woman eat with the girls yet.

As he stopped the car, he saw his ex-wife at the front door with someone. She leaned over and kissed the man just as Tasker turned off the car, and then he saw it was Nicky Goldman, her on-again, off-again boyfriend. He felt his stomach turn in a visceral reaction to seeing the attorney receive any affection from his gorgeous ex-wife.

He gently woke the girls and stepped out of his Monte Carlo as Donna walked toward him and Nicky hustled over to his Porsche parked in the street.

"Am I early?" he asked, eyeing the lawyer hop into the sleek red convertible.

Donna smiled like no one had just come from her house. "Nope, right on time."

"Then you and Nicky were running late."

Her smile dropped off her face. "No, we were right on time, too. I've never hidden my relationship with Nicky from you."

"No, but you never flaunted it, either."

"That wasn't flaunting."

"Then where was Nicky running off to? He didn't even say hi."

"You make him nervous."

"Nervous?"

"Okay, you scare him."

"What'd I do to scare him?"

"Killed two men, spent years on the SWAT team, stand four inches taller than him and generally treat him like something stuck to your shoe."

Tasker shrugged. "That's fair."

The girls retrieved their backpacks stuffed with clothes and gave their mother lazy hugs.

"What'd you guys do to get so tired?"

Kelly said, "Daddy made us run after a Frisbee for hours."

Emily added, "Yeah. We ran and ran and didn't stay up to watch *Saturday Night Live*."

Donna gave Tasker a stern look and said, "You and Tina Fey. You need to write her a fan letter or something."

He smiled and walked them all back to the neat one-story cinder block house.

Kelly said, "We played a history trivia game with Professor Kling and Billie. They're smart."

Donna said, "The man staying next to you?"

Tasker nodded as the girls darted into the house.

"Who's Billy?"

"His assistant," Tasker said, keeping a straight face.

"Is it confusing having two Billys around?"

"Not at all," Tasker said emphatically.

13 TASKER HAD SPENT THE ENTIRE MORNING RE-
viewing logs of the trustees to see if anyone had been
assigned to the area around lockdown the day Dewalt
had been killed.

As he made notes next to his scattered papers on the longest table he
could find in the administration building, he heard a smooth, deep voice
say, "Looks like you're preparing for trial."

Tasker turned to see Luther Williams standing in the doorway to the
library. The older, solid black man approached Tasker carefully, not
wanting to cause alarm, then sat at the end of the table.

Tasker pushed back the slush pile of time sheets and logs he had been
skimming and looked up at Luther, giving him his full attention.

Luther smiled, showing the expensive dental work that Tasker had
seen so many times on TV when the guy had been explaining how he
and the head of the Committee for Community Relief were going to
save the city of Miami.

Luther said, "I did not intend to make you nervous." His FM announcer's voice resonated through the paneled room.

Tasker smiled. "But you can understand why you'd cause me some
concern."

"You, sir, have nothing to worry about. You did your job, treated me
properly and didn't compound my misery in court. The result of being
here is of my own making."

"You still sound like a lawyer. You should have represented yourself."

"I was a lawyer longer than anything else in my life. I suspect I shall always speak like this. As for representing myself, I'm sure you've heard that a lawyer who represents himself has a fool for a client."

Tasker nodded.

"In my case, I had a fool for a lawyer. That young public defender wanted me locked up till his kids were in a nursing home. And part of me understood why. That being said, I studied the plea and told the young man what needed to be said in court." He placed his thick forearms on the table. "And for that brilliant legal maneuvering, I am an orderly to men who can barely read and take orders from men who don't care." He rubbed the light ridged stripe of scar tissue on his elbow. "Still can't believe this old scar gave me away."

Tasker smiled. "The fact that you were trying to shoot me at the time tipped me off you weren't an attorney."

"Yes, I apologize for my unfortunate actions. You were not the target of my displeasure. In here, however, there are no facades. You are who you are and do what must be done. In here it's more important that I was raised on the streets of East St. Louis and don't care what I do to survive. That's the real me. I may still speak like a recipient of a Juris Doctor degree but the reality is that I left school in eighth grade after I poked out my teacher's eye for not showing me respect. Manatee is the last stop for men such as myself."

Tasker nodded and considered the statement, then said, "Tell me something I don't know about Manatee."

Luther Williams smiled and said, "There are more criminals here than are listed on the state rolls."

Renee Chin was happy that Bill Tasker had walked with her across the compound. Not that she was scared, she just liked the company. It was also nice seeing him early on a Monday morning after such a rough Friday night. He was eventually going to visit lockdown and the psych ward, but had stopped at Dorm A with her to retrieve Leroy Baxter's personal belongings.

Tasker sat on the made-up bunk in the empty dorm as Renee used her master key to open Baxter's locked chest next to his bunk.

Tasker asked, "They keep everything they own in those chests?"

"The industrious ones even rent out space to the other inmates."

"What's in the other chest without a lock?"

"Clothes. The smaller chest with the padlocks can hold your so-called valuables."

"Who has the keys?"

"Any sergeant and above. You never know when we might have to gain access fast."

"Anything new on the escape?"

She shook her head as she poked through a dish containing some coins and jewelry with a pencil. "He didn't strike me as ambitious enough to make an attempt, but you never know." She was about to say something else when she took a closer look at a small silver pendant. The front had the profile of a boy's face. She was careful to handle it only by its edges. When she turned it over, she froze. In tiny letters, it said, *Ricky Dewalt, Third Grade.*

She handed it to Tasker, who also held it only by the sides. "Take a look." She watched as he studied it without changing expression or giving a clue as to what he was thinking.

He handed it back and said calmly, "I think we have our first decent clue."

"I better let the warden know."

"I'd wait."

"For what?"

"I'll run it by the Palm Beach lab and let them see if they can lift a print. Only take a few days. Meanwhile I'll interview the officers from the psych ward and any other trustees."

She considered it and said, "Okay. You're right, better to be prepared."

She liked how he thought on his feet.

Professor Warren Kling had spent Sunday and most of Monday handling administrative matters. He didn't mind that kind of stuff, but greatly preferred writing about the history of Florida and in particular the history of the original people like the Tequesta and Apalachee or the Seminole tribe. Most people thought the Seminoles were native to Florida, not realizing they were a product of forced relocation and war. Most of the Seminoles were from the Creek Indian nation and others from areas north of Florida's panhandle. Trying to get an idea of how Osceola had felt when he was captured while under a flag of truce, or why the Spanish had been so cruel to the natives upon their arrival, was what Warren Kling lived for. Now he loved finding little traces of evidence to support ideas. This wasn't his first dig, but it was the first one he had been in charge of and so far the most productive. The lab techs at the university were chomping at the bit to get the artifacts and carbon-date them, then analyze what had gone into making them. The DNA scientists would test the bone fragments and then Professor Kling would write the text that tied them all together.

He bumped along the narrow trail off the road to the apartment complex in his Ford Ranger, whistling the tune to *Hogan's Heroes* that had crept into his head at some point over the last three days. Maybe it was hearing the TV the FDLE agent next door let play all night while he slept. The guy loved the tiny local TV station that played old shows. The professor recognized the theme to *Hill Street Blues* and then late in the night he'd hear *Hogan's Heroes*.

The state cop sure seemed like a squared away young man. His daughters were well behaved and a lot of fun and Billie Towers seemed smitten with him. The professor worried about his assistant. She often seemed preoccupied. He attributed it to her youth. She meant well. He just hoped she didn't mean to stay at UF for graduate school.

He skidded to a stop in the limestone-and-weed parking space in front of his apartment. It was the middle of a workday and no one was around. Only two other apartments were in use besides Bill Tasker's place. An environmental protection scientist was there analyzing soil and a Department of Agriculture employee was in the last apartment while he taught a series of classes on crop rotation. The professor was just as happy no one was home. He intended to take a serious nap. He had completed an important phase of his work and had earned a quiet afternoon.

He hopped past two of the stairs on the porch, opened his front door, which he never bothered to lock, walked into the front room without looking up—then froze as he came face-to-face with a man. They stared at each other. The professor looked around at the shambles of his destroyed apartment, then back up at the man.

"What are you doing?"

The man didn't answer.

The professor caught some movement out of the corner of his eye and saw another man step into the room from the narrow hallway. This man had something in his hand.

The first man barked, "Not yet."

But he was too late.

**14** IN THE ADMIN BUILDING, RENEE CHIN STARTED to look for Bill Tasker, not because of work, she had to admit to herself, but because of him. The FDLE agent had been on her mind since Friday night after the shooting. He had a subtle sense of humor and didn't spend time trying to impress people. She liked that.

She turned toward the library and saw Luther Williams heading out the side door with a few books in his hands. Tasker sat at the conference table in the outer room.

As she approached him Renee asked, "Were you talking to Luther?"

"Yeah, just catching up." He looked up from his work.

"He's a dangerous guy."

"Yes, he is."

"And you locked him up?"

He shrugged. "He and some others tried to steal some cash and I got caught in the middle."

"That sounds interesting."

"'Scary' is a better word."

"I heard someone recognized him as an escaped con from Missouri. That was you?"

"A FDLE analyst had made up a list of missing persons and escaped convicts from a certain time period. I had the list and descriptions. When we arrested Luther for a shoot-out in Aventura, I noticed the prominent scar on his elbow and remembered it from one of the descriptions, that was all. Turns out that was exactly who he was."

She sat next to him, then scooted the chair closer. She looked at all the reports. "How's it going? Anything to liaison with yet?"

He looked out over the scattered papers. "Not on any of this."

She hesitated, wanting to ask him out, and was about to say something when she heard a wail, well off the prison grounds.

In the distance, to the west, she could hear sirens. It sounded like a police car and the town's only fire rescue truck.

"I wonder what that could be? Sounds like it's coming from town."

Tasker smiled. "Maybe a cow got loose."

They both laughed, but she felt a twinge of anxiety.

Tasker packed up his work a few minutes after Renee had finished flirting with him. He checked out with the admin desk officer and decided to knock off for the day.

He cruised the three and a half miles to his state-owned apartment in about five minutes. As soon as he turned down the unpaved road with the official Department of Transportation sign for Dead Cow Lane he knew something was wrong. He could see the red light from a fire rescue truck reflecting off the stalks of cane along the road. When he pulled into the clearing where the parking lot bumped into the 1950s musty, wooden apartment complex, he saw three police vehicles, an ambulance, the fire rescue cart and an unmarked vehicle.

He stopped his Monte Carlo on the rear track of the gravel-and-lime parking lot and bolted from the car in a fast walk to the police cars. A young uniformed cop who spent too much time on the bench press and not enough on his attitude met him behind a cruiser with his hand already up.

"No one can come in." He was firm and obviously liked it.

Tasker said, "I live here."

"So?" said the cop, and gave him a short shove to make his point.

Tasker felt his blood rise, then saw Billie Towers at the rear of another cruiser, crying, while another, older cop offered her a tissue.

Tasker snapped, "What the hell is going on here?"

"Police business."

Tasker reached for his wallet in frustration.

The movement spooked the cop, who stepped back and put his right hand on his holstered Smith & Wesson nine-millimeter. "Slow it down, mister."

Then Tasker heard another voice from the porch.

"What the hell?"

Tasker looked up to see Rufus Goodwin take all three steps in one bound and arrive at the cop's side in a flash.

"Harold, what're you doing, you fucking moron? He's a fucking FDLE agent."

The bulky cop looked stricken. He raised his hands in front of him. "I'm sorry, sir. I didn't know."

Tasker was still hot. "You damn well knew I lived here. That's no way to treat people." He turned to Rufus. "What happened here?"

Rufus looked at the ground, then in a halting tone said, "The guy who lived there, the UF professor, was killed."

"What? How?"

"Shot in the head."

"Inside?"

Rufus nodded. "I'm sorry. Billie told me you were his friend."

"You catch the killer?"

"Not yet. I got the county guys out at the crossroads looking for strange vehicles and we're trying to piece this together now. The perp won't get far."

"Billie okay?"

"Pretty shook up. She found the body. We figure it happened about two hours ago, based on when he left his site and when she found him. Only about a forty-five-minute window."

Tasker was still in a daze. "What was the motive? Any idea?"

"Looks like he surprised a burglar. Place is a wreck."

"Who would burglarize a college professor? Especially one that lived in a dump like this?"

Rufus just looked at him.

"What the hell did he have that was worth killing him for?"

Rufus kept staring silently.

Tasker said, "We're going to have to jump on this quick."

Luther Williams had heard the sirens earlier and seen the activity of the correctional officers. That's what he called them, correctional officers. They hated the word "guard," so he tried to keep them happy. He came to the visitor pavilion unescorted because of his trustee status. She was waiting for him when he walked into the booth. All one hundred and eighty pounds of her. Her thick hair sprayed and teased into impossible waves and curls. Her stupid grin glued to her face whenever he walked into the room.

He flopped down in the wooden chair across from her and picked up the phone on the wall next to him. Sometimes he was happy there was a glass partition between them.

She fumbled with the phone on her side with her gigantic hands, then cut loose with one of her horse grins. "Hey, you," was all she cooed.

"Hello, my darling," was perhaps the warmest thing Luther had ever said to another human. He supposed he'd told his mother he loved her when he was a child but could not now, in all honesty, recall uttering such words.

"How are you?"

He looked around him. "I am imprisoned, my dear. Aside from that, I am fine."

"What about your appeal?"

"My dear, I assure you, I believe my release is imminent."

Her blue eyes nearly sparkled as they widened.

Luther remained steady. "I just need a few things from you."

"Anything." She had a gasp of emotion in her voice.

"Keep this schedule exactly. Wednesdays and Sundays at four-thirty."

She nodded.

"No exceptions, no excuses."

"You can count on me."

"I know I can, my darling. Also, let me see your keys."

She lifted up a purse that looked more like a duffel bag and started to search through it. Finally she retrieved a key ring with a photograph of her miniature white poodle attached.

"Why would you want to see my keys?"

"I have a small problem that the right-sized piece of metal might solve. Just lay them on the counter. No need to draw attention to us."

She laid the ring with the various keys on the small counter between them.

He pointed at the smallest key on the chain. "That one. Is that your car's trunk key?"

She nodded.

"Do you have a spare?"

Another nod. "At home."

"Excellent. Slide that off the ring, my dear, and when you leave, just drop the key, very casually, mind you, next to the last pole in the rail leading down to the parking lot."

"Drop it on the ground?"

"In the grass. No one will bother it."

"What on earth do you need with a key?"

"Just a simple engineering problem. Nothing you need give a second thought."

She smiled again. "I'm just so excited about your appeal. You think they'll let you walk free on all charges?"

"My dear, I believe I will be a free man soon." He was in such a good mood that he even had to admit she had a pretty, if large, smile.

Tasker woke from an uneasy night's sleep. It took a second to focus as the previous day's events became clear in his head. He had to work to develop the drive to get out of bed. A crime of violence affected everyone, but one so close, almost in his own home, had unnerved

Tasker. And Rufus' assurances that they'd catch the killer in a day or two did nothing to satisfy him. Professor Kling was such a good guy, how would he even tell the girls? And now Donna wouldn't let the girls visit and he couldn't blame her.

He plopped into a chair after making a bowl of bananas and bran cereal. The TV droned on without saying anything of interest. He liked watching the West Palm Beach ABC affiliate because it reminded him of his life with Donna and the kids.

He finished breakfast, jumped in his Monte Carlo and headed down the long access road to US 27. He turned east toward Belle Glade, but instead of making the turn toward Manatee prison he turned right toward Gladesville's police department. He needed to make sure Rufus Goodwin handled the professor's homicide like a professional.

 **15** TASKER FOUND GLADESVILLE'S SMALL POLICE
department attached to the rear of City Hall. The four park-
ing spaces by the entrance were shaded by an old oak tree
with years of unraked leaves clogging the sidewalk and the edges of the
parking lot. To the side was a small wall with a Dumpster behind it, and
next to the Dumpster was the rear entrance to the police department.

Inside, things didn't improve much. The lobby consisted of two un-
matched vinyl couches over some cheap linoleum and the city police
dispatcher/receptionist sitting behind a flimsy Plexiglas partition. A
twenty-inch color TV, secured to the upper wall, played a West Palm
Beach NBC affiliate that anyone on one of the couches and the receptionist could see.

The large black woman behind the counter sat reading a *National En-
quirer* as Tasker walked up. She showed no interest in looking up until he
pulled out his badge and tapped the window with it.

She cut her eyes up to him without moving her head. "Yes?"

"I'm Bill Tasker with FDLE to see—"

The radio console crackled in front of her and she held up one finger
to silence Tasker while she turned her limited attention to the city police radio. Tasker couldn't understand what was said over the static and
hiss, but the lady took an old-style stand-up microphone and said, "Ten-
four, Harold. I'll let Eugene know." She turned back to Tasker, this time
showing him the courtesy of actually turning her head.

"Yes, sir, Mr. FDLE agent, whatchu need?"

"Rufus Goodwin?"

She picked up her phone and spoke for a second, then said to Tasker, "He'll be right out." She didn't wait for a reply, just turned back to her paper.

Tasker looked around the empty lobby. Normally he'd have taken the minute to sit on one of the couches and catch the news or just clear his head, but the events of the last day had turned his normal thoughts upside down. He just couldn't imagine why someone would kill Professor Kling. He'd seen plenty of senseless killings, but they almost always had something to do with the victim being involved with the killer or trying to resist a robbery or home invasion. He didn't see the mild-mannered professor standing up to burglars hard enough to be shot.

The inner door opened and Rufus Goodwin stood in a white short-sleeve shirt with a thick blue, polyester tie. "What're you doin' here, Bill?"

"Came to see what I can help with on the Kling murder."

"What d'ya mean?"

"I mean, what's going on with the investigation and what can I do to help?"

Rufus looked at him. "Nothing and nothing."

Tasker walked to the doorway, knowing his invasion of the Gladesville detective's personal space would move him back and then they could talk this over in the detective bureau.

Rufus stepped back and said, "C'mon back to my office."

Tasker followed him down a narrow hallway to the one-room detective bureau. The lone desk in the ten-by-ten office was piled with police reports and file folders. The cheap bookshelves had out-of-date statute books and texts on police work from courses not offered in the past ten years. A double fluorescent light stretched across the ceiling, giving off enough illumination to see through cardboard.

Rufus stopped and shoved a stack of reports from one of the two chairs in front of his desk, then tiptoed through the mess on a well-worn path to his old, straight-backed wooden chair.

He looked at Tasker and said, "I appreciate your concern for the investigation, but this is a Gladesville homicide investigation, not a big-deal FDLE operation."

"Rufus, we need to find this killer. I don't care who gets credit."

"I'm workin' on finding the perp. You need to work on your own homicide investigation."

"Rufus, you know as well as I do that the first few hours of a homicide are vital. My case is six weeks old. Nothing new is going to happen while I help you on this."

"If the mayor thinks we can't do our own police work, he's gonna find some new policemen."

Tasker took a deep breath and gave the Gladesville detective the benefit of the doubt. He remembered what it felt like when the FBI swooped in and stole one of his cases. Finally he said, "Okay, Rufus, will you at least keep me updated on what's going on?"

"That, I can do."

Renee Chin stood at the front of the admin building, looking out the large plate-glass window. She had been drinking her morning coffee waiting for Bill Tasker to arrive. She'd called him the night before after she heard about the murder of his neighbor. He'd seemed all right, but she could tell the FDLE man was not one to go on about emotions. He wasn't one to go on about anything, but he had a quick sense of humor to match his pleasant, if infrequent smile. He was unlike anyone she had met in the last few years in Gladesville. Around the facility, she couldn't show her feminine side very often. Both the inmates and the correctional officers might try to get over on her if they thought she was soft. The men in town weren't much better. She'd dated a teacher from Belle Glade for over a year until he'd had a chance to teach English in Bosnia. She wasn't sure if he had left to find adventure or because of the adventure. After that, Rufus was the only interesting man she had seen. He may not have looked like much, but he was smart and had some ambition. He was only nine hours short of a degree and he always had his eye on a chief of police job. Too bad he couldn't keep it in his pants.

Renee watched the man from the State Division of Management Services work outside on the lights in the grass. She'd seen him around a number of times, but had never met the heavyset, balding man. Nance was his last name. She knew that from running his background to make sure he wasn't related to any inmates and didn't have a criminal history.

He squatted near the walkway from the visitor center and picked through the grass as he adjusted the lights. She never could've had his job. Too bland, not enough human contact.

She turned and found Luther Williams at the far end of the corridor, watching her. She didn't get the sense he ever watched her with an eye toward lust, more like he was sizing her up. He seemed to do that to a lot of the staff. She might have to set his ass straight one day real soon.

B ill Tasker was vaguely uneasy about his visit with Rufus Goodwin. The Gladesville detective hadn't sounded like he was going to beat the bushes on this case. He made his way past the few stores on Gladesville Avenue and then through the industrial section where they had chased the escaped inmate on Friday night and then onto the Manatee Correctional grounds.

Tasker worried about Billie Towers. He didn't know how the professor's death might affect her.

He pulled his Monte Carlo into the last available visitor spot next to a step van with the State Department of Management Services logo across the side. Tasker, like most state employees, dreaded dealing with the bureaucratic dinosaur responsible for keeping up state buildings. It took a memo and ninety days to have a framed photograph hung on an office wall. The kicker was that no one but a DMS worker was allowed to hang framed photos in a state building.

Tasker took the path near the visitor center as a shortcut to the administration building. With his ALL ACCESS identification and badge, he found that he could travel around the facility much faster. He passed the stooped DMS man working in the grass at the end of the path and turned toward the admin building. He noticed a tall figure in the wide picture window and, as he came closer, realized it was Renee Chin. Her brilliant smile was visible from twenty yards away even through the glare of the window. He gave her a wave, which she returned, and he felt his spirits lift as he headed toward the main entrance. He had already pondered the ethics of asking her out before he finished his report and had decided to wait, at least for a while. He wasn't sure if it was the ethics, the fact that he was also attracted to Billie Towers or the fear that she'd laugh in his face that kept him from taking the plunge.

He caught himself almost smiling as he made the final turn toward the administration entrance. She was really having an impact on him and he had to admit it. At least to himself.

She met him in the hallway near her office.

"I'm so sorry about your neighbor." She took both his hands.

Tasker nodded.

"Is there anything I can do?"

"No. I'm just gonna keep working on the Dewalt case."

"What's next?"

"I'm going over to the lockdown facility to compare photos with the real thing and make a few sketches. I figure it'll be nice to be away from people for a while. It's pretty quiet over there."

"No one will bother you, that's for sure. Sometimes one of the inmates in the psych unit will be loud and you can hear them in lockdown, but it should be quiet."

"That's what I need: a quiet afternoon."

E ven though he was still on administrative leave for the shooting, Captain Sam Norton walked along the north fence with Sergeant Henry Janzig waddling hard to keep up. Norton knew the older man had problems, keeping up a fast pace with his arthritis and hip problems, but it was just so damn funny to see him move his stubby legs fast and try to keep up a conversation that he couldn't help himself. They never talked about non-department business inside unless it was an emergency. This way he let the perimeter officers see he was on the prowl, even in jeans and a plain white T-shirt, and he could talk with his partner without fear of being overheard or recorded.

Janzig huffed and puffed, then finally said, "What do we need to talk about way out here? Everything on track with the business?"

"Yeah, Henry, don't worry. We're in good shape there."

Finally Janzig stopped walking and reached up and grabbed Norton by the shoulder. "Let's take a break and talk right here."

Norton let a smile slip over his face. "All right, you old coot. The boys in the tower are gonna think we're having a lovers' spat the way you just stopped me."

"They'd think that more if you had to give me CPR. You walk too damn fast. Now what's goin' on?"

"It's the FDLE agent."

"Tasker? What's that dickwad done? He's just lookin' into the Dewalt kid's death. I know he and Renee found the goddamn pendant I stuck in Baxter's stuff. They gotta be wonderin' why he had it."

Norton looked at him. "They're keeping it quiet. They haven't even told me about it yet."

"They will, and it should lead him to the right fucking conclusion." Janzig laughed. "That boy Tasker does get into things, doesn't he? He works the murder and jumps in on our escape."

Norton looked down and said, "He's doin' a few other things, too."

"What else is he doin'? Renee Chin?"

Norton glared at him. "Don't you talk like that."

"Why not? Ain't it obvious to you?"

Norton sighed. "Don't matter. He's causing other kinds of shit. I need to have a good scare thrown into him."

"Why not a beating?"

"Either way, I just need his ass heading back to the coast. Soon."

"I'll talk to the Knights about it."

"Naw, you use them shitheads too much. They might talk. What if he just gets stuck in the wrong place at the wrong time?"

Janzig scratched his chin. "He's around the hatch and lockdown quite a bit. Might be we could work out something over there."

"You handle it, but keep it quiet."

The pudgy man paused, then asked, "What if he isn't scared by an unfortunate incident?"

"Then we have to set up something more drastic. That's his option. He leaves on his own or in a box."

Janzig nodded and smiled. "I know exactly what to do."

Norton knew better than to ask.

Luther Williams replaced the book he had just retrieved from Dorm D. One of the numskulls had checked out a book on surfing. Luther knew the man had twenty-two years left on his trafficking-in-cocaine sentence. Was he optimistic he'd be able to surf at an advanced age? Luther could see why most of these guys got caught. He sorted through the other books on his cart and was glad he'd done the favors he needed to do to be assigned such a cushy job and given trustee status so quickly. A little legal advice here and a few documents created there and suddenly he'd skipped five hundred men waiting for a job like this.

He shuffled over to the doorway of the library and looked down the hall at Inspector Renee Chin. She had her back to him as she looked out a window, but he knew who it was. No one else looked like that from behind, not in this place. He found himself imagining what it would be like to have those incredibly long legs wrap around him and squeeze. Though maybe not squeeze all the way, because Luther had seen what that girl could do to an inmate who crossed the line. She was as feared as any man in the prison, except Captain Norton. Norton ran a tight ship and he was not a man to put up with bullshit. Luther admired that in a man, even one whose job it was to keep him locked up. Captain Norton was all right to him because of their arrangement, but Luther knew not to push it. He had seen what had happened to Rick Dewalt and the lesson hadn't been lost on him.

As Luther finished sorting some books on his cart, a short, bald man who worked for the state walked into the large hallway with a six-foot folding ladder in his hand. He turned toward Luther and smiled as he set up the ladder next to him to check a fluorescent light in the ceiling. The man's white shirt had the letters DMS across the left chest, with the name Marty underneath. He scooted the ladder back and looked over his shoulder.

Luther watched Inspector Chin turn and head out the end of the hallway, apparently to greet the FDLE agent he'd seen walking toward the front. When the hallway was empty, Luther said to the man, "Did you find it?"

The man nodded and smiled as his hand came from his pocket and he opened his fist, revealing the small, silver key Luther had asked his girl-friend to drop in the grass after her last visit.

Luther said, "Not here. They'll search me when I head back into the facility."

The man put his hand back in his front pants pocket. "No problem. I gotta check the AC unit in Dorm A. I'll leave it on the fuse box next to the dorm. You know where I'm talkin' 'bout?"

Luther nodded. "Mr. Nance, you have done a fine job. Thank you, my man. You just earned your cousin another six months' free rent."

The man seemed satisfied and headed up the ladder as Luther strutted toward the service main gate to the facility. Everything was coming together.

16 BILL TASKER SAT IN ONE OF THE BARE CLOSET-sized rooms attached to the main lockdown area inside the fence at Manatee State Correctional Facility. There were four empty, doorless rooms containing a simple metal table and two chairs. One office sat at each corner of the wide, empty entryway to the secure lockdown area. Renee Chin had told him that the thin green carpet throughout the lockdown facility had been Captain Norton's idea. Another tribute to Stephen King. Tasker figured if the place needed a carpet, why not make it green.

The correctional officers used the small rooms, like the one where Tasker now sat, to write up paperwork or take a break from the constant noise of the inmates. He was looking at photos taken after the murder and making rough sketches of the lockdown facility, which took up most of the building. He always made notes and sketches on cases and rarely had to refer to them. Once, in court on a drug case, he'd brought his sketch of an arrest scene to the trial. When he'd looked at the two-year-old picture of a house off Seventh Avenue in Miami, he hadn't been able to make any sense of what he had written. He still did it on every case, though.

The eight single cells in lockdown were under constant observation, and were used to keep troublesome inmates in complete isolation. There were ten more cells farther from the control/observation room in which prisoners were separated but could still talk through the bars. This part of the facility was personally supervised by Captain Norton, and it showed. The place was clean, the officers right on top of things, and it looked like the extra security area ran smoothly all the time. Norton was expected back tomorrow after his mandatory three days' administrative leave following the shooting of the escaped inmate the Friday before. He could have used up to ten days of admin leave and sick leave after that if he wanted, but Tasker didn't think the sour captain was too broken up over the shooting.

Shooting incidents affected everyone differently. Tasker had been told to take the full ten days off after the bank shooting, but some of that had had to do with everything that had happened to him in the last six months.

After the FBI had investigated him for the bank robbery that first put him in contact with Cole Hodges, he'd thought he'd never recover. He'd been back in five days. After he'd stopped Daniel Wells from blowing up half of downtown Miami, he'd been out a month, but that had been for physical injuries, not emotional. The director had told him to look at his assignment out here as an extension of that rehab. But the image of the dead robber still popped into his head once in a while. Just like the mental picture of the pretty bank manager lying still on the marble floor with the small hole in her forehead. Maybe he'd snap one day. No one had any way of knowing what trauma would haunt you the rest of your life. Maybe he'd dream about them every night. Now it was just part of his world. One more thing he had to deal with day to day.

Right now he was using his assignment as a way not to think about someone shooting Warren Kling. He focused on his drawings of the facility and his stick figure representing Dewalt's body. He had to remember that this was a homicide, too, and that Dewalt's family was still grieving.

Tasker had been fully briefed on the building. He needed the info for his investigation into the murder. He had been told that the lockdown area was attached to the housing for mentally disturbed inmates. This was technically a role for the medical unit, but for safety reasons an inmate deemed unstable was housed in one of the comfortable holding cells with a simple pad for a bed. If the condition was determined to be chronic, the inmate was transferred to a facility better equipped to handle a case like that. The prison located the two units together so correctional officers could move between the units if there was a problem.

Tasker paused and found himself staring out the door at the reflected sunlight entering through the only barred window in the common area of the lockdown and psychiatric area. He wasn't sure if it was the gloom of this place or his shock over Professor Kling's murder, but he couldn't concentrate and his mood was extremely somber. He'd felt like this quite a few times since his unceremonious transfer from West Palm Beach to Miami four years ago after a questionable shooting incident. An incident that had indirectly led to his divorce. But over the last few months he'd felt like the clouds were lifting and he was regaining his old, more positive outlook. Although he was still a little hung up on his ex-wife, Donna, he could admit it and deal with it. Besides, only a dead man wouldn't be attracted to her. He had moved past her and started to date. He used to think these dark moods were acceptable, but now he resisted them and realized they would pass.

A shadow passing across the light snapped him back to the present. He blinked his eyes and looked into the dark common area. He figured the lights were low to keep everyone calm. It took him a few seconds to realize that someone must have been moving outside the little room, must have cut across the square of sunlight. He peered out into the area, then stood and stretched. He kept looking outside, but saw no more movement.

He felt an odd tingle, though, and stepped around the small table with his notebook on it, then to the doorway. As he took the first step out into the common area and turned his head to the left, he suddenly felt someone grip his right shoulder with incredible pressure. In pain, he turned his head just enough to see the white gown of an inmate from the medical facility and a black face with large brown eyes. The man was taller than he was, maybe six-foot-three, and his fingers dug in like a set of pliers. He felt himself start to lose consciousness and fought it as he tried to call out for help, but as he opened his mouth, the man's other hand closed around his throat. This sucked.

Luther Williams found the key right where the DMS man had said he'd leave it. The small silver key used for the car trunk of his—he hated to think it—girlfriend's Cadillac CTX. The thin key was easy to slip into his sock and soon would be hidden in the metal frame of his cot. The metal detectors at the front gate might have picked it up. He'd probably have been able to explain why he had it, but they wouldn't have let him keep it.

He walked down the breezeway toward his dorm like a man who just won the lottery. It wasn't what you had in life, it was what you did with it. He intended to use the little key, in conjunction with a number of other things, to turn around this setback in his life.

Billie Towers pulled out her clean University of Florida T-shirts and slammed them into her open duffel bag. She'd stopped crying, but was still deeply troubled by Professor Kling's death. She wanted to get out of this shitty little town and never think of it again.

As soon as she had that thought, she plopped down on the edge of her bed and started sobbing again. She knew she couldn't leave yet. If she did, she'd keep thinking about some of the better aspects of town. She really did have friends here, not like at UF where the stuck-up sorority girls ignored her because she wasn't white. They didn't even know what her ethnic background was—most people assumed she was Cuban—but they knew she wasn't white.

She'd also miss out on a chance to make enough money to start a new life. She dried her eyes on the bedspread and sniffed as she calmed down. The old-style rotary phone on the nightstand rattled and dinged its quirky ring. She picked it up

"Hello?"

"You all right, baby?" said a man's voice.

"What do you think?"

"I think you need to stay right there until we can talk."

"I'm packing." She made her voice sound firm even though she wasn't.

"Then unpack."

She hesitated.

The voice said, "Be there in a few minutes. Don't worry, I just want to see you happy."

Tasker felt his legs start to give out from the lack of oxygen and the pain. He knew if he hit the ground, it would be all over. He blinked hard to clear his head and tried to gasp for oxygen so he could think. Eleven years as a cop and he couldn't get out of this? He took both his hands and grabbed the large, strong hand on his throat. He could block some of the pain in his shoulder, but he needed air and needed it right now. He peeled back the man's fingers first, then, once the hand was off his windpipe, twisted the wrist, making the man's palm turn completely around. He could feel first the tendons, then the wrist bones, pop and crack as he kept the pressure up.

The trauma of having his wrist snapped caused the man to loosen his grip on Tasker's shoulder enough so that he could back away from the attacker.

He turned to face the man and saw something that really did surprise him. The loose hospital gown on the large black man was only partially tied in place. He stood tall staring at Tasker. Poking out from below the gown was his long, dark, erect penis.

Tasker realized that this was one of the mental detainees and didn't want to hurt him, almost as much as he didn't want to have contact with the man's giant penis. The man stepped forward and Tasker stepped back, holding up his hands. "Whoa there fella, look at your arm. Let's call it quits."

The large black man was not finished. After inspecting his hand briefly, he dismissed the injury, even though his hand hung uselessly at an odd angle from the end of his right arm. His eyes cut from his hand to Tasker and he smiled as he started to spring toward the panting state cop.

Tasker sidestepped back from the lunging man and yelled out for the correctional officer in the control room. "Hey, control room, look up!" He dodged the man again. "Little help here!"

Now he had room to maneuver in the center of the common area for lockdown and the mental ward. He took a second to regain his composure, controlling his breath and clearing his head. Through hard experience he'd learned what jumping into a fight without calming down a little can do to you. The scar on his shoulder was from a rotator cuff surgery after a fight in which he'd gotten winded and, when taking the man down, hadn't had the energy to keep himself from flopping on the ground next to him. His resulting shoulder injury had calmed him way the hell down.

Tasker stole a quick glance around the place and saw no one was coming to help. He couldn't dodge this guy forever. The man stepped forward and paused, gripping his own penis and stroking it a couple of times. Tasker took that moment to creep to his side and deliver a devastating knee spike into the man's leg. He aimed for the peroneal nerve running down the side of his naked leg, and apparently hit it because the man dropped straight to the ground.

Tasker saw he wasn't getting up anytime soon and decided to let the control room monitor know he was there. He took one of the metal chairs from his small room and flung it as hard as he could at the grating above the window to the control room. The young man in the room snapped his head up from his magazine, and seeing the man sprawled on the floor, sprang to his feet with a radio already in his hand. Tasker leaned against the bars and slid to the floor, gasping as he heard doors clang and men running.

 **17** TASKER SAT IN THE WARDEN'S OFFICE WITH ICE
around his bruised neck as he listened to the warden and
Renee Chin apologize for the hundredth time.

The warden leaned on his desk, his face creased with worry lines.
"Agent Tasker, believe me, this sort of thing is not common here at
Manatee."

Tasker replied, "Forgive me, Warden, but I'm here because of the
same thing, aren't I?"

Renee said, "Bill, what can I do?"

Tasker spoke quietly because his throat still hurt. "Nothing. I'm
gonna head to the apartment for now. Can we discuss it tomorrow?"

The warden said, "Captain Norton will be back. Whatever Inspector
Chin and the captain want to do is fine with me. We'll investigate this
fully."

Tasker's head pounded and his throat burned. He nodded as he stood,
still holding the clear bag up to his neck, and headed for the door. In the
hallway he kept moving toward the main door, as Renee trailed trying
to see what she could do.

At the door he faced her and held up his free hand. "I'll be fine. Just
need some sleep." He opened the door and stepped out onto the small
concrete landing. "Tomorrow we'll figure this shit out." He turned
without another word.

Luther Williams had some of his belongings out on his cot as he contemplated his plans. The dorm was empty right now, as a class on "developing a spiritual mind" was being offered for the inmates in the small chapel in the center of the complex. Only a few of the dorm's residents cared about any form of development, but everyone wanted a few minutes in the cool chapel with padded pews.

Luther liked the time to himself. That was one of the worst parts of being in a place like this: you were never, ever alone. He had liked his solitary existence prior to his arrest. As chief counsel for the Committee for Community Relief, he had handled day-to-day affairs from the comfort of his Brickell Avenue office. He'd lived alone for the most part and enjoyed the quiet, private life. Unfortunately, like with so many other times in his life, he hadn't appreciated what he had until he'd lost it. Now he was thrilled to be alone in a large empty dorm room kneeling next to a creaky metal cot with an air conditioner that didn't cool the room past eighty-three degrees.

He found his trunk key and held it up to the light, admiring the beauty of the small mechanical wonder. As he was about to clean up his stuff, he heard a voice say, "Whatcha got, old man?"

Luther didn't turn, not wanting to give the man the satisfaction of acknowledging the insulting name. He knew it was Vic Vollentius, the dope dealer who fancied himself a white leader. The muscular, bald man had a crazy look in his eyes most of the time, but had never bothered Luther until recently. Now he felt like the Aryan Knight was around every corner. Like all the white supremacists, this guy was a bully. Luther was just surprised that he'd try to bully him without any help.

Luther stood and turned toward the man, who was several inches shorter than Luther's six feet one.

Vollentius said, "Looked like a key. We're not supposed to have anything like that in our personal belongings."

Luther remained silent, assessing the man and his intentions.

"What else you got that you're not supposed to have? What if I told?"

Luther didn't have the patience for games. "What do you want, Mr. Vollentius?"

"What do you got?"

"A short temper. Now get to the point."

"How 'bout some of that powder you bring in once in a while. The coke you wouldn't give me to find out why the Aryan Knights are right around the corner every time you go out."

"Yes, I remember your offer and I'm as interested now as I was then."

"But I need some coke to shut my yap about the key. What about it?"

Luther thought about it and said, "That's fine, Mr. Vollentius. You will receive one quarter of one ounce upon my next delivery."

"Now."

"What?"

"Now, you cocksucker. If you use that key to escape or something happens to you, then I'm out my dope."

Luther smiled. He never would've thought this poor excuse for a biker would have the brainpower to think that all the way through so effectively.

Luther said, "Fair enough, Mr. Vollentius. I will access my inventory tonight and make payment tomorrow. Is that satisfactory?"

The bald man smiled. His pale forehead reflected the light as a bead of sweat formed from the warm dormitory air. "Okay, Williams, you got till tomorrow."

Luther nodded and said, "Meet me in the rear of the kitchen right before lunch tomorrow. Just you, none of your racist friends."

"I'll be there alone if you will."

Luther didn't telegraph a single thought. "You have my word."

The late afternoon sun cut through the pine trees on the western edge of the apartment complex, throwing a series of complex shadows across the empty rear yard. Bill Tasker sat in an Adirondack chair, just letting his mind wander. Instead of looking at clouds and making up shapes in his mind, he looked at the shadows dropping across the scraggly grass. Unfortunately, most of them reminded him of long, erect, dark penises and he had to find something else to occupy his mind. The low sun, time of year and slight breeze made the outside temperature perfect and the clear sky like an oil painting.

The experience at the prison that afternoon had definitely shaken him. He'd been in dozens of fights over the years, winning most but recognizing you were always bound to get clocked once in a while. That was the price of going out in the street every day. He shuddered at what might have happened to him had he been beaten today. He was also curious as to what Captain Sam Norton would have to say. Although the burly captain was still on leave, Tasker had the feeling that not much went on out there without Norton's knowledge.

He took a deep breath, almost immune to the faint burning smell that always hung in the air from some distant cane field fire. He had to admit he liked the atmosphere out here. There was none of the pettiness he felt on the coast. No one looking to pass you on the road every minute or banging into your grocery basket at the store. If it weren't for the murder next door and his stale homicide investigation at the prison, he might grow to like this place.

His cell phone played "The Stars and Stripes Forever," jolting him out of his calm reflections.

"Bill Tasker."

"Billy, it's Sally Brainard. You okay? Sounds like you have a cold or something."

"Sore throat."

"Know what I like to do for a sore throat?"

"What?"

"Massage it."

"I think a massage is what gave it to me." Then he said, "Sally, haven't heard from you in a while. I dropped off something at your lab the other day and asked for you, but you were out."

"I heard. That's why I'm calling. I went ahead and processed the little pendant for you."

"Already? Sally, you're the best."

"Glad someone thinks so."

"Everyone thinks so."

"Then why am I still single?"

"Thought you and the ATF guy were serious."

"Alex? He can't see past a case. Just when things are going well, he gets caught up in some bombing or gun case and forgets he's got a girlfriend."

Tasker cringed, having heard the same thing about himself a number of times. He just moved on. "Any prints on the pendant?"

"Yeah. I already compared them against the one set you gave us."

"Leroy Baxter's?"

"Yeah. He wasn't on them anywhere."

Tasker had given the Palm Beach County crime lab a card with a set of Baxter's prints because he hadn't wanted to waste anyone's time by running them through the National Crime and Information Center.

Tasker asked, "You get anything?"

"I got a good thumbprint from the flat back of the pendant."

"Sounds like you matched it."

"Only because I ran it through the employment prints for the county and state. Wanted to eliminate someone who had a reason to handle it."

"And?"

"Sorry, Billy. Just a sergeant for the Department of Corrections. Henry Janzig."

Tasker thought about it. "Yeah, I see his name on things out there. Think I know who he is."

"Probably touched the pendant when they found it."

"Could be." He thought about that possibility. He thought Renee Chin had been alone when she went through Baxter's belongings. He snapped back and said, "Thanks a lot, Sally."

"You got it. Stay safe while you're out there. Lot of cops underestimate how dangerous the Glades can be."

Tasker put his hand to his throat and said, "Tell me about it."

Florida Department of Corrections Captain Sam Norton tossed his German shepherd, Hannibal, a piece of grilled sirloin. The dog snatched it cleanly out of the air. Department of Corrections Sergeant Henry Janzig clapped his hands at the trick he had seen hundreds of times. The stout sergeant was older than Norton by fifteen years, but the two had become close friends during their mutual assignment to the Rock.

Janzig said, "You shoulda seen him. White as a fuckin' ghost, eyes puffy like a girl that'd just been dumped."

Norton said, "Good, but is it enough? Think he'll mind his own business now?"

"I think he'll want outta here right quick. He's got Dewalt's pendant. He'll look around a little more and decide Baxter killed him and be back on the coast and out of our business by the end of the week."

Norton smiled and nodded. "Good. Tell Lester he done good, too."

"Still don't like him here at all. You'd think we could handle an in-custody death investigation."

"Looks better this way. It was arranged at a higher level than us."

"Still don't like it."

"Henry, you worry too much." Norton checked his watch. "Ain't it past your bedtime?" He smiled.

Janzig scowled slightly, although it was hard to tell when he wasn't scowling, and then headed back between Norton's house and the next building toward the row of double-wide trailers that housed sergeants without dependents. Because the older man had a slight limp from years of standing on hard floors, he had a crazy swivel in his hip as he walked. Norton had to smile as he saw his surly friend leave.

Norton was looking forward to getting back to work tomorrow. He was not suited to sit idle. His experiences watching his dad recover from massive hangovers had taught him to work and work hard. Unfortunately, his wife hadn't liked all the time alone in the various isolated postings he'd been assigned to over the years.

He had to admit that, at this moment, with or without his promiscuous wife, he was happy at work. The Rock was a good institution, which he had had a big role in building. The prison had been new enough when he arrived that there was a lot he could fix. He'd transferred any correctional officer too close to the inmates and any officer who had complained about how the institution treated the inmates. That had left a lot of openings, and Norton had filled them with officers he could trust.

What concerned Norton about Tasker was his reputation for not letting things go and his interest in business outside the prison walls. Norton didn't like the way Renee Chin looked at him, either. That girl deserved someone who could take care of her, not some cop who'd move back to his house on the coast somewhere.

Norton cleaned up the plastic plate he'd been eating his steak from and the two empty cans of Mountain Dew. As he stood to head back into the thick air-conditioning, away from the gnats and breezeless evening, a vehicle rumbled into the parking space in front of his bungalow. When the lights shut off, he saw who it was and couldn't keep the wide smile from spreading across his face.

He set the garbage back on the small table and trotted down the steps. "I didn't expect you tonight."

"We have got to talk."

He didn't like the edge in the voice.

It was late, after ten o'clock, when Tasker heard a knock on his front door. The old wooden door rattled at the knock as Tasker turned and tried to decide how to answer it: ready—paranoid and gun in hand—or casually. He swallowed and felt the pain still in his throat and opted for his Beretta crammed into the small of his back. He'd kept the automatic handy since the professor's murder. Tucked in his nightstand, no one would notice it unless they were looking for it. Now it took only a second to pull the gun from the small drawer past the thick novel. He slipped it into the rear of his shorts and pulled his T-shirt over it.

He paused at the door. "Who is it?" he called as he stood to the side. "Billie Towers. I'm sorry it's so late."

He unlatched the door and let it swing open, and smiled at her small figure and big brown eyes. She let a shy smile slide across her face, too.

She said, "I couldn't find your number and really wanted to talk. Is it a bad time?"

"No, no, not at all." He motioned her inside. He watched her gracefully stride inside and to the old couch. "I was going to call, but couldn't find your number. Can I get you something?"

She smiled and shook her head.

"Excuse me one second." He slipped back into the bedroom to return his Beretta to the drawer, then darted back to the living room.

He sat down next to her. "You doing okay?"

"Just sad about Professor Kling and wanted to see how you were doing."

"I'm fine. I'm gonna get after the Gladesville detective, Rufus Goodwin, about the investigation. I just wanted to give him enough time to sort things out and realize I just want to help."

"Shouldn't you finish your own murder investigation?"

"I'll get it done." He looked into her dark eyes and said, "Man, seems like everyone is more interested in my death investigation than the professor's."

She looked like she wanted to say something, then started to cry. "It's just so terrible."

He put his arm around her muscular shoulder. "I know. Cry all you want."

And she did for almost five minutes, then it turned to sniffles, then to an occasional sob. When she stopped, she reached across and kissed him gently on the cheek. "You're a sweet guy."

He knew he was grinning, but couldn't stop.

She said, "So, any progress on your case at Manatee?"

And he started talking.

18 LUTHER WILLIAMS ARRIVED IN THE KITCHEN half an hour before he'd told the Aryan shithead Vollentius to be there. He knew the bald racist would be on guard, but also knew, like any human, his greed would override his common sense. Luther had his best shiv, a razor-sharp, flexible metal band, hidden in his waistband. He had his shirt pulled out to cover any telltale signs of a weapon. The momentary lapse in fashion disturbed him more than what he had planned for this nosy Nazi. He had no intention of providing him with any of his precious cocaine. He didn't care how much he had or how cheaply the Aryan Knight could be bought.

Luther surveyed the empty rear kitchen. He'd already made sure that anyone who saw him walk through the main kitchen would keep their mouths shut. He'd been lucky and the only inmates in the kitchen were black guys. They wouldn't say boo about one of the Aryan Knights having an accident.

Luther turned on the water in one of the floor sinks. The eight-inch-deep, two-foot-square sink was used to clean out the grease buckets with steaming hot water. Luther used that water now.

Next, he paced off a few steps from the doorway to a spot five feet from the now-filled sink and smeared a round wad of grease that looked like a urinal cake onto the floor. He'd taken the round cake from one of the drainage filters in the vents coming from the kitchen. He slid his foot across the slick floor and smiled at the lack of friction.

The trick to chores like this was making the investigating authorities find the answers quickly and easily. It didn't matter if it was the right conclusion, only that it was an obvious conclusion.

Luther heard some loud voices in the kitchen and stepped carefully to the doorway, his foot with the grease on it slipping on the way. From the opening he saw Vollentius arguing with one of the dishwashers, who had told him he wasn't supposed to go into the rear kitchen. The fireplug of a man pushed past the dishwasher, calling him a foul racial name as he did.

Luther noticed the dishwasher smile, knowing what was about to befall the Aryan Knight. Luther tightened the grip on his shiv still hidden in his waistband. It was more instinct than a conscious act. He moved to the side of the doorway behind some cardboard boxes containing paper towels.

The Aryan Knight walked through the doorway and into the rear kitchen without even a glance around.

Luther smiled. He couldn't believe how easy some people made things. He took two quick, quiet steps behind the Aryan and, just as he reached the slick section of the floor, gave him a hard shove toward the sink.

The man flailed his arms as he slipped, then went down face-first, catching himself on the edge of the sink with both hands at the last moment, his face inches from the scalding water.

Luther didn't hesitate. He was on him in a heartbeat and with one hand on the back of his bald head, slammed the man's face into the water and hard onto the bottom of the sink.

Luther used all of his strength because he wanted only one mark on the man's forehead. One slip and fall. One bruise on the body.

He froze in his position on top of the man and felt for any movement as he kept the man's face under the steaming water. After thirty seconds, Luther relaxed, realizing that between the head trauma, hot water shock and lack of oxygen, it was likely this man was no longer considered a living inmate at Manatee Correctional.

After a minute more, to make certain, Luther released his hand and let the man's face stay in the cloudy water. He backed away and grabbed a hand towel off the nearest crate of potatoes. He ran the towel over the floor where he had stepped, in case someone tried to take shoe prints in the grease. Then he wiped the soles of his shoes and casually strolled out through the main kitchen.

He winked at the dishwasher on his way out.

Henry Janzig was over near the main dining hall when his radio crackled and one of his officers said, "Hey, Sarge."

Janzig pulled the out-of-date radio from his hip holster. The three-pound monstrosity was one of the reasons his damn legs ached all the time. He squeezed the button and said, "What is it, Junior?"

"You might wanna come over to the main kitchen. I found something you'll want to see."

"On my way." Janzig didn't ask questions. Junior was a good boy. If he'd found something valuable, he might not want everyone listening to the radio to know it. Neither would Janzig. You never knew what the officers uncovered in surprise inspections.

Janzig hustled toward the solid block structure that housed dining, the kitchen and food storage. His hips swiveled at an odd angle the faster he tried to walk. He slowed down inside the empty dining hall. A couple of the kitchen workers lounged at the table closest to the kitchen door.

"You inmates don't have enough work to do?" yelled Janzig.

One of the workers, a dark black man named Moambi, said, "Officer Hayes told us to wait out here, sir."

Janzig pressed on toward the first kitchen door. "Junior? Where are you?" he shouted.

"Back here, Sarge."

Janzig scooted toward the rear swinging door. As he came through, he saw the big correctional officer leaning over a body at the back of the room. "What the hell we got here, Junior?" he said, taking a step toward him. His feet slipped almost out from under him. "What the shit is this? You can't even walk on this fucking floor."

"I think that's the problem." He looked back at the body.

Janzig knelt with him. He looked down at the face of a white inmate with a shaved head. He couldn't immediately tell who it was because the face had been badly burned. Huge blisters had formed and popped on the man's nose, forehead and cheeks. Janzig could see the lower levels of skin and even some blood vessels near his eyes.

"What happened here?"

"Looks like the guy fell coming through the door and ended up in one of the cleaning sinks. Musta had some hot water for the grease."

"You figure he just happened to land right here?"

"What else, Sarge? He had to land somewhere."

Janzig saw the simple reasoning to this, but still thought the odds were a little high for the man to land in a sink full of hot water.

"You talk to the kitchen workers?"

"Yes, sir. Near as I can figure, it happened after eleven. That was the last time anyone came back."

"Who put the hot water in the sink?"

"The dishwasher. Robert Moambi."

"They see who this was?"

"They said Vic Vollentius came through before lunch. That's who it looks like to me."

Janzig looked at the body and had an idea pop into his head that instantly made him smile. He turned to the hulking officer and said, "Junior, go get Inspector Chin and bring her right back here. She'll wanna see this."

"Yes, sir," said the officer, as he pushed off his knee to stand up and then hustle out of the kitchen.

Janzig struggled up as well, then pulled his small notepad from his breast pocket. Vic Vollentius had friends here in the prison. Mainly the other Aryan Knights. They were one badass group and if they ever had a hint that someone had killed Vollentius they could cause a mountain of shit. Janzig also knew that no one around the Rock could keep a secret. No one except him and Norton. All he needed was to start the right rumor and some of his problems might be taken care of. He ripped out a sheet and scrawled a note across it. Then he rolled up the tiny note and turned toward the disfigured body. He winced as he opened the corpse's mouth with his squat fingers and shoved the note way back against his molars and gums.

He looked down at his handiwork. He chuckled at how clever he had become. That was twice in a week he had influenced investigations that were supposed to be conducted by smart people. Janzig had applied for inspector positions all over the state, but younger sergeants like Renee Chin always seemed to get the cushy jobs. This showed just how smart they really were. She may not arrest old Luther Williams for murder based on his little note, but she sure as hell would talk about it. And eventually the right people would hear about it. Once the Aryan Knights got done with Luther Williams, that shifty lawyer som-bitch would never be able to tell anyone how he had helped out Norton and Janzig.

Henry Janzig was sitting up on a barrel of solvent, resting his weary legs by the time Junior got back with Renee Chin. He watched as she inspected the area and surveyed the body. Finally, she turned to him.

"What do you think, Henry?"

"Looks like an accident to me."

He kept smiling while she did her silly investigation thing.

19

BILL TASKER SAT IN ONE OF THE HARDWOOD, straight-backed chairs in front of Captain Sam Norton's large matching hardwood desk. Most of the furniture was marked with a small P.R.I.D.E. sticker, indicating that it had been made in Florida state prison facilities. No loose paper, books or photographs rested on the wide desk. The morning sun was coming in the large bay window of Norton's second-floor office, hitting Tasker in the face like he was being interrogated in an old movie. Renee Chin sat silently in the chair next to him, her long legs crossed, her foot swinging in nervous frustration. Norton, like a king on his throne, stretched out in the soft, reclining leather chair behind his desk.

Tasker hadn't told anyone about the lab results on Dewalt's pendant. No one would expect that it had already been processed. Right now his problem was who to trust. If the only fingerprint on the silver pendant was a DOC sergeant named Janzig, there was no telling who else might know about it. The question that kept popping into Tasker's head was why there was only one print on the pendant. Maybe Baxter had shown it to Janzig? He'd eventually ask the sergeant after he had checked him out through Renee Chin. Now he let his concentration go back to Captain Norton.

The thick captain kept reading a report of the attack on Tasker the day before. The warden had turned the entire matter over to Norton, and the captain of the correctional officers didn't seem too worried about the run-in.

Norton's small brown eyes looked up at Tasker. "So you met old Linus the hard way." He chuckled and added, "No pun intended."

Renee spoke up. "Sam, you know this isn't a joke."

He held up his hands. "Hold on, hold on there, Renee." He used a warmer tone when talking to the prison's inspector. "Linus done this before and every time the most that happens is he messes on someone's leg." He looked at Tasker. "I heard you got blood on my green carpet in there."

Tasker didn't acknowledge the question, as he tried to figure out where this guy was going.

Norton tried to look serious. "After something like this, Linus gets on his medicine right and goes back to the general population. Shit, they sent him back so many times from Chattahoochee that it's easier just to keep the man locked down in Psych till he's back on track. He's never hurt nobody. He's here on a serial burglary rap."

"He had a pretty good grip of my throat." Tasker opened the collar of his polo shirt to expose the purple stain of broken blood vessels that clearly showed finger marks.

Norton leaned closer for inspection. "That he did, Mr. Special Agent, that he did. But you must've gotten in some good shots, too. Linus' leg is swollen up like a watermelon and his right arm has a compound fracture with ligament damage."

"Next time one of your inmates tries to kill me, I'll try to go easier on him."

"I been tellin' you he didn't try to kill you." He sat back in his leather chair and ran his hand over his face like he was frustrated. "Look, things happen in prisons. People get hurt. That's why none of 'em is manned by the Boy Scouts."

"I understand."

"Do you? Do you really? Just since I been gone—that's three days, mind you—we got a dead Nazi that looks like he slipped and hit his head, a shiv attack on a inmate in Dorm H, a domestic between two officers that got the husband locked up at the county jail, and this shit that happened to you. Some events that don't concern you, but I still gotta make sure you're safe while you look at another death. I still gotta keep things runnin' here. I don't see the governor sending people to help us with them problems."

Tasker kept his cool. "I know things happen you can't control. I just want to know if this could've been controlled."

Norton stared at him and a complete change in mood came over the captain. "You think someone let him loose on you on purpose?"

"That's one conclusion I came to."

"That's a mighty serious conclusion." He looked at Renee. "That's something Inspector Chin would have to look into, and if it's true I'll personally twist the balls off of anyone involved."

Tasker stood. "I appreciate that attitude, Captain. Hope I'm wrong, but if not, Inspector Chin will find out the truth."

Norton softened slightly. "You find out who killed Rick Dewalt and head on home and everyone'll be happy."

Tasker looked at him, using his best cop street sense to see if the guy was on the level. It troubled him greatly that he couldn't tell with this joker. The captain was either a great guy or a total lying psychopath.

R enee Chin walked with Bill Tasker to a small office in the admin building where he could look at the time sheets and write his reports on the investigation. Tasker was very quiet, just asking Renee as they walked into the office, "No one works in here, do they?"

"No, why?"

"I could use a desk until I'm finished."

"How long will that be, do you think? I mean, it looks like Baxter might have done it."

He looked at her and hesitated. Then he said, "I looked briefly at Dewalt's personal effects a few days ago."

"Yeah, so?"

"Something in the back of my mind keeps telling me I had seen that pendant before."

"Where?"

"Let's have a look at Dewalt's personal effects and I can either confirm this feeling or dismiss it."

"Let's go."

Renee didn't know what was on the state cop's mind, but she was fascinated with the process. She looked into deaths and thefts and everything else that went on at the prison, but this was a different perspective.

In a room next to her office were shelves of evidence and contraband she had taken from inmates. It took only a second to find the plastic bag with Rick Dewalt's personal items in it.

Tasker took the bag and looked in the open end. "This is everything?"

"We disposed of any clothing and turned any cash into a check. When everything is resolved, the family will get the bag. No one keeps much around here."

"Was the bag always open?"

She nodded. "I have a small safe to lock up anything real valuable."

"Is there a log of what was in here?"

She reached over and pulled a single sheet off the shelf. "Anything else?"

Tasker looked down the short list. He looked at Renee and said, "Item eight says small medallion with face on the front. Think that a medallion and a pendant are the same thing?"

Renee looked at the log. The officer on duty in the dorm the day Dewalt died had filled it out. What was Tasker getting at?

Tasker said, "Show me that medallion or pendant in this bag."

She took the bag and emptied the contents out onto an empty shelf. There was no jewelry of any kind.

She looked up at him. "I don't mean to sound stupid, but what's this mean? Someone took it after it was stored here?"

"And then planted it in Leroy Baxter's stuff."

"But why?"

"To make us think we had found our killer."

She considered this and then, before she could stop herself, asked, "Who?"

"The only print on it was of a sergeant here named Henry Janzig."

"I don't understand that at all. Why would Henry want you to think Baxter killed Dewalt?"

"First I'd check to see if Janzig was in a position to kill Dewalt. Then work from there."

Renee didn't hesitate. "Believe me, I'm on it."

Luther Williams had been a successful attorney as Cole Hodges. He had raised money by the carload for the Committee for Community Relief, even if they had only received about twenty percent. He had been a successful armed robber in St. Louis years before, until his unfortunate arrest when a patrol car had rear-ended his parked getaway Trans Am and the fat uniformed patrolman had called for help because he thought he was paralyzed. Every cop in the city had responded only to find Luther backing out of the large grocery store with a pistol in his hand and the cop's giant gut stuck under the wheel of his patrol car.

Luther had been a success at the Missouri State prison, running the gambling and homemade liquor concession for three years until the chance to ride a laundry truck out the gate had come up. Now he found he was a success again. He had a nice cocaine distribution network, as well as a small protection racket worked out to keep some of the brothers safe who were hooked up outside but didn't have enough horsepower to scare anyone in a place as pleasant-sounding as Manatee Correctional.

His successful elimination of Vollentius proved he could get things done. Vollentius had been discovered a full two hours after his unlucky slip in the prep kitchen. By the time he'd been found, his face was scaled half away, his skull was fractured and he had drowned in a mere eight inches of water. Luther chuckled out loud.

Walking down the main breezeway toward his job in the administration building, Luther passed Robert Moambi, the dishwasher on duty the day before when the Aryan had had his accident. Luther nodded.

Moambi stopped briefly and mumbled, "They're calling all the staff together to ask us about what we seen."

Luther said, "And what did you see?"

"Nothing."

"Good. I'll remember that." Luther patted the thick, dark young man on his arm and continued on his way.

Once he was through the main gate and in the admin building, he saw the lovely Renee Chin. He heard her say to the officer closest to the door, "I've got to run over to the medical examiner for Vollentius' autopsy. Should be back in a couple of hours."

The seated officer nodded, but Luther took note. He'd watch for her return and see if her face gave anything away. She was one of the few who knew her shit around here. He'd hate to have to change his plans almost as much as he'd hate to eliminate that ebony beauty. But he knew he'd do what he had to do.

Renee Chin wasn't sure if she was sorry or relieved when she discovered that Henry Janzig had been in Tallahassee the day Rick Dewalt was killed. She had confirmed it with paperwork and phone calls to the training coordinator in the state's capital. It left questions but didn't point to the funny-looking old man as a killer. She sat on Tasker's new desk and finished telling him, then asked, "Where does that leave us?"

"Nowhere, really. Eventually I'll have to interview Janzig and see if he has a good excuse for why his print is on a pendant that should have been in that plastic bag."

"This means you'll be here awhile."

Tasker shrugged. "Unless someone confesses, it'll take me a couple of weeks to check out everything and write up the investigation. There's not much to work with."

"Unless someone talks."

"Right. Unless someone talks."

"Someone always talks in here. It just takes time."

"Time isn't an issue with me. I'm here. This is my assignment."

She couldn't hide a smile. "In that case, I have a key for this office. Use it until you're done. I'll even get you a name tag."

He smiled as he settled in behind the desk, his notebook and some papers on his right. "Will you visit me occasionally? I feel like *I'm* in lockdown now."

"The warden doesn't want to risk another incident. You can bet you'll be safe here." She checked her Timex. She never wore anything expensive to the facility because sometimes it seemed like she was surrounded by thieves. "I've got to view the autopsy on the inmate that died, Vic Vollentius. Make sure it really was an accident. Then I'm gonna check out the mental ward and lockdown to see if I can get a handle on what happened yesterday. Can I buy you an early dinner?"

"You bet."

20 RENEE CHIN MADE THE LONG DRIVE INTO THE Palm Beach County Medical Examiner's Office in the correctional facility's five-year-old Ford Taurus with questionable air-conditioning. She found her mind wandering as she drove east on the boring, straight US Highway 80. The endless fields of cane waved in a decent breeze from the east and few cars passed her going toward the Glades. She fiddled with the air-conditioning controls and then cracked the window-to supplement the substandard Freon.

She pushed the rattling older Ford a little for a couple of reasons. It was warm inside the mildew-smelling vehicle and she wanted to get back for dinner with Bill Tasker. A smile crept across her face as she thought about him in the small office, so concerned about doing a good job and studying photos and interview reports.

As she came within sight of Lion Country Safari, a sure sign of the civilization to come, she noticed another car behind her. It was a Florida highway patrol trooper in a brown-and-tan Crown Vic. Where'd he come from? Then the light bar on his roof came to life and she pulled onto the shoulder of the road with her rearview filled with the whirling blue lights.

She cranked down the window as the tall, white trooper with a wash-and-wear haircut lingered at his open door, speaking into the radio mike clipped to his shoulder. He reached back into his car and pulled out a giant Wendy's soda cup and took a long slug, replaced the cup in his car, then started his slow stroll up to the car with his metal ticket book already out. Renee wasn't certain, but thought the Taurus had a state tag on it. The trooper stopped belt-high in front of her window.

"What's the problem, Officer?"

"Do you have any idea how fast you were going?"

"Maybe eighty-five?"

He paused. "Seventy-nine."

"Is that all? Good, I wouldn't want to be unsafe." She looked up at his boyish face and cut loose with the best smile she could.

The trooper said, "License and registration."

She would have to step out of the car for her feminine side to be more obvious. She reached across to the glove compartment and found, like any other vehicle from the prison, that it had no paperwork. She turned back.

"Sorry, this is a pool car from Manatee Correctional. The registration is probably in an office. You know how the state is."

He barely acknowledged her as he stepped to the rear of the car and started to write in the ticket holder.

Renee opened the door and was standing outside the car before the trooper could protest.

She smiled as she eased back toward him. "C'mon, you're not gonna write another law enforcement officer, are you?"

"You're a cop? I thought you worked for Corrections."

She threw out a little laugh and touched his arm. It was only a matter of time, she figured.

The trooper, a couple of inches taller than her, looked her straight in the eyes. "Save it. You were speeding and I own this highway. My job is to make sure people drive safely and don't get killed between here and Belle Glade."

She thought about turning on her female charm to full blast, but that went against her grain. She'd had enough of this redneck.

"Look," Renee said in a calm, firm voice. "I'm on my way to the ME's office for an autopsy. I'm sorry I was speeding, but the state has not seen fit to fix the air in that piece of shit."

"So that gives you the right to speed?"

That was it. Renee took a step back in case she wanted to punch the smug trooper. "I just explained my situation. If you're gonna write me, write me, but I've got a lot to do and talking to an arrogant, self-important asshole is not on my schedule."

"You blew it."

"I blew it? What did I blow?"

He held up his ticket book and showed her a note he had written out on a plain sheet of paper. It said, *Dinner Friday night? Tom Miko.* Then it had his phone number.

She stared at the trooper. "Oh my. I . . ." She really didn't know what to say. She was away from the prison and not on her usual guard.

The tall trooper said, "I just thought you were cute. You'll never know what you missed."

He simply turned and walked back to his police car.

Renee watched him walk away and thought, Damn, he does have a nice ass.

Luther Williams made sure everyone who had to talk to an investigator about the Aryan Knight's death saw him walk by and noticed he knew who was in the group. He had already made arrangements for the dishwasher, Robert Moambi, to get full trustee status and a job in the administration building with him, starting that afternoon. They were going to need the help after he left. Luther smiled at the thought of his freedom. It was almost as sweet as his plan to live on the outside. After a few errands, he had a lot of plans. He'd finally visit Tallahassee and make the visit he'd put off for fifteen years. All he needed first was a stop in Miami. There were people who owed him money in Miami, but more important, there was a man who could work miracles. If you needed a new identity or a place to start over, Mr. Neil Nyren was as good as any saint in performing miracles. And unlike some saints, Nyren knew how to keep his mouth shut.

After making sure the kitchen staff saw him, he kept his casual pace as he walked past D Dorm where there were always four Aryan Knights sitting at the small picnic-style table. If more than four inmates gathered, they were in violation of the facility's rules. The Aryans were dumbasses, but at least they were smart enough to work around the system.

Luther turned and made a show of nodding to the four surly-looking young men. All were, no doubt, mourning the loss of their comrade. None of them returned Luther's pleasant greeting. Their usual distaste for anyone without white skin prevented normal social interaction. But there was something more behind the ice wall. The way all four sets of eyes followed him made Luther realize he was being sized up. Was Vollentius planning his own hit when he went to the kitchen? Luther decided not to put off any plans he had already set in motion.

As much as Tasker wanted to focus on the six-week-old homicide, his mind kept drifting. He thought about Renee and her new death investigation. He'd like working on that with her, but Captain Norton had made it clear he didn't want Tasker tied up in it. He didn't think the governor would order the FDLE to investigate a Nazi's death. He thought about the professor's homicide investigation. He really wanted in on that, too. But Rufus was actively opposed to help. He was stuck on this. There was no lack of death investigations out here in the quiet countryside. Tasker hadn't been close to this many homicide investigations since a gang war in Liberty City. But right now it was time for lunch. That was the one thing he was sure of.

He left the building, used to the correctional officers' feigned indifference as he passed the reception and safety desks. Even Luther Williams, walking in with a younger, very dark man, nodded and smiled to him.

Tasker made the long walk out to the visitors' parking lot and backed his Monte Carlo out of its spot and headed into Gladesville, a couple of miles to the south. As if pushed by some unseen force, Tasker found himself turning toward the tiny Gladesville PD.

All four spots in front of the station entrance were taken, so he decided to use his police privilege and pull around back with the other police cars. He saw an unmarked Crown Vic and thought it might be Rufus Goodwin's. The back door was up a flight of stairs next to the oversized Dumpster. It obviously hadn't been emptied in a while.

As he reached the bottom of the stairs, the rear door opened, and Rufus Goodwin, dressed like a detective in a short-sleeve shirt and a wide, polyester, nasty rust-colored and cream-striped tie, stopped and looked down at him.

"What're you doing here?" asked Rufus.

Tasker hesitated because he wasn't sure himself. "Anything new on the case?"

"Not since you asked me yesterday. You need to worry 'bout your business and let me worry 'bout mine."

"We're in the same business."

Rufus said, "But not the same company."

Tasker took a step up. "Why does it seem like you're stalling the professor's murder case?"

"Why does it seem you ain't workin' on your own murder case?"

Tasker felt his face flush and his heart rate increase. Something wasn't right with this, and this son of a bitch wasn't doing his job.

Tasker said, "I won't forget about the professor." He turned without another word and stomped back to his car. As he backed out, he saw Rufus walk back inside the building with his cell phone to his ear and gesturing with his free hand.

**21** RENEE CHIN PARKED THE RATTY OLD TAURUS in one of four visitors' spots in front of the entrance to the Palm Beach County Medical Examiner's Office. The operations officer, Tony, was just about the most helpful guy in Palm Beach County law enforcement, followed closely by the rest of the staff at the small building stuck in the parking lot of the ever-growing Palm Beach County Sheriff's Office. The little structure looked like a mistake thrown in the middle of the huge parking lot.

She followed Tony from the administrative office to the detached building where the autopsies were performed and all evidence with human remains was stored. As soon as she walked in the rear building, the chemical salt smell rushed over her. Sometimes it was so strong she could taste it in her mouth.

Tony saw her reaction. "You get used to it."

"That's the formaldehyde, right?"

"Yeah. It chemically cooks the tissue and leaves that odor. Won't hurt you though."

Tony said that as they entered the procedure room and a thin man in surgical scrubs added, "Yeah, and that smell turns you into a chick magnet."

Renee snickered at that. "Hello, Dr. Freund, how are you?" She glanced around his feet to find his trademark buckets by the procedure table.

"Could not be doing better, Inspector Chin. It's been over a month since you came to visit. I spoke to Bill Tasker last week about the other case."

She couldn't hide a smile. "He's reviewing the Dewalt death."

The assistant ME nodded. "He's a good man. I've known him for years."

"Yes, he's impressed me. I mean us. That is, out at Manatee."

The ME smiled and moved across the room. "What about this gentleman?" he said, as an attendant wheeled a gurney with the naked body of Vic Vollentius on it.

"We think it's an accident. I'm just here per policy." Renee was affected differently by every autopsy. Sometimes they were fascinating. Sometimes, depending on her mood and what she had eaten, they made her ill. She liked Dr. Freund and he always explained stuff so she wasn't worried. It was his one quirk that often got to her. She once was nauseous for more than two days just thinking about her visit.

The assistant medical examiner made notes into a microphone attached to his lapel that fed into a small tape recorder in his pocket. He finished and stepped up to the station, then positioned a bucket on each side of the gurney. He looked at Renee, who knew enough to step well away from the thin, forty-two-year-old doctor.

"Shall we?" he said, picking up a small metal probe and starting to examine the outside of the body for any obvious wounds.

The only thing that stuck out was the disfigured skin on his face. Neither the doctor nor Tony even mentioned it. They had seen the preliminary reports and knew what to expect. Renee was always amazed at the incredible professionalism that came out of this office.

Tony said, "I've got my own work. Just hit the intercom if you guys need me." He made his quick exit before any cutting, like most of the cops who had been through it with Dr. Freund before.

Dr. Freund said, "Let's do the cranium first." He examined the face and then the sides of Vollentius' head. The rough, splotchy skin still on his face framed exposed bone and muscle in a couple of places. "Looks like all the damage is on the forehead. According to the report, this scalding is from hot water."

He studied Vollentius' bald head carefully, then ran a surgical gloved finger over the one mark on the forehead. He studied the wound, then stepped back from it.

Renee asked, "Problem, Doc?"

"Hard to say. That's a pretty good crack on the head for slipping into a tub of water. Doesn't it seem a little convenient to you that he'd slip right there and fall into a tub of water?"

"The way things work around the kitchen, if you weren't familiar with it, and he wasn't, anything could happen. That's why I'm here."

Renee nodded as she watched him pick up a handheld Dremel rotary tool-like saw with a five-inch-round blade. She took another step back as he flicked on the electric saw and slowly lowered it over Vollentius' forehead just above the wound.

Renee flinched at the sound of the whirling saw against the thick bone of the skull. The slight burning smell caused by the friction of the blade on Vollentius' skull turned her stomach, but she knew that was minor compared to what was about to happen.

As soon as he had circled the head once with the saw and worked the top of Vollentius' head loose, exposing the brain pan and blood, Dr. Freund casually leaned over and vomited into the bucket at his feet. He was so practiced that he hardly stopped working.

"This is a tough one, Inspector. Could be a simple fall, but it could be a little more force was used when his head hit the ground. Let's see what else we find."

Renee watched as he worked down the body to the chest cavity, where he made an incision down the middle of Vollentius' chest. As he used the rib spreader to expose the internal organs, he again leaned down to spit up in a well-placed bucket.

Renee said, "How do you keep any weight on at all?"

"My wife feeds me like a fatted calf."

"You never got over the sight of blood?"

He stopped and looked at her. "Does it look like I did?" He paused. "I know, an ME who gets sick at the sight of blood is funny, but it's been six years. You guys should be used to it by now."

She smiled. "I'm sorry, it's just so . . ."

"Interesting? Sexy? Macho?" He scrunched his eyes and used his forearm to push up his glasses.

"I was thinking 'weird.'"

"That's fair," he said and went right back to work. Over the next hour he explained different aspects of the corpse to Renee, none of them particularly remarkable. He commented that the Aryan Knight had one of the smallest brains he had ever seen on a grown male. He vomited twice more and then finally, after rinsing his gloved hands in the nearby sink, stood erect, arched and stretched his back and looked at Renee.

"I'll check the cavities and take a few more samples and we're done."

Renee, feeling a pain in her knees from standing on the cement for so long, smiled with relief.

He checked the body's ears with a small penlight, then his eyes. He used a small spacer to hold open the mouth and probed it with a metal rod as he shone the light inside.

"What the hell?"

Renee stepped closer as he reached for a pair of long tweezers from the table.

"Lookie here," he said as he extracted a white rolled-up piece of paper from Vollentius' mouth. He examined it, then used the tweezers and his free hand to open the tiny scroll. "A note. That's incredible. I've never seen anything like this before."

Renee said, "I've seen it a couple of times."

Sam Norton nodded while he listened on his phone. He was starting to get frustrated because no one wanted to just get things done. Everyone wanted to bitch.

Norton said, "I got things handled here. You gotta get things handled up there."

"How?" asked a male's voice.

"You know better than me. Having people nosing around is not good for any of us."

"It's gone further than I thought it would."

"It hasn't gone near far enough if it means we're gonna miss out on a big payday. You just get ahold of who you need to and have us left alone again."

"I'll do my best."

"As long as your best gets it done, that's good enough." Norton hung up, tired of talking to people who thought they were in charge but weren't.

Tasker sat in a booth at the Lone Wrangler, a steakhouse between Gladesville and Belle Glade where Renee had asked to meet for dinner. It was now seven-twenty, twenty minutes after she said she'd meet him and he was smelling a stand-up. It had happened enough to him that he'd thought he was immune, but it still hurt.

He nursed his Budweiser, since his choices were Bud and Bud Light, and read the menu for the fifth time. What a day this had been. When he'd gone out to his car, he'd found two tires punctured. It had taken a couple of hours to have his car towed and new tires mounted. He had not finished any more reading of the disciplinary reports, and with Renee off the prison grounds for the day, no one had spoken to him.

Now he contemplated his options. Leave and show her he wasn't a pet, but then risk her not speaking to him again. Stay and risk his self-respect. Or call Billie Towers and see what she was doing. The last option wasn't in his personality. He'd never been one to play with people's emotions and never dated two women at once, if you could call this a date. He yanked his Nextel from its plastic clip and suddenly realized the phone was turned off. Oh shit! He hadn't turned it on after he took a short nap before dinner.

It felt like an eternity before the screen showed power and signal. Then a screen that said "message." When he called to retrieve it, the voice said there were three messages.

The first was from his daughters saying they'd be at his house Friday. Their voices in practiced unison made him smile.

The second was from Renee saying she was running late from the autopsy. The last one was also Renee saying she was on her way. Before he could hear the end, she came through the door. He was almost speechless. Partly due to his own stupidity and the things he had just been thinking, but more because Renee was in a tight, short, stunning black dress with stiletto heels. This was definitely no business meal.

He stood to greet her and was surprised by a kiss on his cheek. He didn't care if the words "Manatee prison" ever came up tonight.

Renee took a breath and said, "You get my messages?"

"Yep, no problem. You see Dominick Freund?"

"That's why I had to take an extra-long shower."

"You mean the puking during autopsies?"

"Four times and he never missed a beat."

"They have to make a musical out of him. *The Medical Examiner Blues* or *I left My Lunch in San Francisco.*"

She laughed, showing her near-perfect teeth.

"What, besides Freund, held you up at the ME's office?"

"A little wrinkle in the simple explanation for Vic Vollentius' death."

"Like what?"

"He had a note hidden in his mouth."

"Like a message to others?"

"No, who he was meeting."

"You're shitting me. Who does that?"

She looked at him carefully and said, "Don't use that phrase with me. My mama hated it and my brothers and me are conditioned to hate it, too."

"Sorry."

She smiled. "Just a family quirk. But the practice of hiding notes on your body in prison isn't unusual. In case something happens, you can testify from the grave, so to speak."

"Sounds like something out of a Stephen Hunter novel."

"Who?"

"A writer I like. So tell me 'bout the note."

"Hidden in his mouth. I've seen them in the crack of an inmate's ass and the fold off his balls before, but this was the first mouth."

Tasker gritted his teeth in mock frustration and said, "What did the note say?"

"'If anything happens, I'm meeting Luther Williams.'"

**22** BILL TASKER SAT AT THE FORMICA-FINISHED
dining table, which had been included in his free rent. He
had a glass of tropical fruit Powerade next to him and the
local weekly paper spread out, trying to understand the world into
which he had found himself dropped by forces greater than himself.

He was still in his shorts and sweat-drenched T-shirt from his morning run. He liked running off-road out here because in the mornings it
wasn't too hot and he always liked exploring new areas. This morning
he'd gone fifty-five minutes and run the small trail behind the apartments that cut through the cane field all the way to US 27 heading
toward Clewiston to the west.

It was a little later than he was used to leaving for the prison, but he
needed a break from that place. He wasn't sure what he'd be working on
today. Renee Chin was looking into the death of the Aryan Knight that
didn't look much like an accident anymore, and interviewing people working the lockdown area where Tasker had been attacked earlier in the week.
He could justify working on either investigation because they were both in
the prison. Who could argue that he should only look at the death of the
son of a rich man? Just like who could argue about him trying to find out
if someone was out to get him? He realized his bosses and their bosses
could. He'd get back on his own homicide case, but now he had to admit
he wanted to talk to the lockdown officers because he was still pissed off.

As he was getting ready to drag his ass to the shower, the apartment
phone made its noisy, clattering ring.

"Hello?" The only one who had this number for him was . . .

"Billy, you takin' a nap?"

He smiled at the FDLE Miami regional director's voice. Tasker said, "Hey, boss."

"Things workin' out all right out there? Is it peaceful enough?"

"I wouldn't exactly call it peaceful, but I'm adjusting."

"I hear you're sliding into old habits, though."

"What habits?"

"Working other people's cases. Are you involved in some half-assed death investigation that occurred outside the prison?"

"Who told you that?"

"No, you don't understand, Billy. I ask the questions and you answer. Now, are you harassing the local cops about a single-jurisdiction, single-victim homicide?"

"I wouldn't call it harassing."

"Look, Billy, just work on the fucking homicide of that Dewalt kid for Gann and the governor's office."

"I am, boss. The victim in the other homicide was my neighbor. Just offering assistance."

"Remember who you're talking to. I know once you're locked onto something, someone's in deep shit. This time I'm afraid it's you."

"But—"

"The only things you should concern yourself with are inside the walls of Manatee Correctional. Understood?"

"Yes, sir."

"And, Billy."

"Yes, sir?"

"How tough is a prison named after a floating cow?"

Captain Sam Norton smiled at the sight of his friend Janzig belly-laughing over what he had done to the so-called "investigators." Janzig caught his breath and leaned on the outer fence of the Rock in their usual private business area. "You know, I feel like God sometimes, making them think what I want 'em to. First making Baxter a killer after he was already dead and then making Luther responsible for the Aryan Knight." He spit, then added, "I'm here to tell you that college doesn't do a goddamn thing for you. Them two both went to college, but neither could find their ass with both hands."

Norton said, "Now hold on there, Henry. Renee is sharp, you have to admit. That note you put in Vollentius' mouth was more to get the other Knights worked up. I haven't seen her bite on it yet."

"You think they don't know about Baxter?"

"They haven't said nothin'."

"I'm telling you, that FDLE guy is stalling. He likes it here."

"Why would he like it here?"

"'Cause his partner is tall, smart and ain't got a dick."

Norton considered that, then said, "We may need to send that boy a stronger message."

"Stronger than having Linus Hardaway choke the livin' shit out of him?"

"Something off the prison grounds. Maybe if he doesn't feel like he has a safe haven to go to, he'll just leave."

"Maybe. Whatcha got in mind?"

"We could use some 'graduates' of this fine institution."

"Like who? The Mule brothers? The hairy one can make some kick-ass explosives."

"What about some off-loaders'. Guys smart enough to know they may be back in here one day and want to stay on our good side."

Janzig nodded. "I know just who to call. Where should they make it happen?"

"Not at his house. Needs to look more like a chance encounter, but he'll figure it out. Maybe a bar or something."

Janzig gave him a big smile with a third of his teeth either missing or starting to rot. "I'll take care of it, boss."

Norton smiled. "I never doubted it."

Tasker hustled after his phone call. A call that bothered him, not because of what was said, but because he didn't know who had complained. It had to be someone with some juice for the director even to bother to call. He was showered and heading out the door in a matter of minutes after he'd hung up the phone.

The five-minute ride to Manatee gave him a chance to calm down and dissect the call. Maybe the chief of Gladesville had called his director, but that didn't make sense. First, the local chief would've talked to him personally, and second, the chief of Gladesville didn't have the influence to make a director for FDLE call like that. Something else was going on around this place and Tasker was going to find out what.

Renee Chin had five correctional officers sitting in the library, down the hall from her office. She also had an officer who wanted to be an inspector doing some research at a nearby table, with instructions to report anything unusual he heard. Renee had been a correctional officer and a sergeant so she knew how protective you became of one another. This might be the first time any of them realized they were under investigation. That was her favorite tactic: Call everyone involved at once. Don't give them a chance to compare stories until you had a way to listen.

She had them wait not only to let them stew, but to give Bill Tasker a chance to be involved. He said he'd like to see how in-house investigations were conducted. It was now almost nine and he wasn't in yet. She might have to start without him.

She reviewed the time sheets and entry logs. There were four officers in that area of the building, two in lockdown and two in the psychiatric ward. She would focus on the two in the ward. They would've been in a position to let Linus Hardaway out and point him in the right direction. She could talk to Linus, but it would be a few more days of medication before he could speak coherently.

A knock on the door brought her attention up from the entry logs. FDLE Special Agent Bill Tasker stood in the doorway as casual as he always was. Dressed in Dockers and a polo shirt, he didn't fit in around the crew cuts and uniforms.

He said, "Sorry I'm late. Can I still sit in?"

"You bet. Have you given any thought to the Luther Williams situation?"

"I have. You say the Aryan or someone else could've set Luther up, right?"

"It's one possibility."

"Or he could've killed him and made it look like an accident?"

"Exactly."

"Why don't you let me talk to him? Just feel him out."

"I can do that. I'll hold my report on the autopsy for a few days." She stood and walked toward him, felt like kissing him but recognized this as a place of business and passed by to the hallway. She called into the library for the first officer and waited while the gangly young man stood and came down the hallway, his eyes so wide it looked like he thought he was going to the electric chair.

Luther Williams had gathered a lot of information in the last two days. He wanted to make sure no one thought he had anything to do with the Aryan Knight's death. He had the only viable witness, Moambi, the dishwasher, working right in the admin building with him, and when he approached the admin gate to report for his work assignment, they let him through without a second thought. His concern was the mounting suspicion that the damn Aryan Knights were getting ready to make a move on him. But at least the prison officials were as blissfully ignorant as ever.

Now he felt even more confident, because the four correctional officers that Inspector Chin had waiting in the library had nothing to do with the kitchen. They were all lockdown officers and wouldn't know anything about the death.

Still, he might have to move up his plans. If the remaining Aryan Knights decided to do their own investigation, he might have to do a lot of things. One definitely included annoying the good Captain Norton. That was a man who needed to be taught a lesson. While Luther had never been a schoolteacher or even pretended to be one, he'd hold a class for that vicious son of a bitch. Maybe he could find a use for the FDLE agent after all.

Tasker had sat in on three interviews and let Renee do most of the talking. He had talked to three of the officers in relation to the Dewalt death. It was routine, but they had all been on duty in the psych ward or lockdown the day Dewalt's body was found. Tasker didn't believe any of them had any useful information, but he'd learned he was only human and could make mistakes. He wasn't like the cops on *Law & Order* or *CSI*. His instincts were good but certainly not infallible. His assessment of Daniel Wells before he had become a fugitive and caused Tasker so much anguish had been as wrong as wrong could be. Now he usually kept an open mind even after he had interviewed people on a case.

He was impressed by Renee's ability and instinct for interviews. Most people think that you ask questions and whatever people say happened is what happened. Tasker had learned over many hard years that people rarely say what they mean even if they don't mean to mislead you.

The body language of this last correctional officer, a tall youth of twenty-four named Lester Lynn, made him look guilty. He fidgeted and wouldn't look directly at either of them.

Tasker sat back to let Renee question the young man as effectively as she had interviewed the other three. She had led the others down a line of questions and was satisfied, like Tasker, that they had nothing to do with his unfortunate encounter with Linus Hardaway. There was something different about this young man. He couldn't put his finger on it, as Renee led him through the opening questions, then led him to his job that day.

"Where were you assigned?" asked Renee, keeping her eyes on him, watching for the telltale signs of lying: twitches, pauses, swallowing. Courses like the Reid School of Interviewing ingrained them in students' heads.

Lester's protruding Adam's apple didn't make it hard to tell when he swallowed. It rose and dropped like the ball in Times Square on New Year's Eve.

"I was, um, I was assigned to the hatch and relief over to lockdown. I been at the hatch for almost a year now."

That was the first time Tasker had heard that phrase and he just looked at Renee.

She said, "Some of the COs refer to the psychiatric ward as the 'booby hatch' or just 'the hatch.'"

Tasker nodded, surprised he hadn't seen the obvious, if ignorant, connection.

Renee stayed on her subject. "You had that assignment the whole shift?"

"Yeah." His eyes darted slightly as he answered. He shifted in his seat again.

"From eight that morning?"

"Yeah, I said the whole shift."

"Who assigned you?"

"Sergeant Janzig. He was in charge of lockdown while the captain was on leave for capping that boy who run off."

Tasker caught the name of the sergeant whose print was on Dewalt's pendant. Was this just another coincidence?

Renee continued. "So you were in the area about noon when Linus Hardaway attacked Agent Tasker?"

"I guess. I mean, I heard the control room officer screamin' over the radio about a fight. By the time I got there, Mr. Tasker was sittin' down and poor old Linus had been beat stupid."

Tasker flinched slightly at the characterization of his defense.

"Was that the first time you saw Linus that day?" asked Renee.

"I guess."

Renee sighed and rose from her seat. If Tasker didn't know better, he'd have thought she was about to strike the arrogant shithead. Then, remembering her action on Rufus Goodwin, he got ready for contact. Instead she walked to a neutral corner of the room.

She said, "You guess that was the first time you saw him?"

He shrugged.

"How many inmates were in the psych ward that day?"

"I dunno, five, maybe six."

"And you didn't take the time to check on each of them at least once before lunch?"

"Is this a job evaluation or something? If it is I think I might need me a PBA attorney."

Renee stepped closer. "You might need someone, but it won't be an attorney."

The young man flinched, apparently familiar with Inspector Chin's ability to kick ass.

Tasker stood quickly to diffuse the situation. He stood his ground against a withering glare from Renee.

She took a breath and said, "Lester, how long you been here at Manatee?"

"Almost eighteen months."

"What assignments have you had?"

"General for the first few months and the hatch since then."

"Did you like working general assignment?"

He shrugged his narrow shoulders. "I guess."

"Where do you want to work?"

"Sergeant Janzig and the captain have been letting me try the control room on the weekends. They say I do a good job in the hatch and I can transfer."

"Is letting Linus Hardaway out doing a good job?"

"I didn't let him out. I told you that."

"If you're telling the truth, then why are you sweating so bad?"

The correctional officer said, "You make me nervous. I don't feel like I can talk."

Renee let out her breath and looked at Tasker, who nodded. "Okay, Lester. What if I take a break and you talk to Agent Tasker alone for a little while?"

Lester nodded. "Okeydoke."

She looked at him and said, "He's all yours."

Tasker waited for her to clear the room and shut the door, just a little too hard. He grabbed his chair and scooted it closer to Lester, hoping to take advantage of his obvious role as good cop.

"So, Lester, is there anything you're more comfortable telling me than telling Inspector Chin?"

The young officer smiled. "You bet."

"What's that?"

"She has got some nice titties."

Tasker knew the interview was over, but at least he'd gotten the young man to tell the truth.

 **23** THE SUN WAS JUST DISAPPEARING BEHIND THE
sugarcane field to the west of Tasker's apartment. He was
now the only resident—the other two had finished their
jobs and left. He stretched his legs in front of him as he relaxed in the
shaky Adirondack chair on the front porch. He had just cracked an Icehouse beer. By Gladesville standards, Icehouse was an imported beer. It
was not unlike a Friday night at home. He did not intend to visit the
prison or work on the case over the weekend, just have fun with his
daughters. If he accomplished that, he'd have to point it out to Donna
on Sunday night.

What a week he'd had: the murder, the attack, the call from the director. He was looking forward to Monday. He'd find a quiet moment to
feel out Luther Williams on the death of the inmate in the kitchen.
Nothing formal or overt. Maybe just get a feel for his reaction to the
question. He was already locked up, it wasn't like he could flee the
charges. Renee had agreed that it was a good move prior to her official
investigation. He smiled at the thought of her. She had said she might
come by this evening, just to check on him. He had told her the girls
would be here but she was welcome, and she'd seemed interested. He
smiled at the thought of Donna and Renee meeting. It would be the
first time Donna had actually seen a woman Tasker was interested in. To
his knowledge, Donna had never met her match.

Tasker watched from his porch as Donna and the girls pulled up in her familiar minivan. She was right on time, at least for her. She had said she would bring the girls around five-thirty. It was now after six. He didn't care about the details as he saw the two blond heads pop out of the passenger side of the van and make a beeline for him. They both hit him at once, almost knocking him down. Donna was her reserved self, fifteen feet behind the ecstatic girls.

After some minor settling in, the girls were out the back door to explore the area nearest the cane field, which was as far as the outdoor floodlights reached.

Donna joined him on the rear porch and even accepted a beer.

She flopped in the chair next to him. "This is nice. Maybe we can have a few minutes without a prison alarm going off or someone being murdered."

Tasker winced at the insinuation that Gladesville was unfit for the girls. "I was upfront about Professor Kling's death. Believe me, it bothers me, too."

"I know. And I also know you'll be with the girls the whole time they're here."

"Every second."

"I just worry, that's all. I was afraid Emily might take the news about the professor badly since the bank shooting."

"You said you told them that the professor died, not that he was murdered."

"I did. They were upset, but they had only met him that one weekend. They were worried about Billie."

Tasker nodded.

"Why didn't you tell me Billie is a girl?"

"Does it matter?"

"Just curious. Seemed like a detail you might add. Something like: 'Billie, this beautiful girl who works for the professor.' That sort of thing."

"Did the girls say she was beautiful?"

"They described her. I concluded beautiful."

Tasker smiled to himself.

"Is she?"

"What?"

"Is she beautiful?"

He considered the question and answered honestly. "Yes, yes, she is."

"Are you seeing her?"

"No."

"Why not?"

"Haven't had the time." He left it at that and looked out at the girls as they cut in and out of the shadows. As he was about to mention that Billie was in her twenties, he heard someone on the front porch.

"Hello?" drifted back.

He sprang up, recognizing Renee's smooth voice.

He looked at Donna in the chair and said, "I'll be right back."

At the front screen door, Renee stood in a pair of tight jeans and a white tank top. Tasker managed to keep his eyes in his skull and thought, This should be good.

She smiled. "I'm not interrupting, am I?"

"Not at all."

"I assumed, since you're the only one living here, that you had guests." She looked over her shoulder at the tan minivan. The glow from the single light in the front parking lot gave her light brown skin a rich color.

"Yeah, my ex is dropping off the kids. Come out back and meet everyone."

"You sure?"

He smiled. "Oh, I'm sure." He led her through the apartment to the back porch and his ex-wife, still in the chair.

"Donna, this is Renee Chin. Renee, Donna."

Donna stood and said, "I remember wondering if you were a Chinese man when Bill said he was going to meet someone named R. A. Chin. Boy, was I wrong." She extended her hand.

"Bill doesn't talk about his work out here?"

"He forgot to mention you."

Tasker just smiled. This was exactly the reaction he had hoped for.

Even though it was petty and immature, he acknowledged it and felt quite satisfied.

Sam Norton stood on his porch, enjoying the Saturday morning chill and the fact that his two daughters were sleeping in the spare bedroom. A whole weekend with them while their mother was off with that damn *Sun-Sentinel* reporter. The guy had written some sort of half-assed mystery novel and was traveling around to promote it. Norton laughed at such foolishness. He was careful not to taunt her about the relationship or the impending divorce. He still harbored hope that they might work it out. They had overcome a lot together. Not many of his family members had approved of the interracial marriage after he had met her while on vacation in Daytona. A tall, sleek black girl with a New Jersey accent. At first his dad hadn't known what was more disturbing: that his boy had married out of his race or that he'd married a northerner. They didn't call them "Yankees" much anymore, but his family sure didn't have much use for anyone from New York or New Jersey. Especially if their name ended in a vowel or their skin was more than two shades darker than their own.

After six years and two kids, maybe his family had been right. He hoped it was just a phase and that she'd come home to him one day. Of course, if that day was soon, he'd have some serious explaining to do to the other woman in his life, and maybe to his wife, too. He'd do what he had to do, like always. But he wouldn't be happy about it. He thought about his wife and smiled. He did have a weakness for certain types.

Hannibal, his German shepherd, came trotting back from his favorite grassy area near the main perimeter fence. Not only did that keep his little land mines away from the house, it let the inmates know that wherever Hannibal was, the boss was not far behind. Hannibal wasn't a work dog. He was too unpredictable. Usually he'd listen to Norton, but there had been times his instinct got the best of him. The worst incident had involved an inmate who had been cutting the grass near the officers' housing. He'd made the mistake of running when he saw Hannibal trotting out the door in front of Norton. By the time Norton had had the dog under control, the inmate had lost his left hand and three fingers from his right. Norton still chuckled at the sight of the yard man with no usable hands. Luckily, he had put the fear of God into the inmate and he'd never made any kind of complaint. Now he had a cake job delivering bedding and knew not to say anything.

Norton's youngest, Lanya, crept out the front door toward her father in a long T-shirt that went all the way to the ground, covering her feet. Her light brown, kinky hair waved off her tiny head in tiny spirals. Her eyes were still at half-mast.

"Papa?"

"What?"

"You got a girlfriend?"

He paused and looked into her dark eyes. "Why would you ask that?"

She shrugged. "You got ladies' things in your closet."

He knew he did. "When was you in my closet?"

"Last night. Playing hide-and-seek."

He thought about his answer, knowing it would get back to his wife. "Those are old things. They was here when I moved in and I haven't gotten around to throwing them out. Now you two don't go poking around in my stuff. Understand?" He gave a father look, not a captain look.

The little girl just nodded her head.

He looked at his daughter and thought how nice it would be to have his wife back, but he wasn't crazy about looking after kids. This might be their last visit until he got the whole family back.

Luther spent his Sunday afternoon sorting books in the library. The quiet admin building gave him some time to think and assess things. He had his new protégé, Robert Moambi, cleaning the offices used during the week. The two inmates worked virtually unnoticed by the small staff in the building on a Sunday afternoon.

It had been almost a week since he had taken care of Vollentius, and

Luther didn't think anyone in authority had any idea of his involvement. He had even heard two of the dorm correctional officers joke about the circumstances of Vollentius' death. The joke was something to the effect that they knew some people weren't good in water, but this was a new record for poor performance in a water environment. Luther had to admit that, on the face of it, drowning in a few inches of water was somewhat comical. All he worried about now was the prison inspector, Renee Chin, figuring something out. She was smart and she knew it. She might even take a death like that personally and work harder than the Aryan Knight was worth. Luther would make the right decision when the time came.

Luther stretched in the chair where he was looking through some newly donated books. Robert Moambi came into the library with a broom in his hand. There was a ring of sweat around the neck of his shirt.

Moambi said, "Nice to see someone has an easy job."

Luther ignored him.

"I should have me a job like this. Sitting in a nice room all day reading books."

"I earned this job."

"And I didn't?"

"Not yet."

"What about keeping my mouth shut?"

"That got you from in there"—he pointed to the main secure prison—"to in here. You're not washing dishes any longer. What're you complaining about?"

"Not complaining. Just wonderin'. Wonderin' if I should be in here reading?"

"Stop wondering. This is a one-man job. Be happy where you are."

"One man that would be out of a job if I let something slip."

"If you let something slip, you won't be the man filling this job." Luther gave him a good look and could tell he had gotten his message across.

Moambi remained silent, then changed the subject quickly. "Your lady friend coming in a couple of hours?"

"How'd you know I have a lady friend or that she's coming in a couple of hours?"

"Everyone knows you got a big white woman that comes by Sundays and Wednesdays at four-thirty."

"Everyone knows?"

The younger man shrugged. "Yeah, everyone."

Luther smiled and said quietly, "Good."

**24** TASKER ROLLED INTO THE PARKING LOT BE-
fore eight o'clock Monday morning. He felt fresh after a
good, hard run through the cane and a surprisingly hot
shower. After taking the girls home the night, before he had come
straight back to the apartment and fallen asleep before ten. He'd awak-
ened on his own near five in the morning and started his day right.

He had spent the weekend appreciating what he had instead of
brooding about Donna. Although Renee had only come by Friday night,
she seemed to like the girls and they were in awe of this tall, strong,
beautiful black woman who told them about her days of playing basketball at the University of South Florida. Kelly connected with the smart
role model and Emily with the athletic side of Renee.

Now Tasker felt ready to tackle the loose ends on his death investigation, then casually run across Luther Williams. Although he had been
told to lay off the Gladesville investigation into Professor Kling's death,
no one had said not to help on prison-related cases. Not that Tasker intended to drop the Kling case. He just couldn't say anything to Rufus
Goodwin. He owed that much to the professor and to Billie Towers. Billie had been scarce the last week, but he knew she was still in town. She
had left a note on his front door while he was driving the girls back to
Donna's, just something saying she was by and would be back. Now that
he could clearly identify an interest in Renee Chin, he looked at Billie
as a friend. A very attractive friend.

A couple of hours later, after ten, he took a break and stood and stretched. Renee Chin had popped in to say good morning earlier, but he needed to deal with Luther before he went on any pleasure calls.

It didn't take Tasker long to find the dignified former fake lawyer in the library, two piles of books on the table before him.

"What are these," asked Tasker, "fiction and nonfiction?"

Luther let out a snort. "Try shit and more shit." He shoved one pile off the table into a large box with fifty more hardbacks in it. "We get the books Goodwill and the Veterans Administration don't want. Thirty-five-year-old encyclopedias that still call Sri Lanka, Ceylon."

"How do you decide what to keep?"

"I keep all the fiction—the boys love a good story—and any nonfiction that is reasonably current or doesn't go out of date. Gardening, woodworking, that sort of stuff."

"What fiction writers do they like?"

"What else, crime fiction. They love Elmore Leonard, John Sandford, Michael Connelly. And anything that mentions women."

Tasker laughed and nodded at the obvious requirement. "Not as glamorous as your last job." Tasker settled into the chair across from Luther.

"My last job was cleaning the toilets in lockdown. You must mean my last job on the outside."

Tasker nodded.

"You take what you can get."

"Good attitude." Tasker waited and then added, "Could be worse."

"How so?"

"You could've had an accident like that fella in the kitchen."

"The Aryan Knight? He was no loss."

"Still a tough way to go."

"Agent Tasker, I really don't know of a good way to go. Especially when you've done the things I've done. I'm not particularly looking forward to judgment from any higher authority."

"You know the victim, Vollentius?"

"Sure, you get to know everyone in here."

Tasker paused, formulating his next question.

"Save your breath, Special Agent Tasker. I'd never give you a hint about any crime committed by an inmate. Even if I knew something."

"You once implicated some people in Miami. I was there."

"That's different."

"How so?" repeating one of Luther's phrases.

"They weren't inmates."

Renee Chin had lingered in her office hoping Bill Tasker would pop in before lunch just to give a glimmer of hope that he saw her as something other than the liaison to the prison. He had already told her that he got nowhere with Luther Williams. That meant she'd have to open a full-blown case and see what she could do to corroborate the note. She'd have Luther pulled from trustee status in a few days as she gathered her info. She didn't want to spook him until she had facts to confront him with. At the very least, he would lose all his privileges, even if she never proved he killed the Aryan Knight. In the back of her mind, she was trying to figure out how to get Bill Tasker assigned to this death investigation, too. She needed more time with him.

If her mother had seen her in action Friday night, dressed in tight clothes and wearing too much makeup, she would have told her she was acting like a ho. Her mom viewed the world pretty much in terms of proper young ladies and hos. Her job here at Manatee fell somewhere in between, but her mama gave her the benefit of the doubt.

At least she hadn't gone back and stalked him over the weekend. After meeting his ex-wife, Donna, she'd felt a little intimidated for the first time in her adult life. That was one good-looking woman, and she definitely had no confidence issues. Renee bet she had never had a man stolen away from her. What she couldn't figure out was how a woman obviously as smart as Donna would let a guy like Bill slip away? Hadn't she seen the other fish in the sea? There was a bunch of similar tuna, too many fat grouper, and only the rare sleek, good-looking snapper like Bill.

Now she had to concentrate on her report to the Secretary of Corrections. She called it her spy report. It detailed the efforts of FDLE Special Agent Bill Tasker in relation to his investigation of the Rick Dewalt death. She had been ordered by the secretary directly to write a report each week and send it only to him via e-mail. No other DOC employee was to see it. At first she'd been thrilled, seeing a possible ticket to ride in the fast lane of careers. Then, as she'd gotten to know Bill Tasker, she'd felt dirty sending it off. Now, she saw that no one could fault the hard, thoughtful work of the FDLE agent as he really tried to follow up the little information there was on the unexplained death.

A knock on her door frame made her heart skip until she looked up to see one of the tuna, Captain Sam Norton, in his dull, white-and-brown, short-sleeve uniform shirt. His brown hair was combed to the side exactly as it was every day and his small potbelly hung slightly over his standard-issue belt. His small eyes were filled out with pleasant laugh lines as he smiled.

Norton stepped inside the corner office and said, "You look fine this morning, Renee."

She couldn't resist a smile. "Thanks, Sam. What brings you down the hall?"

"Just saying hello, wonderin' how everything was going."

"Good. What about you?"

"Monday, you know how that can be." He sat down in the single chair in front of Renee's desk. "I had my girls this weekend, so it went by too fast."

"Anything new with your wife?"

"Naw. She seems happy in Lauderdale. The girls, too."

Renee sighed. "What can you do?"

He shrugged. "One day I hope to have enough money that I'm not floating from one facility to the next begging for a promotion."

"Well, I hope you hit the lottery, Sam."

He smiled. "Hell, maybe we both will."

Norton left the lovely inspector's office and wandered through the hallways making sure everyone was doing what they were supposed to be doing. He spent a lot of time inside the fence, the way he thought a captain should do his job, and as a result he felt like some of the administrative types didn't always work as hard as they should.

After a few minutes, he came up on the tiny office the FDLE agent had been assigned and found him comparing trustee records and time sheets.

"Police work ain't as exciting as it looks on TV," said Norton.

Tasker smiled. "You never know what's gonna happen or what you'll end up working on."

"You should be pretty near finished with the case, right?"

"Every time I think I'm making headway, I find something else I have to investigate. Some other things slowed me down, too."

"You still upset about that Linus Hardaway thing? I thought you and Inspector Chin already looked into it."

"But didn't find any answers."

"Sometimes there's nothing to find."

"Always something to find. Sometimes it's the simple answer, sometimes not."

"Your investigation sure seems to be taking a long time."

"Got distracted for a while. The murder in my apartment complex threw me."

"Old Rufus Goodwin will figure that one out. I wouldn't worry 'bout it."

Tasker looked up at Norton and said, "I worry about everything."

Right then Norton knew everything he had heard was true. This guy didn't let go of things. Maybe Norton could get things so he'd ask to be let go.

Luther Williams lingered over his dinner of canned ham and canned sweet potatoes. He knew the only reason they were feasting on something other than hamburger, Salisbury steak or meat loaf was that the purchasing agent had scored some deal on surplus, out-of-date hams. He had seen the hams stacked in the warehouse along with pureed sweet potatoes, industrial-size cans of yellow corn, carrots and beets. He hoped to miss the beets. As he sat alone, at the end of one of the long mess hall tables, sipping a plastic cup of orange Kool-Aid, Luther pondered his options. He knew the FDLE agent was trying to rattle him by mentioning the Aryan Knight's untimely death. Somehow he and no doubt Inspector Chin had figured out the Knight's "accident" had been enhanced. It could have been forensic evidence, something the Knight had said to someone before he came to the kitchen, or, more likely, a witness had come forward. Whatever the case, they didn't have enough to pin it on him yet. If they did, he'd be in lockdown and his plans would be in disarray.

Luther was bumped out of his private world by the form of Robert Moambi plopping into the seat across from him. Unlike the other inmates, many of whom were afraid to approach the former attorney, Moambi assumed he had the right to, now that they worked together in the administration building.

Moambi had the identical meal to Luther's slopped on his tray. "Long day of sweepin' floors builds an appetite."

Luther nodded.

"Least I get to look at some pussy once in a while over there."

Another nod.

"What's with you? Cat got your tongue?"

"Just going over some problems."

"What problems you got in here? Room and board are free. You know what you'll be doing tomorrow. Got fine company like me. Shit, I thought you just killed any problems you have." He gave a short laugh at his own joke.

Luther looked up at the younger man. He was now pretty sure what he had to do. If he only had enough time.

On Tasker's ride into the prison the next morning, his cell phone rang with a Glades number he didn't recognize.

"Bill Tasker," he said into the static and hiss of a low signal.

"Bill, it's Billie Towers."

"Hey, where've you been?"

"Just busy. Have you heard?"

"Heard what?"

"The police arrested the professor's killer."

Tasker almost spun the car at the news.

"Where?"

"In Gladesville."

"When?"

"Last night. He was a homeless guy. Guess he had a record of violence in Iowa or Ohio. Somewhere in the Midwest."

"How'd you find out?"

"TV news this morning."

"Rufus Goodwin or someone from the police department didn't call you?"

"No."

"Where can I reach you?"

"I live at the Sawgrass apartments on Barson Street by the Piggly Wiggly food store."

He could hear her speaking to someone else off the phone.

She came back on the line and said, "I gotta go. I'll call you later."

Tasker stored the phone number under "Billie" in his Nextel as he drove. He turned toward town and headed straight to the Gladesville PD.

25 TASKER CUT THE CORNER TIGHT HEADING INTO
the Gladesville Police Department, causing the wheels of
his Monte Carlo to squeal. He hadn't intended to display
his frustration that way, but didn't care either. He was out of his car and
up the first three outdoor stairs in a matter of seconds. He paused as he
opened the front door. The waiting room was crammed with people. He
realized it was all media. Two West Palm network affiliates, the *Palm
Beach Post* and the local weekly rag.

The media people turned toward him like they were waiting for
someone to make a comment on what could arguably be the biggest arrest ever made by the department.

The local ABC reporter out of West Palm Beach, Eliot something,
recognized Tasker and said, "Is FDLE involved in this case?"

Tasker shook his head, although he wanted to say, "Not officially."
The reporter had always been a pretty good guy. Tasker specifically remembered him as not piling on when he was under investigation for the
case that got him sent to Miami.

Before anyone else could ask him a question, the door to the interior
police administration offices opened. It was the arrogant road patrolman
from the professor's murder scene. At least he knew Tasker. He turned
and said to the uniformed cop, "Thanks, I was waiting to see Rufus."
Before the cop could protest, Tasker was through the door and headed
toward Rufus' little windowless rat hole.

He caught Gladesville's lone detective behind his desk and on the phone, which he hung up as soon as he saw Tasker.

"What're you doing here?" He sounded like a New York bookie.

"Why do ya think? I'm interested in your arrest." He plopped into the chair in front of Rufus' cluttered desk. The flickering overhead, full-length fluorescent light made the room feel like a cheap disco. "I can't believe you didn't call me."

"I don't work for the damn FDLE. Last I checked, the only man I had to tell things to was my chief and he knew all about it."

"Dammit, you know how I felt."

"And I did what you wanted, I made a fuckin' arrest. What are you so worked up about? We got the guy who killed Warren Kling in custody. End of story. Or, better yet, case closed."

Tasker caught his breath and tried to calm himself. After all the counseling he had undergone over the past few years for the various problems he had survived, he couldn't believe that the only coping mechanism he had for relaxing and controlling his anger was counting to ten before he spoke. What fucking genius had come up with that one?

Finally, he asked, "Who's the suspect?"

"Local guy. See, I was wrong and I admit it. I thought it was migrants. Turns out it was a homeless guy I see every day out by the old Woolworth's."

"What's his story?" Tasker had to squint in the flickering glare of the overhead light.

"Name's Peter Rubie. No idea where he's from. Just a nut that we noticed eight or nine months ago. Ran him and he has an arrest for assault in Ohio. We're checking it out now. Sometimes puts on this fake English accent, but usually just panhandles and searches through the Save-A-Lot's Dumpster."

"What kind of evidence you got?"

"What is this, a case review?"

Tasker sighed and said, "Look, Rufus, I'm just interested. It's your case, your arrest, just fill me in."

Rufus nodded. "Fair enough." He rummaged through some papers on his desk, found one and started to go over some details. "He tried to use one of the professor's credit cards at Eckerd drugs. Tried to buy some Grecian Formula and inserts for his shoes. The clerk knew it wasn't his card and called us."

"That's it?"

"He had on a pair of the professor's shoes."

"How'd you know they were his?"

"Canvas with little orange UF Gators on the heels. Besides, Billie Towers identified them as missing from the professor's apartment when I called her."

"You did call her? Good. I thought she heard about the arrest on the news."

Rufus waited and then said, "She did. I called after she had heard."

Tasker decided to let it slide. "He confess or make any statement?"

"In his own way."

"What the hell does that mean?"

"It means I'm tired of talking to you and have my own problems." Without another word, Rufus stood up and stomped out of the bright room.

Tasker waited a few minutes, then started to make his way out of the police department. Walking past the remaining media people and through the front door, he heard someone call his name. He stopped at the base of the stairs and turned toward the voice over on the sidewalk.

Billie Towers, in jeans and a bright, form-fitting shirt, stood smiling. Tasker said, "What're you doing here?"

"Running some errands." She came closer. "You okay?"

"I can't get used to the way things are done around here."

She stepped next to him and put her small hand on his face. "You look frazzled. Want to get some coffee?"

He felt some of the tension seep out of him and smiled. "Yeah, that sounds like a good idea."

The small town had no lack of early morning diners. Little mom-and-pop places with names like Lulu's or Mabel's Home Cooking. He had noticed there were no Denny's or other chain restaurants and he didn't miss them. Billie led him to a place five blocks from the PD called Jacqui's. A beautiful Dominican woman ran the place with an iron fist. She greeted them with a smile before turning a sharp glare to a lanky teenager who scooted under the scrutiny, and then quickly led them to a table next to the bay window overlooking a cane field.

Billie reached across the small table and took his hand. "They caught the killer, what're you so upset about?"

"I'd feel better if I could verify some of the evidence. Rufus made it sound pretty thin."

"He used one of the professor's credit cards."

"And he had on the shoes."

Billie looked at him. "What shoes?"

He stared at her. "I thought Rufus confirmed it with you?"

"Oh, he did. I'm just so tired and ready to move on."

Tasker looked at her, but he knew the feeling.

She said, "How close are you to being done with your investigation and ready to leave?"

He sighed. "Who knows? Maybe a few more weeks. Haven't even interviewed prisoners yet." He didn't mention he had several reasons for not leaving immediately.

She leaned over and ran her tiny hand through his hair. "You look beat. You should wrap it up and get on with your life."

Tasker nodded. "Maybe you're right. But for now I still have a lot to finish up at Manatee."

He wasn't sure if he saw disappointment in her face, and if it was from his not responding to her touch or something else.

Luther Williams had the books he had been sorting for four days stacked neatly in seven groups. On the wall around the library were a dozen boxes with the discarded old texts he had evaluated as if they were exhibits in a museum in which he was the curator. The rejects included *Ben-Hur* with more than a hundred pages missing; four copies of *The Crash of '79*, because the prison had plenty; a Tom Clancy novel that had been defaced with obscene drawings on a number of pages; and a box full of cookbooks that only served to remind the inmates what they were really eating on a daily basis.

Just as he was finishing the stacks of how-to books, historical novels and nonfiction, his apprentice and would-be usurper, Robert Moambi, strolled in from the west hall of offices, which held the finance and purchasing people.

"You done gone through every book?" asked Moambi.

"Every one," answered Luther, without looking up from the copy of *Wired: The John Belushi Story.*

"I coulda done it quicker."

"But then we'd have books we didn't need and good books tossed out."

"How can you be so sure?"

"Because you're an ignorant ass."

Moambi looked like he was offended until he remembered who he was talking to. Before it could escalate, Captain Norton came from the hallway that led to the senior correctional officers' wing.

"What are you two bickering about?"

"Nothin'," they said together, the standard answer to a query from a correctional officer.

Norton's small brown eyes cut from Luther to Moambi, then around the room. "C'mon, Luther, you had to be arguing about something. Smart fella like you doesn't get worked up over nuthin'."

Luther remained silent and looked down at the cheap carpet on the floor as Norton circled them like a shark.

The corrections captain stopped in front of Moambi and stared at him for a moment. "What's your name again, inmate?"

"Moambi, sir. Robert Moambi."

"How long you been a trustee?"

"Less than a week, sir."

"You supposed to take orders from this man?" He wagged his head toward the motionless Luther.

Moambi said, "No, sir. Officer Spirazza gives me my orders."

"Then why are you even in here talking with him?"

"I'm sorry, Captain. I was out of line and won't do it again."

A smile spread over Norton's lips. "You hear that, Luther? That's respect. Here's an inmate that knows his place." He looked at Luther. "Well?"

"Well, what?" asked Luther.

"What do you have to say about that? You think it's right that this new trustee shows more respect than you?"

Luther thought about how he'd have handled someone who talked to him like that on the streets of Miami, but for now he just shrugged.

"Why should you get to keep your job?"

Luther looked the captain in the eye and said, "Because we had an agreement. I helped you and—"

Norton cut him off. "You're getting a little bit of a big head. Maybe a few months' kitchen detail will shrink it." He looked at the poker face Luther gave him. "We'll see what happens in the next few weeks."

As Captain Norton slowly sauntered out of the library, he leaned into one of Luther's neat stacks and knocked the books onto the floor in a heap. At the door, he turned and said, "Moambi, go ahead and take a break in the admin lounge with the TV. Tell 'em I said it was okay." He turned his head in Luther's direction. "Get this library cleaned up now."

Luther felt the bile in his throat as he watched the stout, arrogant man disappear toward his office. He had an idea of how to get back at the captain with just one phone call. He'd wait until he was gone, just so there'd be no repercussions. He wished he could use the captain in his current plan. Before he could think it through, he heard Moambi.

"You heard the captain. Clean this shit up. I'm going to the TV lounge." The younger man smiled and turned down the hallway.

Luther realized he already had his current plan filled with the proper candidate.

**26** BILL TASKER LEFT HIS SMALL APARTMENT JUST after dark, about six-thirty. He had on nicer clothes than he normally wore, nice jeans, a long sleeve Oxford button-down and a sport coat. He had bought the blue blazer at Burdines on sale and had worn it twice. Tonight made three times. He didn't even know why he had packed it, but had thought the winter in the Glades might give him a chance. Now he had it on just for a simple meal at a sports bar. A simple meal with Renee Chin.

He pulled into the near-empty parking lot of the Green Mile a little early and checked his gelled hair in the mirror. Sport coat, gelled hair. What was happening to him? He slid the belly bag with his Sig into the large glove compartment and locked it. He made it a rule never to bring a gun into a bar where he intended to have a few beers. Instead he reached between his console and the driver's seat and retrieved his state-issued ASP. He rarely went anywhere without the eight-inch metal tube that extended to a formidable nightstick with a flick of his wrist. He had used it a couple of times, but the sound of it opening was usually enough to frighten someone into compliance, or at the very least scare them into running.

He slipped the matte-black ASP into his right rear pocket, the same place he always carried it, and made sure the coat covered it completely.

He didn't see Renee's little Jeep Liberty but wasn't worried. She had proven to be reliable if not punctual. Inside, the place was unchanged from his first visit there the night he arrived in Gladesville. The only difference between that Saturday night and this Tuesday night was the crowd. The first night he'd seen couples on the dance floor and most booths and the whole bar filled; tonight there were only a few booths filled and no one at the bar.

Sidling up to the bar, Tasker didn't wait for the bartender's offer of Bud or Bud Light. He beat him to the punch. "Bud Light."

The bartender with a bandit's mustache nodded his agreement with the order and produced a bottle of Bud Light almost instantaneously, then wandered to the other side of the bar where he had a basketball game on one of the overhead TVs.

Tasker sat down and took a sip from his beer, then glanced at his wristwatch. He was five minutes early, which meant Renee wouldn't be there for twenty more minutes at least.

Two guys in jeans and old, over-washed T-shirts settled in on stools near Tasker. They looked familiar. Tasker had noticed them around town. He was amazed at how fast you got to know people in a small town like Gladesville. One of them, a tall guy with a little gut and a ruddy face, shouted across the bar to the bartender, "Two Buds."

The bartender made no motion that he had heard the loud man, but opened the cooler closest to him. He took his time walking them over and setting the beers on the bar.

After they were served, the two men rotated on their stools to survey the empty dance floor. They leaned back with their elbows resting on the bar.

The larger one, a good three inches taller than Tasker at six-three, snorted then said, "Shit, Tommy, not enough people for a damn softball game."

"Not even a good basketball game. Only white guys."

They both laughed at the dark-haired man's redneck wit.

Tasker didn't bother to look over at them, just kept them in his peripheral vision. He heard one say, "What's a matter, mister, you don't think that's funny?"

Tasker heard him, but didn't bother to acknowledge him.

"Mister, you deaf?" asked the tall man.

Tasker saw him stand up, but still didn't turn. He had learned that a drunk or bully ignored is a drunk or bully deflated. When the man took a step in his direction, he had to look at him. He did it slowly, showing the man he wasn't afraid, even though he felt the anxiety in his stomach. He'd been in enough fights to know that the old saying that no one wins a fight was essentially true.

The big man stopped at the stool next to Tasker and said, "You deaf or just unfriendly?"

Tasker kept a straight face and said, "What?"

He spoke up. "I asked if you was deaf or unfriendly?"

Tasker put his hand to his ear and repeated, "What's that?"

The dark-haired man, smaller than Tasker, maybe five-eight and a hundred and fifty pounds, said, "He's makin' fun of you, Joe."

Joe looked at Tasker with no humor now and said, "That true? You makin' fun of me?"

Tasker turned his body on the stool in case he had to act. From instinct and many hours of practice, his right hand fell to his side, then to his rear pocket, where he could feel the end of his ASP with his fingertips.

Tasker said, "I'm not making fun of you, I just don't want to be bothered by you."

"Too good for us?"

Tasker could try to ease his way out of this. He could look for the bartender to call the cops. Instead, growing tired of the bully and his toady, he said, "You caught on, Joe. Now leave me alone."

Tasker figured trouble was coming, but it didn't happen like he'd predicted.

The smaller man, Tommy, threw his beer bottle at Tasker from behind Joe. Tasker jerked his head out of the bottle's trajectory and rolled off the stool, using his hands to keep from falling and losing touch with his ASP. As Joe stepped toward him, Tasker grabbed the stool between them and yanked it toward him so the metal legs hit Joe in the shins. Joe stepped back in pain, bumping into Tommy.

Tasker took a second to scan the room and realized that with the music and TVs blaring, hardly anyone had even noticed the start of the scuffle. He sure wanted to keep it that way if possible.

He advanced on the two men as Joe untangled himself from Tommy. Tasker threw a quick, hard punch into Joe's solar plexus, knocking every ounce of air out of him. To ensure he was out of the fight, Tasker followed with a quick knee into his groin. He had to grab the big man to keep him from hitting the ground. He shoved him onto a stool and stepped past him, confident he had no fight left in him.

Without a pause, he moved toward the surprised Tommy, slipped a looping right cross thrown by the smaller man, then grabbed his extended arm and threw an uppercut into the nerve center under his arm. Tommy instantly pulled back and held his arm. Tasker followed, grabbed his skanky shirt and twisted him onto the stool next to his buddy, Joe, who still didn't know what to worry about more—his lack of breath or his lack of feeling in his testicles.

Tasker did another spin to check the room. The bartender had seen the fight and it looked like he approved of how Tasker was handling the situation. Several other men had noticed, but kept it to themselves.

He stepped between the two whimpering men and put his hands on their shoulders like they were friends talking.

"So, fellas, what have we learned?" He waited but got no reply. "First we learned there's nothing wrong with my hearing, right?"

Both men nodded.

"Next, we learned not to bother strangers, right?"

Again they nodded.

"Now, unless you want to learn to walk on broken legs, you're going to calmly get up and wander out the front door, right?"

Again they nodded.

"I don't want you two morons to bother anyone else tonight. Is that clearly understood?"

Tommy said, "We ain't finished our beer."

Before Tasker could comment on this monumentally stupid reply, Joe said, "Tommy, don't be a dumb-ass. Let's go."

Tasker eased back onto his stool and watched the two men hobble out the front door.

The bartender came down to his end of the bar and said, "Them two just skipped on their tab."

Tasker said, "It's my fault. Guess I'm just bad company. I'll pick it up."

The thin bartender smiled, showing a missing tooth at the side of his mouth. "Don't worry about it. In fact, you get another on the house. Like your style."

Tasker smiled and then noticed Renee Chin come in and head straight for him. She was her usual stunning self out of the frumpy Department of Corrections gear.

She slid onto the stool next to him and gave him a peck on the cheek. "Sorry I'm late. Girl stuff, you know."

"I don't really know, but I don't mind."

She looked around and said, "It's not exactly hopping tonight."

"No, pretty quiet."

She said, "I just saw one of Manatee's former residents in the parking lot."

Tasker looked at her. "Coming or going?"

"He and a buddy were leaving. They looked drunk, stumbling to their truck."

"Big blond guy and a smaller dark-haired guy?"

"Yeah, the big guy is Joe Kinder. I think he was an off-loader on a pot shipment that flew into the Clewiston area. Why, did you talk to them?"

"Sort of." Maybe he was getting paranoid, but Tasker looked at the incident differently now. Was it random or part of someone's plan? He'd keep it to himself for now.

27 TASKER HAD SPENT THE LAST FORTY MINUTES driving directly into the rising sun over West Palm Beach. He had left his little apartment at six-thirty to make sure he would have enough time to do what he had to do. It had killed him to turn in early the night before. The dinner with Renee had been terrific. She was funny and they shared a lot of interests—one of them sports. The girl knew her Miami Dolphins history and had strong opinions about the coaches since Shula.

Tasker had waited for Renee to invite him home after dinner, but the invitation had never come. They'd spent a moment kissing good-bye in the parking lot of the Green Mile, but that was it. He had actually been a little distracted keeping an eye out for the two men who had assaulted him in the bar. He was afraid they might have lain in wait for him, but he had been paranoid. The worse feeling was Renee saying, "See you tomorrow," and driving away.

He was troubled by his encounter with the two men at the Green Mile. If they were just drunk rednecks, it was no big deal. He had dealt with drunks plenty of times. The idea that they were former inmates of Manatee and might still have connections to the facility was what bothered him. What were the chances that in the whole town they would have a run-in with him? Had someone sent them as a threat? Tasker was getting the uneasy feeling that he was no longer welcome in the little town by the big lake.

Now, his mind came back to the task at hand. As he came to a stop a few blocks from the Palm Beach County Jail almost thirty-five miles east of Gladesville, he remembered how many prisoners he had booked into the nine-story facility. Some of the old-time deputies still called this the "new jail," even though it had been over ten years since the first inmate spent the night in Palm Beach County's only crossbar hotel. The older, much smaller jail sat in front of its newer sister. They both had the unmistakable look of a building you didn't want to enter.

Tasker took a second to shed himself of his Sig and ASP and lock them in the glove compartment. He emptied his pockets, including the cash he always kept folded inside his identification. All he kept was his shield and ID. It was his sincere hope to get in and out without anyone taking undue notice of him.

He avoided the main, public entrance and walked downstairs to the large sally port where a cop would normally bring in prisoners. He walked up to the control room with the thick Plexiglas and held up his ID.

A stern black woman in a deputy's uniform pointed to the little drawer, then pushed it out toward Tasker. He knew the drill. He signed the clipboard, stuck his identification in the drawer and stood there.

"You booking someone?"

"Interviewing a prisoner."

"Why didn't you go upstairs?"

"He's in holding down here. I didn't want to waste anyone's time." He stuck to the story.

The woman shrugged and opened the giant outer sliding door. He entered and the door shut completely before the inner door slowly slid to one side. He walked straight to the main desk. It was so early two deputies were standing and talking, something there usually isn't much time for on their detail.

"Can I help you?" asked a deputy with a gray mustache and a map of the moon around his eyes.

"Bill Tasker with FDLE. I need to talk to Peter Rubie before his court appearance."

The deputy nodded and referred to his list of occupants of the many holding cells on the ground floor of the building.

Tasker could hear the constant chatter of the mopes picked up the night before, waiting for first appearance, the drunks wishing they hadn't driven their cars, the crack addicts who only wanted to score and the punk, wannabe gang members who'd watched the movie *Colors* and thought they were tough. They'd all learned that cops don't have to be tough to make arrests, just numerous.

The deputy looked at Tasker and said, "You got about fifteen minutes until we start chaining them up for transport."

"No problem."

"Take that first interview room and we'll run him down to you."

Tasker said, "Thanks," as he was already turning. He just needed to be sure this guy was the one who'd killed the professor. He didn't want to fuck up Rufus' case. He wouldn't ask anything that he'd have to testify about. He just wanted a feel for the guy. He stepped into the closet-sized interview room and took the chair next to a small table. He had no notebook, nothing to write with, he just wanted to talk.

Three minutes later, two deputies were at the door with a small, smiling man with graying hair and a bushy mustache that made him vaguely resemble a walrus. He had a pleasant look, the kind of guy who charmed women rather than stunned them with good looks.

One deputy with a complexion slightly darker than an old-style chalkboard said with a Jamaican accent, "You the man needin' to speak with Mr. Rubie?"

Tasker liked the professional, clear tone of the jail deputy. "I am."

"You have him for twelve minutes, then we must ready him for court."

"Understood."

The deputies receded from view, but left the door slightly ajar. Tasker wasn't sure if it had to do with security or reminding him they'd be back in twelve minutes.

Tasker didn't waste any time. "Mr. Rubie, my name is Bill Tasker. I'm an agent with the Florida Department of Law Enforcement."

"FDLE? Good show. The big men." Rubie revealed his crooked but engaging smile. He looked like a happy chipmunk.

"Where are you from?"

"Melbourne."

Tasker nodded slowly and said, "Australia?"

"No, Florida."

Then Tasker remembered Rufus saying he liked to put on an English accent. It was a pretty good accent, too.

Tasker said, "Mr. Rubie. You don't have to talk to me, but I'm interested in your case."

Rubie remained silent.

"Will you speak with me?"

The smaller man gave a barely perceptible nod.

"Good. Now, where did you get Professor Kling's credit card?"

Rubie just stared at him.

"The one on you when they arrested you?"

"The magic card?"

Now it was Tasker's turn to stare. "I'm sorry. Why is it magic? What can it do?"

"People give me things if I show it to them."

Now Tasker had an idea of who he was dealing with. If it was an act, the guy was convincing. The accent made everything seem reasonable, but it was just another layer of weirdness.

"Where'd you get the magic card?"

"My friend gave it to me."

"Which friend? What's his name?"

"I'm not sure, but he's always nice to me."

"What's he look like?"

"He has a puzzle face."

"A what?"

"A jigsaw puzzle face, mate. What're you, an idiot?"

Tasker took a moment before moving on. He was no expert on mental illness. He knew that when a guy lived in a fantasy world like this he could do some wild stuff. It wouldn't be a question of right or wrong, more of perception. Maybe this little nut thought he was slaying a dragon or sending a demon back to hell. But for now, the smiling man before him seemed unlikely to have killed Professor Kling, or anyone else for that matter.

"What about the shoes you were wearing?"

"Which ones, my old ones or new ones?"

"The shoes that have the University of Florida logo on them."

"You're a bit of a loon, mate. All I have is my nice flip-flops and the tennis shoes."

"What kind of tennis shoes?"

"The kind we use to play tennis in." He rolled his eyes like he was dealing with a nitwit. "Nice, soft ones with an alligator on the heels."

Tasker's head snapped up. "What about those? Where'd you get them?"

"The man at the hospital gave them to me."

"What hospital?"

"The one I was at until I came to this hospital."

"The other jail? The Gladesville jail?"

"Calm down, mate. You need some tea."

"I'm sorry. Do you remember who gave you the shoes?"

"Sure. The friend of the man with a puzzle face. The chubby one."

"Can you remember anything more than he was chubby?"

Rubie thought about the question. "Oh yes, I remember now."

Tasker leaned forward. "What do you remember?"

"He gave me shoes, too. Yes, that's it. He was chubby and gave me shoes."

"Did he say anything?"

"Yes, yes, he did."

"What did he say?"

"Here are some shoes for you."

Tasker sat back and sighed. He thought he saw what had happened. Someone, probably Rufus Goodwin, had wanted to make sure they had enough on this guy, so he'd given him the professor's shoes from his personal effects. It didn't mean Rubie hadn't killed him, but it did mean Rufus wasn't looking at any other possibilities.

Tasker was at the end of his patience, but this poor guy wasn't the reason. He took a deep breath. "Where are the tennis shoes now?"

"The other hospital orderly needed them. He said I'd get them back when I was admitted again."

"Here's a simple question: Do you know why you're here?"

"Yes, of course."

"Why?"

"Rest, old sod. Rest and recreation. I'm a busy man, mate. I'm married to a beautiful Broadway star, I have a little baby. I'm a busy man. You're lucky I have time even to speak to you."

Tasker stared, unsure of what to say. If he had met this guy in a restaurant, he'd sound perfectly rational. He might have been a little short to attract a beautiful Broadway star, but he definitely had a cool accent and a degree of charm.

Rubie looked at him with deep blue eyes. "Is that all you needed, mate?"

Tasker didn't want to ask the easiest question, did he kill the professor? This crazy little bastard wouldn't know if he had. Tasker did wonder about his prior arrest. "Were you ever arrested in Ohio?"

The pleasant-looking man gave a small smile. "I'm sorry, mate. Never heard of him."

"Who?"

"The Queen's boyfriend."

Tasker was almost relieved when the big Jamaican deputy appeared at the door. "Time's up."

Rubie stood and looked at the exasperated Tasker and said, "Chin up. Things will work out for you, mate. Just hang in there."

Tasker nodded as they led the cheerful little man away. If a judge didn't see this was the wrong guy, then Tasker might have to help him. The best way he could do that was to find the real killer.

Luther Williams had the library in spectacular shape. He believed that if you undertook a task you should do it to the utmost of your ability. He had certainly done that for the Manatee Correctional library. He wasn't giving notice, so he wanted it in good shape for the next trustee.

The useless books in the boxes had all been disposed of in the past few hours. The catalog was up to date and organized. The room was even clean. Luther took a rag and ran it over the shelves closest to the window and then paused as he came to his favorite shelf. It had volumes of Shakespeare and Twain. That was about it as far as classics went. It also had a metal support bar that Luther had taken out several times over the past six months. The rod was slightly thinner than a pencil, about seven inches long, and really didn't affect the integrity of the shelves. It was an add-on the manufacturer had thrown in for peace of mind. It slid under one shelf for reinforcement of a heavy load. That's why Luther kept the classics on that shelf; at Manatee, that was never a heavy load.

Now he removed the support and inspected the edge that had been ground to a rough point. Luther would scratch it on cement surfaces when he had the opportunity until he had worn it into a pointed end like a tiny arrow. It was a good shiv, but he never would have gotten it past the front gate inside the wall. That was why he kept it here. He knew he might need it one day. Today was that day.

He slipped the metal rod back in place and checked the clock. He needed to make his move about four-twenty. He had some time to kill. Then he had something else to kill.

Bill Tasker sat in on the court hearing for Peter Rubie. He didn't see any representatives from the Gladesville PD. Even the state's attorney knew he was a nut. The only question was: Was he enough of a nut to kill someone?

His past arrest was a DUI in Cincinnati fifteen years ago. He'd appar-

ently vomited on the cop and been charged with assault. Tasker wondered if the poor guy had ever had a real life. Why had he lived in Ohio?
Did he have a job? What had happened? Where had he come up with
the bullshit about being married to a Broadway star? Questions like that,
although not generally important to a criminal case, always interested
Tasker.

After a thirty-five-minute hearing, Rubie was remanded to the psychiatric ward indefinitely for treatment and evaluation. Maybe that was
what it took to get treatment nowadays: kill someone. Or at least be ac-
cused of it. Tasker was relieved that they weren't going to automatically
charge Rubie with murder. It tended to take some stress off the situation. Rufus may have done the homeless guy a huge favor.

Tasker nodded hello to a couple of lawyers he had known from years
ago and then headed out to his Monte Carlo.

Tasker had spent the ride back from the jail thinking about something
other than murders and prisons. He thought hard about what he was
feeling for Renee Chin. It wasn't that she was beautiful. It wasn't that she
was smart. He knew a lot of smart, beautiful women. She just had something else, something that made him feel like the only problem in the
world was whether he'd get to see her or not.

The problem he had now was: Why hadn't he said anything remotely
related to his feelings? He hadn't just discovered them on the ride from
West Palm. He had known for the last week or so. He had seen her, been
alone with her. Even been to dinner with her. What was the problem?

Then he remembered: He was a dumb-ass.

An hour later, as Tasker was wandering the halls of the admin building at Manatee Correctional, trying to think what he should say to Renee Chin, if he said anything at all, he was stopped by Captain Sam
Norton.

"Where've you been, Agent Tasker?"

"Checking on a few things. Did I need to advise you of my activities?"

"No, sir, but I hear just about everything that happens around here anyway."

"You ever hear if your officers let Linus Hardaway out of the psych ward on purpose?"

Norton's face darkened. "It shouldn't have happened."

"Lot of things in this town that happen shouldn't."

"Your Miami is better?"

"At least more obvious."

"I think you need to finish your damn investigation and head on back to the big city."

"No argument here. I was in West Palm this morning and didn't miss the smell of burning cane at all."

"What was you in there for?"

"Curiosity."

"I heard that curiosity killed the cat." He smiled, but it wasn't warm or friendly.

"I'm interested in who killed my neighbor."

"The professor from UF?"

"Yeah."

"Heard they got someone for that."

"Saw his court appearance. It'll never stick. He's some poor signal twenty who has a good fake accent."

"Signal twenty?"

Tasker forgot that correctional officers didn't learn the ten codes and signals that Florida cops learned. "Signal twenty is a mentally unbalanced person."

Norton nodded. "Ain't your case, what d'you care?"

Tasker shrugged. "It's my job."

"Thought your job was finding out who killed Rick Dewalt."

"I can do both."

Norton gave him a dirty look and stalked off to his office.

**28** BILL TASKER WAS ALREADY TO THE GATED
main entrance to the correctional facility when he realized
he still had his ASP in his back pocket. In the baggy Dockers he hadn't noticed it, and neither had anyone else. The officers who
ran the front gate had searched him the first twenty times he entered.
Ten had been legitimate and ten were to break his balls. Then they'd
given up the searches because it was more work. Now, they hardly noticed him. If he'd had a gun on, he would've said something and walked
all the way back to the admin building to store it. But now he was just
going to sit on the bunk assigned to Rick Dewalt. Captain Norton had
suggested the late afternoon because most of the inmates would be at
the dining hall. All Tasker wanted to do was look around the psych ward
where Dewalt usually worked, then he wanted to just sit on Dewalt's cot
in Dorm E. He had nothing in particular to look for, just wanted to see
what was on the way. Maybe something would jump out at him.

Tasker was waved through the main gate and then had to wait in between the outer and inner doors a few minutes before being given access
to the inside of the prison. He knew the wait was just to show he could
be stranded in the facility by any correctional officer at any time. He
didn't bother to wave as he entered, since virtually no correctional officer ever acknowledged him anyway.

He knew the way to lockdown and the psych ward. His last experience in lockdown had seared it into his head. This time he entered

from the main, east door where a correctional officer sat at the desk by the door.

"Yes, sir?" asked the pudgy black officer.

"Gonna look around. That a problem?" Tasker kept his hand on his hip to hide the ASP.

"No problem, sir. We were told to give you any help you needed."

Tasker looked at him. "Unless I'm being choked by an inmate."

The officer looked down. He hadn't been interviewed, so he must not have been in the ward the day Tasker was attacked, but he knew what the FDLE agent was getting at.

Tasker headed down the clean, empty hallway with five doors on each side. He looked in each of the cells. Five were occupied. One of them held Linus Hardaway. Today he sat dozing in the sparse room with a mat for a bed. He must have been back on his medication.

Tasker wandered through the three doors that led to the outside door where Dewalt's body had been found. He opened the door and looked outside, then came back inside and looked at the empty entry room. If he turned right, he'd go into lockdown; left, he headed back to psych. He was impressed by the clean walls and wondered if Dewalt might have been killed in there, then dragged outside.

He let his eyes follow the walls and the floor line. Nothing caught his eye. He walked through the first door toward psych. The smaller, empty hallway was just like the entry room in that it was bare and clean. He searched the room again. Then he froze as his eyes caught the smallest of scratches in the door leading to the psych ward. He could reach it by extending his arm. It was really two similar marks on the top of the door almost in the center. He opened the door and looked on the other side. There was a brown scuff corresponding to the scrapes on the other side.

Tasker stepped into the ward and found a small plastic chair and used it to inspect the top of the door. The mark went from one side to the other, changing from a scratch to a scuff. It was probably nothing, but he noted it. He nodded to the officer at the desk as he headed out to the dorm.

He used his long, quick stride to cover ground and got to Dorm E in less than a minute. He noticed a few inmates milling around, but nothing seemed out of the ordinary. At the entrance to E, there were four men talking in a group directly in front of the door.

Tasker stopped and waited for the men to notice him and move. They kept talking and treated him like the correctional officers did. If he wasn't so secure a person, he would've started to get a complex.

Tasker said in a loud voice, "Excuse me, fellas."

The men didn't look over at him.

He stepped closer and said, "I need to get in the door."

Still no reaction.

He started to feel his heart rate rise. Did these guys realize they were inmates? This time he left no room for doubt. "Move away from the door, now."

The men casually looked at him and split up. The largest of the four white men, a bruiser more than six-three, with a bandage around his gigantic right bicep, stayed right in front of the door.

"You say something?" asked the big man.

"You heard me."

"Around here people don't talk to us like that."

"I don't live here." Tasker sensed the other men starting to circle him. His right hand instinctively dropped to his rear pocket. Calmly he felt the end of the closed ASP with his fingertips, thanking God he had forgotten to leave it outside. This was the second time in two days he had had to do that. He was starting to see a pattern.

Luther Williams checked the clock. It was four-fifteen, time to get this show on the road. He was taking a few things on faith, but he felt confident the whole plan would work. It would either be a complete success or a total failure. There would be no middle ground. If he could've followed his own timetable, he would've waited another two weeks and spent the time ensuring everything was in place. But the suspicion on him for killing Vic Vollentius was too dangerous to ignore. At any time, Inspector Chin and her FDLE friend Tasker could have him sent to lockdown until they finished their investigation. At the very least he'd lose his trustee status and the freedom that gave him. No, it had to be today. Right now, actually, if things were to work properly.

Luther went to the classics shelf and removed the sharpened support. He slid it into his waistband and then leaned out the door into the main hallway. He was prepared to go looking for the big-mouthed Robert Moambi, but was pleasantly surprised to see the younger man just down the hall leaning on his broom.

Luther didn't speak, he just rapped on the wall with his knuckle.

Moambi's head snapped up and he gave Luther a puzzled look.

Luther motioned him toward the library with his right hand, like he had something he wanted to show the other trustee. Then Luther stepped back into the library and pulled the shiv from his pants.

Moambi popped around the corner and said, "What do ya got? Something good?"

"I think so," Luther said, and casually swung his left hand over Moambi's back and grasped his head firmly. At the same time, without telegraphing the move, he swung the shiv straight up into the soft flesh under Moambi's chin. The combination of shoving his head down and driving the shiv up resulted in a devastating blow.

Moambi never even gave any fight. He went from surprised to motionless in seconds, so fast that Luther checked his pulse to see if he had merely knocked the man unconscious. There was no pulse, and as a result, very little blood seeping from the metal rod that was wedged five inches into Robert Moambi's head. Luther thought it must have penetrated his brain. No small feat considering the size of the target.

Luther muscled the dead man to the window onto the entranceway. He set him in a sitting position, like he was looking out the window. Even with the metal rod sticking out of his head, he looked completely natural. The correctional officers were so used to seeing him lounge around instead of work, the whole scene just felt right. Too bad that wasn't exactly what Luther needed right now.

He checked the clock. Four twenty-two. He needed to get a move on.

He glanced around the room quickly. Then he saw some of the twine that had been used to secure the boxes of books to be thrown out. He tied a loop around Moambi's arm and then strung it across the doorway to the admin hallway. He tied it off on a chair that sat right next to the door.

He stepped back and surveyed his handiwork. Everything looked right, he just needed to catch a break or two.

Luther did one more check of the room. Aside from a body with a metal rod sticking out from under its head, everything looked in order. He checked his pockets. All he had was the key, which his lady friend had left for him. The same key he had killed Vic Vollentius over. It had been tough to get *into* the prison, but no one ever searched him coming out. He was all set and headed to the front door. Things would start hopping soon.

Lester Lynn had been a correctional officer for three years and generally just did what he was told, no matter what the policy or cops might say. Here in the control room, his dream job, he had failed to mention certain things he'd seen on the monitor, but it was all minor stuff with inmates. This time, Sergeant Janzig had just told him to ignore anything he saw on the monitor looking over Dorm E. Lester had figured it was another lesson they had arranged for some inmate who didn't know his place in this fine world.

Lester had noticed the Aryan Knights. Those were the guys the officers used most often when they needed someone's ass whipped. What surprised Lester was their target. He happened to glance at the monitor and saw the FDLE agent walking up to the dorm, and now he was squared off with the great big Aryan Knight who was in here for beating up a cop.

Normally, Lester would've worked his radio by now, attempting to short-circuit the brewing situation. Instead, he used all his willpower to look at another monitor so later he'd be able to say he hadn't seen a thing.

Bill Tasker took in the scene. The odds weren't that good if it was just him and the big guy, but the other three made him a Vegas nightmare: No one would've bet on him. His hope was to make it last long enough that someone noticed his situation.

He shifted his weight to his rear foot slightly and followed the big man right in front of him as the man looked to move one way or the other.

Tasker let his right hand slip into his pocket and grip the closed ASP. No matter how he looked at it, things were going to get ugly.

The standoff continued for over a minute and Tasker started to wonder why no one had seen him. Why had no correctional officer passed by or why had no one seen it on a monitor? Maybe it was like the lockdown attack. If it was, he was on his own and this time there were four attackers.

After finding no opening, the big man just lunged straight ahead at Tasker.

It was showtime.

 **29** LUTHER WILLIAMS ACTUALLY SMILED AT THE correctional officer sitting at the reception desk at the front door to the admin building.

The burly officer said, "Done for the day, Williams?"

"Yes, sir. Sergeant Janzig told me to be back at the dorm by four-thirty."

"You better shag that black ass if you want to keep that ornery som-bitch happy."

"Yes, sir. On my way."

Luther kept his cool walking out the door, hoping that someone didn't find his surprise too early. Outside the admin building, he turned like he was going to the visitors' center. Everyone knew he had a certain visitor every Sunday and Wednesday at exactly four-thirty. Let's hope she knew it. This was his biggest gamble—that his so-called girlfriend would be in the lot with her Cadillac at four-thirty. He needed the diversion to confuse everyone just long enough for him to turn toward the lot instead of the visitors' center.

Luther slowed his stride as he untied the orange trustee vest over his drab, gray uniform. There were two correctional officers walking toward him, so he kept his course and nodded to them as they passed.

"Sirs," was all he said.

As usual, the big white officers didn't even acknowledge his existence. They kept right on toward the admin building.

Luther didn't have a watch, but knew he had to make his move soon. He couldn't believe no one had run across Moambi's body yet.

He slowed as the walkway cut off toward the parking lot.

Captain Norton couldn't sit still in his big leather chair. There was too much going on right now to be calm.

He stood and stretched at his desk, then decided to check in with the lovely Inspector Chin. Her smile usually took his mind off his day-to-day problems.

When he found her office empty, he cut down the hallway toward the front desk to see if anything was new. He didn't want to go inside the perimeter right now. He came to the library and turned into the doorway. One step in, he felt something on his ankle.

"What in the hell is this shit?" He bent down like a frustrated parent picking up after a messy child. He held the twine that he had stepped into and then froze. Could this be the trigger to a bomb? He held the line and let his eyes follow it up to the form of a resting trustee.

"Luther? You napping on the job?" He straightened and realized the man was not Luther Williams. He stepped toward him as he jerked on the line. The sudden tension in the line pulled the man off the windowsill onto the floor with a hollow thump. Norton took a quick step and knelt by the man. That's when he saw the metal rod coming out of his chin and realized it was the new trustee, Moambi, and he was as dead as a rabbit in a burnt cane field.

"Shit." He jumped to his feet and yelled, "Bobby, go to lockdown, go to lockdown, right now."

Within a few seconds, the alarms all over the facility started to sound and every correctional officer had a job.

Tasker let the big man charge him, then in one motion raised his hand with the closed ASP and sidestepped the lunging bull of a man. Tasker brought his hand down hard, the force causing the ASP to extend on the way down, catching the big man across the shoulders and neck. He froze in mid-stride and dropped to the ground in a heap.

Tasker immediately turned to the other three men with the extended ASP. "Who's next, gentlemen?"

Before he had to deal with the obviously eager men, a siren started to blast.

One of the remaining inmates looked at another and said, "Shit, lockdown."

Before Tasker had a chance to vent his frustration, all three men were running toward their dorm.

As soon as the alarm sounded, Luther turned calmly toward the parking lot and started in a quick pace toward the visitors' lot where he hoped to see the Cadillac parked. If he was real lucky, his lady friend would already be at the visitors' center and have to walk back to the car.

He skidded over the rough gravel-and-lime lot searching for the pearl-white car. His heart started to race as he considered just making a run for the road. Where in the hell was she?

Then, in the third row, he saw the car. It was empty. To one side he saw several correctional officers fanning out toward the edges of the prison grounds as per policy. One had a Remington shotgun.

Luther ducked low between two cars and made his way to the Cadillac. He reached for his small silver key and slid it into the trunk. It opened easily. Damn, Cadillac made a good car, Coupe DeVille or not. He opened the lid a few inches so as not to draw attention to the lot. The trunk had boxes of pink merchandise that looked like Mary Kay bullshit. He didn't have time for comfort so he just climbed in on top of the boxes, which gave way under his weight and actually formed a comfortable cushion. The trunk was completely void of light except for the glow-in-the-dark safety release over his shoulder. Luther could hear his own labored breathing. How long would he have to wait? Would they search her car? It didn't matter. So far he had done all he could do.

Tasker stood over the man he had clubbed with his ASP, waiting for someone to come help with the beaten inmate. He checked his pulse and breathing. The big guy was half-conscious and moaned as he tried to shake off the blow.

"Just lay there," Tasker said. "Someone will come back to help us out soon."

He was right; within minutes two correctional officers, trotting toward Dorm E, stopped and stared at Tasker and the man.

"Little help here, fellas."

"What happened?" asked one of the officers.

"He attacked me."

"What'd you do to him?"

"Hit him with this." He held up the ASP.

The officer stepped forward and snatched the ASP out of Tasker's hands. "You the reason for the lockdown?"

Tasker shrugged. "I guess."

"You better come with us." The two officers leaned down and helped the inmate to his feet, then led him toward the medical section with Tasker trailing behind.

Correctional Officer Fitzhugh Simmons had been at Manatee Correctional his entire two-and-a-half-year career with the Florida Department of Corrections. It was much nicer than the facility he had worked in in his native Jamaica for eight years, though not nearly as lucrative, because the administration here actually frowned on bribes and gratuities.

This was the third full lockdown in the past few weeks. Over his radio he heard it was because of a murder, not an escape, so he wasn't as concerned. His job now was to walk the three visitors who hadn't checked in yet back to their cars. Visiting hours were canceled. The two big white women were crying a little, but the elderly black man almost looked relieved that he didn't have to deal with whoever he knew that was locked up here.

The small group paused as the first lady stopped at her pickup truck. He looked in the cab and the bed was empty, so he just let her ride off. The old man had a Toyota Camry. Again Fitzhugh just glanced in the passenger compartment. He didn't want to bother this man to open his trunk. It was too small to hold a full-grown adult anyway.

The third visitor, a big white lady in a loud flower print dress, blew her nose at the door to her nice little Cadillac CTX. She said, "Thanks," like he had done her a favor, and got inside. Fitzhugh saw the passenger compartment was clear and she didn't seem the type to hide anyone, and after all the alarm was for a murder not an escape. He let her drive off, too.

He watched as the Caddy headed out the main row and slowed near the standing officers with shotguns. Fitzhugh waved to them and gave them a thumbs-up as the Caddy approached.

They signaled the lady on past.

Fitzhugh Simmons started the long walk back to the visitors' center, where he figured this whole thing would be called off and he could get back in the air-conditioning.

 **30** BILL TASKER KNEW SOMETHING DIDN'T FEEL right. He saw Renee a few feet away, mocha skin, smooth and as flawless as he had imagined. Her long, slender legs melding into her lovely hips and black pubic hair. She hadn't said anything as he stood there, staring at this remarkably beautiful woman. Then he heard something, distant but powerful. He tried to ignore it, block it out of his mind as he became aware of what it really meant. The pounding became more defined, and then he heard a man's voice yell, "C'mon, Tasker, answer the door." He gave up and let the pounding seep into his conscious mind.

He opened his eyes and now, still in bed, alone, he heard the loud knock on his door again. "Fuck," he muttered, as he rolled out of bed and rummaged in the dresser for a clean T-shirt. Out of a habit developed here in Gladesville, he grabbed his Beretta from the nightstand and crammed it in his shorts at the small of his back.

He padded from his bedroom, through the living room to the front door. He opened the old wooden door a crack and peered out. Rufus Goodwin stared back at him.

"C'mon, open the door."

Tasker stepped back and complied. He was still exhausted from helping the staff at Manatee look for the missing Luther Williams. A thorough search of the outer field and Gladesville had failed to produce the missing inmate. Likewise, the dogs had failed to pick up much of a scent.

Tasker wasn't surprised the wily Luther Williams, aka Cole Hodges, had outsmarted the staff of Manatee.

Tasker stood at the open door looking at Gladesville's lone detective. His eyes were bloodshot and his white short-sleeve shirt had coffee stains on it. His usual clip-on tie had been discarded altogether.

"What's wrong?" asked Tasker.

"You mean, besides an escape at Manatee?"

"I was out most of the night, too."

Rufus said, "That and talking to my suspect must've worn your ass out."

Now Tasker realized the source of the hostility coming from Rufus. "Look, Rufus, c'mon in." He motioned him into the small apartment. "I wasn't trying to cut in on your case, but I had to see the guy you thought killed the professor."

"And what did you learn?"

"You know what I learned." He looked at Rufus for a reaction. "Why'd you grab a poor stiff like Rubie?"

"I don't know what you mean."

"Give me a break, Rufus." Tasker flopped down on the couch. "I didn't just fall off the turnip truck. That little crazy fucker is no more re-sponsible for killing Warren Kling than you are."

Now Rufus had to sit down. He took the lone padded chair across from the couch. He rubbed his eyes and kept his mouth shut.

Tasker knew he wouldn't get much, but he pressed the detective.

"You under that much pressure that you'd stick a homeless guy with a murder charge?"

"Look, it wasn't like that. He *is* a suspect. A vagrant. Had the credit card."

"That someone gave him."

"So he claims."

"Did you fucking check out his story?"

Rufus just sulked.

Tasker said, "So this thing is wide open again?"

"The judge is having Rubie evaluated by a psychologist."

"Then what?"

"The state attorney said he'd probably be cut loose." Rufus sounded like a beaten man.

"What now? You got any other leads?"

"No, nothin'."

"You offer a big enough reward and things tend to happen."

"The university has put up five grand, the county added a thousand and Dewalt Construction threw in another five grand."

"Dewalt Construction, why?"

Rufus shrugged. "They do a lot of building out here. They often kick in on rewards like this. Why not? They got the money."

Tasker just said, "Yeah, I know."

Luther Williams stretched his sore back and spread his arms as he got used to his new clothes. He had borrowed a pair of jeans and a nice work shirt from a clothesline off Fifty-fourth Street near the Scott projects. He'd left his prison uniform on the same clothesline, hoping someone would be smart enough to report it to the police. He didn't want to hide the fact that he was in Miami. At least for a day or two. He figured a few days of watching his ass down here, contacting a few former associates, collecting some debts, that sort of thing, would serve him well after he left. While the cops were scouring Miami for the escaped convict, he'd be safely off to another big city. A big city not in Florida. But first he'd stop in Tallahassee.

His ride from Gladesville had been harder than he imagined. While the CTX had decent suspension, the engineers weren't as concerned about passenger comfort in the trunk. In addition, the boxes he had lain on contained various Christmas ornaments and crockery, which tended to break and splinter as the trip proceeded. The result was that when his lady friend stopped at the gas station off the 836 near the Golden Glades interchange, he'd decided to make his exit and risk a hike into Liberty City. He would've had a rougher time making it from her condo over on the beach, so it had worked out well. The government-ordered safety latch on the inside of the trunk helped enormously. She never saw him or knew a thing, which he was counting on for when the cops came to question her. He figured it'd take a day or two to run down the visitors that had been seen in the lot, then make the connection to Luther. He pictured the dogs searching out his scent back in Gladesville.

After a restless night's sleep between the Dumpsters at the gas station, he decided to make the next leg of his trip. The trip from the gas station had been as lucky as it was easy. He had merely rolled in the back of a lawn-service truck among the cut grass and oily lawn mowers. The fiberglass bed top had kept him out of view of the general public. He'd rolled out at the Scott project. The sprawling complex of subsidized housing had been the center of activity for the area since before Luther had arrived in Miami. No one took notice of him strolling down the narrow road that crossed the property. Watching the ground as he walked in the early morning light, he noticed an old shish kebab skewer on the ground. It was broken and had been discarded, but after Luther's experiences with shivs over his recent stay at Manatee he snatched up the old utensil. It tucked easily into his waistband. He thought, You never know when you'll need something like this. He patted his belly where the shiv was hidden and continued on his way.

Now he finished his conversion to ordinary resident of inner-city Miami by snatching up an old pair of basketball shoes on the front steps of one of the small single-family houses that surrounded the project. He left his prison work shoes in their place. He started toward Fifty-fourth Street in a casual gait, unconcerned that he'd be noticed.

He headed east, then crossed the street at Seventeenth Avenue. Even though it was early on a Monday morning, he knew just where to go to get his new venture moving again. He needed some walking money.

Sam Norton was exhausted as he lay in his bed. The sun was up and shining over the Rock and he had only been horizontal for about forty-five minutes. He had organized the search of the surrounding area and pulled out all the stops to find Luther Williams. He had even called the sheriff's office and hadn't commented when the FDLE agent, Tasker, joined a team searching the same industrial area where he had shot the last escapee a couple of weeks before.

His mind turned over all the problems this would cause him. No one wanted to live with the stigma of being in charge when a facility lost an inmate. It was hard enough convincing people the Rock was a tough facility when the state had given it such a sissy name. Now the other captains from Everglades Correctional to Union Correctional would be giving him shit if he didn't find this guy.

Then there was the flip side. Without being able to control him, there was no telling what Luther Williams might say or do on the outside. Either way, it made for a bad night.

He tossed to his right again, twisting the covers from the warm naked body beside him.

"Hey," she said.

"Sorry, baby."

"You need some sleep."

"I need to get that son of a bitch back inside."

"You will," she said, the sleepy voice making him smile despite his situation.

The phone next to his bed rang with the extra loud ringer he had installed to make sure he heard it in case of emergency.

He snatched it up before it rang again. "Norton," he said, silently praying for good news.

It wasn't.

**31**

AS SOON AS RUFUS WAS GONE, BILL TASKER SET about waking up and laying out his day. He knew there'd be more to do on the escape, but there were a few things he wanted to check out on Professor Kling's murder as well. Now that it was wide open again, he didn't want the case falling through the cracks. He would see if there were any migrant or labor crews close by on the day of the murder and maybe see if the FDLE crime scene unit from Fort Myers might come over and process the apartment. He'd have to keep it quiet.

He ate a quick breakfast of instant oatmeal and a banana, then dressed in jeans and a T-shirt that identified him as a FDLE agent. That seemed an appropriate dress for the day. He walked onto the back porch and gave Hamlet his usual dosage of food pellets and changed his water. The little mouse who now masqueraded as a hamster seemed to like the rear covered porch. The girls were convinced he wanted a view from his cage. Tasker had initially been worried about birds or other predators coming onto the porch, but he had secured the cage with a bungee cord to the small table it rested on and checked the sturdy cage. He didn't think anything could get to his little friend.

Everything secured in the apartment, Tasker trotted out to his car. It was almost ten-thirty and he wanted to see how the search was coming. As he came out the front door, he was surprised to see a nice, deep blue Crown Vic parked next to his Monte Carlo. It was a second before he recognized the man who emerged from the big car.

"Hey, Billy, nice hours," said the director of the Miami region of FDLE.

"Hey, boss. What brings you out here?" He came down the stairs to greet the well-dressed Latin man.

"You, my friend."

"I don't usually leave so late. I was working the escape last night."

The tall director smiled and said, "I know, I know. I'm sending out a couple of agents from the West Palm office to help. They're gonna have a thousand leads to check out before nightfall."

"That's why I'm in the tactical shirt. I was gonna help in the search."

The director shook his head. "Negative, Billy. You need to finish the Dewalt investigation."

Tasker stopped for a second as the director eased into a chair on the porch. Tasker followed his lead, scooting the other chair to face him. "You came out here to personally tell me to work on a stale homicide?"

He nodded.

"I thought this was more important for now."

"Nothing is more important. Not an escape, not another homicide, nothing."

"Who has the juice to get you to drive eighty miles to tell me that?"

The director hesitated. "I came because I'm concerned about one of my agents. Apparently you didn't hear me when I told you over the phone to drop the outside homicide inquiry."

"I heard you, boss, I just—"

"You just had to look at it. I know, Billy, when things aren't right, you have a hard time ignoring them. Well, guess what? You're not the only cop in the world. Others can solve crimes, too. What I need you to do is finish this goddamn investigation into this fucking kid whose fucking father has the fucking governor's ear." He paused and caught his breath. "Finish it, come back to Miami and I'll turn you loose on the criminals in Dade County. Fuck around any more and you and I will both be out of a job."

"It's that serious?"

"It is that serious and more. Fucking Ardan Gann told me to order you just to write up whatever you have. I argued for a few days to tie up loose ends and give you some breathing room."

"Boss, can I explain what's going on?"

The director said, "I know about the murder right here. I know you liked the guy."

Tasker told him about Peter Rubie and his interview. Then he said, "What's the rush on the Dewalt case? You told me to take my time and go slow."

The director nodded as he stared out into the field.

Tasker continued, "I've been getting little signs about my presence out here, too."

"Like what?"

Tasker told him about the attack by Linus Hardaway in lockdown, the fight with the ex-inmate at the bar and his encounter with the Aryan Knights.

"Billy, why didn't you call me about this?"

"I kept hoping it was all unrelated. Something stinks out here and I need some time to find out what."

"Are you safe at this apartment?"

"I'm careful now. I don't need to go back inside the prison, just to the administration building. And I have a few friends now."

The director kept contemplating the situation.

"Boss, I'll do what I'm ordered, but you always say, 'Do what's right.'"

The director smiled. "I hate it when you guys use my words against me."

"What do you want me to do? What will Ardan Gann say?"

The director took a long time, looking out over the cane field, not saying a word. Tasker knew the look. He gave his boss some time to consider things. Then, after almost a full minute, the director said, "You know what?" He looked out over the cane again. "Fuck Ardan Gann." He looked at Tasker. "Can you keep looking around safely?"

"I think so."

"Can you finish the investigation?"

"Yes, sir."

"Then do it. Keep a low profile, but do your thing. If you're no closer to resolving it by next Friday, you're done. Good enough?"

Tasker couldn't help but smile. "Yes, sir."

"I'll call the commissioner, who'll explain it to Gann. No one should bitch about a little extra time. But you've got to sort this shit out."

Tasker felt like a new man.

The director said, "What do you need as far as help?"

"I might use Jerry Risto if I come up with anything."

The director smiled and headed for his car. "I was never here."

"Wish I could say that."

Just after noon, Luther Williams found the three-bedroom apartment that he knew was used as a stash house for crack and money. He knocked casually, hoping things hadn't changed too much since he'd been away. He didn't like standing on the exposed landing of a third-floor apartment in broad daylight. This was taking his plan of being seen in Miami a little too far.

"Who is it?" asked a voice from inside.

"Luther Williams."

"Don't know no Luther Williams. Go away."

Luther caught himself and smiled. "It's Cole Hodges. Open the door."

There was a slight pause, then the door cracked open with the chain still on. A young black man in an oversized Miami Heat jersey peered out. "Oh shit," he said and slammed the door.

Luther heard him fumble with the chain, and in a few seconds the solid door opened for him.

"I'm sorry, Mr. Hodges. I thought you was, was, ah, away."

Luther smiled. "I was, son, but now I'm back. Where's Scooter?"

"He's out right now, sir, but he'll be back before too long."

"Fine, I'll wait."

"I'll give him a call on his cell."

"That's all right, son. Don't bother him." He watched the nervous young man and added, "Why don't you stay where I can see you?"

"Yes, sir." He fidgeted at the request, but stayed where he was.

"I can see you in the kitchen if you leave the door open. Why don't you make me some lunch while I wait?"

The young man darted into the small kitchen and rummaged through the refrigerator. He called over his shoulder, "I got some pizza from last night."

"That's fine. But heat it in the oven, not a microwave. I like it crispy."

"Yes, sir, right away, Mr. Hodges." The young man flew at his task like a hummingbird, racing around the kitchen, his shaking hands dropping utensils and knocking over glasses.

This was what Luther had missed. People willing to make him happy. He hoped Scooter was in a mood to help, too. If not, this apartment would smell of more than old cigarettes and pot.

Bill Tasker arrived at the admin building just about noon. Among the other things he wanted to accomplish that day was telling Renee Chin he saw her as something more than just a prison inspector acting as his liaison. He had held his growing feelings back for several reasons: his ex-wife, the circumstances, even his interest in Billie Towers had played a role. Now he knew that Renee was special. He still smiled at the memory of her encounter with his ex-wife. Renee's sunny and positive personality always made him feel lighter. He just hoped she shared some kind of feeling for him. She had given him hints. The quick kiss, the way she dressed for their dinner. He had never been too sharp with women; he'd noticed that guys who thought they knew women were usually the most clueless. He, at least, knew he was clueless.

He had changed into a pullover and khaki pants. He had even tried to rehearse what he might say, but it had been futile. He'd wing it when he saw her.

He had other plans for the day. He'd finish reviewing logs and even interview some possible witnesses in the Dewalt death. So far he had no real leads, but he wanted to take some good photos of the marks he had found on the door in the psych ward. He knew the pendant found in Baxter's personal belongings could throw a wrench in the case if he couldn't find a reasonable explanation. His only clue was the fingerprint that belonged to Sergeant Henry Janzig. Renee had already eliminated the sergeant as a suspect by confirming that he was in Tallahassee the day Dewalt was killed. Tasker knew he'd still have to look into the matter.

He'd show the photos of the marks on the psych ward door to the ME and maybe the sheriff's office crime scene person and see what they thought. Maybe it would lead somewhere. If not, he'd start writing a summary for the governor's office in the next few days. That way he had a week to look at Janzig and also see what the hell was going on with the Kling murder case.

He wandered through the administration building, which was nearly empty. The trustees were in lockdown as a result of Luther's escape, most of the correctional officers were out looking for Luther and no outside vendors had been allowed on the grounds.

He heard Renee Chin's voice down the hall and followed her sweet tone that was now in a professional mode. He found her in the library near the taped-off crime scene where the trustee had been murdered the day before. Everyone assumed the killer was Luther. That included Tasker.

Renee spoke into her cell phone. "No, Captain Norton is handling the escape, I'm busy on the murder." She said goodbye, closed the flip-top Nextel and turned to Tasker.

"How're you holding up?" she asked.

"I'm fine."

"Heard you were out all night with the search team."

"Yeah, but my boss is sending agents from West Palm to help now, so I'm supposed to concentrate on the Dewalt investigation."

"I'm working with the county homicide guys on this. They processed the scene and are processing the murder weapon."

"Looks like Luther, right?"

"Oh yeah. Witnesses, location, even motive. We figured he wanted the murder as a diversion."

"The diversion helped me out, too."

"How so?"

"I had a run-in with a group you guys call the Aryan Knights."

"When?"

"Yesterday, right when the alarm sounded."

"You hurt?"

"No. Just scared the shit out of me."

She laughed.

"What's so funny?"

"You. Most cops would never admit they're scared."

"No way. The cops I know admit it. Only a moron isn't scared some of the time."

Renee seemed to relax and leaned against the long conference table. "Who'd you report the Aryan Knight incident to?"

"A sergeant. Harrison."

"Yeah, Stan. What'd he say?"

"Everything was so crazy he just kind of shrugged and said they were a bad bunch."

"He's right. You're lucky." She smiled and patted his shoulder.

Tasker cleared his throat and said, "Hey, um, Renee. I had something I wanted to talk about. I'm not sure if this is the right place or time." He hesitated and ran his hand through his hair. "I wanted to say . . ."

"Yes?" She leaned in closer.

"What I was going to say . . ."

Just as he was about to blurt out something—he wasn't sure if it was what he wanted to say but at least some words—Captain Norton entered the far end of the library.

"Hello, ladies, anything new?"

Renee pulled away from Tasker and said, "Looks like Luther Williams killed him. Won't have forensics for a few days."

"That boy better be back in the can in a few days." He looked at Tasker. "Harrison says you had a run-in with some Aryan Knights."

Tasker nodded.

"You hurt?"

He shook his head, trying to will Norton to leave so he could finish his conversation with Renee.

"You didn't do any favors for one of 'em. He's over at the infirmary with a broken shoulder and a concussion. Was that called for?"

Now Tasker was involved in the conversation. "Look here, Captain, that's the second time your inmates have tried to hurt me. I did what I had to do. Hit him once. Just one time across the back as he came at me. Didn't any of your ace correctional officers see it on a monitor?"

"My question is why did you smuggle an ASP inside the perimeter?"

Tasker was about to give him the honest answer when a better one popped into his head. "I was testing the entry security. Guess what? You fucking failed."

This brought Norton up short. He looked at Renee. "Inspector, we have a lot to go over. I'm sure Agent Tasker wants to finish his investigation." He turned and stormed out of the library.

Renee took a few steps, turned and said, "How about dinner?"

"When?"

"Saturday night."

Tasker grinned and nodded. He'd be better prepared to talk to her over dinner.

32

SAM NORTON CAUGHT UP TO THE SEARCH TEAM covering the residential area to the east of the Rock. The captain didn't need to check on them because Henry Janzig was there and he ran a tight ship. His boys wouldn't get lax, even though Norton was afraid it didn't matter anymore. Luther Williams was probably a hundred miles from Gladesville by now.

He found the short, stout frame of his most trusted associate near the edge of the abandoned US Sugar housing units, screaming at some young correctional officer.

Janzig had the taller man cowering by a department pickup truck. "Boy, you hold a fucking shotgun that ain't aimed at someone straight up in the goddamn air. You hear me?" Janzig's round face turned red as he screamed.

The young man with a crew cut and still a smattering of pimples nodded his head before scampering off to join the others going through backyards and toolsheds.

Norton got out of his own state-owned pickup and walked over to his friend. "I hope the moron pointed the gun at you for you to get so bent out of shape."

"Careless som-bitch. He was gabbing with the female, the cute one, what's her name?"

"Manfredi, Angela Manfredi."

"Yeah, that's the one. What's a girl like that doing out here anyway?"

Norton snorted at his friend. "Trying to make enough money for college. Her daddy is a teacher in Belle Glade. She does a good job. What's crawled up your ass and died?"

"You sayin' I ain't sensitive to females? Hell, I'm sensitive all to hell over 'em. But I got a job and no part of my job requires me to know about people's personal problems."

"Whoa there, sailor, it's me. Now what's really wrong?"

Janzig stopped and looked around to make sure no one was near them. "Having Williams on the loose spooks me."

"No one likes an escape."

"You know that ain't what I mean."

Norton nodded. "Yeah, I know. We're doing everything we can. I had the inspector from the South Florida Reception Center go with a couple of FDLE guys to Luther's girlfriend's nice Miami Beach apartment. You know the heavy white woman."

"Yeah, I seen her."

"She didn't know shit. She let them search her place and car. Nothing."

"Damn sure is a coincidence she was here when he got out."

"Henry, he's a sly one. He might have planned it like that just to throw us off." He patted his friend on the back. "Don't worry. We'll get him."

On his way back to the prison, Norton saw Rufus Goodwin at the town's only coffee and doughnut shop, Dinkin' Delights. It even used the same colors as the corporate doughnut shop that had lasted all of two years in this town. He pulled the truck across US 27 and into the lot next to Rufus' Crown Victoria.

"Isn't it a stereotype to see a cop at a doughnut shop?"

"Only when the cop hasn't eaten in fifteen hours."

"Problems?"

"Our murder case is falling apart."

"Why?"

"One reason is that nosy FDLE agent. That asshole must be some kinda retard because he sure can't take a hint."

Norton nodded. "Ain't that the truth. He does give new meaning to the word 'determined.'" Norton knew he'd have to step in on this matter. It had already gone too far.

Luther finished his three slices of pizza and two cans of real Coke. Not Chek soda or some other store brand but real, honest-to-goodness Coca-Cola. He was starting to realize how much he had missed in his visit to Manatee.

The young man from the apartment dozed as he watched cartoons on the big plasma TV. Luther had forbidden him to leave his sight until the real resident of the apartment, a certain Scooter Brown, returned.

Three short raps on the door sent the young man scurrying. He unchained the door and in walked a muscular man of about thirty. His defined biceps and tapered back showed the man worked out on a regular basis. His coal-black skin showed off the gold-and-diamond earring in his left earlobe.

Luther stood to greet the renowned organizer of crack and cheap marijuana distribution.

Scooter said, "I heard on the news you had taken a vacation. Didn't think I'd see you down here."

"C'mon, Scooter, you didn't *want* to see me down here."

"No, sir, Mr. Hodges, I never had no problem with you. You did some good for the community, and most importantly you never tried to sell no crack."

Luther shook his head. "Scooter, all those years at University of Miami and you still use poor grammar?"

The sleek, tall man said, "As long as I caught the long ball or could run back a punt, they didn't care if I spoke good or well."

"You should speak well. You're an example to our community."

"No, sir. I was, until the Jets passed on me in the draft 'cause of my knees. Now I'm just a businessman who does what he has to. Not proud of it, but I don't deny it, either."

"A fine attitude, I'm sure."

"Mr. Hodges, I need to ask why you're here."

"In Miami?"

"In my stash house."

"Oh, yes, of course. I'm here to collect the debt your former employer owes me."

Scooter hesitated. "You know Odell is dead, right?"

"I am aware he succumbed to the competition."

"And a nine-millimeter in his eye."

"That'll do it. But the loan was not a personal one. I invested in your organization. He was making payments. Now you, as the manager of this enterprise, are responsible."

Scooter looked at him.

Luther continued. "No, my boy, not on a monthly basis. A onetime fee to set things right."

"How much of a payment?"

"Let's say two hundred and fifty thousand."

"Let's say, no way."

Luther smiled his "I'm impressed" smile. "A negotiator, excellent. I could be convinced to accept two hundred large and call it even."

"Sir, I respect who you used to be."

"I am who I always was. Is that understood?"

The crack dealer hesitated, considering his options. "Yes, sir, you are, but I can't pay out two hundred grand. I don't got it."

"That's not a problem. I'll give you two days to get it."

Scooter eyed the older man. "I'm sorry, Mr. Hodges, I don't think we should have to pay. Especially since you ain't got no juice here no more." Scooter eyed his assistant, who had kept Luther company for the past two hours. The young man stood up from the kitchen stool he had been perched on and casually sidled up next to Luther. Scooter continued. "I'll extend you one courtesy, Mr. Hodges."

"What would that be?"

"I'll let you leave here alive if you promise not to bother me again."

Luther nodded, careful not to telegraph his next move. He let his right hand slip to the waist of his newly acquired jeans. His fingers carefully felt for the end of the shish kebab skewer. It had been broken in half, but the end of the five-inch rod had a vicious point. In a flash he yanked out the steel rod by its wooden handle and thrust it straight through the assistant's heart. The young man dropped straight to the floor without a peep. Luther immediately slashed up with the weapon, catching Scooter across the throat and face. The incision spread open wide, showing the depth of the cut. Scooter tried to back away, but the shock of the attack and knowledge of his wound slowed him. Luther slashed downward, severely slicing three fingers on Scooter's right hand.

Luther followed the stricken man to the floor, his face inches from the injured man's. "Now, Scooter, I'm gonna extend a courtesy to you."

Scooter's eyes shifted to Luther's face. They showed the shock that was coming over him.

"You tell me where your cash is hidden in here and I'll let you live. Clam up and I'll wait as you bleed out." Luther threw in a smile to show there were no hard feelings.

Scooter got a look at the blood seeping into the cheap shag carpet and said, "Bedroom closet. There's a safe in the wall near the floor."

"What's the combination?"

Scooter started to pass out. Luther slapped his face to bring him around. "Scooter. The combination?"

He gasped for air. "It's a keypad. Six, six, six. Ain't no two hundred large."

Luther stood up. He looked over at the corpse next to Scooter. He wiped the skewer across a napkin with some pizza sauce on it, then stuck it back in his waistband.

The bedroom was a disaster, with clothes stacked everywhere and all the dresser drawers open. The closet was stuffed full of hanging jogging suits and sweatshirts. On the rear wall near the floor was a two-foot-by-two-foot safe, right where Scooter had said it would be. He knelt down and tapped on the 6 key three times. He tried the handle and sure enough the door opened wide. Luther smiled at the stacks of bills. He pulled out the twenties and tens. Maybe ten grand. That'd work for now.

Luther trotted out through the living room, dodging the casualties of ignorance, and made it to the door.

Scooter called out from the floor, "Wait. I can't get to the phone. I need help."

Luther assessed the man's situation. "I concur. I also think you handled this whole thing poorly. Consider it a lesson."

"What good is a lesson if I die and can't use it?"

"Good point." Luther took two steps to the portable phone sitting on the coffee table. He picked it up, mashed nine one one and heard a voice say, "Nine one one, please state your emergency."

"A disrespectful man has been stabbed and is bleeding badly at 5662 Seventeenth Avenue. Send fire rescue."

Luther turned to the door and on his way out said, "That's the best I can do."

He was out on the street and on his way several seconds later.

 **33** TASKER HAD SPENT THE DAY AT MANATEE DO-
ing just what he was supposed to be doing: trying to deter-
mine who killed Rick Dewalt. This investigation had the
least number of viable leads he had ever seen. It was like the guy had just
died on the spot. If it weren't for the forensics, Tasker would swear it was
a death by natural causes. No one knew anything, or at least, no one was
talking. But that was rare. Someone always talked. Especially in a prison.

He still had the marks he had found on the door of the psych ward he
wanted to check out. The confusion of the attack and the escape had
made him adjust his priorities. Now he knew what his priorities were
again. He'd talk over the marks with Dr. Freund and see what the assistant medical examiner had to say.

The other thing that kept bouncing around in his head was the Dewalt company posting a reward for Professor Kling's killer. Big Rick
Dewalt didn't impress him as a community activist, unless the action
was developing land. Rufus Goodwin said it was common, but Tasker
kept wondering anyway.

Tasker's mind may have wandered to Professor Kling's homicide investigation and Luther's escape and the lovely Renee Chin, but his ass
stayed in one seat as he studied interviews and crime scene photos.

By midday, thirst drove him to the officers' lounge down the hall.
There were a couple of vending machines and a TV. He needed the
break.

The room already had an occupant. Tasker nodded to the round, puffy sergeant named Janzig. Since Renee had discovered he had been in Tallahassee the day of Dewalt's death, Tasker hadn't really worried about him. He was going to talk to him, but it wasn't vital right now.

Tasker mumbled, "Need a break," as he headed across the room toward the machine with Powerade in it.

The surly sergeant hardly took his eyes off the Fox news channel. He was leaning on a chair, giving the impression he didn't intend to be there for long. "Break from what?"

"Looking at photos and reading interview transcripts."

"You need a break from readin'? What the hell would you do if you worked on a farm?"

"I like the outside."

"Even if it's shoveling cow shit and harvesting crops?"

Tasker realized whatever he said this old geezer was going to give him a hard time. "You're right, it's not too bad."

The sergeant turned toward him. "Not too bad? You sayin' I don't know shit?"

Tasker just stared at him.

"I don't need no sissy FDLE agent tellin' I'm a dumb-ass." He turned and headed toward the door.

Tasker assessed the shorter man. "Sergeant, I don't know what your problem is, but we can talk off the record if you want."

"Off the record. When are you on the record? Thought you were looking to see who killed the inmate Dewalt. I see you doin' everything but that. If it ain't running off on escapes or beating up our inmates, you're worried about other things. Shit, I coulda solved this case in three days."

"Is that so?"

"It is."

"How?"

"Inmates talk. They say that Leroy Baxter killed that boy."

"They're not saying it to me."

"What about Dewalt's jewelry Baxter had? Everyone knows you found it."

"Does anyone know the only fingerprint on it was yours?"

The old man froze and stared at Tasker. Then, slowly, he said, "What's that mean? I handle a lot of stuff around here. It's my fucking job. At least I do my fucking job." Janzig spun on one foot and marched out of the lounge.

Tasker just stared at the door the old guy had stormed out of. Maybe there was something there.

It was five o'clock and Renee Chin was closing down her office, getting ready to help a search team cover another section of Gladesville in their effort to find Luther Williams. No one really thought he'd still be in the vicinity, but they had to show they were trying. She liked work as long as it was interesting. And this was definitely interesting.

She had firmed up her dinner date with Bill Tasker for Saturday night, but was unsure what she would say. She wanted to tell him she had developed feelings for him, but didn't want to scare him off. She wondered if that conversation might be better after she had landed him in bed, at least once.

Right now she had to concentrate on work; she couldn't worry about her crush on the FDLE agent.

As she was headed down the hallway past Captain Norton's office, she leaned in to say goodnight.

Norton was talking to Henry Janzig. He motioned her into the office. "What's up?" she asked.

Norton said, "Henry was just sayin' how the FDLE guy, Tasker, called him a dipshit and berated him today."

She looked at the short sergeant. "He used the word 'dipshit'?"

Janzig hesitated. "Not in so many words. No."

"That doesn't sound like Bill. I haven't seen him be disrespectful to anyone here."

Norton said, "Tell that to Linus Hardaway."

She just looked at him.

Janzig said, "You guys know me. I'm sweet as pie. I'd never start a ruckus."

Renee looked at Norton and then had to suppress a smile. "No, you're right, Henry. You make Pat Sajak look mean."

Once Norton started to laugh, there was no point continuing.

I t was well past eight in the evening, and the team Tasker was helping, despite his orders to focus on the Dewalt investigation, had finished covering the far side of Gladesville. They had uncovered every crevice Luther Williams might use to hide in. Tasker knew no one really thought he was still in the area. The rumors had him as far north as Atlanta and as far south as Costa Rica. Tasker seemed to think he was somewhere in between. The correctional sergeant who was running the team told them to knock off for the night and be ready to go at eight in the morning. Tasker knew this didn't apply to him. No one even acknowledged the FDLE agent's help. He hadn't volunteered for the recognition, but a "thanks" wouldn't have hurt, either.

Tasker rode in the back of a DOC pickup truck back to the prison and then started throwing his gear in the trunk of his Monte Carlo. The visitors' lot was well lighted and he had no problem sorting out all of his gear in his trunk. He always had two pistols. His Sig Sauer P-230, which he carried most of the time because it was small and light, and his bigger Beretta 92F .40 caliber, which he usually stored in the nightstand at his apartment. The larger, much heavier pistol was issued by the department and he had found that he was comfortable with the Italian import.

As he slammed his trunk, he heard someone say, "You're here late." He turned to find Renee Chin standing right behind him.

"Just finished the last search for the night."

"Yeah, I collected the issued handguns from all the search parties. Now there's no one left out there."

"Hungry?"

"Not really. Just tired."

Tasker nodded. "Guess I am, too. We ate some fried chicken the prison sent out to us about six."

Renee smiled. "Yeah, that's Don Seiker's recipe."

"Who's Don Seiker?"

"He's in on his second ten-year term for running a chop shop. Specialized in Cadillacs. No one was sorry to see him back in the system because he was such a good cook. A lot of the officers knew him from his last stay at Glades. Anytime something like this happens, the captain has him make up a load of his fried chicken for the officers."

Tasker noticed that even though she had been at work for at least twelve hours, she looked good. "What about a beer at my little state-owned palace?"

A smile broke across her face. "That sounds like a winner."

Tasker's heart raced on the ride from the prison west on US 27 to Dead Cow Lane. Maybe now he could tell her what he had been feeling for her. Maybe, with no one around and no interruptions, he could finally express himself.

The entire complex was dark as he pulled his car into the spot in front of his corner apartment. Renee parked her Jeep Liberty next to him. She fell in right behind as he opened his door with a key and flipped on a light.

"You need lights out front," said Renee.

"Yeah, it'd help. They have floodlights in the back. Looks like the prison at night." He walked through the kitchen, stopping to grab a couple of Icehouses from the fridge. "C'mon out back. We can have these on the porch." He flipped the switch for the rear lights, and a set of four floodlights as well as two lights under the covered porch came on.

She strolled out to the edge of the porch, taking a long drink of beer.

He stayed right next to her, gulping almost the whole bottle. He thought of a way to bring up the subject of his feelings, but his mouth refused to open. Renee helped by leaning her head down across his shoulder.

"This is nice out here," she said.

"It is now." He cringed at his comment.

Her head came off his shoulder and she took one step down the stairs toward the backyard. "Who was killing rabbits so close to the apartment?"

Tasker looked at one of the familiar rabbit fur balls at the base of his stairs.

"That's a new one. There are a bunch closer to the cane, but I don't remember one up here." He came down all three stairs and looked at the white fur spot and froze. Unlike the others, whoever had killed this one had left the body. Tasker noticed the odd yellow streak running across its back.

He charged up the stairs and went straight to Hamlet's cage. It was empty and the door was open.

"Motherfucker." Tasker didn't mean to say it out loud.

Renee rushed up the steps. "What's wrong?"

"Someone killed Hamlet."

She looked at the cage and understood what had happened.

"What'll I tell the girls?"

Even though it was just a mouse he had found in the apartment, Tasker felt like this was the worst thing they had done yet. He'd proven he could deal with attacks against him, but this was low. Now things were going to get very ugly if they had to.

34 LUTHER WILLIAMS WATCHED THE SUN RISE over the condos off South Beach. He had stayed up all night, seeing old acquaintances, collecting a few more debts and in general making sure people knew he was around. In a few minutes, he had a breakfast meeting with the one man he really needed to talk to. Neil Nyren was a powerhouse. Few people knew his name, his address or even a reliable phone number. That made him valuable. Luther had called the pay phone with a downtown Miami exchange where a Latin kid always answered in English saying, "Yes?" If someone answered otherwise, Luther knew to just hang up. When he had heard the "Yes?" the night before, Luther identified himself and told the young man he needed to meet Mr. Nyren for breakfast at a little diner off Biscayne. Two hours later, he called the same number and had his appointment confirmed.

About midnight, Luther had traded Scooter Brown's nice but tricked-out and very identifiable RX-7 for an understated and stolen Buick LeSabre, a nice blue V-6, 3800 series. Luther then found another LeSabre—this one parked in the lot outside a Muvico in Aventura—and switched the tags. It would be months before the old white lady who probably owned the LeSabre realized the tag on her car was not her own.

As Luther settled in at a booth in the diner, he took a quick stock of his situation. With all the debts he had collected, he had about twenty-one thousand bucks. Today he'd clean out any bank accounts he could get his hands on and be up close to forty. After a nap, he'd start to head north, careful not to be profiled by some ambitious Florida highway patrolman or Volusia County sheriff's deputy. He'd drive a few miles over the speed limit and stay the night in a hotel near Daytona. He still planned a stop in Tallahassee for a visit that was long overdue. He owed it to himself.

There was one thing he had to do right after this meeting. A phone call to set right a few indignities he had suffered in the past year. But that was for later.

Now he saw the tall, dignified Neil Nyren as he came through the front door. His insistence on always wearing a dark suit drew attention in a town like Miami, but he pulled it off. It made him look like a successful lawyer or banker. Talk about not judging a book by its cover. No one knew exactly what Mr. Nyren could do, but everyone knew if he said he could do it, he could.

He walked straight to Luther's booth and extended his hand. "Mr. Hodges, how nice to see you again."

"Believe me, Mr. Nyren, it's nice to be seen here." He smiled and offered a seat to the man who many considered the most dangerous person in the city. His smile was disarming, but Luther noticed he never seemed to have any competition in whatever business he decided to pursue.

Aside from dressing well, there was nothing remarkable about his lifestyle. That was the mark of a professional. Someone who didn't have to draw attention to himself.

Nyren said, "Tell me, Mr. Hodges, what is it that I can do that you can't do for yourself?"

"I like that, no bullshit. Straight to the point."

"We are both businessmen. Time is a precious commodity. I'd bet you are in quite a hurry about now."

"I am. I also require absolute secrecy on our transaction."

"When has that ever been an issue?"

Luther smiled. "Exactly why I called. I need two things: identification and a safe, truly safe, place to stay outside of Florida."

Nyren was silent, then nodded his head. "That's it?"

"Believe me, that's enough."

"After we eat, follow me to a studio where we'll take your photo. You can choose what state you are from at the studio." He paused. "I know a number of groups that would appreciate a mind such as yours and eschew any contact with organized government. However..." He fell silent.

"Yes?"

"Most would not appreciate the simple matter of your skin color."

Luther scratched his chin. "I understand. I'm assuming these are acquaintances or business contacts and not friends."

"I can assure you, Mr. Hodges, I in no way share their antiquated belief system."

Luther appreciated anyone in Miami who could turn a phrase and use the breadth of their vocabulary. It didn't surprise him that such a man would not hold the base and simple prejudices of the former South.

Nyren said, "I know of one group. Tax protesters, I believe. A group that resides in a comfortable enclave near Baton Rouge. I could make a discreet inquiry."

"That would be of great benefit."

"Please, Mr. Hodges, consider it done."

"And what might these two services cost me? In today's market. In U.S. currency."

Nyren rolled his eyes into his head as he calculated the cost of his business associates. "Five large for the identification and, if the group could really use an attorney, for non-courtroom work of course, I'll get my end from them."

"Most kind of you, Mr. Nyren. Most kind."

"You've helped me over the years, whether you know it or not."

"How so?"

"Let's just say some of your competition was a threat to my interests. You handled it for me."

"Good enough."

They shook hands on their renewed association.

Luther added, "Now, you'll understand that as part of our verbal agreement, you cannot disclose my identification or whereabouts at any time to anyone."

"I understand."

"Do you understand the consequences?"

"I am afraid I do."

"Then we're off to your studio. I need to buy a prepaid phone card to make a few calls. Is there a service station between here and your studio that would have some for sale?"

Nyren smiled. "I guarantee the studio has plenty of cards."

"Excellent. I need to make an important call about eight."

Bill Tasker had tossed and turned all night, thinking about how someone was trying to scare him out of this little one-horse town. Renee had seen how upset he was and left after only one beer to give him some time alone. It was probably for the best. They were still having dinner tomorrow night and the girls were coming tonight. They had to be back at their mother's by tomorrow at three. He still wasn't sure what he was going to tell them about Hamlet, but he knew it wouldn't be the truth. They didn't need to know how sick people could be. If he hadn't told them or their mother about his recent assaults, he could justify keeping his mouth shut about a pet mouse.

He had scooped up Hamlet's remains and then couldn't bring himself to just throw him in the garbage. Instead, he dug a hole in the cane field and actually gave the mouse a short burial service.

He cleaned up and was out at Manatee before seven-thirty. He wanted to race through his duties so that he could spend some time on other things before he was forced out of town next Friday. He knew his director was sticking his neck out for him and he didn't want to disappoint him. He'd finish the report and make sure Rufus had everything he needed to work the professor's homicide before Tasker left town.

About eight, after he had made a decent dent in his work, he sensed someone in the doorway. The young correctional officer who always worked the front reception desk to the admin building but who had never acknowledged Tasker said, "Sir?"

Tasker looked at him. "Yeah?"

"You have a phone call at the main switchboard. Would you like me to transfer it to the phone in the library?"

Tasker stood up, saying, "That'd be great." As he walked down the short hall to the library, he wondered who would call him on a hard line in the prison instead of on his cell phone. The phone on the corner table of the library was ringing by the time he entered the room. The crime scene tape was still looped around the windowsill. He picked up the old handset.

"Bill Tasker."

"Agent Tasker, how nice to hear your voice from so far away."

Tasker immediately recognized the deep voice and professional delivery of Luther Williams, aka Cole Hodges.

Tasker played it cool. "Hello, Luther. Calling from anywhere in particular?"

"I am, however I'll keep that information to myself."

"What made you run?"

Luther paused, then said, "Let's just say I executed an escape clause in my contract with the good state of Florida."

Tasker said, "Look, you need to come back. We can work this all out."

"Agent Tasker, please don't diminish the esteem in which I hold you. You and I know a number of reasons why that is impossible."

"Such as?"

"Robert Moambi and Vic Vollentius, for two. I knew something had tipped you off about the Aryan Knight's accident. Would you mind if I ask what?"

Tasker weighed the answer and thought, What the hell. "Vollentius had a note hidden in his mouth saying he was meeting you."

Luther gave out a loud hoot and said, "The oldest trick in the book. I should've checked, but he didn't strike me as the jumpy kind."

"Don't be too hard on yourself."

"A reasonable attitude, which is why I chose to call you."

"I'm listening."

"You have proven quite bright in piecing things together. In addition, you seem above the normal weaknesses of other officials."

"Thanks, I appreciate the recognition from the opposition."

Luther chuckled, then said, "I would suggest that you check Captain Sam Norton's name on a list of corporations with the Secretary of State. You might be surprised how industrious the good captain is in his free time."

"I could do that."

"That's all I suggest. Knowing you, I believe that will be a sufficient start to a thorough investigation."

Tasker listened carefully to the brief silence, seeing if he could pick up any background noise that might provide a clue to the escaped convict's location. There was nothing.

Tasker said, "Any hints as to where you are?"

"Oh yes, plenty. I would suspect you'll hear rumors before the end of the day." There was another silence, and then Luther added, "We should not, in all likelihood, see each other again, Agent Tasker. It was been a privilege to meet you on the field of battle."

Before Tasker could answer, the line went dead. He was on his cell phone dialing his Miami office before he even stood up from the stool in the library.

Luther Williams was on Interstate I-95 near West Palm Beach in his comfortable Buick LaSabre when he realized it was late afternoon and he hadn't eaten anything since breakfast with the extraordinarily helpful Mr. Nyren. He felt like some Cuban food, maybe a sandwich to bring along, and decided if he turned east on Forest Hill Boulevard he'd run into a Cuban restaurant before too long. One of his dorm mates from Manatee had been a young Cuban lad who had been part of a botched home invasion. Luther had appreciated the boy's respect for his elders, something he found in most Cuban families. He had done some minor legal work for him and advised him on his wife of only four months' petition for divorce. The young man was from this south end of West Palm Beach and often spoke well of the neighborhood and his family. He said it was a poor choice of friends that had led him to a fifteen-year sentence at Manatee. Luther thought the sentence had more to do with the fact that the West Palm cops were known to be efficient and effective in dealing with violent crime. In Miami, things got lost in the giant shuffle of victims and crimes. In a town like West Palm Beach, the cops still took home invasions personally.

On the corner of Forest Hill and Dixie, Luther saw a place named Havana's. He felt quite comfortable with the assumption that this place served Cuban cuisine. One of the reasons for his urge, he felt certain, was that his next residence was not likely to have Cuban or any other Caribbean food. True to his word, Mr. Nyren had found a group off the beaten path and anxious for someone to review documents and bolster their legal team. Clearly, Luther could not appear in court or hold the high profile he'd once had, but reviewing contracts and deeds beat the hell out of keeping a library clean and stocked.

Luther decided to go inside the restaurant rather than risk an observant cop seeing him at the outside counter favored by the older Cuban gentlemen.

He placed an order for two Cuban sandwiches and an extra large Cuban coffee. He figured that would keep him wide awake for another day or two. He smiled at how things had changed for him since he'd arrived from Missouri more than twenty years before. He had never tasted Cuban coffee or even heard of it then. Now he found it was one of the things he missed deeply when he was away. The strong taste and caffeine was unlike anything else on Earth.

A very attractive blond woman in her early thirties burst into the restaurant with two little girls. She was obviously in a hurry and barked orders before they were all inside.

"Kelly, take Emily to the restroom and I'll get you a sandwich to split. Your dad will expect to have dinner with you, so I don't want you to fill up too much."

She smiled as she looked up at Luther. He nodded.

"We have a long ride and they're already complaining about being hungry."

Luther said, "That's thoughtful of you to stop. Do your daughters normally eat Cuban cuisine?"

"They like the sandwiches and they're not too messy in the car."

"Very resourceful."

He watched the fine form of the young woman as she ordered a sandwich and two Cokes to go. Her hair came down her muscular back in a loose ponytail and she had exquisite, large breasts. He hoped they were real. Too many younger women felt the need for enhancement nowadays. He did so appreciate naturally large breasts.

The waitress handed a bag across the counter to Luther, who gave her a ten-dollar bill and said, "Keep the change." He turned to the young mother. "Have a safe trip."

She smiled a dazzling white smile and said, "Thanks very much. You, too."

"I hope to. I'll be on the road some time, but I hope to."

"Where are you headed?"

"Louisiana."

"That's nice. I've only been to New Orleans once. Loved it."

"I'm headed to quieter parts, but it's exciting to me just the same. Have a nice evening." Luther came out the front door and turned toward his Buick. He knew she probably thought of him as a kindly older man. He was old but not dead. Women like that were one of the reasons he had to take a vacation from Manatee.

**35** BILL TASKER HAD CALLED THE MIAMI OFFICE OF the Florida Department of Law Enforcement four times looking for his friend Jerry Risto. The sixty-year-old man occupied a vital role in FDLE—he was a crime intelligence analyst. Normally the analysts supported investigation by running computer checks and criminal histories. Jerry Risto took it to a new level. He was more like a magician than an analyst. Now the magician had disappeared on some errand and Tasker was anxious to find the friend who had bailed him out of other trouble over the past year.

Tasker said to the secretary, "When will he be back?"

The tired voice with a Cuban accent on the other end of the phone said, "Same time I tol' you an hour ago: I don't know."

"Will you tell him I called?"

"Bill, I tol' you I'd tell him three calls ago. Now stop bothering me and do some work." The line went dead.

Tasker had made his own notes on the message from Luther Williams. What did it mean if it was true? So Norton was in a corporation? Big deal. It had to be some kind of big deal for a wanted fugitive to risk having a call traced.

Tasker could've called any analyst, but aside from being a genius with the computer, Jerry Risto had pulled his ass out of the fire on several occasions. One time, when Tasker had been suspended, he'd done it off the record, under circumstances that could have gotten him fired. Tasker decided it was worth waiting.

He used the free time to straighten up his apartment for the arrival of the girls. He felt the pressure of being under a time constraint by his boss, but he thought he had it all planned out. The girls had to go home the next day by three. Then he had his date with Renee. Yes, he could now call it a date. Then Sunday would be spent hunkered down in front of the computer, banging out this damn report. That would give him his final five days to tie up loose ends on the report and see what the hell was going on with the professor's murder investigation.

He used a broom he had bought at the Piggly Wiggly to herd out the accumulated dirt and then wiped down the counters. Even though he had eaten most of his meals on the go, some dirty dishes had piled up. The kitchen took a few more minutes. Every time he looked at Hamlet's empty cage, he got pissed off. He couldn't bring himself to toss it, so he gathered it up and took it into the apartment next door. The place had been unlocked since the crime scene technicians had finished and no one had felt there was anything in there worth stealing. Some UF people had come in and packed up the few things the professor owned, and since then no one had been by. Tasker set the cage on the small coffee table and felt himself choke up a little at the thought of his friend.

The sound of his cell phone ringing on his own kitchen counter caused him to hustle back into his apartment.

He grabbed the phone on the fourth ring. "Tasker."

"Billy, what're you crazy? Calling me so late on a Friday."

Tasker smiled at Jerry Risto's gruff voice.

"Sorry, Jerry."

"Let me guess, you need some kind of monumental favor?"

"Actually, it's important, but not too hard. A bonus is this is sanctioned by the director."

"Has that ever affected me before?"

"No, I guess not."

"Let Mr. *GQ* come up here and work the computer for a few days and then I'll be impressed when he wants something."

"C'mon, you gotta like that guy."

"I do, but it's not a good day today."

"What's wrong?"

"Nothing that losing twenty years and thirty pounds wouldn't cure. Now, what have you gotten yourself into this time?"

"Got a tip from an unusual source."

"Am I allowed to know the source?"

"Luther Williams, who you know as Cole Hodges."

"You're shittin' me."

Tasker paused. "You're who I picked that phrase up from."

"What phrase? 'You're shittin' me'?"

"Yeah. It offends a certain young lady I'm interested in."

"So blame your old fart friend. Now cut the shit and tell me about this snake Hodges, or Williams. I know he escaped."

"And he called me this morning."

"You're shit— You don't say."

"I do. He told me a captain out here at Manatee Correctional is in a corporation."

"And?"

"And you don't stop to call a cop when you're on the run unless it's important."

There was a long silence. "You may be right. Give me what you got."

Tasker gave him all the identifiers he knew on Norton and the prison.

Jerry was silent another minute and said, "Tell you what. Give me till Monday morning and I'll get this stuff, as well as anything else I dig up."

Tasker smiled. "Jerry, you're—"

"Don't say, 'the best.'"

"A big help. How's that?"

"And you're a big pain in the ass."

Tasker smiled again.

Jerry added, "Hey, kid."

"Yeah?"

"Watch your ass out there."

"Don't worry about that."

Donna Tasker pulled out of the Cuban restaurant near her house in a good mood. She liked chatting with nice people like the older, dignified black gentleman who had wished her a safe journey. It turned out to be a safe and pleasant journey. She listened to the audio version of a Randy Wayne White novel while the girls played a game with their Game Boys linked. They hardly made a sound after eating their sandwich.

After several trips, Donna no longer had problems finding Dead Cow Lane off US 27. She pulled up to the apartment complex right next to her ex-husband's Monte Carlo.

The girls raced ahead, and by the time she came to the front door they were wrapped around their father like a mink stole.

Donna joined the group hug and gave Tasker a kiss on the cheek. She glanced around the living room of the small apartment. He had kept it very tidy. She noticed the notebook computer with some paper around it on the dining room table. Good, she thought, he's focusing on his report.

But there was something wrong. He looked tired. She wondered if it was professional or personal.

He knelt down and looked the girls in the eyes. "I'm afraid I have some bad news, girls."

They stared at him.

"Hamlet passed away the other day."

Emily gasped. Donna was afraid the cumulative effect of the shooting, the professor's death and now her hamster's death might be too much for an eight-year-old.

Kelly asked, "How'd it happen?" She slung an arm around her younger sister, who had started to sob.

"I'm not sure, but it could've been old age."

Emily slowed to a sniffle and asked, "Did he die in his sleep?"

Tasker smiled a little, "Yeah, we were watching his favorite show and he dozed off."

Emily asked, "What was his favorite show?"

Donna and Kelly answered together. *"Hill Street Blues."* That made them all laugh and even Emily acknowledged it with a brief smile, then returned to sniffles.

Tasker said, "I gave him a nice funeral in the cane field and we'll find you another hamster on the way back to Mom's house tomorrow."

Donna shot him a sharp look.

He added, "But he'll still live with me."

"We have his cage at least," said Kelly.

"We'll buy a whole new setup. And you guys can name him anything you want."

Both girls brightened.

Donna stepped in. "This is all part of life, girls. Hamsters have a short life span, so you have to be ready."

Tasker added, "It's a good reason always to be nice to people and animals. Emily, you'll remember the last thing you did was kiss Hamlet on the head. What a nice memory."

It was one comment too many and the little girl started to wail and fled into the bedroom. Kelly followed for support.

After a minute, the cries subsided and Tasker sat on the couch with his ex-wife.

She said, "There's more than just the mouse."

"Hamster."

"Billy, I'm not an eight-year-old or an idiot. I know a mouse when I see one."

Tasker smiled.

"And that story about dying of old age is bull. You gonna talk to me?"

He hesitated, just like he did whenever there was a problem from which he wanted to shield her and the girls.

She ran her fingers through his light hair and said, "C'mon, you can tell me."

"Things are kinda tense out here."

She looked out the front window at the cane field and thought of the light traffic on the way out. "How?" was all she could ask.

"It's not what it looks like."

"You mean the escape. I saw on the news that they think he's long gone. Maybe in Miami."

"Luther Williams? Yeah, God knows where he's at now. He may just want us to think he's in Miami. He could be in South America by now."

"He's the one that used to go by Cole Hodges, right?"

He nodded.

"I thought it was ironic that he was at the same prison you were working at. I mean, considering your history together."

"And that's part of it. But there are things going on that"—he searched for the word—"disturb me."

"Billy, you're scaring me."

He took her hand and smiled. "Nothing to worry about. I can take care of myself."

"I know, but who'll take care of Gladesville?"

Tasker and the girls had their usual Friday night of games and food. It started with a short game of toss in the backyard after Emily had recovered sufficiently from the loss of Hamlet. She liked a small football—she could wrap her tiny hand around part of it and catch it like Jerry Rice. It sometimes frustrated Tasker that her mother wouldn't let her play peewee football. Then, as the sun set and the mosquitoes came out, they moved into the apartment, where they started an Uno tournament.

After a few rounds of the card game, near seven o'clock, Tasker asked, "What do you guys want for dinner?"

Emily shrugged, but Kelly said, "Do they have barbecue here?"

"Oh, girl, do they." Although it was against agency policy, he herded them into his state-issued Monte Carlo and headed for Sonny Boy's, the first place he had eaten upon his arrival in Gladesville.

Tasker attempted to keep his mind on the present as they settled into an empty booth in the corner and caught up on the week's events. He never wanted to admit that his ex-wife was right; he did always think of work. But try as he might, he puzzled about the marks on the door in the psych ward, about Luther Williams' escape, the professor's murder and Dewalt Construction's sudden show of community spirit. He snapped back to the conversation in time to hear about how Emily had broken the pull-up record at school and Kelly had started clarinet lessons. Tasker was relieved to hear she had forgotten her new clarinet at home.

A blond waitress with a bright smile and warm blue eyes brought them some sodas and promised to return. They reviewed the menu and found the right combination of ribs and chicken.

After a few minutes, Tasker noticed that Emily had grown unaccustomedly quiet.

"What's wrong, sweetheart?"

Her blue eyes turned up to him, making him smile as usual.

"I was going to ask you something."

"What?"

"If you like that waitress?"

He shrugged and said, "Yeah, I guess."

She started to cry and her sister, somewhat taken aback, slid closer to her on their side of the booth.

"What is it, Em?" asked Kelly, throwing an arm around her smaller sister.

Tasker thought he knew, but his youngest daughter answered.

"Last time I asked Daddy about liking a woman, it was the bank lady that got killed."

"Nothing like that will happen again, sweetheart," said Tasker, reaching across the table to take his daughter's hand.

"I know, Daddy. Not to me. But what about you? It's your job and Mama says you never give up on your job. What happens if someone shoots you?"

Like most cops, he didn't have a good answer for that. He patted her hand and told the same lie he'd heard other cops tell their kids.

"Don't worry. I don't do that stuff much anymore. I mostly handle paperwork now."

She quieted down until the waitress returned and she started to cry again. Tasker had to ask himself what he had done to his little girl.

Donna Tasker looked at the clock and bolted out of bed. She jumped into the shower without waiting for the water to heat up. As she walked back into the bedroom, fastening a bra as she headed for her panty drawer, she looked at the lump in her bed.

Nicky Goldman rolled over and she could see only his face and the white belly with black hair growing like an orange grove into one thick line down to his navel. A single sheet twisted around his stubby legs.

He opened his eyes. "What's the rush, baby? Thought a nap was supposed to relax you."

"I want to be ready in case Bill and the girls get here early."

"They're not supposed to show for another hour, and your ex never cuts things short with the girls."

"Just in case," she said, pulling up some black, conservative panties.

"I think I'm gonna slip back into peace and quiet for a few minutes."

"Think again," she said, swatting him on his wide butt. "Get dressed."

"Why?"

"Because you need to be on your way before Bill gets here."

"I thought we weren't hiding anything from Bill anymore."

"We're not."

"Then why am I hustling out of here?"

She finished dressing by pulling a blouse down over her head and looked at her boyfriend. "Fine, then you have to answer the door when he gets here."

She saw him consider the chore, then he sprang up and was in shorts and his god-awful Hawaiian shirt in a flash.

Donna Tasker actually had over an hour alone before her ex-husband walked through the door with their daughters.

She gave him a kiss, this time on the lips. "Wanna stay for dinner?" She had already started marinating some extra flank steak.

"Sorry, I gotta get back."

She frowned and said, "C'mon, Billy, it can't always be work, work, work."

He hesitated and said, "It's not."

Somehow that was worse than saying he had to work.

 **36** TASKER STOPPED AT A FLORIST IN BELLE GLADE
and bought a bouquet of flowers to give to Renee at din-
ner. He wasn't taking any chances. He knew he felt something strong for this girl and wanted to impress her. Too bad there wasn't
a nicer place to eat in Gladesville. He'd offered to take her into West
Palm, anywhere, but she had picked the Green Mile. She liked it and
that was good enough for him.

He pulled into his apartment complex near four in the afternoon and
started an unusual primping routine. He rarely did more than shower
and shave, but today he found himself trimming his nails, using some
nice aftershave and brushing his teeth like he was restoring an historic
building.

He cleaned out the car, pulling out two old Taco Bell soda cups, a
Subway wrapper and enough old fugitive info sheets to make a medium-
sized book. He had two sets of handcuffs he moved to his gear bag in the
trunk, then swept crumbs from the passenger seat before retrieving the
four dollars and eighty-two cents stuffed between the cushions. He had
told Renee he'd pick her up at her place around seven and planned to be
on time. At least she couldn't stand him up in public.

As he went about his tasks, his *chores,* as his mom used to call them, he
couldn't stop thinking about Luther Williams' call. Here he was about to
go out with a bright, beautiful, exotic woman and he was thinking

about a clue to something that could, in all likelihood, not really be his business. At least officially.

Then there was the business with Henry Janzig. Why was his print on the pendant? Renee had checked the paperwork and Janzig wouldn't have handled it. Had Leroy Baxter killed the land surveyor or was there another, obvious answer he was missing?

Then there were the subtle threats he had received. He took stock of his defenses. Basically he had his MP-5 in the Special Operations locker in Miami, his shotgun locked in his town house in Kendall and his two pistols with him. He had his Sig Sauer P-230, which he carried most places he went. The little gun had proven effective in the bank six weeks ago. He also had his department-issued Beretta 92F, .40 caliber. The bigger, heavier pistol stayed in the trunk of his car most of the time in Miami. Except for his work looking for the escapees from Manatee, he had kept the gun in his nightstand here. He knew it was safe behind the thick W.E.B. Griffin novel. Tasker smiled to himself, wondering if Griffin had ever written a book smaller than a large-frame automatic. He doubted it.

S am Norton sat at his desk clearing the last of the paperwork he hadn't gotten to during the week off the wide surface. He reached across and turned off his banker's light, which he had bought with his own money to improve his vision in the large office. A voice at his door startled him.

"You closing down the command center?" It was Renee Chin.

"Yep. Old Luther is long gone. We turned everything over to FDLE. It's their problem now." He stood, taking a second to enjoy the full-body view of Renee standing in his doorway. "What're you doing here on a Saturday?"

"I had to catch up on paper. Spent so much time working on the murder and then looking for Luther that I ignored everything else."

"You're a good inspector, Renee. We're lucky to have you."

"Thanks, Sam."

"Hope the FDLE keeps us updated on their search for Luther."

"I'll make sure and ask Bill Tasker later."

"Later tonight?"

"Yeah."

"Where will you see him?"

"We're having dinner."

"To go over info on his case?"

"Not really." She smiled from ear to ear. "More like a date."

He nodded, not wanting to reveal his true feelings. His stomach started to burn like someone had poured pool acid down his throat. He got ahold of himself and managed to ask, "Where you goin'?"

"Where else, the Green Mile."

"He really knows how to spoil a girl."

"No, it's not like that. I chose it, because it's a comfortable place and we actually met there."

"I thought you met here."

"Nope. The very first time was the Saturday before he came here."

"What time are you goin'?"

She hesitated.

"I mean, 'cause it's gettin' late."

She looked at her watch. "No, I'm okay. He's not picking me up until seven."

"Have fun," was all Norton could really get out.

Renee met Tasker at the front door to her well-kept, single-family house located in the center of the small town of Gladesville. Her Jeep Liberty was parked in the driveway and the putting-green-sized yard was neatly trimmed. She had two wooden lounge chairs on her porch, which ran the length of the front of her house. She was completely ready, and shut and locked the door without asking Tasker inside.

He followed her to his car, trying not to focus on the incredibly form-fitting jeans or the white blouse over the pink tank top that looked like it had been made for a teenager. He darted around her at the car and opened her door. She smiled as she leaned into the low Monte Carlo.

As he settled into the driver's seat, Renee said, "You look nice."

"So do you."

"Where do you keep your gun?"

He patted the black belly bag sitting on the center console. "Right here."

"Don't you always wear a gun when you go out?"

"Never if I'm going to a bar."

"Why not?"

"Just prefer not to. I'll store my Sig under the seat. You expecting trouble?"

"No, I was just wondering. That's every correctional officer's dream: to be able to carry a gun off prison property."

"I thought inspectors could."

"Usually only when we're on duty."

"I'll remember not to pick a fight with an inspector on duty."

She smiled and he relaxed on his way to the restaurant.

Inside the Green Mile, they took a booth a row off the dance floor. He couldn't keep from looking into her clear, dark eyes. Every time she looked up at him and caught him staring, she broke into a wide smile and dipped her head.

She said, "It's nicer and quieter over here than at the bar."

"I'll admit I'm surprised at the difference."

"Yeah, you probably won't have to punch anyone over in this section."

"With any luck, neither will you." He smiled, uncertain of how she'd take the joke.

"If I hadn't punched Rufus that night, then he would've taken a swing at you."

"He seems to have moved past it."

"I think Rufus hitting you is the least of your concerns out here."

"You hear any rumors about anyone else trying to scare me?"

"No, only jokes about what's happened already."

"What kind of jokes?"

"The lockdown officers refer to you as 'Mrs. Hardaway.'"

"Funny." He took a deep breath. This was the most relaxed he'd been since his arrival. "I can't laugh at some of the other stuff."

"You think the Aryan Knight encounter was staged?"

"Seemed too easy to have four guys spoiling for a fight with an outside law enforcement officer. They would've gotten in a lot of trouble."

She looked off, considering what he had said.

"And someone was snooping around my apartment, then killed Hamlet the mouse."

"I still believe that could've been anyone. Kids fooling around."

"What kids? No one lives within two miles of me."

"Who would you think is doing all this?"

Tasker looked at her. "I'd say Sam Norton."

She thought about that, too. Shaking her head, she said, "It just doesn't sound like Sam. Believe me, I'm sure he doesn't like an outsider working in the prison, but he's a straight arrow. He runs that place clean, and when he came in, he transferred anyone who was even suspected of corruption."

"Who else would do it?"

"Sam doesn't have anything to gain. Dewalt's death doesn't affect him."

He shrugged, trying to look at the problem from a different angle.

Renee reached across the table with both hands and placed them on his. She looked right into his eyes this time and said, "Now, you kept saying you had something to tell me. What is it?"

He smiled and took a breath. This was it.

She added, "And this better not be work-related."

Just as he was about to start on his well-practiced speech, he caught a movement out of the corner of his eye. He turned toward the dance floor and saw Billie Towers smile and wave as she walked toward their table.

He was about to introduce the two women and explain that Billie was Professor Kling's assistant when Renee snatched back her hands and said, "Tell me you don't know her."

"Well, I, um, yes I do."

She looked at Billie. "You have a lot of nerve coming over here."

Now Tasker sensed this wasn't a simple case of jealousy. "Renee, what's wrong?"

"Why don't you ask Ms. Towers here?"

They did know each other. Tasker looked at Billie.

The small woman's eyes widened. "I am so sorry. I didn't recognize you. I only saw you from a distance the last time."

Renee scooted back in her seat like she might jump on Billie. "Yeah, the distance from across my boyfriend's dick and his apartment."

Tasker was shocked to hear Renee speak like that.

He said, "Look, I don't understand."

Renee turned to him. "Then I'll explain it. This is the little whore Rufus hooked up with while we were dating, and apparently she gets around."

Tasker was shocked by this news. What were the chances and how in the hell could Rufus have two women like this?

Tasker said, "You mean she and Rufus . . ."

"That's right. She's the reason we broke up."

"You're shittin' me."

That did it. Renee stood straight up. "I've had all I want to take. I'm going home."

"Okay, okay, I'll take you. Just . . ."

"Bullshit you'll take me. I'll find a way home." She turned and headed straight for the front door with a few eyes following her as she marched out.

Tasker was in total shock. He looked at Billie, tears starting to drip down her face.

She said, "I'm so sorry, Bill." Then she turned and fled out the same door.

He just sat at the table trying to figure out what the hell had just happened.

37 IT WAS SUNDAY MORNING AND JERRY RISTO was actually at his desk looking at the information Bill Tasker had given him. He liked to work an occasional weekend, especially when the director authorized overtime for it. Aside from the money, he wanted to do a good job for Tasker. He liked the kid. God knows things had not been easy for him but the guy still tried to do the right thing, and most important he treated the analysts right. That wasn't always the case with cops.

There were other advantages to getting on the computer in the office on a Sunday morning. The network ran like Marion Jones, no one asked him stupid questions and the phone didn't ring off the hook. In addition, he just needed some time away from his new girlfriend. This one was young enough to be his daughter, but not as heavy. She kept him up half the night until he gave up on the damn Encite and went whole hog with the Viagra. Now he was tired and in dire need of some silence.

He started his search through public records with the name *Sam Norton,* and its variables like Samuel, that Tasker had given him. Risto then took some unconventional turns. He liked mixing official databases with public search engines like Google. After a few minutes, he had a few leads and some possible associates. He knew Tasker would be impressed, he always was.

On Monday morning, Captain Sam Norton stood up from his desk and glanced down into the exercise yard of the Rock. It was still a little early for inmates to be running around down there. He was bone tired. Yesterday was his only day off from the prison but he had other enterprises to work on when he wasn't organizing the schedule or writing reports on Luther Williams' escape.

He headed out his door and down the hall toward Inspector Chin's office. It was the third trip he had made since eight o'clock. When no one was around and he just wanted to check on her, he didn't think it mattered how often he took the short stroll. This time his effort was rewarded by the sight of the inspector at her desk, preparing her first report of the day.

He rapped on the inside of the door frame.

"Hey, Sam," she said, looking up.

Norton was surprised at her appearance. "Man, you look like you been in combat all weekend."

"Wish I were, it might have been more fun."

"Your eyes are all bloodshot. You get any sleep?"

"Yeah, but I need more."

Norton asked, "Everything all right?"

"Just a personal life that sucks."

"Wanna talk about it?" He slipped into the office and took a seat in front of her neat desk.

"No, not really. It's just that men are all the same."

"I'm not the same as other men."

She looked up and smiled and said, "You're right, Sam, you're not."

Just the comment and half-smile boosted his spirits and made him forget about some of his ongoing concerns.

Bill Tasker had tried to call Renee Chin all day Sunday, but she never picked up the phone. He even went by her small house, but the Jeep Liberty was nowhere to be seen. This morning, he had not walked past her office yet, wanting to give her some space. She'd be down to talk to him if that was what she wanted. He knew she was here because he had seen her coming up the walk from the parking lot when he had gone to the restroom. So far he was still alone in his tiny office.

He understood Renee's reaction to Billie. Had she given him a few minutes, he would've explained. Although he would've welcomed a romantic involvement with the young Seminole woman before he had fallen for Renee, the fact was that he was only friends with her. Saturday night, that seemed like a difficult point to get across.

While he was working up the courage to walk the fifty feet down the hall to explain everything to her in a calm, rational manner, his cell phone rang its odd little "Stars and Stripes Forever" tune.

He answered it, "Bill Tasker."

"I hope so, that's who I was calling."

Tasker had to smile at the sound of Jerry Risto's voice.

"Hey, Jerry, what're you doing in the office so early on a Monday?"

"I got news for you, hotshot. I was here yesterday working on your shit."

"You're a champ, Jerry. Find anything?"

"C'mon, I always find something. This time, though, there was a lot to find."

"Give me some specifics. Is Norton in a corporation?"

"He is, with a few partners. Norton is listed as the president of the GM Corporation. The corporation was formed about a year ago and its listed headquarters is in Gladesville."

"Okay, what's the corporation do?"

"Far as I can tell, it owns some property in its name."

"That's it?"

"That's all that I can get to. It has a parcel with an address of 19650 US 27, Gladesville. You'll have to find that yourself."

"That rings a bell." He looked in his desk, then started to root through the canvas briefcase he had left there. "Go ahead, what else you got?" He listened to some details while he felt through the briefcase.

Jerry went on, "Norton has been with the Department of Corrections twenty-three years. Looks like his wife filed for divorce about four months ago."

Tasker just kept saying, "Uh-huh, uh-huh," not really interested in the guy's personal problems. He pulled out his digital camera from the case and fumbled with the review button. He scrolled through the few photos, then found the one he took of the professor when he visited his archaeological dig. Behind the professor's smiling face was a crude sign with the numbers 19650 on it. This was the proposed site for the private prison near Professor Kling's archaeological dig.

"Jerry, I found it. The property is one of the sites being considered for the new private prison."

"You're shittin' me. And this mope owns it?"

"Looks like it. That's what all this heat has been about. Not the death but the site. He doesn't want me poking around anymore." Tasker thought of the possibilities. "But why?"

"Got me, kid. There are some other partners. I didn't really look into them."

"Who's that?"

"Henry Janzig."

"Yeah, he's a tough old sergeant out here. They must be looking to retire rich."

"Aren't we all?"

"Who else?"

"R. A. Chin. He work out there, too?"

Tasker froze. Just as Jerry said her name, Renee Chin appeared at his doorway.

"Yeah, Jerry. He does. Hey, listen. Can I call you back for the rest of this?"

"One of 'em just walk in the room?"

"Exactly."

"Good luck, kid."

"Think I'm gonna need it." He kept his eyes on her, but this time it was for a different reason.

38

RENEE CHIN STOOD AT THE DOOR TO THE TINY office the warden had let Tasker use to work on his report. He was on his sleek little cell phone and all she heard him say was, "Exactly," and "Think I'm gonna need it." Some part of her reacted like he was talking to that Native American slut Billie Towers. The rational side of her didn't really believe that. She didn't think he was that kind of guy. It was just the sight of that perky, perfect smile coming toward him that made her flash back to the day she caught Rufus Goodwin at his house, on a Thursday evening. That whore coming out of his bathroom naked. Naked. That had almost been too much.

Now she forced a smile as Tasker folded his phone and re-holstered it on his hip holder.

"Hi," she said, looking down at the clean, cheap carpet.

"Hi," he answered.

"Did you try to call me yesterday?"

"Couple of times." He nodded, doing a good job of keeping cool.

"I didn't answer the phone." She paused, then added, "Yesterday."

Tasker just looked at her without saying a word. She felt like his blue eyes were looking inside her. She hadn't seen this from the FDLE agent before.

Renee said, "You'd have to know the full history I have with that girl."

"I pieced it together pretty well."

"But you don't think that's an excuse."

"You're an adult. Your behavior is your own choice."

She nodded and turned away from the door, thinking, I blew it.

An hour later, Tasker was in his car. He didn't really know where he was headed, but knew he had to get away from the prison. Jerry Risto's phone call had hit him hard. He could easily accept that Sam Norton and his crony, Henry Janzig, were involved in a scam of some kind. He had already suspected them of setting him up with the inmates. They wanted him to hurry the investigation and it looked like they were hiding something in the Dewalt death.

The news that Renee was involved with them was much more troubling. It brought up the question of whether she was only interested in him to find out about the report. This wasn't the first time a woman had used Tasker to further her own financial situation.

Tasker pulled into the lone Chevron station in town and started to pump some medium grade into his state car. He could sure use a beer, he thought, but realized it was the wrong time and he was still on duty, although he had no idea how he'd concentrate on anything at the prison. He had to piece this thing together and then tell the director what the hell was going on. Realistically he needed to ask for help or maybe hand it off completely, but in his gut he knew he wanted to see it through.

As he contemplated his options and pumped the gas, his cell phone rang. He opened his Nextel and saw the name *Billie* on the screen.

He answered, "Hey, how're you?"

"Good," said a male voice. "This Bill Tasker?"

Tasker held the phone at arm's length and looked at the name again. It clearly read *Billie*. He said, "Yeah, this is Tasker. Who's this?"

"Captain Norton."

Tasker was confused, but answered quickly, "Didn't recognize your voice."

"I needed to pass on some info on Luther Williams and didn't know who at FDLE to call."

"What's the info?"

"That he has a gun."

"Who, Luther Williams?"

"Who else would I be talking about?"

"Where'd you hear that?"

"One of the inmates. He had a contact on the outside that spoke to Luther."

"I need to talk to the inmate."

"No can do. He's my snitch. I'm the only one he'll talk to."

"Need to verify some facts."

"Then ask me and I'll ask him. But it seems to me that knowing an escaped inmate is armed is something the cops lookin' for him would need to know."

"I'll pass it on and I'll give them your phone number if they have any questions. How's that?"

"That's fine. Give 'em my office number. I just called you from my house. I'm on lunch."

Tasker made the connection immediately. Billie had called him from Norton's home phone last time. Was everyone in town in on this scam?

Norton hung up on the FDLE agent, looked up at his friend Henry Janzig and started to laugh.

Janzig said, "What'd he say?"

"He'd pass it along. Gave me some shit about talking to the snitch, but I just brushed it off."

Janzig took another bite of his turkey sandwich as he sat back and enjoyed the cool air in Norton's kitchen.

Norton said, "If that don't scare those FDLE guys chasing him into shootin' first and askin' questions later, then nothin' will."

"Yeah, them boys'll shoot, too. They got them MP-three machine guns."

"MP-five."

"Whatever. It'll kill old Luther just as quick as a flash."

"Then that'll be one less problem we'll have to worry about."

"Told you we should've got a real attorney to draw up them papers."

Norton scowled at the older man. "Number one, we didn't have to pay him nothin' but a cake job in the library. Two, we didn't know what a lawyer on the outside would say. We could control Luther. At least when he was inside. And number three, it's done. We can't go back, so stop worrying about it, you old goat."

The corrections sergeant laughed and took another bite of his sandwich.

Tasker eased his car into the rear lot of an industrial park that gave him a clear line of sight to the back road that led to the housing for the prison personnel. The hodgepodge of cheap, plain buildings and manufactured homes served over half the prison employee population. He took his big Tasco binoculars and realized he could see all the way down to the first row of trailers along the rear fence of Manatee. He had to be sure. He didn't want to think that Billie would be involved with this group, but if she'd been in the trailer once, she'd be there again.

He sat and watched, knowing he'd get no backup or relief. This was something he'd do himself until he was satisfied. He made some notes on a legal pad so he could adequately brief his director when the time came. He had a little chart at the top where he wrote Norton's name in a square, then added squares for Janzig and Renee on either side. This was the corporation he had hard info on. Then at an angle on the page, he wrote Billie Towers in the corner. He gazed at the paper and tried to think if anyone else could be involved.

An hour after he started his surveillance, the first vehicle came out of the housing area. He picked up his heavy-duty binoculars and zeroed in on the big sedan moving toward him on the dirt road. He could clearly see the driver was an older black man in a brown DOC uniform.

Over the next hour, he saw three more cars, all leaving and none of them occupied by anyone who looked even remotely like Billie Towers. Then, in the late afternoon, he saw a blue pickup truck cut off the highway and zip down the road. The truck moved so fast he didn't get a good look, but he saw dark hair and a small frame. A few minutes later, the truck came back out the road, giving Tasker plenty of time to use the binoculars to clearly see what he didn't want to see: Billie Towers driving the old Ford pickup they had used on the professor's dig.

**39** TASKER SAT AT THE SUB SHOP OFF US HIGHWAY
27 near the prison, picking at a turkey on whole wheat. In-
tellectually he knew he had to eat, but emotionally he
didn't want to. Was everyone in this town in on Norton's scam and using him? Renee was bad enough, he had feelings for her, but Billie Towers? He never would've guessed she was a crook. Now the motive for the
professor's murder was in question, as well as the suspect. Had he discovered the scheme? Tasker didn't want to try to figure out that line of
reasoning past what he already knew.

He grabbed his large Coke and tossed most of the sandwich as he
nodded to the cute high-school girl behind the counter. His Monte
Carlo was on the far side of the parking lot to take advantage of the
shade from a black olive tree in the swale. It was getting late in the afternoon, but keeping cars cool is a way of life in Florida. It becomes a
habit.

As he approached the car, he noticed a movement on the far side.
Then he heard a small pop and hiss and the car's angle changed. He
quick stepped to the rear of the Monte Carlo, careful not to crunch in
the gravel. He peeked around the edge of the trunk and saw a man
crawling toward the front of the car. Tasker took a quick look around to
make sure the guy was alone, then quietly crept up directly behind him.
Tasker watched as the man placed the tip of the blade of an open buck
knife against the front tire.

"Do it and you'll be digging that knife out of your ass," said Tasker, now slightly turned to kick the vandal hard in the head if he had to.

The man turned, sat up and looked at Tasker. He said, "I got the knife."

Tasker jerked the drawstring of his belly bag, exposing his Sig P-230 automatic. "I gotta gun." He swiveled his head again to make sure the vandal was alone. "Listen, dumb-ass, right now that's enough reason to shoot you."

The man opened his hand and let the knife drop onto the ground.

Tasker nodded. "Good move." He realized he recognized the young, thin man. "Shit, you're an officer at Manatee. What's your name? All I can think is Loretta Lynn."

The young man swallowed and looked at the ground and mumbled, "Lester Lynn."

"That's right. We have some issues, don't we?"

The man remained silent.

Tasker said, "Look, I'm out of patience with you guys. I'm gonna ask some questions and you're gonna fucking answer them or—"

The man made a quick grab for the knife on the ground before Tasker gave him the options. Tasker didn't even draw his pistol. He just stomped down hard on the man's hand, feeling the small bones of his fingers snap under his running shoe.

Tasker reached down, grabbed the man by his ear and hoisted him upright, the man squealing like a little kid the whole way. Tasker shoved him against the car and then patted him down roughly as the man nursed his crushed fingers.

"You were gonna try and stab me? What made you think you'd be able to do that?"

"Had to try and scare you. I ain't gonna answer no questions."

"You're not?"

"No, sir."

"We'll see."

"When?"

"After you change my tire."

"You crazy? I can't change nothin', my fingers is broke."

"Didn't say it wouldn't hurt." Tasker shoved him toward the rear of the car and opened the trunk, keeping his eyes on the man.

"Okay, Lester," Tasker started. "You got the tire in front of you. I know there are no guns in there, so it's time."

"Time for what?"

"To get to work."

Sullenly, the man reached in the trunk. He fumbled, using his left hand to free the tire, then yanked out the jack and tire iron.

Tasker took a step back, half-cautious and mostly enjoying the man's suffering. A little payback for the problems he had caused.

After half an hour of effort, Lester, face blackened with dirt, shirt smeared black, finished the job.

"We're even, satisfied?"

"You have got to be shittin' me." Tasker shoved him around to the other side and then into the passenger seat of the car. He came back around to the driver's side, zipped up his gun pouch and then hopped in the car. He pulled out onto US Highway 27 and headed west toward Lake Okeechobee without acknowledging his passenger.

After a few minutes of driving, the young man asked, "Where are we goin'?"

"To a place where I can question you properly." He kept his eyes on the road, never turning to the flustered vandal.

"I got nothing to say. I wanna call me an attorney."

Now Tasker let out a little smile. "You're mistaken. I don't arrest people for misdemeanors. You're not under arrest."

"I don't wanna go nowhere with you, so you're kidnapping me."

Tasker said, "Now you're finally catching on."

Luther Williams had spent the night in a lower-end, oceanfront hotel in Daytona Beach. As rough as that town was, no one would notice a nicely dressed, middle-aged black man checking into a cheap hotel alone and paying cash. He had tipped the clerk an extra twenty to keep him quiet if anyone came looking for him.

The ride north on I-95 the next morning was uneventful as he stayed about six miles over the speed limit and usually kept with traffic. His Buick LeSabre wasn't going to attract the attention of too many cops. He took Interstate 210 near Jacksonville past the Naval Air Station, then ended up heading due west on Interstate 10. Now it was just a straight shot across a few states to his new, temporary home.

The light traffic on I-10 encouraged him to pick up the pace a little, still staying with the few cars on the road but now riding near eighty miles an hour. The newer Buick had a fine, smooth ride and the stereo had a good bass as he listened to an oldies station out of South Georgia. He relaxed as he made good time. In the trunk, he had hidden two pistols he took from Scooter Brown's house. The two automatics were both nine-millimeters, one a Browning Hi-power and the other one of those Czechoslovakian CZs. They were both loaded and ready to go. Up under the bench seat fold-down armrest, he had the Sig nine-millimeter he had bought from a guy he knew from his days as legal counsel to the Committee for Community Relief. The big model 226 packed a punch and was easy to handle.

Just west of the turnoff for I-75, near Lake City, he passed a Florida Highway Patrol trooper's vehicle sitting in the median of the highway.

"Shit," Luther said to himself, as he quickly checked the rearview mirror to see if the brown-and-yellow marked car came onto the highway. Just as he thought he had made it away cleanly, he noticed a vehicle in his rearview closing the gap quickly. It was the damn trooper.

Briefly he considered trying to outrun him, but knew that would never work. He lifted the armrest to see the black pistol underneath and then moved over into the right lane. The trooper followed right behind him, then turned on his overhead flashing blue lights.

Luther immediately pulled to the shoulder of the road, his eyes in his rearview watching the trooper pull in behind him. He had some decisions to make. The trooper would run his tag, which would come back to the owner of the Buick from whom he had stolen the tag. He had no idea who that was, so he couldn't even lie about the name. The Florida driver's license he had would hold up. Mr. Nyren's contacts were the best. They used legitimate DL numbers that matched the name you were given. In Luther's case, he was now Louis Drexler. He liked it because it was a little different but not outlandish. He saw the trooper slowly emerge from his Crown Victoria. A tall, blond cop, about thirty. Luther moved the pistol under the armrest slightly so he could grab it quickly when he had to.

Luther lowered the window as the trooper walked up. He knew he should grasp the pistol now and shoot before there was any chance the cop knew what was happening. As soon as he heard the cop say, "License and registration," he'd pick up the pistol and put a nine-millimeter slug in his face. He didn't want to, but he'd come too far to go back now.

The trooper stopped, then leaned down, looking into the car before he spoke.

Tasker turned down a dirt road he had chosen at random. He pulled in toward the dike that surrounded Lake Okeechobee. The grass-covered, earthen mound had been shoved into place at different intervals over the years by different groups of men who thought they could control the giant freshwater lake. They had been wrong a couple of times, and Mother Nature, in the form of a hurricane in 1928, had shown them that the lake wasn't always going to stay right where they wanted it.

With each passing mile, Lester, nursing his three broken fingers, grew more nervous. "Look, let me off here and we'll call it all even. Sort've my punishment for playing a prank."

Tasker kept quiet. He knew setting had more to do with an interview than almost anything else. If taking the time to find the right setting also served to unnerve Correctional Officer Lester Lynn, then all the better.

"C'mon, Mr. Tasker. I didn't mean nothin' by it. Just having a little fun."

Now Tasker stopped the car. A path in the brush led to the top of the dike. It was nearly dark and they were at least three miles off the highway. He shut off the car and then, without a word, climbed out and walked around to Lester's door. He opened it and grabbed the startled correctional officer by his shirt, then pulled him out of the car.

"Wait a minute. Where you taking me?"

Tasker shoved him toward the path.

Lester had to take some wide steps to keep his balance. He let his right hand touch the ground to keep from falling, but his damaged fingers made him yelp. Once he had his balance, he picked up his pace. He darted up the path ahead of Tasker.

Tasker calmly said, "Nowhere to run, Lester. We're not near anything at all."

Lester realized the truth of the statement and stopped running. Once Tasker caught up to him, they walked together to the rim of the dike. The top was wide and flat like three lanes of a running track. The open black water spread out toward the north and west. There was nothing in the water nearby. No trees or small islands, just water. Like a calm ocean. With the sun now gone, the water had no color to it. Just blackness. The rising moon gave off enough light to make Tasker feel alone out there.

Tasker looked toward the water, ignoring Lester like he was no threat whatsoever. He stretched, reaching his arms high like he had learned in yoga. He cut his eyes to make sure Lester was as beaten as he seemed. He didn't want to be surprised if the tall correctional officer took a swing at him. He was satisfied the young man was open to a real talk. He also had waited long enough that he no longer wanted to kill somebody.

He kept looking out over the water and said, "So, Lester, how do the fingers feel?"

Lester hesitated. "Sore. You broke 'em."

"You realize that if you don't play ball with me, that'll be the most pleasant thing that happens to you tonight?"

"What kind of cop are you, anyway?"

Tasker turned toward him now. "A pissed-off one. I've been fucked with since the first day I came to this shithole. Now I want some answers. Understand?"

Lester took a step back, nodding his head.

"First things first. Did you let Linus Hardaway loose on me in lock-down?"

Lester was silent.

"Nothing is gonna happen to you. I just need to know."

Lester started to speak, then stopped.

"Lester, the longer this takes, the more pissed-off I get."

The young man mumbled, "Yeah, it was me."

"Good. Now, wasn't that easy?"

Lester nodded.

"Now the question is, who told you to do it?"

"No one."

"You know how I can tell you're lying?"

"How?"

"'Cause you're screaming." He grabbed two of Lester's damaged fingers and squeezed. The young man screamed like a lightning siren on a golf course.

Tasker stayed calm. "Now, who told you to do it?"

Lester took a few seconds to settle down and catch his breath. Panting, he said, "Sergeant Janzig just told me to let something happen. I thought of Linus myself." He sucked in some more air. "I woulda done anything to get a transfer to the control room."

Tasker never took his eyes off the correctional officer. He sure looked like he was telling the truth. "So you let me fight off a crazed inmate to impress your bosses."

"Yeah, I guess."

"What about the Aryan Knights? You have anything to do with that?"

"No, nothing, I swear to God."

"Then who did?"

Lester kept his mouth shut.

"I know someone did. I didn't just run into a group of thugs who only wanted to kick my ass and not anyone else's."

Lester remained silent.

Tasker grabbed him by the shoulders and nudged him toward the dark water.

"Wait, wait, wait. I didn't have nothin' to do with them crazy Nazi guys. They're Janzig's boys."

"He tell them to go after me?"

"Don't know what he told them, but he told me to ignore it on the control room monitor."

"I thought you worked in the psych ward?"

"They're letting me work the control room when it suits them."

Then Tasker looked at him differently. He remembered talking to him briefly about Dewalt, then dismissing him. "You love that control room job?"

"Yes, sir."

"And you would've done anything to get out of the psych ward?"

"Yeah, I guess."

Now Tasker got ready to throw out the big one. He had the pieces. The forensics, the marks on the psych ward door and now a motive. Tasker looked at the young man and said, "You'd even cover up Rick Dewalt's suicide?"

The young man just stared at him silently. He didn't have to say anything. He sank down, then plopped to his butt on the grass.

Tasker squatted next to him. "C'mon, compared to the other shit, it's not that serious. You found him hanging from the door and moved him, right?"

Lester started to cry. "I'd just been there so long and I knew the sergeant would be pissed. Dewalt was dead. What did it matter if they thought someone killed him and dumped him outside?" He started to sob.

"He ever say why?"

Lester caught his breath and said, "He was always down about being locked up. He said his dad was some big shot who was embarrassed by him. I never thought he'd do anything like that. I mean, the look on his face with that belt he'd taken from the officers' station around his neck."

"Then what happened?"

He shrugged. "Nothing. I got him down. Took the belt and used some old rope to tie his hands so it looked like he was murdered. I just tossed his body out the door so no one would see me."

Tasker stood up. "Shit, son, compared to some of the people at Manatee, you're a fucking model state employee."

Lester stood up, too, sniffling. "I swear I had nothin' against you. Janzig and Norton call the shots."

Tasker nodded and thought about that info. It still came back to Norton. And Renee. Shit. Then Tasker said, "So you guys set me up in the prison. That I understand. What did Professor Kling's death have to do with it all?"

"Death. Are you crazy? No one had nothin' to do with a killing."

Tasker thought about tossing him in the water, whether he was being honest or not. "Then why are you guys picking at me with slashed tires? That doesn't do much to scare me."

"The captain told me to do your tires. Said they just needed to keep you occupied until Friday when you have to leave. Said getting new tires would use up some time."

"So he just wanted me occupied until Fri—" Tasker froze. How did Norton know he was leaving on Friday? Only one person knew of the timetable. He had to ask the obvious question. "How does Norton know I'm leaving on Friday?"

The young man shrugged. "He don't tell me shit. He says harass you, cut up your tires, put sugar in your gas tank, I do it."

Tasker had enough info for one day. "All right, Lester. I'll take you up on your offer."

"What offer?"

"I'll leave you right here and we'll call it even. We'll deal with moving Dewalt's body another day."

Lester didn't protest.

"And don't you tell Norton about our talk."

Lester nodded.

"And you come tell me if he tells you to do anything else."

"But he'll whip my ass if I do something like that."

"Then there's only one thing you have to remember."

"What's that?"

Tasker reached out and grabbed Lester's broken fingers again. This time he fell to his knees as he screamed.

Luther Williams' right hand gripped the Sig Sauer P-226, waiting for the phrase "license and registration" to come from the trooper. Once he knew there was no going back it was gonna be lights out for this cop. To his surprise, the first thing the trooper said was, "Hi, how're you today?"

Luther gathered himself and looked at the young man with his big blond head leaning in Luther's window like a puppy. "I am fine today, Officer. How are you?"

"Good, good." The tall man pulled his head back from the window. "Sir, could you step out of your car, please."

It was not a question; it was a command. A polite command but one nonetheless. Luther looked up at the trooper. He looked like a tall Tasker with the same light coloring and pleasant face. His eyes weren't as intelligent-looking as Tasker's.

Luther considered his options. Since he had allowed the trooper to step back, the immediate shot was no longer a sure thing. He had no desire to kill this young man, but his survival instinct was his overriding drive. He put his left hand on the door handle and his right remained on the grip of the pistol.

The trooper said, "I wanna show you something."

Luther slammed the armrest down on the pistol and slid out of the car. This wouldn't have been a consideration in his younger days. He decided he could always say his wallet was in the car and reach for the gun if he needed to.

He stepped out and stood up. He was a good three inches shorter than the big trooper. "Yes, Officer?"

"When you passed me a while back, it looked like your wheel was about to fly off. Now that you're stopped, I see the problem." He pointed at the LeSabre's left front tire. "See."

Luther looked at the black wall tire and didn't see anything out of the ordinary. "I'm afraid I don't see, Officer."

"Look here." He squatted by the car and rapped the hubcap with his knuckles. "You got a good dent in your hubcap, and at high speed it looks like the damn wheel is floppin' around. Scared me pretty good."

Luther smiled. "I guess it did. Should I remove the hubcap or just risk that few people will be as observant as you?"

"I'd yank it off. Might pop off itself and it could hurt someone."

"I'll take care of it."

"Just give me your tire iron and I'll pop it off for you. No need you get all dirty on account of this."

Luther was stunned. Here he was in what many called "lower Alabama," a black man, and a white cop was offering to help him. Times had changed since he first arrived in Florida. He scooted to the driver's compartment and retrieved the keys. As he leaned in, he looked down at the armrest where the gun was hidden. He hesitated. Could this cop have tricked him? He looked through the rear window. The big trooper wasn't on his shoulder mike to his radio. Luther decided to ride it awhile longer.

He straightened out of the car and jingled the keys. "Got 'em right here."

The trooper stepped back and said, "Where are you heading?"

Here it was—the start of an interrogation. Luther paused at the trunk. "Tallahassee."

"Too busy there for me. Where you comin' from?"

"Miami."

"Way too busy there."

Luther popped the trunk and started to raise the lid when he glanced down and saw the Browning nine-millimeter sitting on the floor of the trunk. He risked a quick look at the trooper and saw he was looking down the highway at a Camaro that had just swooshed by. Luther reached in, grabbed the pistol and shoved it to the side. He slid a rag over it and found the tire iron loose on top of the spare. He snatched it up and closed the trunk.

"Here you go."

The trooper took it, still tracking the Camaro with his eyes. Then he snapped out of it. "Take one second." He squatted again and used the straight black tire tool to pry the hubcap in several places and then pull it off. He even checked the lug nuts to ensure Luther's safety. "All set." He stood up with the dented hubcap in his hand.

"Here, I'll take that."

"It's pretty grimy," said the trooper.

"Nonsense." Luther snatched the metal hubcap from his hand. He popped the trunk and opened it only a few inches as he slid the hubcap inside.

The trooper stepped back toward his car. "Have a safe trip to Talla-hassee."

"Thanks for everything."

"Sure." The trooper paused. "Why're you goin' to T-town?"

Luther almost made a beeline for his Sig in the car. Was this guy so subtle or was he just chatting?

Luther said, "My daughter is at FAMU."

"Oh yeah. What's she study?"

"She wants to be a pharmacist."

"Outstanding. Good luck." The trooper turned and was in his car be-fore Luther. He was down the road before Luther even started the car. Luther took a few breaths to calm down and clear his mind. That was freaky.

**40** BILL TASKER WAITED BY THE FRONT DOOR OF
the Gladesville Police Department. He didn't want to just
walk in; he wanted to surprise Rufus when he came out for
some reason. The place was small enough that the town's only detective
would have to wander out into the lobby area soon. A few cops had come
from the back to the lobby for one reason or another, but not Rufus.

Tasker hadn't slept much since his unofficial interrogation of the
slow-witted Lester Lynn. The one thing that had spooked him was
Lester's knowledge that he was leaving at the end of the week. Tasker
had spoken to only one person about leaving at the end of the week and
that was his boss, the director. How had Norton found out?

Tasker grew impatient waiting for his target to come out. He noticed
the door to the inner offices was slow to close after someone came
through. He waited until a clerical worker with glasses and hair that
looked like an African anthill came out into the lobby. He saw her head
toward a soda machine and deposit some coins. Tasker stepped inside
and then as she went back through the door he followed right behind.
No one noticed him.

He headed down the main hallway, nodding hello to a public service
aide like he belonged in the building. She smiled back. He turned and in
a few steps was in the doorway of Rufus Goodwin's train wreck of an
office. The frazzled detective was reviewing some paperwork at his desk,

surrounded by stacks and stacks of paper. He didn't even notice Tasker until he cleared his throat.

Rufus' head snapped up. "How'd you get in here?"

"I'm a cop. I thought cops could come back here."

"What d'you want?"

"What do you think?"

"Look, I'm doing the best I can. I thought the nut did it. Now I'm back to square one."

"What if I had some info? Would you check out the connection?"

The detective perked up, his half-mast brown eyes opening ever so slightly. "What d'ya got?"

"I found out some of the correctional officers at Gladesville are in a corporation together."

"So?"

"This corporation owns some land locally."

"Stop with the drama. So what?"

"The land is one of the proposed sites for the new prison. The site next to the professor's dig."

Luther considered this. "I'm still not sure why this would relate to the murder."

"Neither am I, but it's something we can't ignore."

"I told you there is no 'we.' I'm working this homicide."

"Then you better start moving on it, because I have a feeling some shit is about to start happening."

Rufus rubbed his face and said, "You sure do get stuck on stuff. You ever think where you'd be if you concentrated on your own job?"

"All the time," was all Tasker could say.

Sam Norton prowled the corridor outside the main entrance to the facility. Everything was in order, but the officers needed to see him walking inside the fence or they might get slack. He had enough problems in his life without his officers going soft.

He walked with a slightly faster gait that morning because Renee Chin had gone out of her way to say hello and check on him. She had appreciated his concern for her and their little talk the day before and now she noticed him as something more than just the captain of the correctional officers. He liked that.

As he turned toward the stairs for the second-story control tower where he knew Lester Lynn was working, he found the young correctional officer coming out the door, almost slamming into the much shorter captain.

"Whoa there, boy. Where are you headin'?"

"Infirmary." He raised his right hand to show the captain his three heavily bandaged fingers. "Emergency room said the nurse should check the dressing today. I told them I worked here." He smiled at his intelligence to tell the hospital about his job.

"What happened?"

The young man paused. "I broke 'em."

"How?"

"Closed the trunk of my car on 'em."

Norton shook his head. "Dumb-ass. What about Tasker's car? You cut up the tires?"

"Only one."

"Why only one? He can change one tire."

"I found him over at the sub shop off 27. I got one tire real good, but he came out."

"Did he see you?"

"Nope. I'm pretty slick."

"Well, Slick, why didn't you call me last night like I told you to?"

"Lost my phone."

"What 'bout the phone at home. Your mama stop payin' the bill?"

"No, sir, it was just late, so I didn't call."

Norton glared at him. Was this kid really that stupid? He looked at him closely and decided he was.

"Okay. I'll let you know what we need to do next." He stalked off before the young man could answer.

Tasker pulled up to the apartment building where Billie Towers lived. The truck she drove was parked in the street. Since talking to Lester and Rufus, he was concerned that everyone in town knew his next move. That would've surprised him because he didn't know his next move.

He checked the mailboxes posted outside the front door. There were eight apartments. All of the downstairs apartments had names clearly typed on the boxes. They were the longer-term residents. The upstairs apartments had two names filled in with blue ink. One was Lowesen, the other started with a *P* and had five unintelligible letters. He headed upstairs. The two unmarked rooms were at the top of the stairway.

He tapped lightly on the first door and then held his hand to the thin door to feel any movement inside. Nothing. He knocked on the door across the hall more forcefully. After a few seconds, he felt the vibration of someone walking. Then he heard Billie's soft voice say, "Who is it?"

"Billie, it's Bill Tasker."

She opened the door a crack to peek, then all the way. "What're you doin' here?" She had a sly smile on her face like she knew.

"Can I come in?"

"Sure." She stepped to the side to give him free access.

Inside he surveyed the modest apartment. It had a small living room with a kitchen built into one corner, a bathroom and a separated bedroom that from his angle he could see looked tiny. He settled onto the lone, uncomfortable couch and she flopped next to him, turning to face him with her legs crossed.

"What's up?" She let loose with one of her brilliant smiles.

"You tell me."

"Tell you what?"

"What's up."

"Billy, you're not making any sense. I told you the other night I didn't mean to upset your date. I guess she explained how we met at Rufus' house."

"That's old news." He looked into her dark eyes and hoped she had nothing to do with the growing conspiracy he had stumbled onto. "What about your new boyfriend?"

"What new boyfriend?"

"I know about the captain. Now I need to know about his plan."

She looked at him, her throat moving as she swallowed hard. At least the girl wasn't a skilled liar like some of the crooks he generally had to deal with. He just looked at her and let her come to her own conclusions about what he knew and how he found out.

"I shouldn't have flirted with you, Billy. Not while I was with Sam Norton."

"Now that we have the bullshit out of the way, can I get some answers?" He watched, but she didn't flinch. "You just happened to be around asking questions at the right time?"

She kept staring with her eyes wide.

"A young girl like you hooks up with Norton and Rufus. C'mon, all I want is the truth, not one of your chameleon tricks where you morph into the girl I'm most comfortable with. You need to talk, and now."

She looked off into space. "You just don't understand, Bill."

"Every time we were together, you asked about my investigation or why I was so hung up on the professor's murder. How much did you tell Norton?"

"That's not how it was."

Now Tasker started to raise his voice. "What did Professor Kling do to get killed?"

Billie was flustered. "I didn't have anything to do with that. I . . ."

"You what? How long has that asshole Norton been getting you to do his spy work?"

She started to cry, but he wasn't sure if it was sincere or a play for time. She leaned toward him with her head on his shoulder, then blew snot onto his sleeve. She seemed pretty sincere.

Renee Chin sat in her office thinking about Bill Tasker and what he was doing right now. He wasn't at the prison and he wasn't answering his phone. She didn't want to swing by his apartment because it might look like she was stalking him.

In front of her were two official reports she was updating and they had something in common: Luther Williams. In one report she listed all the evidence about the killing of the Aryan Knight Vic Vollentius. The other clearly stated that Luther was the only suspect in the Robert Moambi homicide. For an older inmate, the guy had caused a lot of trouble in a short period of time. She had searched through his personal belongings looking for clues as to where he might have gone, but so far nothing had panned out. The big white woman who visited him was under surveillance because she was the closest link, but Renee didn't think that would lead anywhere. The cops needed to think outside the box a little more. Luther was unpredictable and his girlfriend was too obvious. He was on the move now and she knew it.

Although she liked the distraction of thinking about her job, it didn't hide her feelings for Bill Tasker. Sure, the report might have gotten in the way of a relationship. She didn't know what he would write or even how he viewed her professionally. That didn't seem to matter because he had avoided her since yesterday morning when she tried to apologize. It was tough trying to understand a man's sensitivities.

Tasker let Billie cry and cry hard for almost twenty minutes before she pulled away. His shoulder and sleeve were soaked with her tears. She stood up and walked to the small kitchen. Tasker followed her with his eyes. She was a suspect now, not just a good-looking girl. She blew her nose and wiped her eyes with a napkin, then slowly sulked back to the couch.

She said, "Okay, I'll admit to falling for the wrong guy. He's a lot older than me, but that's always been my weakness."

"I'm sorry. Which older guy are we talking about?"

"Sam Norton."

"How long you been together?"

"Almost as long as I've been here. Maybe four months."

"I thought Renee caught you with Rufus about a month ago."

"She did."

"The older guy thing again?"

She shrugged. "Sam Norton needed me to find out if Rufus was serious about Renee. Said it was all business. All I did was test the relationship."

"And Norton sent you after me, too?"

"Not all the time. But, yeah, a couple of times."

"What about the professor?"

"What about him?"

"You give info to Norton about him?"

"Not that kind, but I did tell him what we found on the site."

"Why did he care?"

"I don't know."

"What'd he want to know about me?"

"Everything. Mostly how far along you were and when you were going to leave."

"Did he kill the professor?"

"I swear he said no."

"Do you believe him?"

"I'm afraid not to."

"Do you know what's going on with the site for the prison?"

She shrugged.

"Can you keep this conversation from Norton?"

"Not if he asks me."

At least she was being honest now. Tasker said, "Fuck it. He knows I'm looking. Tell him I'm ready for him now."

**41** BILLIE TOWERS TOOK MORE THAN AN HOUR TO regain her composure after Bill Tasker left her ratty little apartment. She felt ashamed for her actions and embarrassed that the good-looking cop had caught on so easily. Did money mean that much to her? Maybe she did it all for love? Was Sam Norton who she wanted to spend her life with? She liked Professor Kling, and the thought that he'd died so they could all get rich was becoming more and more difficult for her to swallow. Maybe it was a good thing it was coming out into the open. She hadn't really done anything wrong. She had done what her older lover had told her to do. Any judge would look at her and feel sorry for the little Seminole girl caught up in something over her head. Suddenly she started to feel better.

As she got up from the couch to wash her face there was a knock at her front door. She hesitated but turned and took a few steps toward the door. She stopped and checked herself in the mildewed mirror that hung on the wall next to the wooden door.

The knock came again.

Billie asked, "Who is it?"

"Me."

She cracked the door to peek outside, then, recognizing her visitor, opened the door wide to let him in.

He said, "You been crying?"

"Some."

"You tell Tasker anything?"

"Nothing he didn't already know."

"What'd he know?"

"'Bout the site. Maybe some other details."

"Where's he headed?"

She shrugged, growing tired of the questioning and starting to feel like she'd been used.

"He coming back?"

"Doubt it." She backed into the living room a few steps, feeling uneasy about her visitor.

"You fuck him or is that for a later visit?" He reached out and grabbed her wrist.

She tried to twist away, but his grip felt like a handcuff. "Let go."

"Now you're *offended* by having to fuck all the time?"

She struggled harder until a big left hand smacked her across the temple, knocking her senseless but leaving her on her feet.

Her visitor said, "I got an idea how to keep you from fucking or talking to Tasker."

He let go of her wrist, but she was still too dazed to try to run. Besides, there was no place to go in the tiny apartment. She felt his hands link together around her small throat and then tighten. Not suddenly, but slow and steady like he wanted her to realize what was happening. And she did. Somewhere in the back of her mind, she thought that this would be a good time for the dashing Bill Tasker to burst through the door and rescue her.

As he tightened his hands, her visitor said, "Keep your eyes open as long as you can. You owe me that."

Bill Tasker avoided the prison and stopped to get something to eat. It was late in the afternoon and he ran through his options in his head. Should he call to get help? But who? If the director had called and told Norton about Tasker leaving on Friday, then he was part of it. He had friends inside FDLE he could ask for help. They'd come like the cavalry.

He figured, with his guard up, he had a couple more days. Then an idea hit him. Maybe one of the more unpalatable ideas he had had in a long while. The FBI. They would have jurisdiction over the corruption aspect of the case. If his director was involved, they would be about the only ones who could do anything about it. But did he really want to involve them? He hadn't had much luck in the past with them. Would they even listen to him, given his history with the Bureau?

He had hoped Jerry Risto might have some more info for him by now. Tasker never knew what the intelligence analyst would come up with. He didn't want to call because that only slowed him down. He was the most reliable guy Tasker knew. If he found something, he'd call.

Tasker drove his Monte Carlo west out US 27, past the turnoff for Manatee Correctional. A trooper's cruiser was on the side of the road. As he passed the police car, he could see it was his old friend Trooper Miko, who "owned the road" and knew it was his duty to keep people safe. Tasker smiled at the trooper's insinuation that Tasker wasn't a "real cop." He drove on to Dead Cow Lane and turned left down the long road bordered by cane fields. He kept his eyes ahead because he didn't want to be surprised. There had been a few new residents in the state housing who came and went over the last week, but he wasn't taking any chances. When he thought like a crook and tried to figure out tactics, he decided if he wanted to ambush someone, this isolated apartment complex would be perfect.

He loosened the string on his belly pack, pulling the zipper open three inches. The hammer of his Sig Sauer P-230 was visible. He wished he had his Beretta with him. Now was a good time to start carrying two weapons. Issued and backup.

He slowed the Monte Carlo as he came to the end of the road that opened up into the parking lot of the complex. There were no cars in the front. To the far right, the opposite side from his apartment, Tasker noticed an unoccupied Ford Bronco with the driver's-side door open. The door to the apartment in front of it was open like a new tenant was moving in. Great, innocent bystanders.

Tasker parked next to the Bronco, out of view of his end of the building. He got out but pushed his door closed to keep from making any noise. He realized he might just be paranoid, but he didn't want to take any chances. In fact, he had decided to grab his stuff and stay at a hotel in Belle Glade the rest of the week to be on the safe side.

Tasker looked through the open door to the apartment, but didn't see any movement. He moved around to the rear of the building and decided to approach his quarters from the back.

He eased past the row of vacant apartments until he could clearly see the windows to his. Everything looked in order. No movement. No lights. He crept up the rear porch stairs, looking in through the small window in his back door. Still nothing. His hand rested on the drawstring to his pack. He was conscious of every creak the porch made as he inched closer to the door.

He froze when he noticed that the door was open an inch. He always locked it on his way out. He jerked the string and opened his bag, revealing his compact Sig. He drew the small .380 and carefully grasped the doorknob. He eased the door open and immediately saw the figure of a man crouched down looking out the front window, like he was expecting Tasker.

Tasker let a smile ease across his face as he realized he had the drop on this asshole. He silently slipped into the kitchen, leaving the rear door ajar. He pointed the pistol at the man by his front window and started to advance slowly.

As he was about to say, "Don't move," he felt movement behind him and then something stuck behind his left ear.

A man's voice, coming from right behind him, said, "Drop the gun."

Luther Williams slept soundly in the old Holiday Inn on Tennessee Street in Tallahassee. He had always found the Florida capital city to be refreshingly simple and pleasant. Confident no police officer had a clue where he was, he had slept as soundly as he had in a year. A comfortable, cool room with a color TV. He never thought he'd appreciate the simple things like this.

After breakfast at a diner on Monroe Street, he headed toward the main campus of Florida A & M University, southeast of the capitol, a few miles from Tallahassee's larger university, Florida State. He took a few minutes cruising through the neighborhood near the school looking for the address he had written on the back of a napkin.

He found the small, gray stone house with a wooden porch wrapped around it on a steep hill about three blocks from the school. It reminded him of his grandmother's house back in east St. Louis.

He pulled the Buick up in front and then climbed the three steps from the road into the yard. Not wanting to startle anyone, he called from the front yard.

"Hello."

A female's voice came back. "May I help you?" Then a young woman, maybe twenty, with dark skin and a beautiful face, poked her head out the front screen door.

"Teresa Powers?"

"I'm Teresa."

"You *have* grown up." He smiled. "I haven't seen you since you were nine or ten."

She smiled back and came out onto the porch. "I'm sorry, I don't recognize you."

"I'm . . ." He paused, not sure what to tell her. "Cole. I was a friend of your mother's."

She came to the edge of the porch.

Luther said, "I was sorry to hear she passed."

"Thank you. Would you like to come in?"

"I don't want to impose, I just wanted to pay my respects." He stepped up onto the porch. As she came closer, he realized how much she looked like her mother and he felt a new emotion. He thought it was regret, but he'd have to think about it.

He took a seat on an old wicker chair on the porch and she followed his lead, sitting next to him.

 **42** TASKER SAT AT HIS CRAPPY KITCHEN TABLE with his hands flat on the surface just like he'd been instructed. Across from him, Henry Janzig leaned on the table with a Smith & Wesson model 10 revolver pointing at Tasker's face. Captain Sam Norton sat at the table to the side, calmly drinking one of Tasker's Powerades he'd taken from the refrigerator.

Janzig let out a hoot and said, "Told ya parking my Bronco at the end would fool him." He narrowed his gaze to Tasker. "You thought you just had a new neighbor, didn't you? Some kinda state weenie."

Tasker nodded slowly. "You got me."

"And you with that fancy Sig auto and all your damn training. I got the drop on you with this old revolver. Hell, the Department of Corrections don't even use these no more." He lifted the old revolver.

"It would've killed me just like an auto."

"That is the gospel truth, it is." Janzig leaned back in his chair, satisfied with himself. "Thought you FDLE agents were used to sneaking around. You ain't very sharp, boy."

Tasker let him see a small smile even though he was scared out of his wits. He wasn't sure what these two rednecks had in mind, but it had already gone too far. At least Renee wasn't here to remind him that he'd been duped by a woman. Again. He addressed Janzig. "It's called tunnel vision. Very common in stressful police operations. Once I saw Norton up by the front window, I focused on him instead of looking around. What can I say, I fucked up."

"Boy, you sure as hell did." Janzig started to cackle. What a ball-breaker.

Norton decided to chime in now. "Look here, Tasker. We can still work something out. We just gotta get something on you so you can't rat on us."

Tasker looked him in the eye. He had read somewhere that it's harder to kill a hostage when they look their captors in the eye. He also realized they were probably planning to kill him, but giving him a ray of hope so he wouldn't resist. It had worked for the Nazis in World War II, but he knew he'd have to make a move soon.

Norton continued. "You just didn't know when to quit and mind your own damn business."

Tasker wanted to know a few things, no matter what happened. "How'd you know I'm leaving on Friday?"

Norton said, "Still got friends."

"Thought I did, too."

"Mine in Tallahassee have a vested interest in what goes on down here."

Tasker tried to determine if this guy was lying. Was it someone from out of town? Could it be that the director didn't betray him?

"Someone in Tallahassee wouldn't know shit like that."

"There's always someone who knows all kinds of shit. You just need to recognize who that is."

Then it hit Tasker. His director had been responding to some kind of big-time pressure. A director at FDLE didn't take shit from too many people. He'd just told them to lay off until Tasker left town Friday. Just to buy time. The director never even realized he was giving info to one of the crooks. Tasker had a pretty good idea who had applied the pressure.

Tasker smiled and said, "Hope Ardan Gann stands up for you when this shit all hits the fan." He could tell from Norton's expression he'd made a good guess. Norton was at a complete loss for words. He had to be wondering how much Tasker had figured out and who he had told. Tasker had to stifle a laugh, he was so satisfied with himself. He would've been more satisfied if he hadn't been so stupid as to walk into this trap, but at least he had solved part of the puzzle.

Norton looked at Janzig and said, "You're wrong, Henry. This boy is sharp." Then he glared at Tasker. "Maybe too sharp. And you definitely don't know when to quit."

Tasker kept his hands flat on the table. "So I was a patsy from the beginning. Just look at the Dewalt's kid's death and get out. No one cared if I found out who killed him."

Norton said, "Dewalt's folks went to the governor. Something had to happen. Gann just figured you were ripe for the assignment when he read about your shooting in the bank."

Tasker thought about it and said, "I know who killed Dewalt."

Now Janzig was interested. He leaned forward. "Who?"

Tasker smiled and said, "First, I got a question or two."

The two correctional officers looked at each other. Then Janzig said, "What?"

"Why was your print on Dewalt's pendant that Renee found in Baxter's stuff?"

"Don't matter if you already know who killed him. Now, who was it?"

Tasker shrugged. He didn't care anymore about the details, he just needed time. "Renee Chin killed him."

Both men were interested now.

Norton said, "Bullshit."

"Is it? She hates to be dissed, and Dewalt dissed her bad."

Now Norton was agitated.

Tasker said, "I know all about you guys and the GM Corporation." He looked at Janzig to make sure he wasn't about to be shot, then asked, "What's GM stand for anyway?"

The older man grinned and said, "Green Mile, what else."

Looking at the two correctional officers, trying to reason out his options, Tasker remembered his Beretta in the nightstand. If he could get into the bedroom, he might have a chance.

He looked at his captors. "Look, I have proof in my room about Renee."

Norton paused. "What's that?"

"A medical examiner's report." He wasn't good at lying on the fly, but he found the threat of death a great motivator.

Norton asked, "Where is it?"

"Bedroom somewhere."

"I'll take a look." Norton started to stand.

"I'm not sure where. I'll look, too."

His captors just stared at him.

"Janzig can keep the gun on me and you'll both be in there with me."

They looked at each other and Norton said, "Yeah, but Henry, you keep back from him so he can't get at your gun."

They all stood and headed toward the bedroom across the small living room. Norton stayed right behind Tasker with Janzig a few paces back. Tasker's heart rate started to pick up as his eyes fell on the small night-stand with the drawer already open a crack.

Norton gave him a slight shove. "Okay, where do you think it is?"

"Check those papers on the dresser. Might be in those."

He let Norton step around him to go to the old, veneer dresser with some magazines and other papers Tasker had intended to recycle. Tasker eased, ever so slightly, toward the bed and nightstand. He stole a quick glance over his left shoulder at Janzig. He was still in the doorway with his gun pointed at Tasker, but his eyes were following Norton as he sifted through the papers.

Tasker casually leaned down toward the drawer, hoping not to spook Janzig. He said, "Maybe I left them in here," as he grasped the knob. His heart beat so fast he was afraid he might pass out. He visualized his plan to calmly grab the gun, then, as he turned, start shooting at Janzig. He'd worry about Norton once the threat of a .38 round in the back had been neutralized. He took one more deep breath and started to pull the drawer open.

Luther Williams settled into the comfortable seat of his Buick LeSabre as he headed west on I-10 from Tallahassee. He wasn't sure, because it was all new to him, but he felt as if this had been the most satisfying afternoon of his life. He didn't know if he did or didn't have anything to do with contributing DNA to Miss Teresa Powers, but she was still a delightful young woman. She had captured his attention from the start with her practical plan to become a pharmacist. She had a decent job lined up with Walgreens already and was doing well in the program at Florida A & M. He envied her simple, realistic goals. Maybe he could've had a life like that if he had been raised in a different environment. It was too late to worry about that now. He had spent a life in pursuit of excess. Excess wealth, excess women, excess violence and finally excess confinement. Now he was on a different path. All the money and women he had used up didn't seem to matter anymore. What had it gotten him? On the run and driving a cheap Buick.

As he passed the sign saying Pensacola 199 miles he picked up his prepaid cell phone and punched in the number to one of his few trustworthy business associates.

He heard someone say, "Hello."

"Tulley?"

"Speaking."

"It's Cole Hodges."

"Yes, sir, Mr. Hodges. What can I do for you?"

"I need you to move some money from one of my old business accounts. Can you do that?"

"Yes, sir, not a problem. Where do you want it sent?"

"To an account for Miss Teresa Powers in Tallahassee. You may have to poke around to find it."

"Do you have her social?"

"No, but her date of birth is November eleventh, 1984."

"I'll find her. How much did you want transferred?"

"Make three transfers over the next year. Each one fifteen grand. Don't let her find out where it's coming from."

"No problem, Mr. Hodges. Do you have a number I can reach you at if I need to?"

"Tulley, are you serious?"

Tasker felt sweat drip into his eyes as the drawer inched open and he prepared to spring into action. The cover of the book, a formation of helicopters, appeared, and nothing else. The drawer was empty. He blinked hard and ducked his head a little to check the back of the drawer. The only thing inside was the fucking W.E.B. Griffin novel.

Norton calmly turned toward him. "What d'ya think, we're stupid?" He pulled Tasker's Beretta from the rear of his waistband. That's why he'd stayed behind Tasker on the way into the bedroom.

Tasker sagged onto the bed.

Norton added, "Billie Towers makes really good reports."

Tasker felt the blood rush to his face. "What'd she say about my date with Renee?"

Janzig cackled at that. "Watch out. Now you hit the magic button."

Norton kept his eyes on Tasker, but said, "Shut up, Henry."

Janzig kept laughing. "His love button."

Tasker said, "You used Billie and now got her tied up in this scheme."

Norton said, "I didn't use her. I included her."

"Why'd you have to kill the professor? You include Billie in that?"

"That was an accident. We didn't expect him in the middle of the day. We just wanted to keep his artifacts from going to the university."

Even though he was scared, he had to smile as everything seemed to fall into place. "It all goes back to the private prison site."

"You're making too much noise. Shut your yap. We need to get going." He grabbed Tasker by the upper arm and pulled him toward the living room, then shoved him ahead toward the front door.

Tasker decided his only chance was to break for the cane fields once he was outside. In this little apartment he had nowhere to go. At least in the open, he might have a chance. It wasn't TV and these two weren't used to handguns. He figured he had a pretty good chance to make the cane and get lost in the heavy field. Then he'd get help. Maybe Rufus Goodwin, or better yet get ahold of some FDLE agents and have them kick some ass. He steadied his breathing to get ready for his move.

He walked out the front door first, with Norton right behind him. It was darker than he expected and he decided to give his eyes a second to adjust to the lack of light.

Now both of his captors were on the front porch with him. Norton had stuck the Beretta in his waistband and Janzig had the revolver still pointing at him. He looked toward the field. If he ran down the porch, he'd have better footing, but he'd be a much easier target. If he jumped to the ground then sprinted, he could be tripped up, but he'd be harder to hit. He weighed the options and took another breath.

 **43** TASKER HAD A DEEP BREATH IN HIM, A PLAN of action and now enough adrenaline to make it down to the parking lot and toward the cane field in one quick motion. Janzig was too far away to strike so he decided to at least slow down Norton. As they headed down the porch toward the far side of the complex where Janzig's Bronco was parked, Norton tried to keep him calm.

"We can still work this out. I'll even give you back your fancy *pistola* here." He patted the Beretta. "We just need a little time. You're gonna have to come with us."

Tasker said, "Okay, I'll . . ." He swung his left arm hard and backfisted Norton right on the nose. As he turned to leap off the porch, he heard a gunshot. He glanced over his shoulder and paused. He took a longer look. Henry Janzig toppled to the ground and his revolver clattered on the porch. Tasker just stared as blood pumped out of a hole in the rear of his head. He let his eyes follow the trajectory of the bullet and saw Renee Chin standing at the end of the porch near his apartment with a modern revolver in both hands, still sighting down the porch. Her eyes were wide as she tried to comprehend what she had just done. Tasker knew the feeling all too well. But she had just saved his life. That might help her come to terms with it.

Tasker looked at Norton, who was leaning against the wall holding his bloody nose. Tasker reached over and snatched his pistol from Norton's waistband. He ran a finger over the barrel to feel the tiny metal indicator showing there was a bullet in the chamber. He hesitated, then raised the pistol to Renee.

"Drop the gun, Renee."

She stared at him, then blinked hard. "Why? I'm on your side."

He raised his voice a notch. "Drop the gun. Do it now."

She lowered the big black revolver, then squatted down and set it on the porch. "What's gotten into you, Bill?"

"We need to sort out who's who."

"I'm the one who just saved you from getting killed. Is that confusing? Do you appreciate my efforts at all?"

"I appreciate it, but I know about the corporation."

"What corporation?"

Tasker shoved Norton closer to Renee so he could keep his gun on them both. He stooped and picked up Renee's pistol as they passed it. He stuck it in his own waistband.

Norton looked down at Janzig's body. "Jesus, Henry, I'm sorry," he muttered. "I had no idea it'd ever go this far."

It looked like the burly captain was going to cry as he looked down at his friend's cooling body.

Norton gulped and said, "He was a good man."

Now Renee cut in. "What corporation are you talking about and why do you think I need to be held at gunpoint?"

Tasker said, "The GM Corporation for the property that you wanted the new private prison to go on."

She shrugged. "Bill, I don't know what the hell you're talking about."

Tasker looked at her, then at Norton. "What about it, Norton? She's on the corporate papers."

Now Norton shrugged but stayed silent, still looking at Janzig.

Tasker said, "You think, after all I've been through, that I won't do something stupid to you?"

Norton looked up and studied Tasker and apparently agreed he shouldn't push things. He looked down at the porch. "I included her."

"Louder."

He spoke up. "I said, 'I included her.'"

Tasker said, "In what?"

"The goddamn GM Corporation."

"Why?"

"I thought she might see the light and didn't want my partners to cut her out."

Renee looked at Norton, then Tasker. "Cut out of what? Somebody tell me what's going on."

Tasker said, "I think this moron has a thing for you and included you in his scheme to rent property to the state for the new prison." Tasker turned toward Norton, who appeared to be a beaten man. "I see what happened. You were too cheap to go to an attorney, so you had Luther Williams draw up the papers. You just threw Renee's name in the mix."

Norton remained silent.

"Pretty sharp. Until you lost control of Luther."

Renee slapped Norton's arm. "You son of a bitch. You implicated me in your crazy scheme. Why on earth did you do that?"

Again Norton shrugged, beaten. "Did it for you. Besides, he says you killed the Dewalt boy. You ain't no angel."

"I killed who?" She looked at Tasker.

He shrugged. "I was trying to buy time and confuse them. At least I didn't list you on a state document."

She looked back at Norton. "Sam, how could you?"

"Once the cash started rolling in, you wouldn't have cared."

"Yes, I would have."

Tasker turned at the sound of a car pulling into the lot. A Crown Victoria's headlights fell across them as it pulled in directly in front of the apartment.

Tasker had the gun in his hand, but relaxed when Rufus Goodwin stepped out of the car.

"Finally there's a cop around when you need one."

Rufus walked toward them like it was an ordinary scene. "What'd you get into now? Why you pointin' that gun at them?"

"Now I'm just pointing it at Norton. He's your killer, Rufus."

"How do you figure?" As he started to climb the three steps to the porch, he noticed Janzig's body and said, "Holy shit. Who shot him?"

"It's a long story."

Rufus looked drained and uninterested in long stories.

Tasker said, "I'll go through it later. You got a set of cuffs?"

Rufus reached behind him and pulled out a set of stainless steel handcuffs. He offered them to Tasker. "You better cuff him because I'm not buying all this just yet. I'd rather not get named in the lawsuit."

Tasker stuck his gun in the small of his back, tucking it into his belt. He flipped the cuffs and positioned them to slap on Norton. He took a step, then noticed Norton smiling.

"What's so funny?"

Norton pointed at Rufus. "That."

Tasker turned and saw Rufus with a gun trained on him.

"Okay, Mr. Elite State Cop, reach for either pistol and you'll be dead before you hit the ground." He looked at Renee. "Step over here, sweetheart. You need to be near your boyfriend."

Norton reached across and reclaimed the Beretta from the stunned Tasker. He then took Renee's revolver from him. "Got partners all over the place, Tasker."

Tasker looked back at the Gladesville cop and studied his face. He said, "You have a jigsaw puzzle face."

Rufus said, "What?"

"Rubie, the crazy homeless guy, said his friend with a puzzle face gave him the card. Now I see your freckles look like a puzzle."

Norton said, "I told you not to pin it on that crazy English fucker."

Rufus said, "He's not English." He said it like it mattered. "And you don't need to worry about it anyway." He shoved Tasker onto the porch.

Tasker couldn't help but smile. He had pieced together more of the scheme and gotten under Rufus' skin, and had the partners exchanging sharp words. Maybe there was a way out of this.

Renee Chin leaned in close to the handcuffed Bill Tasker. They were sitting on the porch in front of Tasker's little apartment next to the body of Henry Janzig. Even as Norton and Rufus discussed their fate a few feet away, she wanted to be certain Tasker knew she wasn't involved in this mess at all.

"Now do you believe me?"

"Yes. I believe you."

"When did you find out? I mean about my name on the papers."

"Yesterday morning."

"Is that why you've been dodging me?"

"Yep."

"I thought you knew me better than that."

"Can we argue about this later? It may be a moot point."

She suddenly felt a little sick. There was no way two men she had known for a long time were planning to kill them. She refused to believe it. Then Norton and Rufus finished their hushed conversation and rejoined them.

Rufus said, "Okay, missy, where's your little Jeep?"

"Why?"

"Because we have to drop you off and we're deciding who to drop first."

She felt a wave of relief. "It's just on Dead Cow Lane—"

Tasker cut her off. "Renee, don't—"

Rufus kicked him in the side to shut him up.

"Oh my God, you *are* going to kill us."

Norton said, "Just relax, babe. We'll figure something out. But we gotta get goin'."

Rufus said, "Get Janzig's car and follow us. We'll all ride in the city car." He waited and, when Norton didn't say anything, added, "Now get going." As Norton walked away with Tasker's and Renee's pistols in his hands, Rufus nudged Tasker and said, "You two get up." He looked over at Henry Janzig's body and said to Renee, "Give me a hand with the sergeant."

She hesitated but realized she shouldn't push too hard. She had never been in a situation anything like this before and had no clue what to expect or do. She hoped Tasker had some ideas.

Rufus kept his pistol in his hand and leaned down to grab Janzig's arm. Renee took ahold of his other arm. It wasn't stiff or cold like she thought it might be. She still hadn't come to grips that he was dead because of her. They dragged the body off the porch, letting his feet drop against each stair with a sickening thud.

Rufus kept looking up at Tasker, his hands cuffed behind his back. Just watching them. "You stay right there," ordered Rufus. Once they had the body at the rear of the car, Rufus looked up at Tasker and said, "Come on down. You can help hoist him into the trunk."

Renee noticed how Tasker never took his eyes off Rufus, like his mind was working out all the possible courses of action. He came down the steps and toward them silently.

Rufus popped the trunk just as Tasker arrived at the car. Renee looked in the big trunk and froze. "Oh, Rufus, you didn't." She couldn't take her eyes off the small body of Billie Towers, her dark eyes still open.

**44** TASKER DIDN'T ACTUALLY SEE BILLIE'S BODY until he had squatted down to grab Janzig. With his hands secured behind his back, it was awkward leaning into the dead sergeant. Then, as he stood, he looked in the trunk and realized what Renee was talking about. Billie looked like a child thrown in the rear of the trunk, wrapped around the outer edge of the spare tire, her black hair framing her face then fanning out over the tire. He dropped Janzig back to the ground.

"You motherfucker." He started to lunge at Rufus, his head down like a bull. Rufus stepped to one side and raised his pistol.

"Save it, tough guy." He waved his gun at them both and added, "Toss Janzig in."

Tasker's mind started to race. Now he didn't just want to escape, he wanted to kill this son of a bitch. But he needed some time. He helped Renee lift Janzig and set him in the trunk, careful not to hit Billie.

Rufus said, "All right, Tasker, you sit next to me. Renee, sweetheart, you're next to the door. And remember, if either of you tries to run, the other one gets shot first." He looked at Renee. "Understand, beautiful? You decide to open that door, your boyfriend won't live to see you start to run."

They both nodded. Rufus watched them climb in the big Crown Vic and then he opened the driver's door. He cranked the car and pulled out past Norton, who had been waiting at the edge of Dead Cow Lane in the Bronco. The two cars stopped at the end of the street.

With his hands cuffed, Tasker couldn't do much but think things through as they turned west on US 27. Everyone was silent as they picked up speed on the paved, four-lane road, with Norton in the Bronco following them at a distance.

Rufus laid on the gas as soon as they were westbound on the empty highway. Tasker stole a glance behind them and saw Norton way back in the Bronco. He had no idea where they were headed, but he wasn't in a hurry to find out.

A mile after they were on the road, Rufus blew past a car on the side of the road. A few seconds later, Tasker saw the reflection of blue lights in the rearview mirror.

Rufus said, "Not a peep or this trooper is a dead man and so are you. You got it?" He showed Tasker the revolver in his hand.

"Let him go, Rufus. He's got no part in this."

Before Rufus could answer, there was a rap on the trunk as the trooper paused.

Rufus lowered the window.

The trooper stepped up, then leaned down to look in the car.

Tasker cut his eyes, then had to turn his head as he saw Florida Highway Patrol Trooper Tom Miko.

"Well, well, well, looks like I pulled over a damn law enforcement brain trust here." He looked at Rufus. "I guess you've heard my safety and speeding speech a few times."

Rufus said, "You mean where you own this highway?"

"That's the one."

"I heard it."

The trooper relaxed a little and squatted down to chat with everyone in the car.

Tasker's eyes cut to Rufus' right hand with the revolver held low. There was no way he'd let Rufus shoot this poor guy. As soon as he made a movement, Tasker was going to do his best to stop him. Cuffed hands and everything.

Trooper Miko said, "I stopped the FDLE agent a while back and the inspector last week. No one in this car much cares about setting a good example, do they?" He smiled, just joking with them now.

Rufus was careful to look straight ahead so he'd catch any movement or signals from his passengers. "Sorry, Tom. We're in the middle of something."

"Need a hand? It's slow tonight."

Just as Rufus was about to say something, Tasker saw the headlights in the rearview mirror and heard the horrible thump as Norton, in the Bronco, swooped in on the unsuspecting trooper.

Tasker cried out, "You fucking assholes," as he saw the trooper fly onto the ground in front of Rufus' Crown Vic and roll to a perfectly still heap about twenty-five feet away. Tasker couldn't tell if he was dead or not.

Next to Tasker, Renee whispered, "Sweet Jesus, what have I gotten into?"

Rufus pulled back onto the road and followed Norton, who had hardly slowed down. "He is certainly a man of action, isn't he?"

Tasker said, "Does any of this shit bother you?"

Rufus was quiet for a minute and then said, "Yeah, I don't like doin' it, if that's what you mean. But the cash will make it all right."

"You guys really think this scheme will still work?"

"It'll work. We just had a few glitches."

After a few miles, they turned left, away from the lake on a dirt road next to a long, wide South Florida Water Management canal heading from a catchment basin near the lake. Cane fields rose up across from the canal as they continued down the bumpy dirt road. Tasker felt his body knock into Renee, then Rufus as he thought about his options. The sight of the motionless trooper stuck in his mind. Then he had a flash of brilliance and took action before he could talk himself out of it.

He lifted his feet and twisted hard, leaning his back against Renee with his legs cocked. He kicked out both feet into a surprised Rufus, driving him hard against the door. He tried to raise the pistol he held in his right hand, but Tasker kicked him again, causing the car to spin one way then the other, heading straight for the canal. He fired his legs again, this time catching the dazed Gladesville cop in the head. Rufus' two front teeth bounced off the side window as blood poured from his split lower lip. Renee reached across to straighten the wheel and direct the car back onto the dirt road.

Somehow Rufus managed to stop the car. He was confused but still had the gun.

Tasker yelled, "Get out, Renee. Run."

She hesitated and he shouted, "Right now."

She was out of the car and heading toward the cane field before Norton in the Bronco had even realized there was a problem. Tasker knew he had only a few seconds to either disarm Rufus or run with Renee. He kicked at him again, but now the cop was fending off the blows more effectively. He had tried to move the gun to his other hand, but it was stuck between the seat and the door. Tasker turned and pushed himself into Rufus so his cuffed hands were against the cop. He hoped to grab the gun somehow, but felt nothing except the keys in the steering column. He closed his hand and yanked, jerking the key out of the ignition along with the others on the chain.

This wasn't working, so he scooted toward the open door, noticed the Bronco backing up toward them, and then jumped out, running in the same direction as Renee into the cane field. He was already panting a few feet inside the cover of the cane when he ran headlong into the stationary Renee, causing them both to hit the ground.

She grabbed his head and kissed him hard on the lips.

Tasker said, "We gotta haul ass. I'm guessing neither of those two can keep up a pace on foot very long." He twisted away from her, offering her his bloody hand. "Here."

"What happened?"

"I grabbed his keys, but the chain broke. I'm hoping the cuff key stayed with me."

She sorted through the half dozen keys and said, "Yes!" when she found the tiny metal standard handcuff key and dumped the others on the ground. In the dim light, it took a few seconds to fit the little key in the hole. "I got it."

He rotated his wrists and the left cuff clicked open. He spun around with the one hand still in a cuff, facing Renee. She opened it with less trouble. Without a word, they started to scurry away from the two cars.

Rufus Goodwin was pissed off. He'd worked too hard and done too many distasteful things to lose his chance at a big score now. Every time his tongue moved over his teeth he felt the disturbing gap where his two front teeth had been. He had checked his face in the car mirror to make sure he wasn't too badly injured but didn't want to dwell on how he looked. He had his big Smith & Wesson .357 out and a four-cell Kel-Light in his hand scanning the outer edges of the cane field. Sam Norton was a few feet away checking the field in the other direction.

Rufus said, "I got an idea." He holstered his gun on his hip and raced back to his Crown Vic. As he opened his door, he yelled to Norton, "Wait right here. They'll be coming back this way in a few minutes." His mouth ached with each word but his speech sounded okay. He had always sounded different from the locals anyway. He retrieved his spare key from his wallet and started the car, turned in the direction they had come in from US 27 and punched it, covering a quarter mile in a flash. At the first break in the cane field, he bailed out and popped his trunk. After a few seconds of frantic searching, he retrieved two road flares. It was night but the moon had developed into a decent source of light.

He ran into the cane field and realized it was a narrow strip that ended about thirty yards east at another drainage canal. He ignited the flares by striking them like giant matches against their rough caps. The red flame glowed on both as he touched them to the base of the cane rows. The blaze grew as more cane was consumed. The brisk wind from the north was going to push the flames right back to Norton and he'd walk up the opposite bank. In a few minutes, they'd have their pigeons, and in the morning some county sheriff's deputy would take a vandalism report from whoever owned this little cane field. Everyone else would be investigating the dead trooper up on the highway. Rufus included.

He stood back and watched the flames grow and spread. This was a lot of trouble, but there were some satisfying parts to it as well. The money would be real satisfying if they could ever get it rolling.

45 THE CANE DIDN'T JUST BURN; IT IGNITED.
Tasker and Renee were on their bellies looking through
the last few rows of cane about fifty feet from where Rufus Goodwin was using a couple of road flares to spread the fire. With
the wind it was clear he meant to drive them to Norton, or at least out
in the open. The idea that someone would try to roast him and Renee
alive pissed him off. He already had a score to settle with this jigsaw-
puzzle-faced New York asshole. Billie Towers may have been tied up in
this scam, but she didn't deserve to die. His concern now was getting
back out to the road to see if he could help the trooper. He may have
been beyond help, but Tasker had to try.

Next to him, Renee lay with her eyes wide. Tasker didn't think she
had ever been in a position where someone had the upper hand. As a
correctional officer, one of the key principles is: Always stay in charge.
Now she was the hunted, not the hunter. She clutched his arm like he
was anchored to this spot in the field. He wanted to shake her off, but
knew she was too scared to be pushed away. But he had to do something.
This sitting still went against his nature.

Renee finally said, "What're we gonna do? Should we try to sneak
past Norton?"

"That's the wrong direction. We need to get back to the trooper."

"So what do we do?" Her voice was taking on a slightly panicked
tone.

He smiled as he saw a clear course of action. "We attack."

"How? With no weapons?"

Tasker's hand had been resting on a fresh stalk of sugarcane that they had knocked flat when they dove into the field. He jerked it free of the broken section near the ground. He felt its surprising weight, slapping it into his other hand. He scurried on his stomach toward Rufus, turning to say in a harsh whisper to Renee, "Stay put as long as you can."

He watched as Rufus moved along the edge of the field, lighting the cane. The flames were moving away from Rufus' car and he crept closer to Tasker as he spread the fire. Tasker eased back into the cane as Rufus came closer. His mouth had blood coming from his lips, and his forehead had a deep gash, too. His revolver was in a holster on his hip. Tasker tried not to focus on the gun, even though that was his goal. He didn't need tunnel vision now. He took a deep breath as Rufus worked his way closer every second.

With the smoke from the fire growing thicker, giving him more cover, Tasker stood, out of sight of the clearing, and hefted the sugarcane stalk like a Louisville Slugger. He tried to steal a look over at Renee to make sure she was still safe and was shocked to see her standing in plain sight, away from the cane. What the hell was she doing? Then he heard her call out.

"Rufus, stop, we give up."

Rufus spun and looked at his former girlfriend. He stood with the road flares still in his hands. "Where's Tasker?"

Tasker stepped up to Rufus, who was looking to his right at Renee, swung the sugarcane and said, "Right here, asswipe." He let the arc of the cane come up between the sugarcane stalks and into Rufus' exposed chin. He felt a solid connection and saw a couple more teeth fly as he followed through like Barry Bonds. Rufus toppled like a building hit by a demolition ball.

Tasker dropped the sugarcane club and stepped over Rufus' motionless form. He yanked the pistol from its holster and resisted the urge to put a bullet in this guy's head right then.

Tasker had the groggy Rufus Goodwin leaning against his car. The fire burned unevenly behind them with the road along the canal open but smoky. Renee stood behind Tasker, who had Rufus' revolver in his hand.

He raised the gun at Rufus' impassive face. "I oughta cap you right now."

When Rufus grimaced in pain, he looked like a jack-o'-lantern with half his visible teeth missing. "Go ahead, smart guy. I'm done anyway."

Tasker lowered the gun. "Because I'm not God, I'd rather let you squirm before a judge. This town won't like this kind of scandal."

"These hicks won't even understand it."

Tasker looked up the road and said, "Where are the keys? I gotta go see about the trooper Norton hit."

Rufus coughed and said, "You yanked the key out of the ignition when you ran. You must have it."

"Shit." He looked toward the spot where he thought he and Renee had hidden before the fire. "They must be over on the ground."

Renee said, "I'll get them." She trotted off before Tasker could answer.

Tasker turned back to Rufus. "All this suffering just to keep the professor's artifacts from being tied to your damn prison site?"

He shrugged like he was in a conversation on a street in New York. "You think the state woulda let us build over an historical Indian village? Lotta money, Tasker. Plenty to go around still." He looked at Tasker.

"At least you're not as incompetent as I thought."

Rufus managed a slight smile and said, "Same here." He wiped his bloody face with his bare hand as the smoke started to drift in all directions. "You sure as hell don't give up easily."

"Why did you kill Billie?"

"She had a big mouth."

"You fucking creep. You're not even a psycho; you killed the professor and Billie for money."

He smirked. "No, I had fun choking the life out of Billie."

Tasker tensed but let it pass. He turned to Renee and shouted, "Find it yet?"

She looked up from the ground and shook her head.

Tasker looked at Rufus and said, "Give me a reason and you're dead meat."

Renee Chin liked her job with the Department of Corrections but she had always watched police shows. This was as close to one of those as she had ever gotten. Bill Tasker seemed to make decisions and act on them in a split second. She had never seen someone take charge like that in her life. She'd been afraid he might kill Rufus when he first surprised him, then again when he was talking to him, but that wouldn't have been in his character and she knew it. She might have agreed with his killing Rufus if it wasn't for her shock at having shot Henry Janzig herself. This wasn't like TV. She didn't feel like joking or going fishing. All she saw when she closed her eyes was Janzig's still body and the blood seeping onto the porch back at Tasker's apartment. What she didn't know was if Tasker was using the threats as a way to get more information out of the befuddled Rufus.

Now she was frantically searching for the keys. Tasker wanted to help the trooper, but she just wanted out of there fast. Then she'd do whatever she could for the injured cop out on US 27.

She found the spot where they had hidden and then saw the metallic sparkle in the dirt. She leaned down and dug out a silver Ford key. As she stood up to yell to Tasker, she sensed a movement, then an arm wrapped around her neck and Sam Norton's voice said, "I'm sorry, Renee."

Tasker saw the spare key as soon as he looked in the Ford. He turned to Rufus and muttered, "Asshole."

Rufus shrugged at his attempt to stall Tasker by lying about the missing key.

Tasker waited for Rufus to scoot in the car when he heard a voice from the cane shout, "Now we can cut a deal." His head snapped up to see Norton with the Beretta to Renee's head as they backed away into the cane.

Tasker didn't hesitate to pull Rufus out of the car by his ear. He had the revolver up, first at Norton, then jammed into Rufus' ribs as he backed to the rear of the Crown Vic.

Norton shouted, "Let us go. It'll take you a couple of hours to walk back and we'll be gone. Nobody wins, but nobody loses, either."

Tasker felt Rufus snicker. The thought of these two walking away, even as fugitives, didn't appeal to Tasker in the least. Besides, he had to get to the road fast. He yelled back to Norton, who was now almost in the cane field with Renee squarely in front of him, "Why's this mope mean so much to you?"

"Have to take care of partners. You know how it is." He shook Renee once. "Just walk away and we'll let her go. Everyone lives."

Tasker looked at the smug Rufus next to him, then across to Renee, who was keeping her emotions well hidden. He wanted to blow Rufus' head off then take a shot at Norton, but wouldn't risk someone close to him again. He couldn't help but think of that split second in the Kendall bank when he had had to act even though he knew his daughter was nearby. His finger tightened slightly on the revolver's trigger. He had never even fired this gun. Didn't know how accurate it was and what kind of rounds it was loaded with. He knew what he had to do.

Tasker raised his voice. "Tell you what. I'll make an even exchange. You send over Renee and I'll let Slappy here come to you."

"Then you clear the way for us to drive out?"

"But I keep the pistol to make sure you keep the deal."

There was a pause, then Norton yelled, "Send him over."

Tasker loosened his grip on Rufus as he peered over the trunk of the car and saw Renee alone at the edge of the field. He knew Norton was in the field right behind her. The smoke from the spreading fire drifted through in thick clumps.

Tasker said to Rufus, "Anything goes wrong and the first round is in your back."

Rufus smiled his nearly toothless smile. "Watch out, it shoots to the right."

Tasker knew the Gladesville cop was just trying to get into his head. Maybe the gun shot left. It didn't matter, because if there was a problem, three rounds aimed in a spread would go toward him. Something would hit.

Tasker said, "Get walking, jerk-off." He shoved Rufus ahead of him and yelled, "He's on the way." He stood up, the pistol pointed at Rufus as he walked quickly toward the cane field. Renee hesitated, either out of fear or because Norton told her to wait, then started toward Tasker at a much slower pace than Rufus. He started to shout to her to run, when Rufus lunged at Renee, scooping her in his arms and fading into the cane field with Norton. Tasker never had a chance to get off a round, but he scampered around the car and raced toward the spot in the field where they had disappeared.

46   NORTON GRABBED RENEE BY THE SHOULDER AS she and Rufus barreled back into the cane.

"C'mon," was all he said as he led them along the western edge of the field, away from the flames.

Rufus said, "Where are we goin'? The highway is the other direction."

"I need my 870p. We can use the Bronco to get back to the highway and let Renee go up there."

Rufus started to pant now at the fast pace they kept up cutting through the cane. "What do you mean, let her go?"

"If Tasker is loose, it don't make a bit of difference to have her free, too."

"We can still get Tasker. You'll have the shotgun. The fire will keep him on this side of the cane. We can get him if we use her as bait."

Norton kept silent as he started to breathe hard himself. He knew he had already lost his chance to give the girls and his wife a proper place to live. He had screwed everything up, and worst of all Renee knew he wasn't the straight-up guy he wanted to be for her.

After a minute of good running and two minutes of fast walking, they came to the Bronco with the driver's door still open. Norton handed the Beretta they had taken from Tasker to Rufus and retrieved his Remington 870 pump shotgun from the rear seat so they could pile in.

He hit the gas a little hard and spun in the soft soil near the canal, then straightened out and raced back to Rufus' car now shrouded in thick white smoke. The Bronco skidded to a stop next to the Crown Vic.

Tasker was nowhere in sight.

Rufus said, "Watch out, he's a tricky bastard. He could be low, next to the car, just waiting to start popping off rounds at us."

Norton kept looking out through the smoke and moonlight. "He wouldn't risk Renee."

"How do you know that?"

"Because I wouldn't if I were him."

Norton eased out of the Bronco with the shotgun in his hand and Rufus scooted out with Renee in tow.

Norton stared as Rufus raised the gun to Renee's head and shouted toward the cane, "Tasker, come on out. Don't risk her life."

Norton had seen how quickly he had shot Professor Kling that day in his apartment and knew he meant it.

Norton just wanted this to all be over. He had seen enough killing. He hoped Tasker would ignore them and they could just leave. Renee would be safe and he'd have to deal with his mistakes.

Then he heard Rufus say, "You got ten seconds. One, two . . ."

Tasker had followed Renee and her captors into the cane when they fled but realized they would have to come past him again, so he stopped. He was hoping for an ambush if they stopped at Rufus' parked car. Now he saw with the smoke screen and low light, that wasn't an option. Then the Bronco skidded to a stop and he caught glimpses of the two men with Renee in the front seat.

Tasker not only heard Rufus Goodwin's rough voice, he could see him and Norton with Renee in between after they slid out of the Bronco. They stood behind the Crown Vic and in front of the Bronco. It was maybe seventy feet. Too long for a shot with a pistol he wasn't familiar with, in low light. The moon provided some illumination but the headlights from the Crown Vic gave him a pretty clear picture of the two men and Renee's tall figure. The drifting smoke was starting to irritate his eyes and an occasional shift in the breeze pushed it between him and the others. Lying prone on the soil at the edge of the cane, he extended his right arm and steadied the big revolver with his left hand, sighting in on Rufus' head. He took a breath as he matched the rear sight with the front.

Then he heard Rufus start to count. No way he was going to get to ten. His hope was that if he somehow managed to hit Rufus, Norton might just flee and leave him and Renee.

He heard Rufus shout, "Five," and then slow the count way down. Tasker's finger tightened on the trigger, smoothly bringing it back.

"Six," yelled Rufus.

Tasker needed to buy some time. Even a few minutes might bring someone checking on the fire. Then they could see to the trooper on the highway. How had he gotten into a situation like this? He felt like he was in a foreign country without laws.

As Rufus reached seven, Norton eased to his left a few steps, almost blocking Tasker's shot. The stout prison captain said something to Rufus that made him stop counting. Then it looked like Renee said something, too. Tasker paused, hoping this might be the lull he needed.

Then he heard, "Eight."

Renee could smell Rufus' musky body odor and squirmed under the feel of his sweat-slicked arm around her neck. The muzzle of the Beretta was snug against her temple and she was terrified. She was terrified but not senseless. She knew she had to do something. Had to think like a cop. She had never realized the huge difference between supervising inmates and investigating crimes at a prison and being actively involved in a dangerous situation like this.

She knew Tasker was nearby. She trusted him and could almost feel him watching her. She knew he had Rufus' pistol. She thought to herself, What would a cop do?

Rufus continued to yell out his count right next to her left ear. He was up to seven when Norton took a step toward them and stopped him.

Norton said, "Let's throw her in the car and get a head start on him."

Rufus said, "No way. We need 'em both tonight. He'll come out. No way he'll risk me capping her. You said it yourself."

Norton looked at Renee.

She steadied herself and felt Rufus tighten his grip slightly. She swallowed hard so she could speak in a calm voice. "Rufus, you gonna kill me like you killed Billie?"

Norton snapped his gaze to Rufus. "You killed Billie?"

Rufus didn't give him time to think about it. "Don't worry about that now. Tasker could be out there right now. You need to be ready with that shotgun."

Just the mention of Tasker made Norton shift his eyes toward the cane field.

Now Rufus loosened his grip. Renee knew, knew for a fact, that Tasker was close and ready to take action. The guy was always ready to take action. She had to help. If she dropped her weight and pushed to the side, maybe Tasker would have a shot at Rufus. She needed only a second to sprint toward the front of the car and be out of the line of fire. She filled her lungs with air and blinked her eyes.

Rufus yelled, "Eight."

She dropped straight down and used her hips to bump Rufus hard. She slid away from the pistol's barrel and out of Rufus' left arm easily, but as she started to sprint, she slipped on the loose soil and felt like a deer frozen in a hunter's sights. She looked over her shoulder to see Rufus turn and point the black Beretta automatic at her face. She saw his brown, emotionless eyes over the front sight of the barrel and knew he intended to pull the trigger.

The sound of the shot was deafening and she felt a hot, spreading pain near her neck and a force like a slap knock her onto the ground as she struck her head against the tires of the Bronco.

Her vision blurred and the bright moon seemed to wobble and she laid her head flat on the ground and blinked her eyes.

 **47** TASKER MADE UP HIS MIND WHEN RUFUS
yelled, "Eight," and squeezed the trigger slowly, still hoping
for a miracle. Then he got one. Renee seemed to instantly
disappear and suddenly Rufus was in the clear. He saw the Gladesville cop
turn and point the Beretta and Tasker knew what had happened. The
gutsy girl had made a move so he'd be able to end this with a good shot.

Then he heard a gun discharge. Not the stinging report of a single
.40-caliber shot, but the blast of a bigger weapon. Rufus flew out of
Tasker's line of vision and fell behind the cover of the Crown Vic. Norton stood with his shotgun still pointing where Rufus had been standing. The only person Tasker could see between the two vehicles was
Norton, so he adjusted his aim. The front sight fell on Norton's wide
chest and he slightly adjusted his hand until the rear sight framed the target as well. He didn't want to risk Norton firing another round.

Tasker exhaled and squeezed the trigger, then immediately reacquired
the target. As he sighted in on Norton for his second shot, he saw him
stumble then fall to the ground behind the Crown Vic. Tasker sprang
to his feet, shook out the cramp in his leg and started a quick advance
on the cars. He had the revolver up in front of him in case someone
popped up and decided to take a shot. Now that the shooting was over,
at least for a moment, he started to worry about Renee and what might
have happened. He still wasn't clear from what he had seen from the
cane field.

He slowed as he came within a few feet of the parked cars. The smoke still drifted in front of the headlights. He crouched and duck-walked to the edge of the Crown Vic. He peeked around the car, then popped back out of reflex and training. They didn't call it the quick peek for nothing. Then he stuck his head out again, taking a longer look at Norton, leaning against the front tire of the Bronco, holding his shattered left elbow, the shotgun a few feet away on the ground. Renee had the Beretta on him and gripped her own shoulder with her left hand. Tasker stood up and walked between the two vehicles. He took a quick glance at the rumpled form of Rufus Goodwin, but the buckshot pattern that had torn out most of his lower abdomen said he wouldn't be a threat. He twitched as his blood seeped into the soil. A gut shot like that didn't usually kill someone so fast, but buckshot was unpredictable. One of the small pellets could have bounced off a rib into his heart. Either way Gladesville needed a new detective.

He turned his attention to Renee. She was on her knees, panting slightly, but had her focus on Norton.

Norton just stared at her. He didn't even notice Tasker. "I'm sorry for all this, Renee. I didn't mean for nothin' bad to happen."

Tasker stooped and picked up the shotgun, then eased toward Renee. "It's all right now," he said softly, as he wrapped his finger around the Beretta and gently pulled it from her hand.

She immediately sat back down and leaned against the Bronco. She kept her hand on her shoulder as a small stream of blood escaped between her long fingers.

Tasker kept his eye on Norton but knelt beside Renee. "Let me see."

She moved her hand like she was a zombie from an old movie, her eyes unfocused.

He inspected the single gunshot wound. It looked small, like a .22, not the .40-caliber Beretta. He felt the barrel of the Beretta. It was cool.

"What happened? Who shot you?"

She shook her head. "Don't know."

Norton slowed his panting to say, "Think it was a flyer from my buckshot. She was too close, but I couldn't wait. He aimed to kill her."

Tasker left the guns next to Renee and scooted over to the wounded corrections captain. He lifted Norton's hand to inspect the bullet wound. It was right at the tip of the elbow and bleeding profusely.

Norton winced and said, "'Preciate you not killing me. Takes a good shot to hit someone in the arm."

It took a second for Tasker to realize what he was talking about. "Yeah, well, I needed a witness. Yeah, that's why I didn't shoot you in the chest."

Norton looked up at Tasker. "It was Rufus killed the professor. I never meant for it to happen."

"I'm going to check on the trooper you hit, so get your fat ass up and in the Bronco." Tasker stood and tugged on Norton's good arm. Renee was already climbing into the passenger seat.

As Norton climbed in, he said, "It was instinct. I saw him and just turned the Bronco into him. I didn't mean it."

Five minutes later, Tasker was pulling in front of the parked Florida Highway Patrol vehicle. The road was silent and dark. He checked to make sure Renee still had Norton covered and then raced to the rear of the cruiser.

He froze at the sight of the trooper sitting up against the trunk of his car.

Tasker stepped toward him. "Jesus, don't move, I'll get help."

The trooper held his smashed handheld radio up and said, "I think my leg is broken. I was going to try to make it to the main one in the car."

Tasker knelt beside him. "Give me your flashlight." He took the long Kel-Light and looked at the trooper's dilated eyes. He checked his head for obvious wounds. "Relax there, Trooper. We're gonna get you some help."

"What happened?"

"It's a long story, but you got caught in someone else's business." Tasker stood up.

He took a look at Tasker in his grim and smoke-covered clothes and his scratched and bleeding face. "What the hell happened to you?"

"Same thing."

The trooper said, "This still doesn't make you a real cop."

"You're right, a real cop would've seen this shit coming a mile away. But I'm still the guy that's going to get you some help." And he did.

Sitting next to Norton as a paramedic took his pulse before transporting him to the Belle Glade hospital, Tasker took a second to check himself for any other wounds.

Norton said, "I can give you the whole plan. I'll cooperate, but I gotta be able to see a chance at a light sentence."

Tasker said, "You don't get off that easy. I need a whole lot more for you not to be charged with felony murder, too."

"I'll give you the big man in Tallahassee, that's all that's left. Henry and Rufus is dead, Luther escaped and the Dewalt kid—he did the land survey—is dead, too."

Tasker nodded. "He killed himself."

Norton said, "No shit. You came and fucked this thing all up over a suicide?"

Tasker nodded as the paramedics lifted Norton into the rear of the ambulance. "Crazy, huh? You never know what you turn up if you keep looking."

"Do me a favor," said Norton.

"What?"

"Keep looking for Luther Williams and see if he turns up."

Tasker watched as the doors to the ambulance shut and it pulled out onto the road.

 **48** FLORIDA DEPARTMENT OF LAW ENFORCEMENT
Special Agent Supervisor Chris Byrd stood on the steps of
Florida's capitol and looked up at the seventy-story building, then at the matching domes on either side. He smiled at the common joke that called the building the "phallic office building." He knew
one thing for sure: In a few minutes, there would be one less dick in
the building.

He motioned to the two agents with him, Charles "Bubba" Tomp-
son, a mountain of black flesh and muscle, and Sue Teis, the opposite in
body shape and size but maybe a little meaner. He flashed his badge to
the capitol police sergeant at the front desk and proceeded to the elevator. His heart rate was up, but he couldn't wipe the smile off his face.
They rode the elevator in silence to the sixty-ninth floor, one below the
governor's executive offices. They turned left off the elevator then entered the corner office without knocking.

The startled receptionist stood up as Byrd headed for the inner office.
"Do you have an appointment?"

Byrd didn't even acknowledge her. He had been waiting for something like this for a long time. Inside the office, he saw a bald man on the
phone absently looking out the window toward the Apalachee parkway.
When the man turned and saw him, he told whomever he was talking
to, "Call you back." As he hung up the phone, he obviously tried to
keep his calm. "May I ask what this is all about?"

Byrd, flanked by his two agents, flipped open his badge case and said, "Mr. Gann, I'm Chris Byrd with FDLE."

"So?"

"I have a warrant for your arrest."

"Are you insane?" Now he was starting to crack.

"I may be, sir, but that has no bearing on this issue." His slight Tallahassee drawl mixed with his monotone earned a quick snicker from behind him.

Gann reached for the phone, but Byrd put his hand on top of Gann's and forced him to hang up.

Byrd said, "You can make a call after you're booked."

Gann snapped, "I'll have your fucking job for this."

Byrd shrugged. "You can have it, sir, but I don't think you'd like it. Pays good but you gotta deal with assholes all the time."

"When the governor finds out about this, you're done."

"Sir, the governor wanted us to shoot you at your desk. It was only my boss being reasonable that earned you a simple arrest."

Gann's eyes searched the room as he considered his options.

Byrd said, "Sir, now you need to stand up and come with us." He pulled out his handcuffs and clicked them through a few times, just to fuck with this guy.

Gann said, "I'm not moving."

Byrd smiled broadly, glanced over his shoulder at Bubba and said, "I was hoping you might say that."

Tasker sat in the FDLE Miami regional director's outer office waiting for the tall man to get off the phone. In the week since he had returned from his exile in Gladesville, things had returned to normal somewhat. The corruption case was being handled by FDLE out of Tallahassee, and Tasker had been given the week to rest at home. They said it was a result of the shooting in which he had hit Norton in the elbow. Tasker didn't care what it was for. He had slept solidly for twenty hours, then lay around his town house another two days.

Jerry Risto stuck his gray head in the door long enough to pat Tasker on the shoulder and say, "You done good, kid."

After a few minutes, the director came from the inner office and signaled for him to come in.

Settling into his high-backed leather chair, the director kept a smile on his face. "Billy, you made us proud."

Tasker smiled, not sure what he could say.

"I'm sorry I let that asshole Gann get to me. I should've left you to do what had to be done."

"I never doubted your support, boss." Tasker hid his smile.

"You can have any assignment you want. Domestic security, narcotics, even protective operations. You name it."

Tasker shrugged. "Don't care, boss. Just want my life back."

"We just want you back here."

By five o'clock, Tasker was on his porch with an Icehouse beer in his hand. He liked his open-air patio, and this time of year he even had a cool breeze from the east. He felt a little uneasy because he had no specific goal right at the moment. It seemed his career was back on track and he liked where he was living, though he knew he had no chance of getting back with his ex-wife, Donna. He may have had a chance, he just wasn't interested right now.

He heard a car pull up in one of the two spaces in front of his town house. The light door sounded like a smaller import. The knock on his front door gave him no indication who it might be. A week ago, he would've answered the door with a gun. Now he didn't even bother getting up from the lounge chair.

"I'm on the patio," he shouted to his visitor.

A moment later, the wooden door to the patio opened and Tasker broke into a broad smile. His visitor walked to him as he sat up and offered a hand.

"Hi, I'm Renee Allison Chin."

Tasker shook it. "Bill Tasker."

"I just wanted us to have a fresh start." She leaned down, then tumbled on top of him in the lounger, laughing.

Tasker laughed, too, until he started to kiss her.

Luther Williams pulled his Buick LeSabre up to the gate of the sprawling complex. He knew he was expected and that the people in the complex were in need of legal advice in exchange for his room and board. It had seemed like a good idea when Mr. Nyren arranged for his stay with the tax-protesting group here in Baton Rogue. One of the few extremist groups that didn't include racism as one of its tenets. Luther could get behind a group opposed to federal taxes. He had avoided taxes himself on occasion. Besides, he needed a safe place to lie low for a few months and these guys were the ticket.

He pressed the button on the intercom. After a few seconds, a voice came over the tinny, static-filled speaker. "Are you the lawyer from Florida?"

"I am."

"Meet you by the main house."

The gate started to open automatically and Luther eased the Buick into the yard. An average-looking white guy in a University of Florida T-shirt, shorts and flip-flops slowly walked from the front door to the passenger side of the car.

The man said, "I'm from Florida, too. I wore the shirt to make you feel at home."

Luther smiled and looked past the man to see two little blond kids at the door to the house. The man was lean with intelligent eyes, and seemed friendly.

He said, "I'm Daniel Wells. Welcome to our home." He stuck his hand in the open window.

Luther paused as he quickly assessed the man. "Luther Johnson, attorney at law." He shook Daniel's hand.

"We all do something here. We can sure use a lawyer."

"Good, good. And what do you do? If I may ask."

"Engineer. Lot of stuff needs fixin' around here. I build stuff in my free time."

"What kind of stuff?'

"Fireworks, mostly. Big-ass fireworks."

Big Rick Dewalt had been recovering from the disturbing news that his son had committed suicide. He didn't like to talk about it, but he still missed the boy. If little Rick hadn't called him about surveying the land for a site for the private prison, he might not have been able to do all he did to influence the state's decision on the new site. He certainly wouldn't have picked this particular business partner.

Now he surveyed the land he and the other members of his investment group had bought out here in the middle of nowhere near Lake Okeechobee. They had lobbied hard to get the state to put a new private prison on the land but it was all that bullshit with the governor's aide, Ardan Gann, that had laid the big contract right in their hands.

He made some notes as his newest partner leaned on the Lincoln Town Car next to him.

Rick Dewalt said, "What do you think, Warden? This gonna be a good facility?"

Robert Stubbs, soon to be retired warden of Manatee, said, "After what I've seen, this should be a fine facility. I'm just sorry they don't want us to name the private facility. We could call it Sawgrass Prison."

Rick Dewalt nodded and slapped at a bug bite, then wiped sweat off his forehead. "I'm glad old Warren Kling was here in the winter. Hot, but not like this." He paused and added, "Too bad he's not here with us now."

Warden Stubbs agreed. "I only met him a couple of times, but he seemed like a fine fellow."

"I guess we really didn't need his Seminole village smoke screen after all. It was a great fucking idea, though, wasn't it? It was our little escape clause if the state tried to use that site."

"Too bad I didn't realize what was going on with my own captain. Norton and Janzig both were a lot brighter than I gave them credit for."

"No one suspected mild-mannered Professor Kling planted that Seminole village shit to eliminate that land as a possible site for the prison. If those two had, he might still be alive."

"But we never would have known about their site if they hadn't used your son as a surveyor. Everyone had a scam going."

Dewalt looked at his partner. "And we don't talk about any of it again, either. We should probably change the corporation's name, too."

"Why? I like the OP Corporation."

"Someone might figure out OP means 'original people.' Warren's cute little name could lose us a fortune."

Warden Stubbs chuckled. "The governor is so busy kicking ass over what Ardan Gann did, no one will look at us for fifty years."

They both started to laugh as they headed to the cool interior of the big black Lincoln.